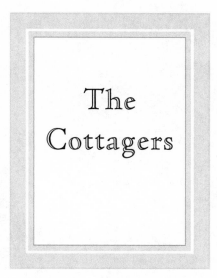

The
Cottagers

The Cottagers

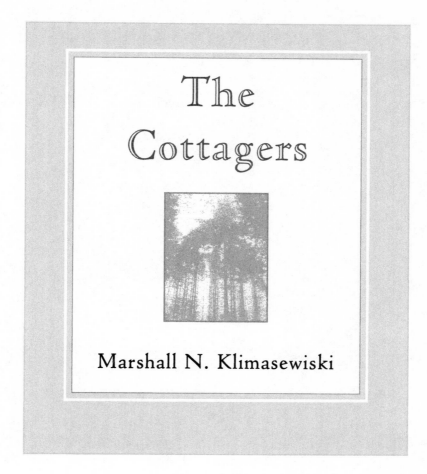

Marshall N. Klimasewiski

W. W. NORTON & COMPANY

New York   London

Copyright © 2006 by Marshall N. Klimasewiski

For information about permission to reproduce selections from this book, write to
Permissions, W. W. Norton & Company, Inc., 500 Fifth Avenue,
New York, NY 10110

Manufacturing by RR Donnelley, Harrisonburg
Book design by JAM Design
Production manager: Andrew Marasia

Library of Congress Cataloging-in-Publication Data

Klimasewiski, Marshall N.
The cottagers / Marshall N. Klimasewiski.— 1st ed.
    p. cm.
  ISBN 13: 978-0-393-06077-5 (hardcover)
  ISBN 10: 0-393-06077-2 (hardcover)
  1. Vancouver (B.C.)—Fiction. 2. Missing persons—Fiction. I. Title.
  PS3611.L557C68 2006
  813'.6—dc22

                                                        2005030992

W. W. Norton & Company, Inc., 500 Fifth Avenue, New York, N.Y. 10110
www.wwnorton.com

W. W. Norton & Company, Ltd., Castle House, 75/76 Wells Street, London W1T 3QT

1 2 3 4 5 6 7 8 9 0

ACKNOWLEDGMENTS

I am very grateful to the National Endowment for the Arts and to Washington University for their generous financial support during the writing of this book. Also to Jill Bialosky and the tireless Elaine Markson; to Barbara and 5 Star Accommodations for the cottages and the hospitality; to Morton N. Cohen's *Lewis Carroll: A Biography* for many of the details in Chapter 13; and to friends who read the manuscript at different stages and provided extremely helpful perspective and advice, including Zachary Lazar and Lynne Raughley. Most of all, I'm indebted to my family, whose support, confidence, and love have been more valuable to me than they can probably guess.

for SAHER

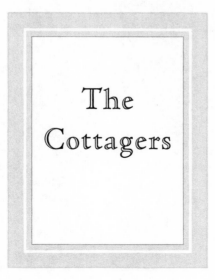

The Cottagers

Our whole happiness and power of energetic action depend upon our being able to breathe and live in the cloud; content to see it opening here and closing there; rejoicing to catch, through the thinnest films of it, glimpses of stable and substantial things; but yet perceiving a nobleness even in the concealment, and rejoicing that the kindly veil is spread where the untempered light might have scorched us, or the infinite clearness wearied.

—JOHN RUSKIN,
Modern Painters, Volume IV

Part

I

1

IN EAST SOOKE there was only one road to speak of—one spine with short limbs dead-ending into fists of driveways—so it wasn't difficult, if you had any motivation at all, to keep track of which cottages were occupied and in what way: which were rented for the week; which were second homes, busy for one month or another between Victoria Day and Labor Day; which were simply lived in. A few were abandoned, visited only by realtors and their parties. Cyrus could tell one-week rentals by the rigor with which they threw themselves at recreation: by the number of watergoing vessels tied to the vehicle in the driveway or tipped against the cottage by the door. If there were little people at all he could figure one week in summer, two at most. He could confirm this easily enough with a look into the windows at night or when the cottagers had packed into the car and driven away to a subdestination (which they would do nearly every day if they were weeklies, no matter how tired the little people got). In the cottage he would see chaos, nothing put what might be called "away": bedroom items in the living rooms and mugs and plates with crumbs in the bedroom, wine glasses scattered and unemptied and clothes in puddles, a lot of wet towels needlessly staining wood chair backs. A house treated this way suggested depression, but also corruption. The only thing that kept the bedlam in check—and the last indication required to be sure he had weeklies—was that they hadn't brought too many of their own possessions: not enough to liven the underfurnished rooms. There would still be the sad, suit-cased, half-empty character to these cottages, and the devastating occu-pation would settle on top of the emptiness somehow, clearly temporary.

This was on the south coast of distant Vancouver Island. Where Cyrus had been born and had always lived—but he had always known it was a place in the distance in any case. At all times there was a map in his head and on the map—it was an animated map, as on a television documen-tary—on this map you began at a place like New York or London or Atlanta or Buenos Aires, and the line wrapped a long way out around the curve of the earth to Seattle, and up the coast across the border nearly to Vancouver. You zeroed in here, the details of the coastline bloomed: the ferry through the Gulf Islands—wavy line in water—and the landing near delightful Victoria. Onward farther west, out of town and past billboards and muffler dealerships, off the main Sooke Road finally, into the cape of land tucked between Sooke Harbour and the Strait of Juan de Fuca. This was East Sooke, where the road just dead-ended into dirt and the low ocean cliff, as not many roads did any longer. Roads ought to dead-end, to Cyrus's mind. They should not relent to the intentions of other roads, or fork indecisively. A dead end was especially satisfying when it resulted in a landscape with a sense of closure. Often Cyrus imagined that Vancouver Island might be moving still—floating, as landmasses do—out farther into the Pacific. Getting more remote. There was evidence. For instance, the Olympic Mountains across the strait became a little smaller every year, and every year you caught more ocean breeze.

One day in early September he watched an unfamiliar car pull into the drive of a decent little rental cottage that often went unoccupied. The owner asked too much, Cyrus believed. The woman who stepped out of this car was a pleasure to set eyes upon and not at all right for East Sooke. Not a typical cottager. She was foreign, first of all, and that set her apart. Her husband—for there was a husband, emerged on the other side of the car—was not. The husband was slim and tall and nearly bald, with eyeglasses and vacation stubble. You would have known he was American before you saw his license plate (New York). His wife had dark, mobile eyebrows, clearly distinguishable from a distance, and a matter-of-fact air of sobriety that one seldom saw at the moment of first arrival. While her husband stretched his arms out and said, "Look at this," already fattening with acquisitive cottagers' pride, she stood still and considered her debut in East Sooke not with disappointment or vacation grumpiness but only poise. As if she were no more or less than exactly where she'd expected to find herself.

Cyrus watched them from the patch of woods beside the cottage. He had been walking along the road, coming down the slope from past their driveway. They hadn't seen him duck into their trees. The trunk of a big Doug fir hid him from the road, and the mesh of brush and branches, plus lack of awareness, hid him from the family. People were remarkably unaware, by and large. So few took full advantage of all that peripheral vision and a little wary diligence had to offer—but then, they had no idea what they'd missed, either. The woman was Indian, he discovered later; that is to say, from India. There was a little person: a girl who was three, very likely, or a small four. Cyrus was invariably correct about such calculations. It was an Indian word of some kind, possibly two, that the woman mixed in with the accent-free English she spoke to the girl: "cha-loo" was the sound. "Cha-loo, Beta, cha-loo"—a little lazy. The girl's name must be Beta, he thought that first day. There are innumerable languages in the country of India—one did not speak "Indian." The woman had long black hair and large eyes (they would be brown eyes, and he felt he had seen their color, but of course he was not near enough for such detail—the mind fills things in, embellishes, which is only the one-thousandth reason not to trust the mind). She had a good figure—slim enough. Curvy to the extent that perhaps a mother ought to be. But what set Samina apart (that would end up being her name; you don't attach false names to these people—it may be handy, but it's imprecise), in addition to the shallow pleasure of an unusually pretty face to look upon, was (1) that she wasn't really American perhaps at all—he didn't know yet she'd be from as far away as India, but he knew she was from an honest-to-goodness foreign location; (2) relatedly, that they had evidently driven here all the way from New York, perhaps from Manhattan, from the streets and taxicabs of a place of real consequence, so that they would settle in here, presumably—one wouldn't make a drive as long as that for a stay of only a week or two—but in the end return to those lit corridors and high apartments and the unimaginable lives they led; and (3) that when the woman, Samina, had the girl in her arms and was rounding the car, her husband ahead of her inside the cottage, she had looked up and right at Cyrus.

He *had* just begun to stand, getting ready to leave. That was probably it. But you don't encounter that sort of peripheral vision every day. It was a point of interest—a kind of challenge. Though he couldn't be absolutely certain she saw him: she took a short, composed glance—he smiled, accidentally—then she turned away. On into the cottage she went, undisturbed.

2

——

ONLY A FEW hours after arriving themselves, later that evening, Nicholas and Samina were joined by friends. Laurel and Greg flew from St. Louis to Seattle, took the passenger ferry across to Victoria and a taxi from the ferry to the rental car, then began driving, along the coast of Vancouver Island, down roads that lost lanes and closed in and wound narrowly past rock coves and glimpses of mountains. You had funny money in your pocket by now—royalty, and large-denomination coins. The cottage must be half an hour at least from a grocery store or a traffic light. Because Laurel and her husband no longer loved one another, Laurel felt, in any enlarging or passionate sense (but there was another sense, of course—she seemed to love him stubbornly and resentfully, as she once might have gone about a healthy dislike), and the life they led in St. Louis (where their home would be tuck-pointed in their absence and their friends would all keep extremely busy with nothing worth recalling) had begun to bore her, and because she had once lived in a place as rural as this—on a lake, among docks, long before she met Greg—and also, most of all, because of the secret request Nicholas had made, the journey out to the cottage became more exciting to her with each stage of conveyance: large plane and then small, ferry, rental car. Leave it to Nicholas and Samina to find such a place from New York. They were people with good taste and great luck in addition to ample money, but someone's lives ought to be as fortunate and lightly worn as theirs, and if you couldn't be those people, next best was to be their friends.

They were generous as well. They had invited Greg and Laurel out for four weeks when they discovered that Laurel had engineered her leave for the same semester as Nicholas's. It was the first "sabbatical" for all of them (a lovely word). Greg was still between positions, or had perhaps proven unsuitable as a teacher—unhappily free, in any case. To him, the location of this cottage was true to Nicholas and Samina also: a bit excessively removed and underappreciated—not Seattle or Victoria, or even the San Juan Islands, which he had heard of. They would be proud of that. It was very pretty, sure, but the ferry was seventy bucks per person, one way, and then you had to pass through customs without the payoff of a proper culture on the other side, only Canada. Nicholas and Samina would go home and tell everyone it was actually better than those places you hear about—in this very specific way, and that—though they wouldn't say "better." They would say it was genuine and render its limitations virtues and leave comparisons implied. They had driven here from Brooklyn, for god's sake. They were too good for Greg, though they wouldn't act it. They would be gracious and generous. A month with these people. The cottage they had found was tastefully weathered but well kept, not ostentatious, nice windows, right on the water. What was wrong with him? Greg wondered. Why did everything he touch turn rotten these days?

"Hello, hello. Would you look at this spot!" Laurel hugged and the men shook hands, but she was disappointed if not surprised to note that Greg and Samina failed to touch. "Hilda, dear . . . so *big* . . . oh, I'll get that, I'll get that." Too many things required attention at once, and for the first half hour Laurel couldn't finish a thought: ". . . it would have been stunning in better—now, did you take that same ferry or—oh, look at this: is this *our* room?" It was the smaller bedroom, naturally (Samina and Nicholas were paying, after all), facing away from the bay, but it was a cozy, impersonal box that pleasantly reminded Laurel of childhood vacations. "Lucky us!" After a quick tour of the rest of the house and the shadowy yard in the last light of the evening, Greg and Laurel retreated to their room while Nicholas and Samina put Hilda to sleep. Laurel shook each piece of clothing out from the suitcase and refolded it into the complex wood smells of the dresser drawers, replaying each shrill and inane word that had emerged from her lips already. *It's probably nothing,* Nicholas had said on the telephone. *But you know how she is. You're the only other person she's ever confided anything to, I think.* Something hissed and bubbled in a pressure cooker in the kitchen. Someone emerged from the other bedroom as Laurel was stacking the empty suitcases in the closet. Greg had flung himself across the bed with his shoes on. It had been years since Samina had confided anything to Laurel, and wasn't it a strangely bad sign that Nicholas didn't know this? But her heart had stopped racing now and she felt prepared for a second try. She took a deep breath. Greg opened his eyes and propped himself up. "Ready?" he whispered, as if they were about to step onstage.

Dinner was served on the deck, between tiki lamps, leaving the quiet house to sleeping Hilda. Oceans and stays in cottages: they talked about tides, gulls, seafood. Made plans. They ought to rent a boat. Or kayaks, Nicholas suggested—they'd seen these two-person kayaks paddle by on the harbor. "But kayaks tip more easily than canoes, don't they?" Samina asked. Greg said, "No one should share a kayak with me." He was tired but persevering. Laurel's own mood had leveled and was quietly surging under the influence of wine.

"Let me tell you something," Greg said. "Water is like a dog—it senses fear, and then it pounces."

"He won't even dunk his face in the shower."

"I don't float," he admitted. "It may defy the laws of physics, but it's true: I sink by nature."

"Lawbreaker," she said, and added, "Surprising," patting his gut, though there wasn't really much of a gut there. *What sort of "nothing"?*

Laurel had asked Nicholas. *What am I looking for? Is there something in partic-ular you want me to ask her about?* She'd been immediately thrilled with the charge. And it had retrospectively explained what had seemed up to then a remarkable invitation—a whole month to crowd this consolidated, impenetrable little family. But Nicholas had said, *I don't know, really. If there's anything there, I have a feeling you'll know it when you hear it.*

"Samina's afraid of the water, too," he said now, glancing at his wife slyly. She was hunched down into her cardigan, seemed sleepy and had hardly eaten. She would likely retire first, as usual. Nicholas wore short sleeves despite the chill and grinned in a way that was dry but surpris-ingly hospitable.

Samina said, "Well, you have to see what's out there. Right there on our beach." Crabs, she said, and jellyfish, all sorts of crawling things. Everybody knows the ocean is full of seals and killer whales. "Killer seals," Laurel added. Nicholas said, "Blood-crazed starfish."

"I'm with Greg," Samina told them, "we'll watch you two from shore." She offered Greg a complicit smile but he frowned and studied the gloomy harbor, and this inspired a pause among them.

Nicholas was not especially good-looking but he could be granted an odd appeal, Laurel thought. His hair had mostly fallen out already, although you could tell he was only in his thirties. His smile was the wide and flat kind with thin lips in a round face which read as ironic but warm. He looked a little like the writer Isaac Babel, and his delicate glasses made him appear smart but not quite stylish. Samina was not so much stylish, either, as sexy—dark and glossy and compact. She was a woman who knew how to wear a shawl. Hilda had seemed to be devel-oping into a nifty combination, with her father's lips and her mother's eyes; her mother's slow, studying regard but her father's quick laugh.

The breeze was cool and just slightly salted. The water made busy, secretive sounds in the dark. It seemed to Laurel that Greg had never given Samina a chance. From the moment they first met he had decided that she traded on a certain affected exoticism and lately he had taken care early in their visits to make it clear his opinion hadn't changed. "Let's cook," Laurel said.

"Right now?" Nicholas asked, the remains of dinner still on the glass table between them. But he asked politely. He was afraid his guests had been left hungry.

"No, no," she said, "I mean while we're here. Let's cook some big, extravagant meal together." And she added, "But no—this was delicious," gesturing to the Indian dishes whose names she'd been given too long ago to recall. "Absolutely delicious."

They were competitive people—that couldn't be avoided. Academics, three of the four (Nicholas was a historian, Greg a biographer, Laurel taught English): they spent too many of their evenings during the school year trading jealous compliments over cheap wine and cubes of cheese. By means of cheerful and diplomatic caution they would get through this first evening, the most difficult, and tomorrow they wouldn't require quite so many smiles or so much fake self-deprecation. Hilda in the room would help. The five of them would quickly arrive at the relaxed and candorless intimacy that they'd shared before, on their once- or twice-a-year weekend visits.

But what would happen after that? It seemed to Laurel that if Nicholas hadn't directed her attention she would have sat across from these old friends with absolutely no sense of intrigue or mistrust lurking between them. On the contrary, they would have seemed to her—as they always had, perhaps right up until the point in the phone call less than a week ago, when Nicholas had left behind last arrangements and begun to speak in a different, quiet voice—comfortably, even boastfully in love. On the plane she'd begun to wonder if Nicholas might know exactly what she was meant to be looking for, had a particular betrayal in mind, and then why he might use Laurel in this way. Was he enlisting her as a witness more than a confidante? And how would she and Nicholas manage it? When would they share the secrets Laurel had deviously collected? In addition to the thrill, she felt a little disgusted tonight, smiling at sleepy Samina. She found that she hoped Nicholas was right—that there was nothing to discover and he had nothing to worry about—almost as much as she wished for something furtive and worthwhile and worse than anything she and Greg had descended to. But later (it was so little later, strangely—only a matter of weeks), when it had all fallen apart and they'd managed to keep their secrets nevertheless—Samina as sealed up, suspicious, and proud as ever, like a refugee wading through the rubble of her life still wrapped in a fur coat—Laurel would look back on this first evening and wonder why she'd envied them, or why she'd never worried, before Sooke, about so much suppression and shallow agreeableness. She should have been kinder, Laurel would always think. Patient with Samina. She should have kept her cool. She could have helped poor Samina, if anyone could have.

3

—

CYRUS HAD WALKED home through the woods that afternoon, past the ponds. His own house was almost silent with the ticking of the clocks and the snap and creak of his father's chair upstairs. There was a tinfoil tray of yeast rolls left out on the stovetop—too brown because Chick had forgotten them, as usual. Nineteen is an age at which geniuses find their minds, by and large. No one knows what a nineteen-year-old is capable of, entirely—he himself doesn't, God knows. God has a fear of nineteen-year-olds that they feel in the back static of their brains—it is the thought that corresponds to the smell of a dentist drilling your enamel until it burns a little. Cyrus heard the parrot speaking to itself on the back porch. In summer, Cyrus's father wrote and researched his book while clothed in only his underwear, which was a practical reply to the stuffy conditions in his study up under the roof, but really too bad as well. Cyrus went and fed the parrot a roll—little pellets between his two fingers. "Chick sucks cock," he said. The bird was mumbling bird words mixed in with "hello" and "parrot." "Hello," it mumbled, "squackle squackle, hello parrot. Squack-swit." No one remembers his own nineteen-year-old mind for long. Who would want to? one supposes. The twenties come and things settle into place—a genius finds direction or lets his genius go entirely or else it kills him. There are examples that can be cited easily enough, from history, though the middle option—the neglected potential—never gets recorded, of course. It's the rule. "Chick sucks cock," Cyrus said to the parrot. The parrot did not have a name, because it shouldn't, although Cyrus's father called it Pickles, unfortunately. Cyrus offered the pellet of yeast roll, then pulled it back. "Chick sucks cock." Offered it, pulled it back. "Chick sucks cock." The bird said, "Chick sucks cock," without any enthusiasm. Cyrus gave him the roll. Does anyone know anything at all about the mind of a little person, though, except God, if there is a God? He heard his father's chair creak—adjusting. Chick was at his desk, in briefs, involved in legitimate considerations. Cyrus would prefer not to know as much as he had gleaned, over the years, about his father's nether apparatus.

Back in the front room the windows were darkening. It would be raining in minutes. The books on the shelves along all the walls were gaining harrowed shadows across the tops of their spines. Cyrus sat down at one of the pump organs—the taller, dark-stained one, which was further out of tune. He pumped the pedals a few times to get a bit of breath up and then laid into a circus waltz. His father began to stomp on the ceiling above him. Cyrus sang out the melody while the parrot squawked and whistled unhappily. His calves began to burn from the pumping. "*Please,* Cyrus," his father shouted, banging with his whole chair now. Bits of something fluttered down from between the cracks in the ceiling. Cyrus flung his fingers away from the keyboard, shook out his imaginary sleeves. Then got up and left the house. Outside you could already *feel* the rain, though it hadn't started falling yet. People have no idea!

He cut through the new clearing on the hill where they would presumably put a new house up this winter. It was a slope with a perfectly acceptable view of Sooke Basin and the cottages along Sooke Road on the far shore. A deforested slope. The trees had mostly been debranched and cut into six-foot lengths, turned into "logs," which had been stacked neatly by a clawed piece of machinery. The tangle of tree limbs was bulldozed into a gory pile. Below the slope, by the water, the Flaherty cottage had a pair of Winnipeg weeklies sucking the marrow out of their last-full-day. When Cyrus got there Mr. Wilson was at the north windows, taking in something on the surface of the bay through a very attractive pair of binoculars. Mrs. Wilson read her book on the sofa behind him. It wasn't a good book. Cyrus had skimmed through it earlier in the week. The Wilsons were perfectly typical cottagers: Mr. had stylishly cut silvering hair and a blocky jaw and Mrs.—she would be his second wife—was put together so carefully you could forget that she was made of armpits and knees just as ludicrous as your own. She wasn't in any way beautiful, though. She actually made you a little sick if you looked at her neck too closely, or if you saw her in too many of her tasteful, strategically casual outfits. There was nothing behind these people of the slightest interest to Cyrus—nothing about them could surprise him. Tonight they had the cottage's many windows open. They had hit their stride—anyone could see that they were thinking of the cottage as their own, imagining that their lives belonged here. Anyone would know that a fishing boat figured into Mr. Wilson's fantasy, and hearty wood-chopping, cozy winter—inane. A sound you could loosely call music, featuring a string section over a rhythm as interesting as a stepladder and a woman tossing her blowsy voice out past it all, spattered through the windows and across the lawn. To Mr. Wilson's mind it must be soulful.

Cyrus walked through the middle of their neighbor's yard, down to the water. He ought to be seen, but knowing the Wilsons, he wouldn't be. The tide was out. He hopped on rocks to the beach at the end of the passway by the Damon cottage. He found a stick of driftwood and beat it against the trunk of a tree until his arms ached. It wouldn't break, though. Objects said "fuck you" to man, from time to time, and even dead ones had this remarkable ability. Finally he shattered it against a sharp, pointed rock and the pieces splintered and flew past him. He felt accomplished in an ironic way. His friends Don and Paula were just then heading home from checking traps. Don saw him and began to turn the boat in his direction. Cyrus dove into the basin and swam out to meet them. His pants were a sort of dreamlike drag on his legs. "You're a fucking idiot," Don said, smiling, when Cyrus got there. Paula didn't say anything because she had had sex with Cyrus earlier that summer and something had gone quite wrong. Once he was in the boat she pointed out that he was dripping on her blouse, which was folded on the seat beside her. Cyrus peeled his sopping shirt off. The breeze was warm, but it did finally begin to rain a little. Paula was wearing a black bikini top that was not sexy so much as thoughtful—a kind of philosophical presentation of remarkable elements. Don stood in the bow and steered them across the pocked, glassy bay toward the far shore and the basin marina. He had the stupidest boat anyone had ever seen: it was assembled out of a camp rowboat that he'd cut in half and the middle length of an old dinghy that had sunk at the marina. He had welded the pieces together and rigged a stand-up helm resembling a podium. There were Dungeness crabs in the tubs by Cyrus's feet, and fish heads in a bucket. Nineteen is too young to be of particular consequence, except in cases of genius, where a great deal has already come together at nineteen but none of it has settled down for the evening yet, or been driven into the chutes of conventional thinking. Cyrus smiled at Paula until she finally said, "So what happened to your face, freak?" Only then—this is another way the mind works—did he feel the tangy burn of a cut on his cheekbone. He touched it and his fingers came away with a dab of gooey blood. He smiled and shrugged, and Paula smiled too, but at her own ungenerous thoughts, probably.

At the docks Don said, "Want to smoke a dooby?"

"No thanks, Don," Cyrus said. "I'm meeting Ginny." He *ought* to meet Ginny, in fact, though the idea had just occurred to him as he said it.

"Is she back?" Don was lifting his tubs and traps onto the dock. Paula had put her damp blouse on and walked down the street to the gas station. It was hardly raining at all but it made a nice splashing sound beneath the tires of the cars on Sooke Road. "Yeah, I think so," Cyrus said, although now he remembered that of course she wasn't, and wouldn't be for at least a few more days, and Don probably knew this. The sequence of thoughts, coming as they did while he stood shivering in his wet pants and sneakers, while Paula fled from him, made Cyrus feel wretched and dumb as can be. He laughed out loud—tried to claw back out—and Don looked at him from the boat and raised his eyebrows. Don knew that Cyrus had had problematic sex with Paula but Don was a sympathetic soul who considered other people's limitations and the difficult angles from which they approached their own lives. He

was loved widely in Sooke for this skill but not deeply, though no one
would have agreed with that assessment had Cyrus ever aired it: *Oh, Don
is loved deeply,* they would have said—*it's you none of us can figure out, or really
care to.* It could make you feel like shit to be near Don in the wrong frame
of mind, so Cyrus left, though he'd intended to help him haul his things
in exchange for the ride across the basin. Don didn't say anything to
Cyrus, not even a polite or teasing goodbye—he would know that Cyrus
wouldn't want him to. Don was an asshole.

Cyrus bought a burger from Toby. He had to wring his bills out before
handing them over. He began the long walk back around the basin, out of
Sooke and home to East Sooke again, cutting the corner on the
Galloping Goose Trail. The rain picked up a bit but he managed to stay
under trees. He tried to hitch a ride on East Sooke Road when it got dark,
but after a few minutes he realized it was the last thing he wanted. What
did he want? What was he waiting for? An unappealing question; more
interesting was to wonder what *they* wanted, or expected to find, coming
all the way out here onto this drifting island in the Pacific at the end of
summer as the rains set in, overshooting delightful Victoria. Cyrus took a
seat on the dipping branch of an arbutus tree, to rest. It seemed unlikely
they were merely more Wilsons—no more than tourists. Also, what does
a woman like that foreign woman look like at nineteen? Was there *genius*
in her, right? That was the question. And then you needed to know, did
she squander it, or willingly set it aside, or already spend it on something
worthwhile? Did she have any idea how she had gotten from there to
here, to a half-empty cottage in Nowheresville with her balding husband
and lovely daughter? What did she think Cyrus was, crouching in her
woods? The way she had not seemed startled still made him think (while
walking again: his wet socks slipped in his shoes) that she had recognized
something she knew about. The walk took hours. The traffic on the road
fattened just after dark and then thinned again. He was starving.

Back at the basin in East Sooke, finally, he washed out the cut below
his eye and slicked his hair back. It was a steady, determined rain by now.
Dry is a condition that is extremely overrated. He found the largest
remaining piece of his stick. The Flaherty cottage was annoyingly out of
his way, and he was just incredibly sick of walking for one day, but he

took his socks and shoes off and then felt refreshed enough to brave it. Do what had to be done. He left his shoes under a fern by the beach. Little sticks and stones dug into his feet and clung. He pulled the socks over his hands and up his arms, almost to the elbows. He tied his shirt over his head and under his chin like a bonnet. A flap of it hung over his face, which he could just half see around. The Wilsons liked to sleep on the pull-out bed in front of the ocean-view windows instead of the big bed in the bedroom. There was a back door in the kitchen with four little panes of glass in it. Through the windows Cyrus could see that the Wilsons were almost all packed up—their suitcases and Mr. Wilson's fishing tackle were neatly stacked in the foyer, but there were dirty dishes left in the sink. Mr. Wilson and his wife were two lumps under the sheets on the sofa bed. Cyrus punched through the little pane of glass and reached for the doorknob from the inside. One of the lumps had sat up, but it was in a shadow too dark to identify. He or she was probably seeing Cyrus at the door already and trying to process the image: the weird shape of the head behind the window and that white-socked, disembodied arm groping in. By the time Cyrus had the door unlocked, the other lump had risen—it was Mrs. Wilson, whose pale breasts bobbled out from the sheet and caught a bit of light through the window. Cyrus threw the door open—it crashed against the kitchen counter—and stood still in the doorway for just a moment. Mr. Wilson said, "Hey!" Mrs. Wilson screamed. People did not scream in life the way they screamed in movies, and Mrs. Wilson was no exception: people had much less breath to devote to the whole endeavor in life, when actually frightened and without any preparation, without the chance to gather a proper lungful. These screams were always a surprise—constricted, breathy, or sometimes squeaky. Cyrus's own scream (ready, aim, *fire!* like an actor) engulfed Mrs. Wilson's. Everything had changed for them now. Up to his scream, they could still hope he was the landlord or a caretaker, that a mistake had been made, that he would say, *Sorry, folks,* followed by something rural and inane. People should sometimes pay—for living half blindly and for trespassing and for thinking their little thoughts: they don't always have to, but they pay so seldom. Mrs. Wilson fell in a clumsy way into a lamp, which tumbled over with a crash. But Mr.

Wilson didn't help her. Women should be told this in advance—they should be shown films of such moments and told the statistics, which said that maybe one woman out of ten (had Cyrus done this ten times yet?) would get any help at all from her husband. Mr. Wilson reached for something to arm himself with or to throw. It was a log from the pile by the fireplace. So Cyrus raised his socked arms like a mummy in an old movie and lunged toward them a few steps—enough to seem to want to catch them, but not enough to cut them off from the route out. He screamed, "Chick sucks coooock!" He never knew what he would scream—or he tried not to plan in advance, at any rate. Once he had heard himself scream, "Who loves you, baby!" but it had had about the same effect. Probably he did know. You don't fool yourself in such matters—that's a misconception. Mr. Wilson flung his log halfheartedly and ran, pushing Mrs. Wilson in front of him, and they experienced the usual difficulty with the door. Cyrus followed them, and punched a larger pane of glass out in the living room to give them some extra incentive. Finally they were out and dashing up their driveway. Mrs. Wilson had managed to keep a hold on the sheet—there's a truly modest person. Cyrus watched them pass by the weak lamp and turn down the road, Mr. Wilson pulling away. Then he went to the suitcases. It took him a minute to find the binoculars. There was an equally good camera, which he decided to take also. He tossed the rest of their things around the room a little—but not too much, no unnecessary damage. He was out of the house in no more than two minutes. He cut down to the beach rocks and walked along in the bay, ankle-deep, for just the breadth of a few dark yards, then turned up into the trees. He was too tired of walking today to stretch the circle out any farther. He took the socks from his hands—a little bloody—and balled them, planted his feet, and threw them into the bay. He threw the camera as far as he could as well. An unimpressive splash.

It was actually natural to take advantage of the cottagers—it was very easy, and something so easy was probably natural and, on some level, meant to be. And they had a large advantage to be taken, in many ways, though not in all ways. Cyrus was a better person than most of them in terms of several vital qualities, including honesty (to self and others), untapped potential, and general awareness (literal—physical—awareness, as well as the metaphoric varieties). Anyone presented with the parties objectively would be likely to agree on these points. But the cottagers treated possessions as if they half hoped they might be stolen (it was probably a sign of guilt), and they were often so readily and predictably frightened that you couldn't help but wonder if the fear wasn't something they wished for, too. Lacked, perhaps, day to day, back at home—like a vitamin. They heard sounds in the night when no one was there; they stared at you fearfully when you walked past their driveways. He felt there really was some satisfaction in his arrival, for both parties. They came here to the edge of the woods and they wanted a glimpse into your wilderness, secretly, even if the narrowest part of them imagined they wanted to find the wilderness not mysterious or awful at all but only pretty and cozy and threaded by well-marked trails. The same people would complain to you about how "touristy" Victoria had become.

Cyrus was almost home when he realized he was still barefoot, had forgotten his shoes under the ferns. Nothing could induce him to walk back tonight, though. His house loomed darkly under the trees at the top of the hill. He took a look at it through the binoculars, approaching, but they made it only more difficult to see—dark shadows enlarged, abstractions. His father would be sleeping or pretending to. His father deserved better than Cyrus—that could hardly be denied. But who gets what he deserves, after all?

4

GREG WOKE THE first night and couldn't fall back to sleep. Insomnia was fairly new in his life but quickly becoming regular. He got out of bed and went to the window facing up the driveway. A bright light hung on the rotting shed, shining down through the fringe of trees—he hadn't noticed it earlier. His mind was oddly unprotected when he woke this way, a vacated fortress open to invasion from any quarter. It was unpleasant sometimes, at other times a relief. Beyond the light a thick darkness hemmed the cottage in: it gathered under the trees and smudged the top of the driveway where the road ought to be. No streetlights or cars. It was very nice to know that the Pacific—the exotic ocean—was just around the corner. Someone else's life.

Something scuttled out of the darkness under the trees (*I knew it*, he thought, despite being startled) but it was only a dog. Or not a dog—a raccoon. He'd never seen a live raccoon but it looked the way one knew it would, with the dark eyes and stripes, walking on paws that seemed too small for its bulk. There was another raccoon behind the shed. They both slipped into the shadows there.

He had brought two suitcases with him to Canada, one full of clothes and the other of paper: the notes and manuscript half chapters—letters and their replies, diary entries, photographs; another man's annotations, reannotated now—which were meant to coalesce into his book. If they did, it would be some sort of intimate and nimble (or else gossipy and diffuse) biography of John Ruskin and John Everett Millais and Julia Margaret Cameron: a writer, a painter, and a photographer—eminent Victorians and friends, more or less, although Ruskin was frightened of the imperious Mrs. Cameron, and Millais stole Ruskin's wife from him or saved her from him (pick your narrator). Greg's feeling lately was, *Who cares?* Biography, he'd decided, was a thorough sham, though for most of his adult life he had taken it to be a partial sham and that much more interesting. A convenient misconception.

It was two hours later where she must surely lay blamelessly asleep, but the worst part of having a younger lover was knowing she'd never be kept awake by thoughts of you. She would never feel so anxious to be in your presence again—to have your voice in her ear and her hands upon you (*dug in*—he wanted great hunks of her elastic flesh between his greedy fingers and in his slack mouth)—that a fine vacation or an unfinished book representing ten years' worth of ambition would be reduced to so many empty hours to kill. All winter his lover had worn a denim jacket with faux-fur at the cuffs and the collar and for much of the summer she had dressed in little patterned shifts with a touch of gauzy cling to them and spaghetti straps across her bare shoulders. How would the poor, stupid biographer taking Greg as an object ever know that what had occupied the best part of his thoughts and ambitions this entire year had nothing to do with Ruskin or Laurel or whatever had befallen the distracting, neglected country around him but these banal textures—her rinds and the fruit he unpeeled them to get to?

The light on the shed clicked off, and Greg wondered if someone else was awake in the house. He stood still listening. But the cottage was silent until Laurel rolled over behind him. "Are you okay?" she asked, too loudly.

"I'm fine." He felt obliged to get back into bed. "Just couldn't sleep."

She propped herself up, looking out the window. She had probably been dreaming—she had a lost, wide look. He ought to touch her. In a minute, she lay back down. "What were you doing?" she asked.

"Nothing."

When her eyes remained open, he said, "There are raccoons out there, hunting something."

"I doubt it. Raccoons hunt garbage."

After a moment, he said, "Okay," and turned away from her.

He closed his eyes. He could begin to hate insomnia, he realized. He turned onto his back and stared at the empty ceiling. Laurel waited for him. He whispered, "What?" and she said, "I want to tell you something. I'm not going to follow you around and baby you for this whole vacation."

He wished he could think of a clever answer.

"If you want to sulk or get jealous of Nicholas's books or make it clear to everyone that you're doing your best to pretend you're enjoying our company, that's your decision. But just don't consider me the slightest bit interested."

She'd never quite understood how to whisper. "How nice of you to let me know," he said, much more quietly.

She propped herself up on one elbow in order to see his face—he could feel this, though he didn't look. "I don't want to have to worry about you."

"Don't, please."

"I'm sick of it."

"Yes, I bet."

She lay back down with a thump. "I'm not going to anymore. Just for a few weeks."

Soon she turned away. Was it over? Her outbursts were still too new to predict, but he couldn't imagine lingering in this marriage long enough to be able to.

A little while later the light filled the window again and threw a block of yellow against the wall behind the bed, almost as if someone shone a flashlight into their room. Laurel would know it was a trip-light; Laurel knew about the habits of raccoons and what to fear from the woods. Greg was still awake when the light went out.

5

I N THE MORNING Hilda sometimes told Nicholas stories that he thought must have been her dreams. "In the ocean was the bear," she explained, patiently and perhaps more to herself than him, "and Mindy was swimming but I didn't want to go. I didn't like the look of him."

She had her morning interest in her own hands, threading her fingers together, until Nicholas set the bowl of wheat germ porridge down. She centered it in front of her and formed a neat spoonful and passed it to him with the meticulousness he found both adorable and a little disquieting. "A good batch," he confirmed. It tasted like sweetened cardboard, as usual. She'd never have been interested in it if it wasn't her mother's favorite breakfast. Mindy was Hilda's best friend. Throughout the ten-day drive across the country and their initial week in the cottage, he and Samina had been waiting for homesickness to catch up with Hilda. But perhaps it never would.

"The bear is a good swimmer," she said, after a first delicate taste of her own. "But I didn't know *which* way he was going."

That Samina would roll over and fall back to sleep most mornings, even if only for an extra half hour, was a symptom, it seemed to

Nicholas. How quickly Hilda had adapted—his was the shoulder she tapped now when she woke. "We'll get you swimming lessons," he said. "Next summer you'll start. You'll be a strong swimmer, I bet."

Hilda allowed this to pass. "Mindy touched the starfish 'cause I told her not to. 'They don't like you to touch them.' I got a rope and tied it."

He punched a straw through her juice box and took the first sip, as she preferred. He had hated to give up feeding her—losing that moment of cooperation each time she parted her plump lips for the spoon he held and tipped her chin down to clear the trough as he took it away—and he would hate it again when she no longer wanted him to sample her breakfast this way. One morning just before they'd left Brooklyn Samina had grabbed his arm in the hallway and pointed and they'd watched Hilda manage to pull the refrigerator door open and stand with her arms folded on the crisper shelf, considering her wealth of options. He'd smiled along with Samina, but he'd been a little heartbroken, too.

It was probably a mistake. Last night he had watched Laurel watching Samina and had already felt guilty and ashamed. Her anxious attention and the complicit half smile she kept directing toward Nicholas had made him certain she was imagining anything and everything but this placid, insinuated gap that was all the trouble between them and all he hoped Laurel might help him fill. She had come here expecting an affair or blowsy arguments. She had searched Nicholas as if for scars. How to call her off now?

And on the other hand, what if Samina did tell her something he didn't know?

He'd slid open the glass door across from the table and the morning smelled complexly green and remembered, even though he'd never been to the West Coast before.

Samina's argument for India rose out of her feeling that the three of them were becoming too selfishly and exclusively attached to one another, and losing track of how to be with anyone else. Ever since the weirdly hypnotic year in which both of Samina's parents had died and Hilda had been born, they'd been losing touch with old friends, not bothering to gain new ones. In the summers, between semesters, they would sometimes go a week without speaking to anyone apart from strangers behind cash registers. Their telephone didn't ring. Their routines were unsocial and unthreatened: newspapers and teas and coffees and Kix, the park or the library, naps, slow and frequent meals prepared with Hilda's complicating assistance, early bedtime and books, movies in bed. Samina was right, of course. They were leading narrow lives. They thought too much alike, he supposed, agreed too often, hardly ever argued about anything more important than what to do for dinner, so that their days usually lacked any friction or accommodation. But Nicholas couldn't bring himself to see this as a problem. And anyway, it wouldn't last. Soon enough, when Hilda went to school, there would be teachers and other six-year-olds plus their parents to accommodate, and when the three of them were evicted from this idyllic, irresponsible shell, whether they were ready or not, it would be permanent. Why not enjoy the idyll while it lasted?

But there was something a little sad about the quiet orderliness as well—he conceded that. They had expected to have another child by now; had tried and miscarried, when Hilda was one. They had wanted to try again, the last time they talked about it (too long ago), but they had wondered if they were rushing things. In the midst of feeling stunned and sad after the miscarriage they'd also felt greedy, and chastened. Then Samina began talking about India instead. Her half-brother still lived in the vast family house in Delhi, with his mother and his wife and sons. It was a house built to allow for the semiprivacy of an extended family and the second-story apartments were unoccupied. Nicholas's sabbatical was assured long in advance and he could take it as one semester at full pay or a whole year at half. Samina had thought they should take the year and try living in Delhi—through the fall and winter, she said, although if those seasons went well perhaps they'd settle indefinitely. Until Hilda entered school, at least (though the right schools there were as good or better than any here, she had added). He might decide to quit a teaching position he wasn't wild about anyway. He could teach there, she thought. It was probably their last chance, she had pointed out, until old age.

"When is Mommy getting up?" Hilda asked between spoonfuls.

"Don't know, deary. Should we wake her?"

Hilda thought a bit, then shook her head no. He couldn't always predict her reactions to his proposals lately—a new development. "Are the people here?" she whispered, meaning Laurel and Greg.

"Uh-huh. You want to wake *them* up?"

She smiled, but didn't dare say yes.

Samina and Nicholas had visited India once, before Hilda was born. (Samina's parents had emigrated when she was two and had never returned, though they were thrilled and relieved when their married daughter decided to go.) It was a trip he remembered fondly in many ways, but he also remembered that they had returned to New York— both of them—half proud to have survived it. There was the minefield of her family, first of all, where everyone was invariably friendly but then unexpectedly touchy on topics he hadn't been able to anticipate. Samina was the child of her father's second marriage, but it was the first wife who lived in the old house in Delhi, along with Khalid, Samina's half-brother. Nicholas was never quite certain where this first wife's goodwill toward Samina began and old resentments left off, and she was a woman with an unsmiling face on which goodwill might easily be mistaken for resentment (especially since he didn't share a language with her). But he also found the extended family's sheer bulk tiring. Samina's parents had chosen and imposed upon her a state of tidy exile, and Nicholas's parents were a bit of a breakaway republic from their own families, too, so neither he nor Samina were accustomed to roomsful of uncles and aunts devoted to working out matters of lineage and packs of children uncertainly attached to cousins. In Urdu there were four different words for "aunt": one for one's mother's sister and another for one's father's, plus two more for the sisters-in-law—*khala* and *phoophi* and *maami* and *chachi*—and then as many again for uncles. Also the confusions of honorary promotion—second cousins referred to as sisters or aunts—plus a complex system in which you used a person's first name only when he was younger than you, except that if you were an in-law like Nicholas then your wife's relative age was the determining factor, not your own. Each day he risked offending dozens, and it was an indication of Samina's surprising investment in this family she herself had never met before that she kept such easy track of them all.

But the crowds of family were just an analogue for the general crush of people and animals on the streets of India. He'd felt dazed by abundance the whole time they were there—elated and depressed, excited and overwhelmed, all at once: by the daily, casual corruption and confusion, the appalling heat, the stink, the haze of air pollution that made even the most pleasantly cool evening dingy and lent a halo to the headlights of the oncoming cars and auto-rickshaws and bicycles and scooters which would, as often as not, be coming at you in your own lane. The poverty was terrible, of course, and in evidence everywhere, not conveniently confined to lesser neighborhoods. He hadn't anticipated the security measures around these old houses and the atmosphere they would create: the high walls and locked gates and guard dogs. It was both draining and enlivening to be exposed to such a disordered medley of daily existence. It wasn't that he couldn't see why Samina might think a return to India was the bracing re-immersion they needed, but he was sure the elation they'd felt on that first trip had been attached to their tourist status and the constant knowledge that in just a few weeks they'd be safely home again. (Viewed from India, America had seemed impossibly orchestrated and half empty.)

"Finish up," he told Hilda. He still wanted another child, but often raising an only child was more intoxicating than he'd imagined (even though he'd been one himself). She could sit across from you at the breakfast table, humming a bit, kicking her legs, taking her meal with her agonizingly slow care, and just *look* at you, without a word—sated on your attention and perfectly content. That wouldn't last with siblings in the mix, one supposed. He didn't hear Samina coming but he saw Hilda's gaze shift past him and her smile break.

"*Assalaamalaikum*, my little dumpling," Samina said. "What are we having for breakfast?" She slept too much lately, he worried, but she'd always woken up in an impressively good mood.

"They're sleeping still," he whispered, reminding her, when she leaned down to kiss him.

"No, they're up. I heard them."

"I want to poop!" Hilda said.

"Well, who can blame you?" Samina replied. "Let's take care of that, my dear."

He cleaned Hilda's dishes and started a new pot of coffee for the guests. Samina and Nicholas had their pattern of disagreement, like any couple: he would resist, gently and steadily, with a variety of reasons (he was frankly afraid to bring Hilda to India at this age; the university expected him to finish his book while on leave and he could hardly hope to over there) all couched in concessions and apologies (he did *want* to go back, of course; he wanted to show Hilda where her mother was born; how about for a month again—a nice visit?) and she would let both pass agreeably, never contradicting him or arguing, but a few days later she would return to the topic with new answers (there was a garret at the top of the house in Delhi that would be a perfect study for him; Khalid's boys were almost the same age as Hilda—and, she implied, enjoying perfectly safe and healthy childhoods there). Nicholas would concede and agree, retreat to plan his next advance. Behind all his objections he wondered if he wasn't just keeping her from her homeland because he found it dirty and disconcerting. That spring, with the sabbatical looming at last, she had let it go—had suddenly stopped mentioning India at all—and he'd suggested Victoria because it was hers, a place she'd talked about and always wanted to visit. They found they could afford more house, and waterfront, in this fishing village called Sooke, an hour outside Victoria. And his last inspiration, when Laurel said she was on leave, too, was to suggest they invite their oldest friends to join them—to remind Samina that they did have friends and roots here, still, and perhaps refresh the friendship in the process. She had agreed and agreed, never letting a hint of hesitation or disappointment show, yet somehow this only underlined his recognition that he had failed her. She had given him the chance to come around to India on his own, finally, fully aware of how much it meant to her. And he hadn't.

It was clear that Samina had enjoyed the drive across the country: they had strung together national parks and cities neither had visited before, and she'd seemed happy and perfectly relaxed. But he was just as certain that she was simply (if truly) enjoying *his* vacation, his choice—his language, if not quite his country now. Together they were living his life, of course. It felt like the first inkling of a separation of spirit, of two paths instead of one, parallel but apart, and what if the paths began to diverge? It would be at a gentle angle, hardly noticeable at first, but over time . . . He had enlisted Laurel mostly just in the hope that she and Samina would talk as they used to, years ago. Greg and Laurel had known that Samina and Nicholas were in love before anyone else had, even their parents. Nicholas could remember the first night he and Samina had invited these friends over for dinner at his apartment: the thrill of playacting in all the adult preparations—the meticulous grocery shopping, Samina's idea to buy candles for the table, cooking together all afternoon—and he'd never forgotten that during dinner Laurel had joked about Greg's snoring (the odd titillation of such a topic, half sexy and half anything-but: settled, middle-aged, banal). After dessert, when they'd all moved to the secondhand wicker chairs and the lumpy futon excuse for a sofa, Samina had sat close against Nicholas and casually wrapped her arm through his. It was their first affection for an audience, and a ridiculously potent confirmation, coming from her. He had pursued her, at first secretly and always timidly, mostly without hope, for more than a year in order to get to that moment. It was almost a pledge. Only a few weeks later they had eloped.

He'd disappointed her, hadn't he? He wanted to know that he had— to have something she might dare to tell Laurel confirm it. They were supposed to have arrived here at the cottage two days ago—a little time to themselves before Greg and Laurel joined them—but the drive had stretched out. They could have used those couple of days. But in a month the three of them would be alone again—as he always wished to be, though she didn't. He half believed that Samina was finally beginning to experience the doubts he'd feared she might come to, one day, about marrying someone like him (not an Indian or a Muslim; marrying into a life so far from anything her parents or even she herself could have anticipated—the doubts attached to this very disarranged marriage of theirs). She'd once promised him she'd never have such doubts. But he didn't blame her for that, of course—he'd known it was a promise she couldn't make then.

6

CYRUS'S FATHER READ two newspapers before his day took shape. "Coffee's on," he said, as Cyrus crossed past the kitchen door. He would not have looked up. In this house they kept track of one another by listening—like moles or maybe bats, some such. Surely there was another lowly animal in the world which operated this way. Cyrus had cleaned the cuts on his hand the night before. They weren't deep, but there was an ostentatious web of them. Now, in the bathroom, he checked to be sure there weren't further injuries in places he wasn't aware of. His father always set the two newspapers down, unfolded, beside his right hand, and reached across with his left to turn the pages, reading and browsing, one section into the next in whatever order the publishers had chosen for him. The Vancouver paper first. He saved Victoria's. For a day or two after these cruel things Cyrus did, he felt weirdly calm and sort of physically saturated, which made him recognize what a powerful thing it was just to act on a sentiment, even a mean one, and how seldom he ever did. He sneezed twice, then he was ready. He strode into the kitchen without bothering to put on a shirt. His father didn't look up, but wouldn't have to. The parrot saw him from the porch and said, "Hello there," cheerfully. Cyrus poured the coffee that had been made just for him. He sat down across from his father with his hand clearly visible on the table. "Hello there," the bird repeated while Cyrus's father read. "Anything in there about me?" Cyrus asked, as he often did. It was a little joke between them.

His father glanced across the top of his glasses and smiled briefly and indulgently. "Rough night?" he asked. Cyrus hated coffee—the taste of it—but it wasn't a bad thing, in fact, to begin a day with a little poison, a little shock to the system. When his father had turned his attention back to the paper, while fluttering one of its long leaves over past his nose and flattening it patiently (he was so one hundred percent predictable it was almost fascinating), he asked Cyrus, "What did you do to the hand?"

Cyrus looked at it himself, as if for the first time. His father's eyes didn't stray from the paper, but he would see the birds flitting by the windows in the front room, at the other end of the house, while never losing his place in an article. "Fucking Don," Cyrus said. The parrot was speaking to itself, quietly—half in its own language and half in theirs. Did it think there was a difference? you wondered. Cyrus sneezed and attached a bit of a sigh and a slump onto the end.

"What's on the agenda today?" his father asked, after a while.

Cyrus sniffled. "Very little." He sipped his coffee. He said, "You may have me on your hands, Chick."

His father pulled his smile out again, unfolded it, then folded it up and put it back. Eventually he said, "Did you find any Vicks in there?"

But Cyrus's mind had slipped away. It was raining again, or still, outside, which was good, presumably—washing steps, cleaning "prints." He didn't know exactly what evidence a person left, doing what he did. He couldn't imagine he might be pursued too extensively for such a small offense, in any case. The local constable was a man who frightened Cyrus, but he was not known to be diligent, and the Wilsons had a ferry to catch, lives to return to. These sorts of things—breaking into cottages, kids menacing the tourists—weren't as unusual as they ought to be. People were cruel for no reason, as everyone knew. Cyrus ought to go get the pair of shoes he'd left, he thought, but not today. He would stay indoors, play it safe. He'd practice the piano and read a book while his father worked, teach the parrot something new, and in the evening he and his father would play their games. They had developed an *über*-game which linked gin rummy, poker, and Monopoly—it involved a complicated and flexible system of betting. Their kind of triathlon, his father liked to say.

"In your hair," Cyrus said aloud. Often, recently, it seemed to Cyrus that he couldn't quite manage to be anything—any one thing in particular. He went and got more coffee. "Sneezing when you're trying to work," he continued. "Cooking fish for lunch. You're in for a crummy day, Chick." He sat back down. His father didn't like to have his son refer to him by name—it was something new that Cyrus was trying out—but he smiled bravely. "Sorry," Cyrus said, meaning it.

His father, Cyrus believed, ended up seeing far too much of the new Cyrus on these rare days together and right about when his dumb, papery heart might rip from disappointment in his son the *über*-game would mercifully end and Cyrus would be careful to give him a few days alone to recover.

The clocks pinged the hour. Chick put his palms down flat on his newspaper and said, "Pancakes," with his awkward cheerfulness. It was an emotion he had no natural aptitude for.

Next day Cyrus went out crabbing with Don and helped bait and haul traps. It was always interesting to handle squid. Don gave him ten bucks and bought him two beers at the marina.

Next day Cyrus thought Ginny would be back and walked all the way out to the dump but she wasn't yet and her father was in a lousy mood, which probably meant he was in pain. Her father was dying slowly of a cancer he preferred not to treat. "Don't need my help today?" Cyrus asked him, trying to make it sound like a favor he was requesting rather than offering. But Ginny's father said, "I need three more hours in the day, Cyrus—can you arrange that?" Cyrus tried not to smile, since his smile invariably came out insolent when he was nervous. "I didn't think so," Ginny's father said. And then, "When do you plan on getting a job?" To which Cyrus shrugged. Ginny's father said, "Do you have any plans for a life of any kind? Anything vaguely worthwhile anytime soon?" Cyrus couldn't keep the grin back, so he turned away. "Soon, Mr. Mallet," he said. Ginny's father went back to whatever he was doing among the tires, but as Cyrus was walking away, he said, "She'll be home next Friday. All right?" Cyrus turned around. "Come back that Saturday, why don't you." Mr. Mallet's voice had shifted—back to his pleasant, dry grumpiness. "Why don't you bring your old man with you?" he asked. "Don't you take him anywhere anymore? Have some dinner with us, for Christ's sake."

Next day Cyrus dug the north pond a new outlet toward a little bare patch of pine needles between trees, then dammed it off for the fun in that since he couldn't get much outflow going. He went by the Flaherty cottage for the first time: No sign of the Wilsons, of course, and there was cardboard taped over the two holes where the panes had been smashed. The Wilsons had had a wonderful week of vacation, far from landlocked Winnipeg, in East Sooke by its lovely harbor, but now whenever they remembered this trip for the rest of their thick, happy lives they would only remember the dread and embarrassment of that last night. Cyrus had ruined the whole story for them, recategorized the whole memory. He imagined the Wilsons considering what had happened to them from a number of angles each evening before they gratefully fell to sleep—remembering the details they had half seen and what they had been thinking in each busy instant, considering what they might have done differently—but not for a minute did they imagine Cyrus properly. He was an atypical looter and marauder, he believed. He fell outside the demographic. He went to the ferns by the shore at the Damon cottage, but his shoes were not there. He searched some bushes in the next yard over—did he remember the wrong spot? Then he had the distinct impression that he was being watched. He pretended to "find" the first thing that came to hand—a seashell—held it up, smiled as if satisfied. Overacting, probably. Then walked up the passway, smiling. A few minutes later he snuck back to survey the area, but couldn't guess where anyone might have watched him from. Where were his shoes, though?

Next day he went to Don's house and they shot dope—he gave Don back the same ten bucks—and they lay down, and Cyrus cried happily and blinked, amazed as usual at dumb, kind Don. "Bastard," Don said affectionately, feeling Cyrus's stare though he hadn't opened his own eyes. "Complete . . . fucking . . . asshole," Cyrus said with all possible sincerity, but he began to laugh and couldn't quite stop. Next day he stayed home with his father and mastered all but the clumsy *Allemande* of a French Suite that had half eluded him for a month. His father had been listening from upstairs, naturally, and complimented him on it that night. Outside, it did rain and rain. Cyrus read a book about Arctic whaling and his father read a book about Oxford College in the 1800s but soon fell asleep. Cyrus kissed his father's forehead, then held his nose closed until a snore burbled out between his lips, but this didn't wake him.

In between these occupations, each morning and each evening after dinner and some afternoons before dinner if there was time, Cyrus went to the woods beside the cottage where the foreign woman and her little party were renting and had a seat to watch them. Like all cottagers they had been quick to develop routines, but theirs weren't typical. Nothing was rented or ventured to. No beaches were visited. They ate most of their lunches on their deck instead of in restaurants, and their excursions were often only down the stairs to the salmonberry bushes in the company of the girl. He was surprised that this second couple had arrived and settled in. He hoped they wouldn't stay long, or he would need to adjust his plans. But this, too, had its appeal: In the early stages of your new life, shouldn't you be at sea a bit? Casting about in uncharted waters, looking for your route and the undiscovered lands? A life ought to gain the focus it had lacked—an objective—at nineteen, before the next decade opens up, and Cyrus had half anticipated change. Or when he had seen this woman step out of her car into his kingdom he thought that he had: cleared the decks a bit, as a matter of fact, cleared his mind, end of summer, the bay emptying out. "My little molestee," the husband called her, one morning when the two of them were alone together. Another day when the husband brought her tea she said, "You're my free radical." Everything about this family seemed as if it might be something new to Cyrus. He'd guessed the woman would be Hindu, which was endlessly interesting—those people had thousands of gods— until the husband made a joke about "the prophet" and another about pork, both of which she smiled at bemusedly. So she might be Muslim?

He used his new binoculars to take a closer look into her lovely eyes.

She had a sweet giggle which Cyrus himself would almost certainly never elicit.

So much could be skipped past when you connected to a person through windows. There was nothing more familiar to him than this satisfaction, but it was the old life. One had to take chances, and exceed one's natural limitations. In a few weeks this family would return to a house he could hardly imagine and next year they would depart for another short stay in another cottage permeated by the local smells of local creatures damp and dead behind the walls, and with another remote and lovely vista laid before it. Sometimes Cyrus wondered if they didn't begin to dream the kinds of dreams he dreamt and feel just a little rotten at the core after marinating a week or two in the smells of East Sooke, looking out at the shabby fog, driving into town to take a slightly stale sandwich at a scarred table on a chair with uneven legs in one of the Sooke restaurants that too closely resembled their owners' dens. You couldn't quite keep hold of the sense it made for them to come here at all. Just when you'd begun to envy these people, you'd lose your grip on the attraction.

Her natural expression when she thought she was alone seemed testy. She read a paperback novel at night, in bed, which he took out from the library in Sooke and found puzzling, a little dull, but well written. He tried to read along with her, guessing the chapter she was in by the thickness of pages between her fingers. It appeared to be a simple life, and it was almost certainly nothing Cyrus would ever know—his future would be unsettled by honest if perilous adventure, and anyway he couldn't really imagine living as long as they already had—but it had surprising, undeniable attractions, all the same. All day they were happily together, the three of them—a complete family, unencumbered, with no one missing—and here were their friends, too, devoted if unworthy.

7

OGETHER, THEY WENT to a steep, stony beach with great blond stumps thrown up and anchored in the sand and clouds caught in sharp mountains across the strait. They tried each of the seafood restaurants in town to see which would earn their tourist loyalties, but their first choice was about to close for the season. Hilda was wary of the few children they encountered on the beach and of the adults who would fawn over her curls and ask how old she was. She stared mistrustfully in reply, but Samina never scolded her for this as Laurel might have. Samina smiled politely. Sometimes Laurel had to answer the question. They all spent evenings on the cottage deck when it wasn't raining and it was remarkable how dramatically the harbor changed character depending upon the light in the sky above it and the wind and chop, what the tide had covered or revealed, and the coming and going of fog, which combed like fingers through the crowns of trees up the hills behind the town of Sooke. Their cottage was not in Sooke but East Sooke, they discovered—the name for their peninsula, across the basin and harbor from town.

When they woke to rain on their fourth morning together, Nicholas dragged Greg off to the library in town, where they would put a couple of hours in with their manuscripts. Laurel smiled conspiringly at Nicholas while waving goodbye (he may not have noticed), but her conversation with Samina—about Nadine Gordimer and houseplants, chicken korma and preschool—offered no back alleys toward intimacy. They were left alone again a couple of days later and this time, while Hilda napped, Laurel tried offering her own confession first. She told Samina about the strange thing that had come over her lately—this exotic sense of composure combined with something you'd almost have to call cruelty. Though it was really only honesty. All summer Greg had been taking small jabs disguised as compliments, doubting anything she remembered, playing devil's advocate to any point she made, chipping away at her. They'd wake up and have a dull little argument about how to manage the alarm clock and another about how to make the bed, then another about who should get the tea water when it boiled—who always did or didn't, who owed whom in the grand kettle-tending tally— and the whole day would more or less go on like this. Without thinking, Laurel had found herself playing her part in it: just locking in on her stand in favor of eating an unwashed peach from the farmer's market; going on the Internet to marshal some hard evidence for her case (since his sourceless conjecture always trumped hers, for some reason—she'd always need to outdocument him). The arguments were perfectly polite, as if they both enjoyed them, and carried to ends with the aid of little jokes and endearments. They didn't shout or call one another names and Laurel had to admit that this was most of what they had left to call intimacy between them. "But one day recently," she told Samina, "we were in the bathroom, brushing our teeth, and he started to complain about my hair—how it clogged the drains and collected in the corners of rooms. How it was all over the bed. It seemed like such a sort of—such a comprehensive complaint. I was all over the house. Evidence of the fact that I lived with him in it was everywhere. That was the real problem. And I just . . . I wasn't thinking this in advance but I suddenly looked at him in the mirror and I said, 'Listen, Greg, don't imagine you can be an extra lousy shit to me just because I've finished my book and you haven't.' "

They were outside now—Hilda had woken and led them down the lawn to the ragged little shoreline in front of the cottage. Samina had been right:

this beach crawled with creatures. Most garish were the starfish, broad hands in plastic shades of purple and orange that allowed themselves to be caught above low tide surprisingly often, clinging to the dry rocks in shriveled fists. At high tide they'd revive and be gone. Giant crabs, also orange, patrolled the algae and fell into skirmishes when they crossed paths. Jellyfish hung in the seawater, more delicate than the East Coast varieties but still ogling and otherworldly. In the strip of sand between the ledges of rock were bug-sized hermit crabs whose shells blended in. You only spotted them when they moved on their wispy, articulating legs, but once you stood still and had picked out one or two you would begin to recognize dozens coming shyly to life on all sides of you, secret and diligent.

"What did he say?" Samina asked.

Hilda bent on her haunches to stare at sand fleas popping from a strip of rotted seaweed.

"Well, he just froze," Laurel said. The rain had dwindled to a warm mist. Samina had always been a lovely listener, as a matter of fact. "He just stood there. It was perfectly obvious in his face that what I'd said was true but I really hadn't been thinking it two seconds before I said it. I mean, I knew he was a little jealous. I probably would have been, too, in his place. But right after I said that I realized how right I was—that's *exactly* what all the bickering and needling had been about, all summer. This really isn't a very impressive revelation, though, is it?"

"No, it's interesting."

"It's awfully petty. You probably never realized how petty Greg and I are, at heart."

Samina smiled. She was a person who never objected to the little self-criticisms Laurel habitually offered her, as anyone knew you were supposed to. "But you know what?" Laurel asked. "I don't think I've ever done something like that before. Isn't that strange?"

"I guess it doesn't sound like you."

"Not at all. Right? I mean, it's not that I go through my days telling lies—I just don't tell the truth very often."

"Careful, *beta*." Hilda beat the water's edge with a stick and cast a prideful look back toward her mother.

Laurel said, "It's just that I'm *nice*. I've always been nice. I hate the word, though, and I've always loved the word 'frank.' " She picked a pretty pink stone from the sand while speaking and showed it to Samina. "My favorite characters in novels have always been the frank characters who go around setting others straight. But the thing is, now that I've started, I can't stop. Not just with Greg. I've suddenly found myself being awfully *frank* with all sorts of poor, unsuspecting people, like our neighbors and the mailman, my mother. You'll be surprised to hear that not everyone takes it well."

Samina laughed a little. She wore a pretty, draping skirt that would have been even better if it were a little shorter. She had her hair pulled back into a ragged bun.

"Not everyone's open to the truth," Laurel said with sarcastic bewilderment. "But I can't tell you how good I feel right afterward. I never would have guessed how satisfying it is. The mailman just drops the mail at my feet instead of handing it to me—as rude as possible—because I've finally told him he needs to buy more expensive cigars, at least, if he's going to smoke them on the job. (Our magazines reek.) But do I feel sorry? Or just angry or fretful, the way I would have before? No! I was obnoxiously cheery for days after that."

Samina laughed—she'd been entertained. But when Laurel smiled at her she was looking past Laurel at something else. It was a boy—a teenager—picking his way toward them around the corner of shore on the rocks. "You've always been better at this, though," Laurel continued (he was still some distance away, after all, and would probably walk right by them with no more than a nod), "haven't you? Don't you find you have to set Nicholas straight now and then?" But Samina smiled in her paltry, public, highly composed way now and waited for the boy. Hilda had come to stand against her. Laurel felt loud and clumsy beside them.

He was looking for a crab trap he had lost, and they knew it was the one they had found washed onto their beach. Samina had left it on a high rock for a couple of days, until it seemed no one would make a claim. Now Laurel ran and fetched it. She had scrubbed the striped buoy and cleaned the gunk from the mesh and hung the trap along the deck railing. *Tourists*, she thought. When she returned to the beach, introductions had already been made. The boy said, "Thanks for cleaning it," not seeming to poke fun at them, but they were too embarrassed to answer.

He asked if they were renting. For how long? Had they come far? "Do you like it here?" he asked.

"We love it," Laurel said.

"It's very pretty," Samina chipped in, and Laurel added, "It's so peaceful." They sounded, Laurel thought, like some sort of act.

The boy looked into your eyes while listening, then at a point just below your chin when he spoke. "Do *you* like it here?" Laurel asked him.

Cyrus frowned and considered. "I live here." He shrugged.

From behind Samina's legs, Hilda asked, "Will you catch a crab?"

"A bunch of crabs." His voice didn't change for her—he was one of those people. "Are you four, Hilda," he asked, "or a big three?"

She buried her face in a fistful of her mother's pants. "You have a good eye," Samina told him. "She'll turn four in a week. Do you have a younger sibling at home?"

"God, no." He smiled.

They were interrupted just then by Nicholas, calling down from the porch—he and Greg home from the library. "Daddy!" Hilda cried, showing off, and Nicholas called back, "Hilda, dear! Come to me, baby!" So Samina and Laurel turned to the steps and there was an awkward moment in which it wasn't clear if this was goodbye or not. Would Cyrus go back the way he had come? He was still watching them, though, and Nicholas called down, "What are we up to?" probably not seeing the stranger. Samina, stranded between them, asked Cyrus, "Do you want to meet our husbands?" This also made him laugh.

There were handshakes, the dip in the pitch of voices, the establishment of facts between men: Cyrus's last name was Collingwood; he lived just down the road toward Metchosin, year-round. Nicholas held Hilda in his arms and allowed her to dig a pudgy finger into his ear while he spoke. "What are the winters like in East Sooke?" he asked.

"Oh, mild."

When Hilda tried to fit two fingers, Nicholas grabbed her hand and kissed it. "Sorry," he said to Cyrus.

Cyrus said, "Yeah, my father and I actually sell firewood. If you were interested, we could set you up with a little supply. Stack it under the deck down here."

Nicholas and Samina shared a look. Hard to tell what passed in it but he emerged saying, "That might be nice." Terms were agreed upon, delivery. Cyrus would determine the proper load for a two-month stay. "Better get along," he said, then lingered. He was a boy with neat edges—a bowl of dark brown hair on his head and small, clean features, small hands, mild eyes. Samina told him, "I'm sorry I cleaned your trap." It seemed to embarrass him: instead of replying he bit his bottom lip and waved—a little low waggle of his hand, by his waist—while retreating down the stairs to the beach.

Before dinner Nicholas volunteered to make a quick run to the store, and Laurel said, "I'll come," even though she had nothing to offer him. He seemed to guess that, though—on the drive they only spoke about the library and the beautiful trees lining the road, and as they pulled into the parking lot she finally had to say, "So your wife hasn't divulged anything to me yet, Nicholas. But we've been having pleasant conversations."

"About that . . ." Nicholas said. He'd been regretting the whole idea, he told her. It felt funny, and anyway, he didn't want to give Laurel the wrong impression. He and Samina were fine, much improved since they got out of the city, and better than ever now that Laurel and Greg were here. "It's just good for her to have someone other than me or Hilda to talk to all day," he said. "I think that's what she really needed." Laurel nodded.

Walter's Lickety Split was the only real business in East Sooke: a selection of groceries meant to provision a hiker or hold a cottager over for the evening, plus fishing tackle, postcards, gardening trowels, lightbulbs. The kind, shy, gray-haired man always at the cash register must be Walter. He had put penny candy into paper sacks of enticingly different weights with slightly different figures—74¢ or 77¢—printed on the front in red crayon. "Mystery Candy!" the sign by the register read. The more Laurel thought about what Nicholas had said, the more angry she became. But she held her tongue and grinned and agreed with the old man's nervous assessment of the weather. Nice.

East Sooke Road was narrow, shoulderless, and tortured. It simply ran out at the head of the peninsula, a couple of miles past their cottage in the opposite direction of Walter's. When she had first arrived it had seemed incredible to Laurel that such a beautiful area was still so sparsely settled:

where were the beach clubs and teeming summer camps, the shingled gas stations and mini-putt? She had a romantic notion that westward expansion was to blame—that fewer settlers had ventured so far yet—but after two days of the lurching drive back and forth from Sooke proper, or even just to this store and back, she understood the real reason: such a short distance on the map, and of course you looked across the water and there was town, a mile away as the crow flies, yet you couldn't get there in less than a slightly sickening half hour. On the whole, it was charming to be so isolated. But she was relieved that Victoria was only an hour away, too.

They drove in silence. The sun must be setting but the cloud cover was uniform and dull and evergreens made corridors of twilight along this road at any time of day. When they were almost home she said, "There is one thing. She told me not to tell you." Laurel looked out her window, not confident of her performance. "But I think she actually wanted you to know."

Maybe you shouldn't tell me, he could say. But he didn't.

You don't pretend to take someone—an old friend—into your confidence and then just shut her off before anything is revealed.

"This afternoon," she said, "before that local boy showed up, I'd been telling her . . ." What was the right way to do this? "Well, I was confessing something myself. Telling her about something between me and Greg—we weren't talking about you guys at all, at the time. But it had to do with frankness—with being honest. And the minute I was done telling my story she said, 'If I was that honest with Nicholas right now I'd break his heart.' "

She let that land. Eventually, Nicholas said, "Really"—a kind of statement more than a question. Did he believe her?

"I asked her what she meant and she started to tell me, a little bit. But I wasn't going to mention this to you at all, Nicholas. For obvious reasons. And I really feel like I can't say too much."

"I understand." But he didn't—he looked a little angry.

"At least not yet. I'm not sure, but I think she might have been intending to ask me to talk to you, until that boy showed up. Because in all the years Samina and I have known each other, I have to say she's never been quite so forthcoming with me as she was this afternoon." They came to the cottage's driveway and he simply drove past it. He believed her. "I almost warned you about this when you first asked me to speak to her. To tell you the truth, she's never told me any secrets about you guys before." She stole another glance at him. "So today—it seemed like she meant to be speaking to you more than me."

He only took them a short distance farther, pulled over at a dirt track disappearing into a vaulted forest. The tires crackled on the pine needles in an old, familiar way. "Maybe you're right. Maybe you shouldn't tell me too much," he said now.

"Well, unless she wants me to, I certainly won't. I'm not interested in whatever this is, you know—whatever little, ordinary misunderstanding is happening. I get the sense it might be something new for you guys, but I'm sure it's probably just the same old familiar . . . whatever. Bump in the road. Something most of us are pretty used to. You guys have been lucky up to now." He believed her so thoroughly that it was clear there *was* something substantial and illuminating he was hiding from Laurel. And that really did surprise her: just having the fact of a betrayal or mis-understanding or mistrust between them confirmed, no matter what she'd been imagining. "I'd rather stay out of this, if possible. I'd appreci-ate it if you didn't tell her I said anything, in case I wasn't supposed to. I just—" What? She didn't have an end to this sentence. She ought to be careful—she wasn't this good at improvising.

Nicholas tapped a single finger against his lips. He was most hand-some like this: when thoughtful or concentrating, in pursuit of some-thing. "Never mind," she said, and felt a touch of remorse, watching him. "Anyway, I'm sure it's not important. You guys are just as in love as always—anyone can see that."

He grinned bravely. "It's true, I think," he said, with rather adorable sincerity.

"I'm sure it is. We're all jealous of you two, I hope you know—all your friends."

"That's not true." He put the car in gear. "I'm sure you're right, though. Bump in the road."

When they pulled back into the driveway (from the wrong direction now), and parked beside the cottage, he said, "So we never spoke?"

She agreed.

8

THE WAY IN which Ginny's father lived, which he had freely chosen (therefore, the way in which Ginny was obliged to live) was, to Cyrus's mind, distinctly Canadian. Abject and stubborn in a distinctly Canadian way. He lived in a "trailer," if that was the word—not a proper mobile home but rather a medium-old, surprisingly large recreational vehicle meant to extend over the bed of a pickup. It was potentially quite mobile, yet weeds grew in a fringe around it. Ten years ago, when Mrs. Mallet was still alive, they had lived in a much older, even smaller recreational vehicle. This one was intended as a step up, evidently. Inside, they had constructed a partition out of cardboard (for God's sake) which Ginny had painted quite artfully (but still . . .) so that she could have something half resembling a private bedroom. Mr. Mallet slept in the nook which would have gone over the truck bed, if there was a truck. That was the only space to the left when you stepped through the screen door: the raised bunk of his unmade bed, with a little rectangular window floating above. Straight in front of you was the kitchen area, and to the right was the abbreviated space dominated by the Formica dining table with the television and a clock-radio and a lamp tucked around it. In another month the kerosene heater would have to fit, too. Then came the cardboard wall with a door cut into it (Ginny was adept at perspective, so that the door seemed to have a frame of molding around it and a Greek pediment above) and behind that was Ginny's "room." The drawers that pushed into the "wall" of the trailer beneath the bunk of her bed hit the cardboard when she pulled them out. Okay, Mr. Mallet was the garbage man. Yes. They lived at the dump—sure. But (1) they did not have to live at his dump—he could drive to work, like anyone else; (2) the dump was, in fact, a lucrative business, probably—he employed two people part-time, after all; and (3) in America the man who ran the dump would compensate, like any sensible person, and probably live in one of those extremely neat and tidy ranch houses with a low, sound roof and a glass case full of untouchable knickknacks and pile carpeting—ugly, sure, but scrubby-clean. Unless Mr. Mallet's cancer made it necessary for them to live here. But he wasn't treating the cancer, so how could it be expensive?

In any case, if they lived this way, certainly they should not have guests over to dinner. Like Cyrus's father, they shouldn't ever host social occasions. This was part of why Cyrus believed that Mr. Mallet had chosen his lifestyle, and was proud of it. And that was quite Canadian. But where did it leave Ginny? The ways in which a mother and a wife were needed in a household were so subtle and various that everyone underestimated them.

Mr. Mallet made spaghetti. He had broad ideas about spaghetti sauce. "Okay," Cyrus said, when the plate was in front of him, "identify the things I'm looking at." It was part of his assigned role, with the Mallets, to be the picky eater. Once it had been only who he was, but now that it wasn't, he played the role with more flair. Often Cyrus felt he was engaged upon a campaign to eliminate all that was natural and therefore messy or unpredictable about his character. He only replaced it with more careful versions of the same stuff, but delivered now, and strategic.

Mr. Mallet said, "Capers, olives, and the mystery ingredient," pointing at different-colored bits. "Mystery ingredient," Cyrus said darkly, "why does there always have to be a mystery?" People laughed appreciatively. He was a reasonably good performer.

Everybody was happy; Mr. Mallet might be drugged. Ginny looked stunning—God, Cyrus had forgotten! She had her hair down and it was both longer and curlier than it had been two months ago, more unruly—perhaps she hadn't washed it recently—and she had new highlighted streaks and tiny little glass beads tied into the ends of certain strands. She had the most generous smile you've ever seen, as usual. She had a new nose stud—purple, like amethyst. She'd been at a music camp in the Berkshire Mountains of Massachusetts, playing her violin with other like-minded geniuses. Ginny's genius had long ago been discovered and delineated, then encouraged—she was one of the lucky ones, but she acknowledged this. Cyrus's father asked her polite and astute questions about the nature of the camp, and about the pieces they had performed (she'd been part of both a string quartet and a symphony, playing in front of audiences—presumably wealthy New England Americans whose ancestors had sailed over on the Mayflower and etc.). She had taken the bus from Seattle across the whole of America and back again. Her father ate perhaps two small bites off his plate, but otherwise you could not tell, today, that he was sick—he very nearly smiled, and fattened out Ginny's stories with the bits of praise or particular accomplishment that she modestly omitted. One person, who was a cellist for the Boston Symphony, said that Ginny had the sweetest tone he'd heard since Isaac Stern. "That's not true," Ginny said, leaning to squeeze his forearm where it rested on the table. "Well what did he say, then?" "He said I played in the manner of Isaac Stern—something like that. He didn't say I was the next Isaac Stern." "Still . . ." Chick replied, in his deep and composed, frail voice, "quite an association." "There were people there much better than me," Ginny said. "My God, you should have seen them, Mr. Collingwood. You would have appreciated them. Especially this one girl, another violinist." She closed her eyes, remembering. Cyrus's father ought to get out more often, Cyrus felt. Everybody found him charming, by and large.

"It's anchovies, by the way," Cyrus said, holding one up on his fork. "I can tell."

There was a general pause at the table. His father said, "A puttanesca, Cyrus."

"Whatever you say."

"It's a classic sauce in Italy," his father informed. "Are you telling me you care for anchovies?"

Cyrus shrugged. "Now I do." He smiled, and tucked the little fish away into the cave. "I take note," his father said.

The fact is, a true conversationalist concentrates on the art of one-on-one dialogue because it's well known that group conversation is generally corrupted, watered down—too many audiences for each statement, too much accommodation—and the corruption enlarges the larger the group. After dinner he and Ginny did the dishes while the fathers sat and mulled. Mr. Mallet asked politely about Chick's book—Chick's answers were evasive as ever. Then Ginny put her arm around Cyrus and led him out of the trailer. Ginny was a touch-oriented person, unlike Cyrus, who was devoted primarily to sight. "We're off to cause trouble," she called behind her. "Don't get arrested," her father replied. It was a thing they said.

Once through the screen door, she put her arm back around his shoulder and squeezed. "Miss me?" she asked—her voice was entirely different now, and not only quieter. *Now* they were talking. This would be conversation. He didn't want to meet her eyes yet.

The dump was Saturday-busy, with people unloading garbage or recyclables and William directing, taking their dump money. She said, "Miss me terribly? Cry every night? Piss your pants with longing?"

"Does your father have an axe or something?"

She took her arm away, hit his head with her open palm. "You didn't miss me a bit, you freak." "Were you gone?" "Fuck you." He had made her laugh. Then he met her eyes. They were okay now—back to basics. He said, "You think he has an axe?"

She led him to the shed and took care of the combination lock. Cyrus had never touched the lock but had long ago noted the combination as anyone would. She asked him what he'd been up to all summer—anything at all worthwhile, or no? Inside the shed there were some very fine tools in good shape, many more in poor shape, and homemade wooden shelves on which rusting or greased small bundles of mysterious and sometimes complicated machinery were delicately heaped, along with Maxwell House cans full of nails, screws, washers, shotgun shells, odd lengths of chain, etc. A duck call, a vacated wasp's nest which someone had carefully cut from wherever it was built and saved. There must have been a reason. Cyrus said he'd been busy. Yeah, at what? The axe was quite nice: it had a pretty wooden handle. He said, Too many important things to list all at once or divulge to a mere civilian, but I'll give you an example. They stepped out and she closed the shed door and locked it up, then looked at him as if to say, *Where now?* He pointed toward the woods with the axe. But then he said, "Oh, hold on a sec," and collected his new binoculars from his father's car. Ginny waited for him. She wasn't a person who asked questions—certain questions: she wouldn't ask, for instance, *Where'd you get the binoculars?* Or *What are they for?* She wouldn't say *New binoculars?* suggestively, as Cyrus's father had. Ginny took things as they arrived. She didn't ask where the two of them were going. While they walked out, leaving the cars and prying eyes behind, he said, "I—for example—did get around to having sex with Paula Peabonnet while you were gone." It was a name they had invented for her. "No you didn't," Ginny said, nicely stunned. He nodded, mock sadly. "Yeah," he said. She said, "Holy shit. And how was that? Wait, did you do this multiple times, or just once?"

He led them through the little meadow, where automobile parts were half entrenched among the weeds like land mines, into the vast woods behind the dump. There was a sort of barrier of brush and blackberry cane at the place where the meadow met the woods—you had to be determined to enter this forest. They thrashed their way through. The axe proved helpful.

He told her about a party Don had organized, after Ginny left town— it was at Dog Pond and there were some guys from Langford who arrived shit-faced and struck out from there. Cyrus didn't drink, on principle, and often that meant he became less welcome the further a party progressed. Paula, however, came with her little sister, who was new to such scenes, so they weren't drinking much, either. The three of them had sat on a log, poking at one of the fires and talking. Paula's sister, who's name was Melanie and who was thirteen, didn't speak at first, and stared at the revelers by the other fire—she was frightened, it seemed to

Cyrus. Probably if the assholes ever noticed her at all they would find her too entertaining to ignore. So he plied her with questions to distract her.

"Like what?" Ginny wanted to know.

Cyrus said, "Well, like, I wanted her to sort of remind me of what it was like to be thirteen, you know? So I was asking her, for instance, like, 'So okay, what *I* remember is that, for one thing, you're a lot smarter than anyone thinks you are—your brain has started working in a really efficient, adult way—but you're just not *knowledgeable* yet, since nobody's chosen to tell you anything worthwhile. So they all think you're stupid because you don't know about home equity and you only have like this shady, intuitive grasp of fractions and such. You know? Is that true for you?' Stuff like that."

Ginny was laughing. "What did she say?"

It was almost chilly under the trees, sweet-smelling. He was half listening to the ambient sounds behind them—he wanted to go deep enough into the woods not to hear the dump or the road any longer. Not to be heard. "She was into it," he said. "I mean, she didn't have very useful answers at first—she's a kid, for god's sake. But I kind of stuck with it, right? And then she started to say some interesting things. Paula contributed."

"I'm surprised."

"I know. But she was like, telling me about menstruation and so forth, and how that figured in. She was telling her little sister—just using me to slip some good info through, right? Sisterly advice. It was cool."

But at the other fire, he said, the white boys were showing off for the natives from Beecher Bay. These two brothers were wrestling, and they stumbled backward and almost fell into the fire where Cyrus and the girls sat. Melanie jumped up and screamed. Cyrus had to push them aside as they were going down. But then people were pointing at Melanie—at her reaction—and laughing, so Paula said, Let's get out of here. She had her car. They drove back to her house. The idea was that they would sneak Melanie into her bed, and then Paula would drive Cyrus home. Melanie seemed shaken up, though. She wasn't talking to them any longer.

Ginny had slipped her arm through Cyrus's while they walked. They finally felt isolated and safe, he thought—the only sound was from a stream coming down the hillside. Cyrus stood still and surveyed the perimeter through his binoculars. Then he took them from around his neck and set them on the ground. He picked a tree—a good cedar, not quite huge—and spat in his palms (as he had seen done). Began chopping. Ginny had wandered from his side. All his life he had wanted to chop down a tree! New things—a new beginning, a new phase opening up. He had priorities to get to. He said, "I didn't want to go in their house," speaking between swings, "—why should I? But Paula said, 'Come with me.' " He felt behind schedule in his life—in a broad but not yet fatal way. "So we go in. The house is dark. Paula was kind of being giggly—trying to lighten the mood. But her sister went straight to her room. Slammed the door." He stopped talking to devote himself full-time to the chopping. Ginny was wandering, perhaps hunting for mushrooms. He *did* love her for not asking questions. She had always followed him. She had always trusted him, despite a number of misconceived endeavors. He was certain that one of the things she liked best about him was that he invariably had something in mind for them to keep busy with. When she wasn't practicing her violin, or in Vancouver with her violin teacher, Ginny was a person with limited ideas about what to do with herself.

The axe was reasonably sharp, but it seemed tiny compared to the tree. In ten minutes he had barely made a dent, so he gave up on the cedar and started into the much narrower trunk of a hemlock, one just a bit wider than the blade. "Then what?" Ginny said, calling from where she'd wandered to.

He stopped for a minute. "So her sister disappears. And then Paula started walking away, too. I was about to head out the door, but then she came back out of the dark and took my hand." He put in a few good swings. He was trying to cut away a wedge—he had an idea that was how it was done. "So in her bedroom we laid down on her bed, and she just started talking about Melanie." This would always be the first tree he had cut down. "About how she hoped she wouldn't say anything to their parents, and Melanie was a really square kid so Paula was trying to take her under her wing. Et cetera and et cetera." He looked at Ginny. He willed her to stop poking about and look back at him, and it worked—telepathy. "I happened to be without words," he said, "because I was lying on Paula Purebred's *bed. She* was lying *beside* me. Right?" Ginny smiled kindly. He went back to chopping. "I mean, we know what she is and all, but she looks really, really good on her bed, Ginny. She was lying on her side, with her head propped up on her elbow. Like this." He showed her. "I was lying on my back, kind of a little lower on the bed than her. I was, like—looking sort of up"—he gestured—"across her breasts and into her eyes, you know? My lips were sealed." He shook his head. Then he got back to the tree. He was making real progress. Wood chips were flying.

When he was out of breath he took a break and sat down on the soft, dead forest floor. Ginny came back to show him a hideous orange mushroom with puke-colored spots. "Nice," he said.

She gestured to the tree and asked, "So what are you doing here, sweetie?"

"Making firewood."

After a moment's hesitation, she began laughing.

"What?"

She said, "This is *not* how you make firewood," laughing.

He made himself smile. "Why not?"

She was still laughing—she had her hand on his shoulder. She sat down heavily beside him. It was cripplingly funny, evidently. Why couldn't he find things funny? When she was able, she said, "First of all—" but cut herself off. "Oh, my dear little freak," she said, and mussed his hair. "First of all, it'll take you all night just to chop that not-very-big tree up. Plus, how are you going to get the wood out of here?"

He said, "We could drag it on a tarp." She was smiling and shaking her head no, and now that he pictured the procedure he recognized she was right. "Your father has tarps," he said, nevertheless.

"And anyway, this won't burn well. It's too green."

He smiled and smiled. "Yeah, oh well," he said. She finally stopped laughing, then tucked her smile away. "Want to finish it off?" she asked him. He said, "Guess so."

He spat on his palms again—just joking!—and laid into it. He swung with a kind of wild abandon. The tree clung to life, and sometimes the axe stuck in its side. But then he landed the deciding stroke and all of a sudden it was falling—toward him, unfortunately, but he moved out of the way. It made a creaking groan and a whoosh up high where the branches were hitting other branches, but then the crown lodged in the limbs of another tree. It came to rest at a forty-five-degree angle. "Well, that's disappointing," Cyrus said. His arms were rubbery tired.

"I kind of like it that way," Ginny said. "Look at the little patch of light you let in here."

"You have a good attitude toward life," he told her.

On the way back out of the forest he tried to walk while looking through the binoculars. It was a part of what it was like to be a lion—or the antelope, for that matter. "Muhammad was an orphan," he said, "did you know that?" "Who's Muhammad?" *He* got to laugh at *her* now. "That Muhammad?" she asked. He'd stopped laughing (it wasn't pleasurable, as a matter of fact). She said, "Well how should I know?" "And a businessman," he told her, "raised by an uncle." She said, "Sometimes you lack transitions, dear. Hate to say it." "I mean caravans," he explained, then agreed with her: "Yeah, I know." They walked on— there was a soft-edged chill in the air—and she said, "Finish the story." So: He had lain still on Paula's bed, looking into her eyes while she whispered, and eventually she had kissed him. Things progressed quickly from there. She got on top of him. They had to be quiet—she kept putting her finger to his lips. "Paula has really great tits," Cyrus said, recalling them fondly, giving up on the binoculars.

"Uh, yeah," Ginny said. "I think I've noticed."

"No, I don't mean just big. They're *joyful*, you know? Sort of bubbly."

" 'So I told her that,' " Ginny said, imitating Cyrus. Poorly. " 'Right? I said, "Paula, you've got very bubbly tits." Oh, she was so pleased!' "

"No, but what I said was she shouldn't have taken Melanie to the party."

"After you'd just had sex with her? What did she say?"

"Actually, while we were doing it."

"While she was on top of you, you told her this?"

"I had a very guilty conscience. Because the truth is, I was kind of hat-ing her that night, you know? The truth is, I did not deserve her great tits. Her sister is thirteen, which is one thing—*I* might have gone to parties at thirteen. God knows you did."

"Sweet of you to say so."

"But her sister is not in that place yet. You follow me? I mean, not at all. And anything could have happened to her. I could imagine a lot of terrible things—they were running through my mind, vividly—and it seemed like almost all of them *had* happened. We had just barely gotten her out of there with that girl's innocence in one piece, right?"

Ginny didn't speak. She was thinking. He could hear the sounds of the dump again and the road past it. It must be almost closing time.

"Can we borrow your father's car?" Cyrus asked.

"What did Paula say?"

Cyrus sighed. "She didn't take it very well." Eventually, he said, "Look, we have circuits, okay? I mean, with you and me, by now—we're so cynical and basically just adult that . . . *you* know." He tried again. "Something happens over there, at arm's length"—he held a hand out, wiggled his fingers, squinted at it—"and it has to do with us, and we take it in, but we can still hold it in our heads the all-important split second and turn it over a little, think about it, say, 'Okay, it's a drunk person—he knows not what he's up to' or 'Okay, this is an insult—now, the right way to take care of this, given that person there and the nature of this insult'—all that wiring we've built. We pick the role to play, shake it out in front of us, step into the legs, pull it up, zip"—he pantomimed this, as if getting into a costume. "You know? *Then* we respond. We're safe as houses. But that girl? Melanie? She didn't know how to do that yet. Do you see what I mean?"

Ginny said, "I guess." Then she said, "I don't think I'm like that, though, sweetie. I don't think *I* know how to do that yet."

"No, you do. I'm just talking about adults."

But she shrugged—she wasn't convinced. They were into the meadow now. They picked their way through the debris. When the holes open—shoom, down you go—they're actually moments of pure clarity. It's sad, it's really remarkably stupid and annoying, but it's the truth, too: you know, in that moment (but secretly, you always knew) that you're just a half-formed jerk with painfully little to offer so what could you possibly be looking forward to? Try to imagine the thing you're waiting for or working toward that makes it worth going on with you—worth it for anyone. Try to. Tell me what it is. When they were back on the gravel apron of the dump, she said, "Let me go get the keys," and ran ahead, a sweet girl with a girl's funny run. Chick's car was gone. Cyrus's father was safely at home again. The worst possible thing, Cyrus thought, waiting for her to come back, would be to somehow learn that even the Ginnys of the world don't follow you, after all—that where you've gone has nothing to do with where anyone else ever goes. That you're just waving to them from across a chasm or from down that hole. You won't be missed.

9

THEY DROVE HER father's station wagon down Gillespie, past Walter's Lickety Split, and into East Sooke. They killed a couple of hours at the headland where the road dead-ended. Cyrus had kept the axe, so he and Ginny took turns trying to throw it into a tree trunk, swinging it from over one shoulder with both hands. There was a large, very expensive development planned for this spot. The last kilometer of East Sooke Road (which was actually called Sooke Sun Drive now—this piece the developer had bought) was newly paved, up to a fancy and useless iron gate that locked between two stone stanchions but had no fence yet on either side and nothing at all to keep one from. It was perhaps meant to suggest the exclusivity that investors could expect when they came to this spot to visit their future house lots. The road's tail would be wrapped around into a neat circle. The place past the gate where the road so satisfyingly hit the sea would be a resort with a spa. There would be dozens and dozens of new houses arranged around it on narrow lawns, four meters apart. It was terrific land: a great view of Whiffin Spit protecting the harbor and clear up the Strait of Juan de Fuca to the west and across it to the mountains of America. They took turns with the binoculars.

Ginny said, "I want a boyfriend." Apropos of nothing—except his story about Paula an hour earlier. That was Ginny. Cyrus said, "No, you don't." "I do, actually. Lately." "You don't need a boyfriend," he said. She said, "God knows *you'd* be jealous." "I would not." "You were jealous of Tony." That hurt, though she didn't mean it to. How could she get him so wrong? He said, "Look, you want a boyfriend? We'll get you a boyfriend." "Oh, you will?" "Give me a week," he said. She said, "What a friend," in a funny way—she was angry at something. She told him about a boy in Massachusetts who was nice, but she had scared that boy. "He was extremely clean-cut, Cyrus. You would not have liked him." She talked at some length about the camp and the people there, but she knew when to stop.

When the lighthouse lit up in its puny way, they got back into the car and drove to the recently cleared hillside near Cyrus's home. He backed the station wagon up the ruts where the heavy machinery had driven. "Don't get us stuck," Ginny said. They attempted to lift a log from the stack of logs, one person on each end, but it was too heavy. Instead, he backed the car up farther, so that the tail came down on the stack. Ginny kept an eye on his house. The lit windows were just visible through the trees, empty light that meant nothing at all, no family warmth, no one waiting or wondering about him, a shell with a couple of tin lives rattling around in it. Cyrus could not remember a single word his mother had ever spoken, yet her voice was in his mind still, aligned with the sensation of loneliness. The logs could be slid down off the stack into the car—three fit, with some shoving, though they hung several feet out the back.

"No sign of your father, thank god," Ginny said when they were driving away.

"Oh, I saw him," Cyrus told her. "I saw him."

He drove them to a year-rounder's house near the top of Copper Mine Road. He passed the house very slowly, surveying, and parked the car under a tree beyond it. "Be right back," he said. Ginny wasn't listening—she was lost in thought. There was a fresh smell to the air. It would rain later. The lights were on in all the first-floor rooms of this house. Creeping through the yard, bent over, he could hear voices already—father speaking to kids. It was a house with a lovely wraparound porch on three sides. The father coughed just when Cyrus was at the porch—Cyrus fell onto his belly and rolled underneath. In the unnaturally chilly and half-haunted crawl space, the family kept two small lawn mowers and old, neglected, or misplaced toys, and a very fine wooden canoe. Also the chainsaw. Cyrus could hear the television above him, on which a movie starring Bruce Willis was playing. A kid called out something from far away, upstairs. The father said, "Just a minute," and sounded as if he was right beside Cyrus. How does anyone ever get to that life? he wondered, for only the one-thousandth time. How many odd things does a person have to do right and wrong, and *believe* in, to end up after dinner one day with sons upstairs and Bruce Willis on the television? Cyrus rolled out from under the porch, crept across the yard without looking back. The chainsaw was heavier than he would have guessed, just as the axe had been. He should have skipped the axe entirely and cut his first tree down with this thing, he supposed. His respect for wood and the integrity of trees was enlarging today.

Ginny didn't look at him when he got back into the car. He checked the saw to be sure it had gas. In a bit, Ginny said, "How do you think my father's doing? Is he noticeably worse?"

Cyrus said, "No."

She eventually said, "God, I'm starving." "Yeah, I know," he said, "but we're fasting tonight." "I was afraid you'd say that," she replied, quite sadly and sincerely.

So he changed his mind, turned the car around, and drove them the wrong way back out to Walter's. Walter was about to close. Ginny and Cyrus collected candy bars and cookies in foil, and pop. Neither of them had any money, but Walter wrote the amount on a sticky and put it in the register. "Oh—tell your father he has a package," he said, without meeting Cyrus's eye. Walter never did, with Cyrus. "Books," he added. "Will do," Cyrus replied.

When they came back out to the car, Ginny said, "Hm. We probably shouldn't be driving around with those logs hanging out like that."

"We'll be okay." Though one day he might not be (he had, right then, what had become his daily, aimless thought for his disappeared shoes). Very soon all this sort of business would be over with and he'd have broken through to that settled stage, or discovered the true nature of and the profitable channel for his talents. He intended to have a future out of spite, as a matter of fact. With a family like his, coming from a place like this, no one would expect it of him, but maybe that was reason enough to keep a vague faith. And meanwhile, Cyrus felt incredibly wealthy, driving back to the satisfying dead end of the road: a car full of wood and candy, soda pop, a good axe, a good chainsaw, a good pair of binoculars. They had the windows down. "We're rich!" he shouted. Ginny smiled, but perhaps without comprehending.

When they got back to their spot and parked, he devised a system whereby she shoved one of the logs a few feet farther out the open back and he used the station wagon as a workbench. Ginny had a flashlight from the glove compartment. "You know how loud that thing is going to be?" she asked, when he was figuring out how to start up the chainsaw. He hoped they were far enough from the last inhabited house on East Sooke Road to be okay. The houses across the mouth of the harbor would hear it, but it would sound too far away for anyone there to quite worry. It *was* true, though, that one day he would attract the wrong attention, and this was why he had to change his life. The saw was loud, but not terrible. And the system worked, by and large: Ginny pushed a log out past the others, and he cut a few feet off the end. The chunks piled up on the ground at the back of the car, and sawdust clung to everything. When all three logs had been sliced, he switched back to the axe to split the chunks, which was surprisingly slow work. He and Ginny speculated at length upon the construction of families and the evolution of family sensibilities—whether it was more primarily nature and instinct or a willed response to circumstances which made one narrow down and settle in, rise to the occasion. They agreed that they were both especially unfit for the conversion, but Ginny said she *wanted* to be capable of it—Cyrus said he did, too. "Since when?" she asked. Since this week, he felt. A woman like her—the foreign cottager, Samina—was a future in and of herself, with all there'd be to learn about her and to tell her. Why was her husband driving past the cottage with another man's wife, then circling back? Did she need Cyrus? "People change," he said. "Try and keep up, Ginny."

In any case, he pointed out, her kids would have to share her with her violin, but she said, "No, I'm done with that." He was shocked. "With what? With playing the violin?" "Don't say anything to my father yet."

She explained that there was this girl in Massachusetts who must have been no more than thirteen, but who played as beautifully as Ginny ever had on her best day, except that this girl did it with the kind of ease that Ginny had dreamt of and had decided must be just an ideal, not something real which a person could possess. Utterly, unthinkingly nimble, Ginny said. Better than Ginny's teacher. She said, "Here's the best way I can express it, Cyrus: her playing was water. Mine's sand. You know? Good days it might be fine sand running through my fingers, but you see what I'm talking about? I'm through," she said.

Cyrus didn't know how to respond, so he explained his new philosophy to her: that everything was about to change for them, nineteen was a pivotal year. He did the splitting—he was getting better—and she held the flashlight and collected the pieces and stacked them in a hidden spot behind some bushes. It did rain, but ever so mildly. It felt just tremendous, in a simple sort of way, to do steady, abandoned violence to wood. When they were done at last he stretched out on the ground and she looked at the watch her father kept in the glove compartment. "It's two in the morning!" she said.

She came over to him and stroked his hair from his forehead. "Arms hurt?" she asked. He nodded. "Come on—I'll drive you home."

"I'd rather walk from here."

Her fingers felt heavenly in his hair—light as can be. Samina's fingers were a feature he hadn't taken note of yet. "So who's the firewood for?" Ginny asked.

"A family," he said. "I'll have to borrow your father's car again—in a few days."

They lay there not moving. A little later she said, "Boy, I really missed you, freak."

10

ONE OF THESE mornings Laurel woke long after Samina and Nicholas and Hilda had, and put her robe on over her nightgown—feeling decidedly short on sexual attention, as she did in the first moments of the day, lately. She stepped from her bedroom and from stiff-sleeping Greg, ready to pick up the battle again, her face unnaturally opened in the way that she never intended but couldn't quite suppress. She was a still-slim woman of only thirty-seven with colored hair—an artificially light brown, shoulder-length—and a modest but tidy figure. Her smile, she'd long decided, was too wide, and her eyes, strangely, too bright. She could still attract a certain man's attention, but it was the wrong kind for her temperament. She thought she would see Nicholas or Samina the moment she stepped through the door, since this had been the case every other morning. The last few days she'd been waking with a bit of active resolve at hand—things would get going, today.

This morning the Green-Naqvi family was collected in the kitchen, none of them in the corner of it visible from the hall. Good: she'd step into the bathroom before emerging for their regard. Nicholas said, "Let's keep moving here, love. Let's make tracks, huh?" He was speaking just above a whisper—it must be to Hilda. "Come on, my little hedge fund,"

he said. Someone fussed with something on the stove—that would be
Samina. "My little long-term investment," he said. He sounded perfectly
serious, sleepy. "Let's reap some earnings here, sweet pea, eh? Daddy's
growing old." Samina laughed a little—Hilda did, too, in imitation.
Samina asked, "Should we suggest high tea?" "Come on, now," Nicholas
said, and Hilda replied, "I'm stuffed." "Would you mind?" Samina
asked him, then took two steps toward the rest of the house. Laurel
tensed, ready to flee or face her as if just up. "I don't care," Nicholas
replied. Then Samina was at the sink again, running water—enough
white noise for Laurel to reach back and nudge the bedroom door open.

Greg lay with his head propped on his arm, staring at the slowly opening door and then at her. He stuck his tongue out. Laurel smiled.

"You're up," Samina said—and Laurel jumped. (The water was still
running in the sink. Tricky.) "I'm sorry," she offered, and at the same
time Laurel said, "Yes, just now." From the corner of her eye Laurel saw
enough of Greg to know he was smiling viciously, sweetly. "They're up!"
Nicholas said to Hilda, around the corner and out of sight. "Yea!"

Mornings were slippery and short. Breakfast came in stages, each a
negotiation between self-service and Samina's desire to provide. The
shower queue was just as worried and prolonged. It was always time for
lunch, at least for Hilda, by the time the last breakfast had been cleared,
and the first excursions of the day were generally in separate directions,
by ones and twos. Someone would invariably be gone already when
Laurel got out of the shower—to Walter's for a newspaper or the latest
essential they'd left themselves short on. Nicholas might be out with
Hilda for their morning walk, so plans for the afternoon would wait.
But if he was gone too long, Greg would slip away next—"Off exploring" he'd say. "Just for a bit." He wasn't sharing his discoveries. Did he
realize they'd all taken note of this? From home, anticipating her vacation (especially before Nicholas's phone call), Laurel had envisioned,
among other things, a ferry excursion to the city of Vancouver and perhaps a weekend drive to Banff. There was also a long strip of national
park—the "Pacific Rim"—on the west coast of the island, not very
much farther down the road that went through Sooke. They might take
a leisurely hike, she had thought, and camp out for a night. Hilda would

love it. Now that seemed unimaginable. Instead, she continued to stay by the cottage all afternoon with Samina and Hilda, where no confidence was ever risked and they succumbed to the particularly profitless and discouraging loss of hours that only a child could induce: the rock between stretches in which Hilda must be distracted or placated and the interim periods, always too short, in which she was occupied enough to be spoken around with at least a semblance of attention. What did they end up talking about, anyway? Only residue—child psychology (you'd think it would be a more interesting topic), and the evolution of Hilda's personality.

Laurel had begun pressing for an excursion of some kind. She was probably right on the cusp of becoming a nuisance. She felt their month together thus far was no more than a series of beginnings, rebeginnings each morning with no middles arising, no depths falling beneath them, though endings would come along easily enough and soon. Nicholas had deftly and thoroughly avoided her all week.

"There's talk of high tea," she told Greg, when she caught him in the bedroom an hour later. She was wrapped in towels and still steaming, her bare feet already icy. "At the Empress Hotel. It's supposed to be very pretty."

"You mean they talked about it," he said. "No one has mentioned it to us."

This bedroom was too dreary, she'd decided—north-facing. She was tired of waking up in it. Greg was putting his shoes on. "Are you running off somewhere?" she asked.

"Did I tell you Nicholas says we 'vent' well, by the way? He admires it."

She unwrapped herself and toweled her skin pink. The window facing the driveway was open, but no one would be able to see into the unlit room from the sun-drenched day there. "When was this? You've probably been complaining about me."

"Not really. This was at the library. Anyway, he says it's 'healthy,' you know."

"I'd love to see them 'vent.'"

"Hm." He sat against a pillow, his shoes hanging tidily off the bed.

"Samina would run roughshod over him." They could both hear her in her bedroom, getting Hilda dressed. Nicholas must be out. "Healthy, my ass," Laurel added.

"What makes tea 'high'?" Greg wondered.

She was half dressed: bra over pants. While she'd been naked and half naked, he hadn't set eyes on her, even for an instant. She said, "Funny to think we still look healthy to someone." She buttoned her blouse. "I really can't stand all that psychobabble. Nicholas is an idiot, in some ways."

"You're looking nice, darling," Greg said, finally turning. "A little wet. Mean and rotten."

For a while he'd responded to her lunges with a different defense each time, but he was beginning to settle on a dependable sarcasm he must be finding protective. He would make it less fun soon.

She said, "They can't wait for us to leave, actually. Have you noticed?"

He stood and stretched. "Think I'll examine the day."

"Despite your charms, Greg," she said to his back. He slipped out, leaving the door ajar.

IN KEEPING WITH the quaintly amateurish ineptitude on display almost everywhere in Sooke, the boy named Cyrus showed up without warning and delivered the wood in the back of a comically overburdened station wagon. Nicholas was home again by then—he and Greg leapt to the boy's assistance, and a wheelbarrow was discovered in the shed and set to work. Samina invited Cyrus to stay for lunch. He washed up by walking into the freezing bay in his shorts—Nicholas followed him, mock reluctantly—but Greg had already washed in the bathroom and looked momentarily embarrassed when he came out to find the other two shivering together on the beach rocks.

At lunch, Cyrus proved capable of meeting Nicholas's demand of Sooke history. He offered the early encounters between the Spanish and the natives, the fraught arrival of the British, and the seven tribes of the T'Sooke. He *was* a good kid, Laurel decided: a little disconnected, but he reminded her of her brothers. He was bluff and shy in the same proportions. What must he make of them? she wondered. *Summer people* was what they'd been called on the lake where she grew up, as if the season ran in their blood.

Hilda took to Cyrus immediately, which was saying something, since she had never accepted Laurel's attentions any more than grudgingly. After lunch, Hilda wanted to introduce him to her crabs. She led him by the hand, with Laurel and Samina following at a respectful distance. Hilda was convinced she could tell one from another and had named them and divided them into crab families. Cyrus said they were looking at three different species: there were the Dungeness (most of these), and rock crabs (they were more red than orange, and the tips of their claws were a soft blue-gray), and one was a graceful crab—the common name. It was smaller (not younger), with a little identifying spine in the middle of its shell. He made the crawling beach seem less menacing, Laurel felt, but he had done that already just by daring to take a swim. "That's my favorite," Hilda said of the graceful crab. He said, "Yes, me, too."

When he had to go, Hilda, transferred to her mother's arms, asked, "When can Cyrus come back?" "Well, soon, I hope," Samina replied, offering him one of her modulated smiles, this one equivocal but not entirely uninviting. Laurel hoped it wouldn't scare him away.

He was gone for two days. The first afternoon, Laurel couldn't help but notice that high tea never was offered, and that a rare cloudless day was wasted in a muddle of house errands. They made pizzas for dinner. Greg and Nicholas embarked on one of their interminable catalogues, this one concerning first efforts down through history—first novels, first albums, first compositions—and the relative benefit to one's broader career of starting well or modestly, with fame or without. Well, fine. Very nice! It was exactly the sort of boring yet awaited evening that they'd all been seeking out and then suffering through together, only to happily anticipate the next opportunity, for years. And what did Laurel expect from Nicholas and Samina, some flash of anger or insinuation? A rush of accusations? Of course they wouldn't expose themselves that way. Not to Laurel and Greg, at least. She found herself thinking that maybe Samina and Nicholas were simply "too too" for her (as Laurel's mother would have said), too lovely and smartly unconventional for such plain company, or for the travel she had looked forward to—for anything so crass and convenient as a guidebook or a scheduled tour, a whale watch or a tidy park—a thought which made her *feel* like her parents, like a person liable to pack a plastic lawn chair for the beach (what was actually wrong with that, though?) or buy a T-shirt that said "Victoria" in script and had a seal blinking through the "V." They were graceful crabs; she was a rock crab. At night, before falling asleep, she'd begun secretly asking Samina the questions she really wanted answered, but never would risk aloud. *So tell me, what did you think of me in college? When you first met me?* What about Nicholas—what had Samina first thought of him? When did she fall in love? It took a long time—for months and months they at least appeared to be no more than friends, and two diligent students (unlike she and Greg) who were lucky to find time for one another as often as once a week. Could one really expect a proper or sustained passion to erupt out of that? *Haven't you found him, well, a touch disappointing? Am I wrong, Samina, or is he not quite a person who might hold one's lifelong interest, after all? You'd have options—you'll always have options available, I'm sure. Have you found someone more intriguing recently?*

Next day began equally disorganized and without promise, but after lunch Samina finally offered high tea, and off they went. It was a second warm and clear day in a row. The drive to Victoria was a kind of ascension—into light and worldly bustle: from narrow and neglected East Sooke Road to Gillespie, where the asphalt was properly lined and maintained and people might be busy in their lawns or driveways. On the main Sooke road there were motorcycles and turn lanes and stands for flowers or firewood, then a short stretch of properly divided and busy highway, and finally a Victoria avenue as familiar as could be: fast food and discount motels that featured cable television; city bus stops with their glass half enclosures and their advertisements for cell phones and condom use. It was like waking from a dream, although downtown proper, so pretty and pressed for visitors, nearly put you back to sleep. The Empress was on ostentatious display before its shining lawns, the masts of the Inner Harbour, and the stately face of Parliament. The lobby of the hotel was out of a Bowen novel—everything Laurel might have wanted it to be. Upholstered armchairs and sofas and small tables had been gathered half haphazardly—the chairs didn't quite fit the tables—and there were fires in the fireplaces at each end of the room. Waiters circulated under the high ceiling with brushed-silver tea sets and tiered trays of sweets or savories. La-di-da—yes, of course, but why shouldn't Laurel admire the reproduction? It was carefully rendered to have this effect on her, but wasn't that all to the better if it was just what she wanted? "Charming," Greg was saying of the Jersey cream—"How ever so charming," Nicholas agreed—and Samina seemed pleased enough, if distracted. But look, this would be memorable, a thing worth mentioning to people at home. Everyone needed to carry some of that back from a vacation, didn't they? Hilda broke loose from their table to join a pack of roving children. The sunlight was available for consideration behind the tall, tall windows, but not invited into the room. They had merely indulged her.

Afterward, they strolled along streets with wide sidewalks and doors propped open. It had become a summer day; they were all overdressed. In a high-ceilinged bookstore ("Isn't this Alice Munro's?" Samina whispered. "Her husband's, I think?" Laurel said) they soon separated. Laurel could feel the fine sheen of perspiration across her back coalescing into a first running drop down her spine, then another—little teases. A phrase came to mind, *slick with desire.* This room had a library's shifty acoustics: voices seemed to carry and bounce from the central hive of cash registers and bargain books, but among the categoried alleys the air was dead and intimate and the wood floors creaked softly. Those people she heard speaking in little more than a whisper one aisle over, just through this screen of books, were her husband and her oldest friend. "Have you read her?" Samina asked—she would be holding up a book. Greg might have come up close behind her to look over her shoulder. "I haven't." "What did you find?" A pause, in which he must be showing her the books in his own hands. A long pause. Rustlings—which could be anyone, passing through their aisle. Would they make way to the same side? Why wouldn't he touch her—lightly, only naturally? Sometimes even deep in the midst of these sexless stretches between them, Greg touched Laurel—at the crossing of a street or to let someone pass—with such perfect, gentlemanly firmness, his hand finding its fitted place on her back, that she understood it was merely his habit and a casual talent and meant nothing at all. Samina said now, "I like this cover. Do you?" She whispered.

Laurel went in search—saw Hilda first, at the back of the store, among the children's books. She discovered him just around the corner. That he was hidden from every important angle—from the open space at the registers and the aisle where Samina and Greg were and even slightly from Hilda—this convenience seemed a sign. Laurel stepped close to him and put her fingers on the back of his neck. When he turned she smiled and held his gaze as long as necessary, and when he began to say something but stopped himself she steered his pliant head down toward hers and closed her eyes and kissed him.

But when she opened her eyes, his were open. He pulled away, unsure what to do with his lips. Smile at a joke? Frown disapprovingly? His eyes had already clouded with guilt and a childish sort of appeal. He wasn't the slightest bit interested in her. He never had been; he never would be. Before he could get a proper hold on his anger or, worse yet, some pitying apology, she took her hand from his sleek skin and turned to face the wall of narrow, waxed, brightly colored spines they stood beside. "There's someone else," she said.

A child—not Hilda—peeked around the corner of the aisle; saw them; retreated.

"I swore to her I wouldn't tell you."

He drew in a great, ready breath, but only managed to produce a confused and conventional, inauthentic "What?"

She fingered the crown of one book's spine. "I don't know *why* I'm telling you," she whispered. "I'm sorry I kissed you. It's very nice to be in your wife's confidence, you know, and anyway I can't figure out why I've been feeling so sure you deserve to be told."

"I don't want to talk about this," he replied now, not whispering— with more authority than she would have given him credit for, in fact. It was better to stand this close to him than she would have imagined it might be, too. The look in his eye now seemed slightly reckless.

"Forget it," she said. "It isn't true. Forget I said anything."

He shook his head. "What are you *doing*, Laurel?" he whispered. "This isn't anything I'm interested in—being told such things by you. I don't *want* your secrets."

"I can see that."

"I don't want to be sneaking around having secret conversations. I don't want to be kissed."

Hilda called to him. Nicholas turned quickly, caught out, but she wasn't there—she called from where she sat. He said to Laurel, "No more," then went to Hilda. Laurel stood still a moment, wondering what she'd done—but more amused than alarmed.

On the way out of downtown there were long lines of traffic at the lights. Hilda sat in her car seat beside Laurel and wished to inform her of the proper way to drive. Wasn't it exactly the way her father drove? Laurel asked. No—you have to go very fast, she said, and you shouldn't stop. "I like a breeze on my face," Hilda admitted, looking wistfully through her open window. "Did you hear what she said?" Laurel asked Samina and Nicholas, in front. They had. "But what if there are cars in the way?" she asked Hilda. It was a funny skill—one she didn't possess, but might like to: speaking to a child this way, with all the adults listening; satisfying both audiences without seeming to mean to. "How can you go fast when the road is full of traffic?"

"You go around it," Hilda said.

"Come on, Nicholas," Laurel said, pretending to whine. "Go *around* it."

"Go *around* it, Nicholas," Hilda agreed, and received general laughter from everyone but her father.

"Finally," Nicholas whispered, as the knot of cars pulled loose before them.

The highway traffic was tightly packed but fast-moving—it did remind you of America. Hilda asked, "Will Cyrus be there when we get home?" Everyone grinned.

"*Such* a nice day," Laurel offered a few moments later. "I'm so glad we got out into it."

He might be imagining that she was either hopelessly thoughtless or a little out of control, but in fact she could see herself very clearly: yes, fine, a cruel, meddling, awful person, pleased to be in the presence of someone else's pain, but she couldn't bring herself to summon a real pinch of guilt and she felt certain what she'd done wasn't particularly unfair or important. Not really. Really, who cares? Instead, she felt weightless, a little self-disgusted yet exhilarated, and simply more capable than anyone around her because she was heedless and collapsed in places where they were still hopefully inflated. He might speak to Samina—he might find he had to, once he'd stewed for some number of hours or days. What would they do when they discovered she'd lied? Would they kick Laurel and Greg out, make a scene? Impossible to imagine. But no, he wouldn't speak to her. He wouldn't say a word, would he? Not Nicholas—not these two. And anyway, what if Laurel's fabrications turned out to be true?

"Is that the Outer Harbour now?" Greg asked. A narrow, meandering strip of water edged the highway. There were little houses with groomed yards and sharp, dark pines.

"Could be," Samina said.

Laurel told them, "No, the Outer Harbour is right next to the Inner Harbour, right in the city. We saw signs for it. Except I don't think it's the *Outer* Harbour, either—isn't it the Upper Harbour?"

"That's your Double Upper Harbour there," Greg said, and leaned into Laurel. Greg could sense something coming off her, probably, some added heat, though he wouldn't guess its source.

There was a wedge of Canada geese overhead, to one side. The car in front of them was going much too slowly for Nicholas. He was already changing lanes to pass it, accelerating, when its brake lights came on again. It was swerving—but calmly, a drift to the right—and where it had been there was a tire in the road, instead. The tire lay flat on the white lines, between lanes, directly in front of them. Nicholas seemed to aim for it. Samina gasped—her hands flew out to brace herself against the dashboard. Perhaps Nicholas braked or perhaps he didn't have time. They would hit the tire—then instantly, they did. It seemed to jam under the car momentarily, or kick up off the road. They almost seemed to bounce on it, an awful screech, then it shot out behind them. Nicholas fought the steering wheel. They headed toward the middle guardrail, but there was time enough to correct this. When they were under control, they realized the engine was off. The dashboard was ornamented with warning lights. "Everyone okay?" Nicholas shouted. "Hilda?" She said, "What?" "Be careful," Samina told him, still braced. While they sailed on, stalled, he shifted into neutral and turned the key back and forth. The engine made metal scraping sounds that didn't offer the slightest promise of ignition. A space had opened up around them—this seemed slightly miraculous. Nicholas cut across lanes to the shoulder, politely using his indicator. He let the car roll off the base of an exit ramp and into the grass and traffic streamed past, undisturbed, as they came to a stop. "My god," Samina said. Nicholas was shaking—with what looked like anger, though it must be fear. He tried the engine again but the sound it made was ugly. "We're leaking," Greg said.

They all got out to inspect the damage. Nicholas took Hilda from her car seat into his arms. The bumper was cracked and half hanging, and the signal light had been smashed on one side, but it didn't look terrible, all in all. Samina rubbed Nicholas's back and said, "You did well." "It was there so fast," he said. "All I had time to do was try to center it under the car."

They walked up the ramp to a gas station and called a tow truck. Nicholas had failed to mention that there were five of them, though, and after much debate, he and Samina went with the truck and with Hilda, back to the Jetta. The driver radioed his garage and had them call a cab from Victoria for Greg and Laurel. She made him buy her some chips and while they sat on the curb waiting, she couldn't *help* but smile.

"Having a ball, eh?" Greg asked.

"But I don't know why!" she said.

Her mood slowly ebbed on the long drive home, but it didn't sour. Darkness fell in stages, encouraged by the closing-in trees of East Sooke, and their harbor was fogged over, although there had been no suggestion of fog anywhere else. "You're a long way out," the driver noted. They had arrived before Samina and Nicholas, and waited in the chairs on the back deck. How quickly the evening turned chilly. Laurel thought, for the first time, that they hadn't chosen the best cottage, actually, or not a very good location. It was so dreary out here, compared to Victoria.

Nicholas surprised her once more that night at dinner—he seemed to succeed at appearing unfazed to all eyes but her own. He imitated the tow truck driver's accent and later told a long story, complete with voices and gestures, about a crazy student he'd once had who pretended to have been in car accidents and wore fake casts. Samina and Hilda laughed the adult and child versions of the same sweet laugh for him, though they must have heard the story before. What had Laurel *ever* known about these people? If he was a performer this adept, who could say what he'd hidden in the past?

Later, alone at last in their room, Greg and Laurel kissed and fondled about as quietly as possible—a slightly painful reacquainting with old appetites and proclivities. They both slept soundly for the first time in weeks.

11

CYRUS CAME POKING, shyly, from around the corner of the house. It had been an open, sunny morning that was closing in toward afternoon fog and patter. Greg and Nicholas had taken the rental car into town together to see about the Jetta. Samina invited Cyrus in for a cup of coffee and she and Laurel asked him questions for as long as Hilda would permit. He lived alone with his father, he said. No mother in the picture. He had just graduated from high school and deferred college for a year to help his father with "the business." (Now, this would be firewood sales? Laurel wondered. Or did the crabbing pay the bills?) Next fall he would be off to Columbia. "Columbia! My goodness, congratulations," Laurel said. Cyrus said, "Oh, sure, thanks."

"What do you think of him?" she asked Samina, when Cyrus had given in to Hilda's frequent requests and walked off hand in hand with her toward the beach. "Seems sweet," Samina replied, watching him out the back window. Still, a minute later she said, "Hilda will never forgive me, but I think I'll follow them."

Interesting, Laurel thought. A typical cottager, afraid of the locals. Cyrus would have sensed it by now—they radiated their fear when you came to their door to ask if their daughter was free to play, or to sell them Girl Scout cookies or raffle tickets; you knocked and then took a step backward and kept your hands visible in front of you. Your voice lifted into that mousy register that would make you sick to remember. But it never worked. There was always the creepy fear coming at you from these people, measuring the threat you posed. *These people,* Laurel thought. Whose side am I on now?

There was no sign that Nicholas had said a word to Samina. Did this indicate their capacity to keep secrets from one another as well, or hadn't Nicholas believed Laurel after all?

They saw Cyrus drive by on a boat another day—on the ridiculous boat that seemed to have been assembled out of two. "There's Cyrus," Laurel said to Hilda, holding her up to see. "Wave to Cyrus!" But Hilda was not the waving type. She glared while he waved with cute abandon for her benefit. "What is he doing?" she asked, and clearly she meant, *What is he doing enjoying himself without me?*

He stopped by the next day, and when Greg asked him about his boat he said, "Oh, that's Don's," as if its construction were thus explained. Samina invited him to Hilda's fourth birthday party, and he obliged. There was colored bunting hung between the doorways. Balloons bobbed against the ceiling. Six party hats, but Hilda would not allow four to be worn: they were for the kids, she explained, meaning herself and Cyrus. On her cake it said, "A Super Sooke Birthday for HILDA!" "The baker's text," Nicholas said. *Text,* Cyrus thought. *What a life!* There was a fat candle in the shape of a four, plus four small pink ones set around it. Cyrus watched Hilda ever so carefully: with little people, there is a wonderful transparency. You can follow their expressions and the bob and weave of their attention, the great betrayal of their eyes, and it's often as if you've seen right through the pupils into their limited minds, where weird movies are unspooled and thrown up and then translated into actions, into little interventions in the big weird movie surrounding them. Her father, way up above them, said, "I'm afraid Hilda needed a playmate in Sooke," and then, "Poor Cyrus." And you could *see* the hard knot of some brief hatred pull together between Hilda's eyes, just for an instant—a thought for some obliteration, no doubt—but an instant later the knot pulled through and her thoughts had fluttered on to edible letters and that pink, translucent, toothpasty gel. What a theater a little person is. He watched something new come to her—some idea took possession of her shoulders, you could trace it flying up toward her lips—and she said, "Cyrus can sleep over for my birthday," then made eyes at her father. Had she influenced the world? Dad must be the softer touch. Oh, if only adults—full of narrower thoughts, after all, less unpredictable in their way—if only they could be read so easily. He'd decided he might follow them to the States. If things progressed apace and he became so very indispensable to little Hilda's happiness he might "go to Columbia"—his new favorite euphemism—and pop over for visits to their stylish apartment on the weekends. Such an arrangement could last for years.

His procedure was to circle past their driveway on the hill above the other side of the road, well out of sight, and come down at the far corner of the empty double plot next to their cottage's property. Enter the trees there, creep close to shore, and finally make his way back toward their house, only near enough to put the binoculars on the windows. There were two people to be careful of: Samina had her impressive peripheral vision, and Greg was a problem, not because he could boast any particular awareness—he was dull as the next man—but because he was suspicious. He didn't trust Cyrus. Anyone would see that. Perhaps he was a suspicious or fearful person by nature. He often went about alone, making quiet calls on Walter's pay phone or walking the enchanting trails in East Sooke Park. Cyrus had followed him.

"Can Cyrus sleep over?" Cyrus said, imitating her. Hilda smiled at him and opened her eyes wide—posing, actually: *cute face.* "Can we stay up all night and blow bubbles and have French toast for breakfast?" he asked her. "Can we can we can we?"

The day after the birthday party all the others went away together and—at last—left Samina alone with Hilda. To test her, he approached from a different direction—from the beach, where no more than the top of his head would be visible past the stairs and the salmonberry cane until he stepped up into her back yard. He fixed where she was—in a kitchen window—before he stepped from cover. His gaze was vaguely on the sky above her cottage. Absently, you would have to say. Five steps was all it took. He must be a blur, a glimpse of hair—less than that, in the corner of her eye; and it was a windy day with a storm coming: everything blowing about, calling attention—yet she looked straight at him! At the edge of his vision he saw her head rise—she'd found him—and he smiled despite himself and had to turn away to hide it. He climbed her stairs. From the top step he searched for her on the deck, then in the living room windows. He hesitated—*Anyone home?* He was playing the part so well he decided to take it a step further: *I guess not. Too bad!* He turned his back and took his first step down the stairs. She could let him go if she wished to—if she was afraid of him, or lacked interest. If she wouldn't want to be alone in a room with him for any reason she could simply let him go. What, after all (he took the second step) could be her interest in him—in a kid from Fucksville, Canada? What did they actually have in common? She was kind to him out of pity and polite instinct and a sense of superiority accompanied by guilt. That was why she would let him go right now and find a way to not quite lie when he came back later and said he'd been by in the afternoon, but no one seemed to be at home. He got down three steps. It *was* down: he was heading down to earth again, down to Sooke and limitless nothingness, a drift out to sea, pure bullshit. *Touch the beach,* he said in his head, *and you're through, Cyrus.* But he almost hadn't finished the thought when he heard the sliding glass door slip open. He didn't stop yet. "Cyrus," she called—that was all. And what a lovely way she had of saying his name! *Off to Columbia,* he thought.

"EVERY YEAR HE goes to this cave. I mean, he'd been doing it for some time, right?"

"I think that's right."

"And then this year, same old cave, but one night—you know, *think* of it. He wakes up and as I understand it there's like something gripping him. I think literally, they mean. Like he's being held in a fist—God's fist. And he just starts speaking the Quran. Which is to say, these words that he's never heard before or even thought of begin to spill out of his mouth, against his will, as if they've been squeezed from him. Like pulp."

"Look at this one!" Hilda said. She sat on his lap and drew princesses in crayon. Cyrus bent over her shoulder to look—purple princess. "Not bad," he said.

"It's very good," Hilda replied.

"Her crown could twinkle with a little more flair," Cyrus pointed out. "You could put folds in her skirt maybe."

Samina milled and fussed among the countertops, preparing dinner. Cyrus had already been invited to stay. "You want folds in the skirt?" she asked Cyrus. "You're a tough critic."

"I'm thirsty," Hilda said, bent to her work again. "May I have a juice, please?"

"You may. Do you want a juice, Cyrus? Or maybe iced tea?"

"Tea, thank you."

"You can go on, by the way. I'm listening."

There was an embarrassing discrepancy developing in his fantasies—he didn't like to face it. Half the time he wanted her to ravage him and the other half he seemed to want her to adopt him. Outside, the wind blew. "I guess you know all this," he admitted, "how he waits two years to tell anybody and all? I guess it's all second nature to you."

She said, "It's been a while, actually." She brought a pitcher of cold tea to the table and mixed in ice and sugar for him with a casual expertise concerning proportions. "And it's not so fascinating when you grow up with it," she said.

"Yeah."

"How long have you been interested in Muhammad?"

"More or less forever," Cyrus lied. "I have a particular thing for prophets." She had deceptively large breasts (seemed to choose clothes meant to hide this fact), which pained Cyrus and gave him comfort, too. He was ashamed to notice them, yet he always did.

"Those are folds," Hilda said, but to herself. Samina admired the drawing. Then she stood and went back to her work in the kitchen. Last night Cyrus had lain in bed unable to sleep, listening to his father's chair creak into the night, thinking of sand and elephants and the Taj Mahal and Arabic script, and he'd wondered if anything of his had seeped into the chemical caves of her brain and if so, how long he might hide there, coming to light again years from now in some distant city that she would have carried Cyrus to. Visiting her in the depths of her privacy.

Eventually, he said, "I do wonder how you keep your mouth shut for two

years, actually." He bounced Hilda on his knees a bit. She made a sound—
"uhhhh"—to hear it shake. "Don't you? I mean, if that had happened to
you in a cave? Although he did tell his cousin. And his wife."

"Was that Aisha?"

My little molestee, she would call Cyrus, approvingly. "Muhammad was
a man who loved women, they say. He was actually quite progressive for
his time."

"So they say."

"Then there's the Battle of the Trench, you know?"

"Remind me." She browned meat at the stove.

"Yeah, Muhammad had his troops dig a trench around the whole city,
which the Meccan cavalry fell into. This was apparently unheard of
then—this was like a great innovation. You have to hope they at least disguised the trench to pull this off, right?"

She smiled. She spoke to him just vaguely as if to a child, yet he
couldn't bring himself to be offended. Hilda made such a bony,
squirmy weight in one's lap that you realized more firmly than ever she
was a real live thing on her steady way toward full personhood.
Muhammad had not been young at all. He was forty when God took
him in His fist. He, too, had had an unhappy youth, without parents or
proper care. At nineteen, what was Muhammad? At some point everything changes—you leap into a new life—but you can't be certain
when it will happen and you can't be patient, either, or risk missing
your chance. "You pray five times a day, I guess?" he asked. "I never
have," she said. "You don't believe?"

She took the measure of him once more from the stove. "It's not that.
I've just never quite managed it." They were quiet together for a
moment. She said, "I'm going to be a pretty disappointing Muslim for
you, Cyrus. Be prepared."

He took comfort from her verb tense. "It doesn't matter."

They sat quietly. Hilda colored furiously and whispered, "You're a
tough critic."

"I think of those two years," he said. "Knowing everything that
way—hearing from God. Must have been hard, don't you think? Not to
tell someone?"

12

HALF AN HOUR later the others bustled in with arms full and descriptions of the gathering storm. "Cyrus is here," Laurel said when she saw him. "Is Cyrus staying for dinner?" She believed he was hers most of all—that was Cyrus's impression; Laurel's impression was that he was clearly devoted to Samina.

Greg put on music—a radio station from Seattle that played jazz and came through with a touch of homely, vacation-worthy static. Cyrus set stacks of dishes and napkins out on the table—a nanny. A disregarded, indispensable part of the household. Dinner was served.

Nicholas, Samina, and Greg sat on the sectional leather sofa, Hilda on Nicholas's lap. Laurel pulled a chair over, and Cyrus settled in the generally neglected wicker chair in its corner. Cyrus's smile appeared ironic, nearly rude, but you had to trust that it wasn't. Outside, the cedar trees bent dangerously—it appeared dangerous, to unaccustomed eyes—and the deck was covered with the brown-gold fingers torn from the trees. The cottagers all felt slightly safer with Cyrus among them. He didn't seem concerned about the storm.

"Cyrus," Samina said eventually (after the weather had been discussed, and the meal), "was asking me earlier what ever happened to the noble ambitions of my youth."

"I was not," Cyrus replied, quietly, though it was true—this was roughly the topic they'd moved on to after Muhammad. She sat directly in front of him on the low sofa. She could turn at the waist to face him, but instead she tipped her head all the way back and looked at him upside down. When she tipped her head up again, she said, "I hardly remember my ambitions. It's a bit sad."

The rain blew against the windows like pins.

"No!" Hilda shouted, when her father offered her the wrong risotto. The adults were set free. "She didn't nap," Samina said, quietly and not to anyone in particular. "Is this Art Tatum?" Nicholas asked Greg, ignoring Hilda and his wife both, and at about the same time, Laurel asked Samina, "What were your ambitions? What can you remember?"

"No, I'm the worst person to ask. Poor Cyrus already found this out."

"You were going to go to Med School—I remember that."

"Not really. I was bluffing."

"Samina," Laurel said to Cyrus—she faced both of them, where she had placed her chair, "was a bit of a bad-ass in college."

"*That* was my ambition, actually," Samina said.

"A bad-ass who got good grades," Laurel explained. "An Indian bad-ass, but still . . ."

Cyrus listened politely but failed to smile. "You went to college together?"

Laurel said, "She had a following." She thought of something—grinned—and said, "Okay, here's what Samina was like—you remember this?" she asked Samina. "George Bush—the elder one—spoke at our graduation. This was during the Gulf War, or right after it—I don't know if you remember the Gulf War, Cyrus. Well, there was supposed to be a big, embarrassing protest: a bunch of new graduates were supposed to stand up in their caps and gowns and turn their backs on him throughout his speech. Everybody was very excited about it leading up to graduation, but when the time came, Samina was the only one who did it. The *only* one. Thousands of people there—everyone's parents, all the deans and professors—and all the graduates are out there in the middle of things, on display. And you stayed standing through his whole speech, with all those parents and grandparents staring at you, murmuring."

"*You* were supposed to stand," Samina said. "As I recall, you were the one hanging fliers all week, not me."

"But you know what I admired just as much?" Laurel said, speaking to Samina now rather than Cyrus. "The way you didn't crow about it afterward or complain about the rest of us. Or try to get mileage out of what a rebel you were, the way any sensible twenty-one-year-old would have. I was a fan," she said to Cyrus. "One of her lackeys."

"I stood," Greg put in, rejoining them.

"Yes, I'm sure you did, dear," Laurel told him. To Cyrus she said, "He wasn't there."

"Oh, that's right," Greg replied.

Second helpings. What were Cyrus's ambitions? Laurel wanted to know. Cyrus said, to rule the world. But failing that, to build a massive dam and flood a canyon. He appeared serious, so he was made aware of how uncouth such an ambition was—by instructive and right-minded Nicholas, gently, and then by Laurel in more strident chorus. "Oh, come on," Greg said, "I think it sounds great. Let's flood a canyon! Have you ever been to Lake Powell? In Utah?" Cyrus shook his head. "It's beautiful. We went last year. It's a great place." Was he kidding? his wife wished to know. Because Lake Powell was a crime. What's it like? Samina asked, and Greg described the canyon walls, which fell below the green water almost as far as they rose above it, visibly, so that in a boat, beside a wall, looking up and then down, you felt precariously suspended. Laurel offered instead the buzzing mess of boats and the grazing lands at the bottom of those canyon walls, the centuries of native culture replaced by Jet Skis, the wild river habitat destroyed. Greg frowned and said (to Cyrus, who had been left at the edges of this conversation), "You know, the first thing you learn writing biography is that ambitions are fine and dandy but mostly a big waste of time. We don't know what we're going to do or what our lives are going to be like. Everybody gets surprised. That's the one thing you can be sure of," he said. "But it doesn't even matter. You just revise backwards. People look back and find all the things that led them here, to wherever the hell they've ended up, and in hindsight they just focus on those things and forget about everything that didn't come true. Samina's right—I might think I remember my ambitions from when I was your age but it's bullshit. Excuse me, Hilda." She hadn't been paying attention—she'd been squirming crankily on her father's lap—but she was momentarily spellbound by the appearance of her name in the conversation.

"Amen," Laurel said, with sarcasm. Everyone was quiet for a moment. Greg picked an olive from his plate and shrugged.

Outside, flashes of white chop on the bay were picked up by the stray lights along the shore. Nicholas said, "I'm not so sure that's really true, though." Greg said, "You want to fight? You want to take this outside, buddy?" Cyrus laughed loudly, though alone.

Nicholas smiled, but he didn't seem to mean it. It occurred to Cyrus that up to now, Nicholas had hardly spoken all evening. He said, "It's just too easy to think highly of the stuff we've forgotten about ourselves, isn't it? Or what we don't know about a dead person—to think he must have had secrets he never told his wife—"

"Yes, I can't imagine that," Greg said.

"Let me finish."

But Greg said, "I'm not claiming we're all deep mysteries or something. I'm just talking about how we organize things—just the nature of memory."

"I know."

Hilda wrestled her way out of Nicholas's lap, broke past her mother's reach, ran down the hall to the bathroom, and Greg took the opportunity of the distraction. "Look," he said, "if you happen to be living a charmed life maybe you don't want to believe that other people keep secrets and skeletons in their closets. But I think you might be disappointed with the rest of us, Nicholas."

Nicholas said, "How are you supposed to know if my life is charmed or not if your claim is that even I can't tell?"

How interesting, Cyrus thought: they don't like each other. Samina said, "There's more salad, Cyrus. Can I get you more?"

Everyone turned to him. "Oh, no. Thank you."

She rose from the couch and collected plates. After a quiet moment, Greg leaned over and slapped Nicholas's knee. "Finish what you were saying."

Nicholas shrugged. But eventually he did. He said that yes, sure, everybody—even your Victorians with their diaries upon diaries and all those letters—even they must only get some small part of their lives down on the page. Of course. But it's just as obvious that they did get down more of what's important. Most of what people forget every day was never worth remembering and surely whatever's essential to us *usually* gets told to someone, somewhere, or happens in front of someone, who probably repeats it later. And what's trivial and what's important in someone's life might flip-flop now and then, but it doesn't happen often. That's the exception, not the rule. Don't the people close to us (Nicholas asked), who spend the most time with us, don't they know us more than they don't know us, and understand more than they misunderstand? Although we're so much more troubled by the misunderstanding than impressed by the understanding that we sometimes lose track of this?

Greg said, "I don't agree," and shrugged. Cyrus wondered who he was rooting for, Greg or Nicholas. Wouldn't it be great if they came to blows?

Greg said that what Nicholas was talking about was all the figment, actually, the fabrication, the autobiography we're all busy telling ourselves all day long, "I think," he added. "I really think we feel somebody 'knows' us or doesn't," he said, "or understands us or doesn't, based on how loyal they seem to be as an audience for our shifting ideas of who we are. Based on how much they seem to buy this autobiographical version of our-selves—this made-up person. Who, I mean—god knows—we believe in, too. *We* believe it's the real man."

Nicholas said, "But you're focusing on the exceptions, not the rule. You're talking about the Nixons of the world now."

"No, I'm not." Greg shook his head and smiled. "No, I'm not. I don't mean people sweeping embarrassments under the rug—"

He interrupted himself: "Listen, this may never have been your expe-rience, Nicholas, I don't know, but let me just assure you that people *are* misunderstood now and again. By good friends, by loved ones—"

"Now you're talking about melodrama."

"—by the same people who are supposed to be remembering what this person was like when he's dead—remembering all the *important* things, as you say, except they may have had the wrong impression about those things all along so what good are those memories going to be? Who's being remembered now?"

"Poor Greg," Laurel said, ostensibly to Samina, "he's so terribly misunderstood by loved ones, you know."

But Greg had continued, speaking over her. "Fine," he was saying, "of course. Everybody knows that—fine. But that's not even my point. What I'm saying is that just as often the autobiography we tell about ourselves, right along the way as we live our lives, is *uglier* than the real person. Or than the person other people get to see. We're an idiot, in our autobiographical version, who has everybody fooled. Or no one fooled. Or we're a coward. Or we're a fuckup who will never get anywhere or ever finish anything important—whatever it might be. And then we change the self-portrait all the time—but gradually, so we end up losing touch with our wife or old friends and falling out of love and imagining that they don't *know* us anymore, but all because they haven't kept up with the revised self-portrait."

Cyrus was a little dazed. He said, "I think that's right!"

He spoke with such conviction that everyone in the room laughed a little. Hilda, when she had come back, had stood by his knees and reached up, and he had lifted her onto his lap. She lay with her cheek against his chest now, sucking her thumb. When they laughed Cyrus could feel his smile unpeeling—and he laughed, too.

Laurel said, "Hilda, dear, you're adorable."

Cyrus said, "I'm with Greg. That's my theory, too."

Nicholas turned to Greg, smirking happily, and said, "Well, you've got *Cyrus* on your side," and this stilled the room. There was a foul note to it.

Nicholas looked down at the glass in his hand, his smirk quickly gone. "Oh, you're probably right," he tried, in a different tone. "I'm sure you're both right."

After a moment, Samina offered coffee and ice cream. Hilda awakened. Up out of their seats. *My goodness, this weather,* they all said, awkwardly repeating themselves. Greg laid a fire—he would burn the wood that Cyrus had split.

Cyrus was the only one who could put them at ease again—he recognized this—and when he felt they had suffered long enough for his sake, he said (to Nicholas, smiling amiably—perhaps even thickly, as if he were a person who didn't know when he'd been insulted), "My father's actually working on a biography. Or something."

"Is that right?" Nicholas asked, grateful as can be. He could look severe and unapproachable with that bald head of his and the just-so glasses, but then his smile popped forth like a *Bang!* flag from a toy gun. "Who is he writing about?" Cyrus said, "Lewis Carroll. Whose real name was actually Charles Dodgson, as everyone in the room knows."

"Is he really?" Nicholas replied. "Is he a teacher, your father?" Cyrus laughed and ate his ice cream. Samina asked, "Has your father written many books, Cyrus?" They used his name too often—all four of them did. That was an indication of certain things, he felt. "No. No, he only writes the one book."

"Just an Alice fan, eh?" Nicholas asked, having assessed the depth of the endeavor already. *Quaint*, he must be thinking. He was thinking, *Those Canadians!*—or so Cyrus thought. "Actually, we're relatives of the Dodgsons," Cyrus said. *He* is *smug, old Nicholas*—somehow Cyrus hadn't noticed before tonight. "My dad has the family stuff," he said. "You know: boxes from the attics."

Laurel said, "Oh, that's fascinating." And Greg, from the fire, asked, "What's your family name again, Cyrus?"

"Collingwood."

Greg nodded—a name he knew, evidently.

Greg, Cyrus decided, was all right. He was certainly smart, and an awkward person will be drawn to another awkward person, it's true: there's nothing quite to be done about it, although who will ever want to be around them, put together? It seemed so obvious, now, that he was as wrong for Laurel as Nicholas was for Samina. It was tempting to deliver Samina from all of them, but it wouldn't do: she liked to be part of the background too much to be alone. She needed someone nearby to take the attention from her, Cyrus thought.

Oh, if only people could be molded—if only their lives could be engineered by a practiced hand, from the outside, by someone with the proper perspective. Samina had been born in a different language, in a third-world country, to parents Cyrus would probably have found baffling and impenetrable, and she had come about as far around the world as you could to reach him here. He hoped to travel as far himself—not as a tourist, sampling, skimming off surfaces, but to live some dedicated life that far in the distance—and he didn't intend to go all that way to end up a bourgeois spouse in an ordinary marriage. Perhaps she couldn't really allow herself to take a clear look at how little she'd settled for. Her dismissive attitude about ambitions as amazing as Muhammad's—that would be self-protective, too, of course.

Or was it possible she'd done some real damage in her day? Had she *failed loved ones?* he wanted to ask her, with an irony she would recognize. Was he only catching her post-eruption, cooled and dormant again? He would have to be patient, and find some way to earn her trust.

Yet he had this terrible fear, too—it was so strong it was more or less a conviction—that he would run out of patience and interest before he ever gained anything valuable from her. Was she really *so* wonderful, after all, so worthwhile? The mind is its own worst enemy, as everyone knows: you beg it to be sensible, to respond to reason or if not reason then how about to earnest provocation (I *want* to know her, you tell it— I'm capable of the dedication required; I'm willing; she likes me, so far), but it replies: Ho-hum. You beg the mind, or try to trick it, rope it in, but the little pissy part of it in back is already, right this minute, saying to you: Look, this is getting old. This is a boring evening. And anyway, you'll never carry through. You'll never take the big chance, commit to the big act—*you won't go to Columbia,* you'll never get out of Sooke, you won't carry through, you never do. Relax, it says. This is how people are. People settle. Nobody does the really hard things. Nobody does what's in his heart. Relax. Why should you be different?

They talked about Chick's great magnum opus, his long and senseless dedication. Cyrus was not mean about it, he thought, but he kept the portrait of his father colorful for their benefit. Then the others got comfortable enough to slip back off topic and forget about Cyrus. They found it easier to talk to one another than to him—he saw this. Hilda fell asleep and Samina carried her away. Perhaps the pissy mind is right, Cyrus thought: I don't belong in this lit room and this dull conversation. He'd much rather be outside now, right this minute, with the wind blowing against one side of him, satisfyingly saturated, sitting in a bush and looking through the French door at Samina in that bedroom as she lay Hilda down and bent over her, casting her spell the way she did each night. There was a little chant she had—he'd love to hear what she said—then she waved a slim finger around Hilda's head in a circle and blew on her softly, ruffling her bangs. Alone with Samina that way. *Know thy place, Cyrus, my boy*, he told himself. *Know thy place!*

13

_____

I T WAS A not very sensible thought—so unlikely, of course; so transparently desperate (nothing more attractive to an author bailing a sinking ship than to spot another boat passing by and swim for it)—but once this Lewis Carroll (yes, dear Cyrus, Charles Lutwidge Dodgson) was in his mind, Greg could not stop thinking about him. He was up half the night wondering what Cyrus's father might have. He knew quite a lot about Dodgson. Like Ruskin and Millais, Dodgson had visited Julia Margaret Cameron and Tennyson on the Isle of Wight. He had crossed paths with Ruskin at Oxford and photographed the older man. Mr. and Mrs. Millais (John Everett and Effie) were friends of Dodgson's. His photographs of them with their two daughters were taken through an open window, doubly framed, husband and wife in profile at each side smiling upon the children in their laps while one of the girls stared skeptically at the camera. Dodgson had, in fact, always been a figure at the periphery of Greg's book, a minor character making brief, ungainly appearances.

But Greg hadn't brought any materials on Dodgson to Sooke, so the day after the storm he made an excuse to get out of his library date with Nicholas. Since Nicholas was still feeling contrite about his moment of nastiness the night before, this wasn't difficult. Greg would have to hurry, taking their only car away—the rental—with the Jetta still in the shop. The driveway was covered entirely with golden needles from the trees. When you drove over them they smelled like downed apples. He went to their library in Sooke first, but had to double back to a town called Langford for the nearest copy of anything suitable. There were fallen branches in the roads but no road crews in sight, and the locals swerved breezily without braking. At the library he found a metal desk by a window and settled down with his book. He didn't think he wanted to bring it home or be seen with it yet. How exciting it was to be at this stage: a new prospect before you, a subject at hand who could still surprise you. It had been such a long time since Greg had pulled a book from the stacks and sat down to graze from it as impatiently as this, and it was ironic that the book, this biography, was one he had already read. But years ago, with different eyes.

In fact, there were plenty of holes in the documentation of Dodgson's life—important, delectable pieces missing from the puzzle. Diary pages had been suppressed. Whole volumes of the early diary had gone missing. Letters, too: he was an inexhaustible letter writer and had kept a meticulous register, but three-quarters of those listed as "sent" or "received" (ninety-eight thousand entries! ridiculous) were considered lost. Most enticing was the mystery attached to what you couldn't help seeing as the moment in Dodgson's life that a sensible biographer might erect at the center to swing the rest of the narrative around. It was the turning point in Charles's relationship with Alice—the real Alice, Miss Liddell, the second daughter of the Dean of Christ Church. A single diary page was missing from late June 1863—a record of three difficult days, evidently. At that point, Dodgson had known Alice (eleven years old) and her lively sisters (Lorina was eldest, Edith followed Alice) for five years. He was an ordained deacon and mathematical lecturer at Christ Church, with his tidy rooms in Tom Quad and a stutter that sometimes receded around his "child friends." The Liddell girls seemed to love Dodgson, and trust him, but as anyone with a passing interest in Lewis Carroll knew, it was difficult to decide how to characterize his affection for the girls. He took them on rowing expeditions to picnics under haycocks and told them stories on these excursions, about Alice down the rabbit hole. The sisters were among his first photographic subjects, and his best. Some of the photos were reproduced in the book Greg was holding. Here was Lorina (Charles called her "Ina") dangling cherries above Alice's parted, impatient lips—Alice grabbed at her sister's arm to pull the treat down; she wouldn't wait. Edith sat behind them with the bowl full of cherries and a complex frown. "Open your mouth, and shut your eyes" was the caption Charles had provided. Here was Alice as the beggar maid, in tatters and barefoot, her hand held out in supplication. Her dress of rags had been encouraged to fall from one shoulder. How coyly she struck the pose—she was a beggar who wouldn't rely on pity alone.

In the spring of 1863, right up to the cliff of June 26, Dodgson was hardly ever apart from the Liddell girls. "There is no variety," he wrote, "in my life to record just now, *except* meetings with the Liddells, the record of which has become almost continuous." On the twenty-third of June he took them photographing—the light was especially good. On the twenty-fourth he accompanied them and their governess, Miss Prickett, to Sanger's Circus—a fine outing. On the twenty-fifth of June, "Alice and Edith came to my rooms to fetch me over to arrange about an expedition to Nuneham. It ended in our going down at 3, a party of ten. . . . We had our tea under the trees at Nuneham, after which the rest drove home in the carriage, (which met them in the park), while Ina, Alice, Edith and I (*mirabile dictu!*) walked down to the Abingdon-road Station, and so home by railway: a pleasant expedition with a *very* pleasant conclusion." In five years of close attendance and friendship, this may have nevertheless been (so this biographer said) the only hour or two in which Charles had ever been properly alone with the girls—with no Miss Prickett or Mrs. Liddell at hand; no party of adults just ahead of them on the path, being adults, exerting their dampening force. Dodgson was always careful to be proper. Even the river trips had depended upon the participation of at least one more adult—one more chaperone, as if Charles wouldn't quite do the trick on his own. What was the train trip like ("*mirabile dictu!*"): having them all to himself in a cozy berth? He wouldn't detail. Alice, Ina, and Edith were delivered home safely that evening. On the twenty-sixth of June it rained, and Dodgson kept busy with neglected work.

And then the page is missing. It had been cut from the diary (the biographer explained), very neatly, close to the spine. If you weren't careful, you might not have noticed it was missing. A niece named Manella Dodgson admitted, years later, to razoring it out, but she wouldn't say what had inspired her censorship. It may have been that the page had covered three days, or only one in detail with the next two skipped past. The diary picks up with 29 June, and there is no mention of any Liddells. In fact, the girls and their mother disappear from the record, as entirely as they had occupied it a page earlier. The change is so startling that it might be another year resuming after the missing page, with an entirely different routine to the days, a different mind divulged. Dodgson neither visited the girls nor referred to them in print (there weren't even private thoughts on them, recorded—or if there were, these hadn't yet been found) for the next six months. Prior to the missing page, it had been a long time since he'd gone six days without seeing them or writing about them. On December 2 of 1863 he went to the theater and spotted Mrs. Liddell and her daughters across the room. "But I held aloof from them, as I have done all this term." He doesn't explain why. Presumably, he *had* already—on the missing page.

Whatever happened in those days—whatever the misunderstanding was, or the argument, the wrong step or the insult or the overdue revelation—it meant the permanent end to Dodgson's friendship (or was it a romance?) with Alice. There was never another river trip or game of croquet between them, and never a second hour alone. She surfaced from time to time across the years in his diary, in passing reference or awkward meetings. He photographed her once more, along with her older sister, in 1870, when Alice was eighteen. They are the saddest, stiffest, most abject photos Dodgson ever took, with none of his art in them—and the one of Alice is by far the worst. Each young woman was set in the same ugly armchair, Lorina cold and primly posed, Alice almost depressive, slumped, her eyes shadowed and cast down, the ostentatious bow in the front of her hair a joke floating over her desolate frown. She had never hidden her feelings from the camera—not from his or Julia Margaret Cameron's. But what was going on in this photo and in this room? Greg wondered. There was every indication that she was a reasonably happy young woman at this stage in her life. In other photos from the period she smiled confidently. In no one's account was she said to be desolate. What made her so that day, while staring at the hooded Charles through the length of the lens? Had something gone wrong (or too right) when he was alone with the girls on the train back from Nuneham? Or the day after that? Well before it? Had something *been* happening for months or years—something that one of the girls had finally revealed to her mother? Neither Mrs. Liddell nor the adult Alice had ever said—Alice had been asked, when she was an old woman, but claimed she couldn't remember.

The biographer said Dodgson had kept different diaries for different purposes at certain times in his life, but those that anyone had yet recovered were meticulously, strangely impersonal. Some scholars wondered if the best diaries had been destroyed by the family, or if they remained hidden.

A niece—one of Dodgson's first executors, along with Manella—was named Collingwood. Mary Collingwood. Her son Stuart had written the first Dodgson biography. A Collingwood had been Ruskin's first biographer, too—it had actually made Greg shiver a little to hear Cyrus say his name. He decided to check this book out after all, along with a two-volume set of the letters. He could hide them in the trunk of the rental car and read them on the beach, alone.

A biographer can't help but think of his own life in biographer's terms, of course, but doesn't everyone, now and then? You wonder what era you're in the midst of now. Which chapter will this be? Will this vacation, for instance—the four weeks he spent in Sooke, when he was thirty-eight—become its own chapter, Greg wondered, while driving back to the cottage: a consequential moment in the narrative to be covered in detail, or a caesura slipped past in a sentence or two? The sentence after that would begin, "When he returned to St. Louis . . ." and then the momentous thing would happen. Or maybe it would be further off: "When he returned to St. Louis, he and his wife were refreshed and relatively happy through Christmas. He had regained his faith, he felt, in both his work and his marriage. But in January . . ." Just as likely, the thing had already happened, and Greg had missed it from his poor perspective in the midst of things. One hot morning in August, Greg had somehow annoyed Laurel, as he could so easily now—over something trivial, he couldn't even remember what—and without any warning she had turned on him and said, "Don't think you can be cruel to me because I've finished my book and you haven't." That was a banal little jab, too, but it had landed because the envy and pettiness she accused him of (while, he admitted, not necessarily out of character) could not in fact have been further from the truth. He had felt just the opposite: immensely proud of her, and relieved that *one* of them had finished, and grateful that she would almost certainly get her tenure now and prop him up a little longer. But the look on her face when she delivered her shot—of pure satisfaction, and release—told him it was something she was sure of, and had been saving up. For a few days afterward he'd wondered if he had miscalculated in his relationship with her at some point far in the past: if he'd always been too honest and open, too willing to document his least-flattering thoughts. He had assumed that she, of course, was the one person who would see through his weaknesses and never forget who he was despite and between his poorest impulses. But probably that was asking too much of a person. He should have been more sensible and discreet. Was it too late now? he'd wondered. Did she know him too well—or, as a matter of fact, *not* know him any longer? Maybe the ugliest part of what he had given her access to had also been the most compelling, and had eventually obscured her view of the rest.

He saw a phone in front of a pharmacy and couldn't resist. But Melanie wouldn't answer any longer. He knew she had caller ID; how sad and desperate to appear as "Pay Phone" in her bright, warm apartment this way. "I just don't like it," she had said, and he'd been wrong— she'd admitted that she hadn't been sleeping well, either, thinking about them and about his wife (whom she had met only once, momentarily, yet developed a complex and far from accurate impression of). She had cried. "I feel *awful*, Greg. And old." He'd felt awful, too—so guilty (for what he was putting her through more than Laurel) that he'd said she was right. But her voice on her answering machine was lighthearted and resilient and by now, a week later, he felt certain they had made a mistake, rushing out of things as quickly as they'd rushed into them. He'd be back soon and there was no reason for them not to dally further. Somehow it seemed only easier as things mysteriously improved a bit with Laurel. He didn't dare leave a message.

He would have to meet Cyrus's father, of course. As soon as possible. He and Laurel were supposed to return to St. Louis in two weeks—too soon. Sometimes these amateurs—the family descendants with documents, the scribblers hoarding their valuables—sometimes they welcomed the professional invasion and were pleased to be freed of the burden. Often they could be persuaded that it was better to be gratefully acknowledged in the introduction of someone else's book, completed and published while you were still alive, than to go down with the ship. Cyrus had suggested that his father had been working on the book for many years already. He *must* have something new. He must have read this very biography that Greg has just checked out, perhaps this same Langford Library copy—he must know what was already out there and what the world didn't need. Greg would simply have to meet the man. His mind, on the drive home, was already turning to schemes. He wasn't about to steal anything, of course, he just needed to know if there was anything there worth stealing. He could become friendly with Mr. Collingwood in these two weeks, then stay in touch from St. Louis. Nicholas and Samina would be here through November—Greg could come back, if necessary. He was a raccoon, of course, rooting through someone else's scraps after dark. It was the biographer's animal, he decided.

But he did want it all to remain his secret at least a little longer. So first things first: he would have to cover his tracks from today. When he'd gotten into the car to drive home he'd found it was two hours later than he'd guessed. He ought to patch things up a bit with Nicholas, play nice. He should offer to show Nicholas the provincial park he'd been visiting alone. He had planned on sharing it, eventually. Fine, then—with Nicholas first. He felt high. Truly high: elated and paranoid, both. Maybe he'd never felt as excited as this about his writing. He'd first been attracted to biography because he'd imagined himself in neglected rooms opening hidden chests, discovering diaries and secret lives—an explorer, tracking across virgin paragraphs that no one had laid eyes upon since the author blotted the page. But up to now, he'd never been so lucky. He'd begun to doubt he ever would be. "Charles, my friend," he said aloud, into the car, "what have you got to tell me?" He laughed at himself, a fool. Oh, dear, dear Cyrus.

14

I T WAS JUST behind them all along, this park—out of sight, beyond
the back lawns and edge trees, hemming the property lines on the
inland side of East Sooke Road. A narrow lane, hardly wider than the car,
led to a deeply shadowed parking lot where the trees were enormous, even
to eyes accustomed to Sooke. There was a path into them. It wasn't a dense
forest, but oddly emptied. Red cedars and hemlocks and firs, their crowns
never visible—the same trees they'd been seeing everywhere, but here they
loomed, dimly, with the lit evening only a figment in glimpses above them.
There were gray alders in clumps where one of the evergreens had fallen,
and dead trees sprawled in all directions, half covered by ferns that were
also enormous. The mosses grew thicker on the north sides of the trunks
and a Spanish moss hung in webs from dead branches. A damp chill clung
to the forest floor, and there was the suggestion of mist gathered between
the trees. Walking in such a forest you seemed to be in a moving pocket of
existence. The webby edges of everything were visible around you but as
bravely as you approached, you never reached them. To Nicholas, it was
exactly what a forest ought to be, though he'd never seen one look this way
outside the illustrations of grim tales.

"You've been keeping this to yourself," he said. He felt compelled to speak quietly.

"I just found it the other day," Greg told him, deploying the vague term.

The fallen trees were pulpy and long dead, but there were new branches knocked down or torn by yesterday's storm. Everything smelled wet. There was a suggestion of openness before the coast became visible. The trail split off to the right or left above the beach. Steps had been cut into the steep slope down to the water's edge, but you didn't quite see the ocean until you ducked through the screen of brush and stepped over a barrier of driftwood. The beach was a crescent of pebbles a couple of dozen paces wide, with another crescent beyond a low tongue of scrubbed rock. The cape was protected by tiny islands on either side. With the tide out you could walk on a causeway of sand to the nearer island and then scramble up through the grove of stumpy trees to the bald top. Nicholas and Greg looked across the Strait of Juan de Fuca at the Olympic Mountains, massive and gray-bodied in the haze and cut off by clouds, and down into the green-blue water in front of the island, where trees of seaweed grew up from the darkness. The sun was hidden but low—it would set soon. "The last time I was here I saw a couple of seals swim by," Greg said, pointing.

"It's beautiful." Nicholas was surprised by how impressive it was—a provincial park that hardly made the map. A container ship seemed still in a distant lane near the Washington side of the strait. "I can't believe we have the whole place to ourselves."

"I've seen other people. On the weekends."

Obviously this was where Greg had been disappearing to some mornings.

They sat watching the water slip by, then wandered back across from the island to the beach and poked around without speaking much. Nicholas took off his shoes and rolled up his pants to wade. He was relieved, and not surprised, when Greg said, "I think I may wander off—down the shore a bit. Do you want to come?" he added after a pause.

"No, no," Nicholas told him, "take your time. I'll be here."

Greg disappeared up what must be a different path, into the trees at one end of the beach. Nicholas skipped stones, then began to recognize how many of them were beautiful. They were small and tumbled smooth, in oranges and reds and rich browns and greens, dove gray, a shiny and impenetrable black. If he didn't believe it (and he didn't) and he operated just as if it weren't true—only exactly as he would have before Laurel whispered a single moist, cloying, obnoxious word to him— then it disappeared. This wasn't a philosophy he could quite believe in, yet it worked in practice. Who could this someone else be, after all? And Samina would argue with Nicholas before she ever began an affair, he imagined, or complain, give him a chance to rectify whatever was wrong and rise to the occasion. There would be clearer signs of disappointment. The signs he had were too tentative, half imagined, he still believed. Some of the stones were calicoed, as if two different species of liquid rock had been stirred together before cooling. Some had thick stripes of a different shade neatly belted through the middle, or scribbled in white like twine embedded in the stone. Volcanic, he supposed? He found one that was translucent and lit from within like an opal. He was walking on the thin-ice surface of a deep, dark lake, he felt. It all scared the shit out of him. The fact was, they had never "communicated" well (they shared a contempt for that term and all the others that came with it). They never spoke about the hardest things, they didn't argue—they didn't need to. That seemed built in. If they needed to argue, something would be lost already. The stones rolled in a throaty tumble when the waves pulled apart from them.

She longed for India and he'd taken her to Canada—to a place where a park as beautiful as this could be deserted on an evening as beautiful as this. It would be nice if Greg and Laurel could just once go off somewhere together for an afternoon—if only for a couple of hours—and leave Nicholas and Samina alone.

Even if what Laurel had said was true, he couldn't think of a better way to combat it than to offer Samina his best and hope he proved preferable. To confront her or plead with her . . . maybe these strategies worked for someone, but he doubted it. Not in the long run. Or to have entertained the suggestion when of course it wasn't true—even for a moment, much less for several days now. It wouldn't help anything for her to know that about him. And any of these approaches would be to sacrifice their advantage and drag what they'd carefully made down to anyone's ordinary marriage. Better to keep secrets, if necessary. Better to lie or not to look too closely.

He would do anything to keep her, as a matter of fact—he would buckle or crimp in any way necessary. Let them go to India. For as long as she liked. Let him bend into the form of her life for once.

15

IMAGINE A HEAD in profile, tipped up, facing northwest on the map: the mouth is open and that open oval of mouth is Sooke Basin and Harbour. The lower jaw is East Sooke. The upper jaw is Sooke itself, along the main road, and if you continued down that road another hour or two you'd come to a second dead end at the tip of the nose: Port Renfrew and the southern entrance to the national park, which would continue up the bridge of the nose on this face and well into the forehead. Victoria is back at the soft spot just under the earlobe.

On the lower jaw, in East Sooke, their cottage was at the front molar, and the point where East Sooke Road dead-ended at the harbor was the bottom lip. The beach with the stones and the tiny islands, where Greg had left Nicholas perhaps an hour ago, was the soft indent just in back of the bone of the chin, under the jaw, and this beach that Greg was at now was the strong point of the chin. It was the corner of the peninsula, jutting into the Strait of Juan de Fuca. The waves rolled down the strait from the open ocean to the west, and as small as they might be at the beach just around the corner, they were almost always substantial here. They rose at the openings of the channels they had cut into the rock, bullied through to the walls at the ends of these funnels, and threw up their spray. Then boiled back out and reconsolidated. There was always a wind in your face here. It was a spot that Ruskin might have loved. Greg could not keep his mind from Dodgson. He was a useless companion to Nicholas at the moment. What had Charles done? What had he done to be banished by the Liddells—what had he done to Alice, or with her—*for* her, he might have thought? He was this perfectly poised figure: his devotion to prepubescent girls, his collecting of them (keeping alphabetical lists of the girls he met each summer at Eastbourne, and lists of girls in Oxford "photographed or to be photographed" with their birthdays recorded beside each name)—all of this was so relatively common and acceptable in his England for a bachelor with an aesthetic temperament that he fearlessly documented the obsession. But on the other hand, he kept so much out of his letters and diaries. You only had to become acquainted with his biography as loosely as Greg was now to get the sense of a lonely life packed with secrets. He had constructed a glass house on the roof of Tom Quad with heavy curtains that could be pulled, when the sun was too bright or when privacy was wanted, but where he could also photograph his "child-friends" on rainy, intimate days. A few photos of nude girls had surfaced, in which they appeared contemplative and posed, relaxed, yet so pale and pudgy and blank you couldn't help but worry for them. It wasn't hard to guess what one would find in these diaries Mr. Collingwood might have.

Greg watched the sun set into the Pacific. It half burned through the cloud cover at the very edge of the horizon, leaving streaks of orange and then lurid pink. Tomorrow he would try to meet Cyrus's father and this fantasy he was indulging might easily be shattered in any number of ways. The ocean in the funnels made deep, gurgling sounds that belonged half to the water and half to the rocks. The green bled out of the ocean's surface and turned gray in the twilight.

He lingered longer than he'd realized, and when he stepped from the open headland back into the cover of the forest, the light went from a subtle dusk nearly to full dark. It was almost difficult to see the path in front of him—the floor of it, anyway; the forest was dense enough here to mark the corridor out. If he had left fifteen minutes sooner he probably would have been fine. But now it was a clumsy darkness. Nicholas would have grown impatient. Greg came around the headland to the other beach and called down. "Nicholas?" He couldn't see anyone down there, in the open dusk past the trees, or on the little island. "Hey, Nicholas!" He went down the slope to the beach. But Nicholas had already left. He must be waiting at the car.

Coming up into the forest again it seemed darker than it had only a moment earlier. That was probably because (Greg admitted) he didn't want to walk the mile back to the car alone. Not in the dark. This part of the path was wide and nearly flat, more easily navigated than the bit of trail between the two beaches, but it was darker, too, more thickly enveloped. There was no sound here except the sound of his own footsteps and his own breathing. Nicholas might be worried about him, or angry, or both. So much for making things up to him. Greg walked as quickly as he could, and broke into a jog for a few steps before returning to the fast walk.

He knocked into a fallen branch he hadn't seen at all—it must have jutted into the trail. He held his ankle in both hands until the dull ache drained away. He was in the middle of a thick silence. Despite the inarticulate shadows, despite this branch, he could almost believe he was in the middle of nothing. He tried to walk more slowly, but it was no use. He felt compelled to sprint. Then an idea occurred to him and he stopped and felt about blindly on the ground until he had two stones in his hands. He banged them together, making a thin, stony crack. It wasn't half as loud as he could have been if he just called something out, some shout or whoop, but that didn't seem quite possible, for some reason. No, the crack of the stones was just right: sharp enough to warn whatever was out there, at the edges of the trail, that he was coming through, but not so loud as to call attention from any distance or attract danger. (Or to let Nicholas know, when Greg got closer to the parking lot, how scared he had been.)

He began jogging and cracking his stones together. His own breathing filled his head. What was he afraid of? What did he really think could be out there? A bear? Not quite (though suddenly he wondered if that *was* a legitimate concern). He was just a scared city kid. He thought he would have to stop jogging but his lungs seemed to expand to meet the task.

The trail was longer than it had been in daylight. Twice he thought he saw the opening that would signal the parking lot, and when he actually did—when he knew for certain that's what it was—he stopped jogging. He dropped the stones into the darkness down around his ankles. Then he wondered why there was no light on past the edge of the forest. He had expected the car to be started, or a door left open for the beacon it would offer. Nicholas shouting his name. He called out: "Hey Nicholas!

"It's me," he called (how stupid it sounded).

The rental car was still parked where they'd left it. Greg had the key— of course Nicholas couldn't be in it. There was the tiniest bit more light—a last shade of dusk still—in the lot, where the web of treetops overhead was thinner, but it was a relief, nevertheless, to start the car up and put the headlights on, even if they rendered the darkness around them that much more opaque. The engine sound was welcome, and the sound of the radio, human intrusions. *Let this be the one*, Greg thought— meaning Cyrus's father and Dodgson. *Let this be my gift, however large the obligation it brings with it, however much of my life it occupies (in fact, the more the better). Let it be something worthy and engrossing—an occupation not so tawdry or disheartening as another Melanie.* He rolled down his windows and called out. "Nicholas!" He beeped the horn—though that was a mistake, much too loud, a violation of the silence and somehow dangerous. His concern for himself slowly got out of the way. Where could Nicholas be?

He backed the car up and pointed it straight down the trail. There were boulders placed across the entrance into the forest but his head-lights shone down the narrowing corridor, a long straight stretch before the first turn. Dead branches leaned into the light from above, weird arms. "Nicholas!" he called, sticking his head out the window. "Ni-cho-las!" He got out and stepped away from the car to listen. He stood in front of the headlights and waved.

It was true that Nicholas had never been in this park before, but the trail in and out was quite clear. (It must have been some kind of road once.) And Nicholas was all that Greg wasn't, out in the wild—he'd be the last one to get lost.

In fact, Greg's best guess, for quite a while, was that Nicholas had sim-ply wandered farther than Greg, probably down the coast in the other direction. *He* wouldn't be jogging back, terrified, afraid of the dark. He might be standing still somewhere, happily listening for owls or communing with the damn bears.

But after half an hour (he listened to National Public Radio, kept the car running and the headlights pointed down the trail, rolled the window back up; it began to rain, very lightly), it finally occurred to Greg that Nicholas might even have walked all the way to the cottage. If he had gotten to the car first and become impatient, he might have—it was probably only two miles farther. Or he might even have taken a different trail, through the park, navigating by sense of direction. Greg wouldn't put it past him. He'd go home, then. If Nicholas wasn't there, he would come back with Laurel and Samina and flashlights. He was resolved, and he put the car in reverse, but he kept waiting an extra moment, expecting Nicholas to appear, just now. How demoralizing it would be for him to get to the parking lot just in time to see Greg pulling away. There was a turn to the right that the trail took at the end of this last straight stretch. Past it, under the trees off the trail, the headlights seemed to give way to an indistinct darkness. Greg kept thinking he saw something move there. Or not move, quite, but begin to take shape, materialize, some portion of the darkness that would break off and come forward, turn into something else instead.

Part

II

16

AT TWO IN the morning, Hilda was in her bath. "I haven't a shoe," she was saying, and, in another register, "I haven't the hiccups" while Samina soaped her shoulders. It was a dialogue between Mr. Brown and Miss Porridge, the plastic figures in her hands. Hard to know what had registered with her—or it seemed so to Laurel, who sat on the lid of the toilet, wanting to speak but too tired by now to think of a new sentiment worth expressing. Samina sat on the bath mat and leaned so that her armpits rested on the edge of the tub. There was the phrase *Where is he?* passing through Laurel's mind again, a message becoming too steadily and pointlessly repeated to gain any contemplative traction. It skittered across the back of the stage behind the other thoughts dutifully playing their parts—not quite a cast member but hardly interrupting the play, either. "God, I'm tired," she said.

No use trying to avoid all the things one shouldn't say, everything that might sound selfish or insensitive. It was as little use as venturing the same speculations and empty assurances again. Laurel was an hour past this realization, but perhaps it would seem less prudent to her in the morning. For now, she had resolved to speak truthfully and to give any assistance she could. She trusted that she would be asked for little and would have to determine how she could be helpful on her own.

"Go to sleep," Samina said, emptily. "I'll wait for Greg."

"I couldn't sleep anyway."

Greg was driving the road one last time, up and down between the entrances to the park. He'd been gone nearly an hour. It was difficult not to think that the longer he was away, the better the news might be, but Laurel worried about him, too.

Greg had arrived at the cottage after dark, after the rain had begun, with no Nicholas beside him. Laurel and Samina had gone to the front door when they heard the car. "He's not here?" Greg had asked, then came inside and told them the story, such as it was. "He's probably on his way," he'd said. "Worst case he may have twisted an ankle somewhere, maybe had to settle down in a dry spot. Or he's just moving slowly. It's warm out tonight, not raining much." None of them wanted to call the police yet, for some reason. They decided that Greg and Laurel would return to the trailhead and walk to the beach with flashlights and first aid while Samina drove the length of East Sooke Road with Hilda. They didn't want to leave Samina on her own, but what was the alternative? They couldn't bring Hilda down a dark trail in the rain, and Laurel wouldn't let Greg go back into the woods alone. "We need Cyrus," she had said. He would know this park, he would know Walter and other people to speak to, they would have two cars again. But they didn't know where Cyrus lived—they only saw him when he appeared. "Walter will know," Laurel had pointed out, but Samina had said, "Forget about Cyrus. Let's just go." Earlier, she had interrupted Greg's story for details: What time, she wanted to know (though Greg hadn't worn a watch), what time was it when he left Nicholas? What had Nicholas said? Did he *say* he was going somewhere else? Why did they split up? What were they doing in this park, anyway? Laurel resisted the urge to defend Greg but was relieved when the two parties separated at the trailhead.

The darkness on the trail, under the looming trees that ticked and shivered with the rain falling through them, seemed complete. "Nicholas!" they called. Greg stomped ahead. His foot sank into the mush of pebbles at the beach. "Tide's coming in," Greg whispered as they crossed a narrow causeway with silvery waves fanning toward one another from both directions. Laurel couldn't be sure what the island overlooked— only a gray region where the water met the clouds—but it must be pretty in the daylight. "How long have you been coming here?" she asked him, accusingly. "Nicholas!" they shouted.

They took the smaller trail, winding and rugged, along the coast. The waves lipped a momentary white before plowing into the rocks. When they wound back again through the bunchy, strange darkness, past the beach with the rain beginning to fall more steadily, they were listening to the sound of one another breathing. Greg relented and took her arm. Something shivered through the trees now and then—a breath of wind. "Maybe Samina found him."

When she hadn't, they called the police. Walter, at the store, had given Samina the home phone number of the local constable. "He said there are cliffs in this park," she told Greg. "Right beside the trail."

"Who did?"

"Walter. Is that true? He said a hiker once fell."

"No," Greg said, "I think he's exaggerating. It's not a dangerous trail."

"But why would he exaggerate?"

"Greg's right," Laurel said, though she knew she should probably keep her mouth shut. "It's a perfectly ordinary trail, Samina. Nicholas wouldn't have fallen off of it."

And suddenly Samina's anger had crumpled into tears. Hilda joined her immediately—Hilda must have been waiting to let loose. Laurel had never seen Samina cry. Her lips had crinkled almost grotesquely. "Why did you *go* there?" she asked Greg, the question lent additional force by Hilda's wailing.

Now, in the bathroom, she'd begun to cry again. This time her pretty face was left intact and her attention didn't appear to waver from the sponge. Her daughter hadn't noticed she was crying, and it seemed possible Samina herself hadn't, either. "Maybe we should put you both to bed," Laurel offered. "There's nothing else to do tonight, and we'll all want to get up at dawn and get back out there. Find him in time to stuff him with a good breakfast."

To her surprise, Samina nodded and stood. "*Chalo, beta,*" she said, and

Hilda let herself be lifted from the water. She let her mother towel her dry while Laurel drained the tub. Mr. Brown and Miss Porridge whispered to one another with more vehemence now, and more secrecy—the words were not quite perceptible any longer and perhaps they were being kept from Laurel, or from Laurel and Samina both. "Come, come," Samina said, steering her out of the bathroom and down the hall, wrapped in towels, turning them both away from Laurel. Over her shoulder, Samina offered a quiet "Thank you," then closed the door between them.

THE CONSTABLE HAD been a British man with a thick head of silver hair and an upright, considerable bearing. He stood a full head taller than Greg. "Constable Cortland," he had pronounced, presenting his hand, and when Greg had introduced them all, the constable had delivered a little speech. Sooke was pleased to have them, he said; it was a town that welcomed "foreigners." It had taken he himself in more than twenty years ago, along with his wife, and hadn't let them loose yet. Not to worry—they would get to the bottom of this mystery in no time and leave them with the rest of their vacation to enjoy. His smile was, if somehow inappropriate, nevertheless pleasant: sly, oddly reassuring. He walked stiffly, and when his speech was through he asked if they might take a seat. "It's the back," he said, referring to his own, evidently. "Should we have a cup of tea?" He winked at Laurel, and passed his charming smile on to each of them in turn. "Now." He took out a tattered notebook. "Nicholas Green is the name I have, from whoever it was called."

"That was Samina," Greg said, indicating. "Nicholas's wife." He watched the man writing in his notebook and said, "Her last name is Naqvi, actually. An *i* on the end."

"But you're married to the missing man?" the constable asked her.

"Yes," Samina replied, disinterested. Anyone could see that she didn't like the constable already.

"Hilda's the little girl, you said? Poor thing." Hilda cried still, and eyed the stranger from Samina's lap. "And what surname would she go by, then?"

"Her father's."

"Excellent." He took his notes. "Now. Who is it would have seen the missing man last?"

Greg recited the same details he had given them earlier. Without prompting, he added estimates of the time of day, explaining quite carefully the calculations he was making, backward, from the first time he'd seen a clock—in the car. The constable wrote and nodded. He said, "Yes," now and again, but at odd moments, midsentence—by way of encouragement, evidently, though Greg (and Laurel, too) kept hearing it as the beginning of an interruption. Hilda fretted. Laurel passed out tea. The constable whispered, "Lovely," to her, while Greg continued to speak, and when she indicated the milk he said, "Ta."

His questions were directed at the particulars of the day: Where exactly, now, and where had they already looked for the missing man? How well did the missing man know the park? What was he wearing and what might he have in his pockets? How fit was he? "In what sort of mood was he?" "When I left him?" Greg asked. "Yes, then," the constable said. "Earlier as well—earlier this week. Let's say 'lately,' if you like."

Greg said that Nicholas was in a good mood this evening. He admired the park. He's been cheerful in general, lately, hasn't he? Greg asked Samina. Since he got here?

And for the first time, a stray speculation crept into Laurel's mind. If Nicholas was not "lost" at all—if he had left—how responsible would she herself be?

Samina sat with Hilda at the far, dark end of the couch. She said, "He's perfectly happy."

A general silence followed. Eventually, Constable Cortland said, "Lovely." He jotted in his notebook. "Now," he said, pressing on, "would you have a photograph of Nicholas handy?"

Samina was not blaming her husband so much as Greg, it seemed to Laurel. Hard to imagine what she suspected him of, exactly—some larger negligence? Of ditching Nicholas on the trail? In any case, Greg had gotten the message. But at bottom Laurel felt certain that Nicholas was going to step through that door at any moment, and that all of this—Constable Cortland, Samina's suspicions, Laurel's own guilty fears—would appear a little ridiculous in hindsight. She hoped no one would say anything ugly that couldn't quite be retracted.

"Well . . . ," the constable finished, sitting back. "That should about do it for tonight. More than we'll need, I'm sure." He closed his note-book and tucked his pen away—each of these little gestures was per-formed elaborately, with an actor's care. It seemed to Laurel that he was playing detective, to some extent—trying on the role, borrowing every-thing from his inquiries to his broad and earnest expressions from books he had read or dramas he'd seen on television. It was an older, quainter notion of the role he was aiming for. How perfect that, as he was about to stiffly stand back up, he said, instead, "Oh—one more question," and paused. Laurel smiled.

"It's only I meant to ask, if I may," he said, "what exactly you're each thinking has happened to our missing man. To Nicholas. What your own theories are, I mean. It can be helpful, you see. We don't always think of everything, try as we may."

Into the quiet which followed this, he added, "For instance, there was a young girl who wandered off once—it would have been five or six years ago, now—and my men looked under hill and over dale for the better part of two days without a trace. Well, we happened to ask the girl's mother for her best theory and she said to us, 'She likes the starfish, you know—little Jenny does. All along,' she told us, 'I've been picturing her mucking about with her starfish in some tide pool.' I don't recall the girl's name, in fact." He had told this story often, Laurel thought. He'd be telling their story soon. Everyone in town would have heard about the American who got himself lost in the park. "Now she'd gone missing," he continued, speaking mainly to Greg, "not less than three tricky miles from any shore, so we hadn't given the beaches more than a passing thought. But what do you know if we didn't head down to the nearest bit of ocean, which was on the basin side with the starfish I'm sure you've seen for yourselves—very tempting oranges and violets, to a child's eye—and there she was, plain as day, the poor thing."

He paused, and Greg asked, "Had she drowned?"

"I'm afraid she had."

"So Mr. Faber?" the constable said. "You first? You know as much as anyone. What's your best guess, do you suppose? Where do you picture your friend Nicholas at this moment?"

Greg said that it would be like Nicholas to strike off in another direction—to want to see more of the park. Greg's voice was quiet and pre-cise—he had, over the course of the evening, modulated it into the very essence of reasonable consideration and attention. Nicholas had either gone farther than he realized, and lost his way, or injured himself in some manner that slowed him or kept him from walking at all. He might have twisted an ankle. Or, heaven forbid (had Laurel ever heard him use that phrase before?), something worse—broken a bone, maybe. "He was only wearing sandals," Greg said. "Oh, I'm just remembering. He wasn't wearing his hiking books—he was wearing sandals. Those new sandals of his," he said to Samina, who did not look up. "Nylon sandals. They were gray and black."

"Very good," Constable Cortland said, jotting this down. "Well, there's something."

Laurel, for her part, agreed with Greg. It was hard for her to imagine any other possibility. But she added that he was the sort of person who was comfortable in the woods, who wouldn't panic. He would find his way, eventually.

She was looking at Samina while she spoke, and Samina had begun to cry again—the quiet, less awful tears that she would cry later, by the tub. Hilda sucked her thumb, her cheek against her mother's sweater, not look-ing at anyone. The constable had turned to Samina, presumably to get her theory as well, but when he saw her he said, "Oh, I shouldn't worry, Mrs. Green—or, ah . . ." He reopened the notebook in his hand, flipped the pages. "Mrs. Naqvi, rather." He stood from his chair, smiled at her bravely. "In thirty-one years, we've managed to find them all, sooner or later."

Laurel asked, "Have many people gotten lost in that park?"

"They certainly have," he said. "My goodness, we've seen all this before. It's nothing new to us, you see." And oddly, Laurel did find this reassuring. He was right: it was nothing new, nothing terrible, only a mis-placed hiker, a mishap to be laughed at in the coffee shop and *tsk*ed over in the grocery aisles. *Tourists,* her father used to say, *they're easily misplaced*—she remembered, suddenly, how this went. She wondered if the constable was playing detective for their benefit—if the earnest man-ner of inquiry he'd adopted wasn't simply to reassure them. He himself probably had no doubt that the man would turn up. He only hoped, very likely, that Nicholas might resurface with a worthwhile story to tell, something richly inflected by his own incompetence, which the constable could get some mileage out of. This thought made Laurel begin to like Constable Cortland.

He had turned to Greg to shake his hand. "No, we'll have him home safe by midday tomorrow," he said. "You have my word." He shook Laurel's hand, too, this time. He touched his cap in Samina's direction. He smelled of cigarette smoke and, vaguely, of gasoline—townie smells. He'd been working on a car, perhaps, earlier in the day. Or fixing his lawn mower. People who owned snowmobiles often smelled this way, in winter: he and his wife would visit a brother in the mountains for a week each December, say. They would drive instead of flying—take the ferry across, pull their matching snowmobiles on a trailer. His truck would have a cab on it, and a toolbox with drawers built into one wall of the bed. Laurel knew him, after all. His accent had hidden the resemblance, but she probably knew him well.

LAUREL HAD FALLEN asleep on the couch, meaning to wait for Greg. She woke to the sound of him coming through the door. For a few seconds she lay happily still, patient for him to reach her—it was an old, pleasant sensation—but then she remembered Nicholas and leapt up. Samina was already halfway down the hall in a long, embroidered nightgown that must be from India. The shape of her breasts was highlighted by the drape of the fabric. She was looking at Greg and then past him, out the door, where the rain fell in a curtain off the roof. The gutters must have been stopped up by the debris the storm had knocked down last night. Greg closed the door with disappointed gentleness and wiped his feet on the mat. "I walked on the trail again," he said quietly. "It's still perfectly dry under the trees. Not so cold, either." He tried to meet Samina's eye. "He'd be smart to stay put for now, actually—stay under cover. He could easily have fallen asleep."

She took one more look at the door behind him, as if it would open or as if Greg had forgotten something. Then turned from them without a word and closed herself back into her bedroom.

17

I T WOULD HAVE surprised Laurel but perhaps not entirely dis-
couraged her confidence in having identified the type to learn that
Constable Cortland had been working on a dune buggy rather than a
lawn mower or snowmobile that afternoon. He had thus far failed to
repair a faulty carburetor. It was one in a fleet of nine identical buggies
which he owned and maintained—four-wheeled, open vehicles with roll
cages and engines hidden under fiberglass faux-jalopy frames. All nine
carburetors had become fouled and been effectively flushed now and
again, but the usual treatment had not worked this time. He was just
thinking, when Mrs. Cortland called out from the kitchen door to say the
telephone was for him, that he would have to obtain a manual of some
kind. A dreary prospect. But then it had been Mrs. Green or Naqvi on
the telephone, quite troubled, endeavoring to hide it, and, miraculously,
he had been set free from such a fate. The boys would be disappointed,
of course—the malfunctioning buggy was a speedy one and numbered 8
(which also made it more popular, for reasons the constable did not
understand)—but they'd be mollified by the news of the missing man. It
was Constable Cortland's present assumption, while driving home from
his interview, that the missing man might prove no more than an inept or

unlucky American with a fractured American this or that and a foul mood, come morning. He would be found, readily enough, slumped somewhere. In short, that Mr. Faber was correct. But there were a number of other possibilities, all more involved and engaging, and with Americans one did underestimate what they were capable of at one's own peril. One couldn't leap to premature conclusions, in any case.

The constable's car—the same for constabulary business and for groceries—was a blue-green Japanese model equipped with a two-way police radio and a siren/light unit which lay between the front seats, by the gear shift, and could be reached out the window and attached magnetically to the bonnet at a moment's notice—à la *Starsky and Hutch*. It was preferable that the car should be essentially unmarked since the bulk of the constable's work, day to day, involved catching speeders, particularly during loading and unloading hours along the short and tempting straightaway that ran past the elementary school. For such work he merely plunked the siren/light unit on the dash, generally speaking. About twice a year he had occasion to reach it through the window properly. He sometimes "fishtailed" out of the driveway on these occasions and waved for Mrs. Cortland's benefit. His wife had been the *Starsky and Hutch* fan—had even kept up with the two actors' later careers, such as they were. There were a number of American magazine publications which came to the house in her name. She always knew when a celebrity was in Sooke—which happened more often than one would guess, thanks to the Harbour House, the mildly famous and enormously expensive inn at the edge of town. Occasionally she dragged the constable across to Seattle, Washington, for a night, where they did just what they might as profitably have done in Victoria, or Vancouver— took their meals in restaurants, where the waiters were condescending and had to be tipped nevertheless, and looked into shop windows without purchasing anything, as the exchange rate was not good, and slept in a hotel room, where the bed was too soft, and looked in on American television, which exactly resembled Canadian television to his admittedly untutored eye—but all of it, for Mrs. Cortland, was touched by a bit of randy glamour simply because it was America. She came away from these visits happy, and that was all that mattered. He tried not to tease.

She had taken them to Salt Lake City once—had wanted to examine the Mormons—and once as far as Los Angeles, which proved quite horrid. First thing when Constable Cortland arrived home this evening and relayed the facts of the case to his wife, she would want to know where in America the parties were from. She would have something to tell him about not only New York City but St. Louis in Missouri. Stored facts and incidents from her magazines. Someone noteworthy would have been born even there, no doubt.

On his radio, he listened to the occasional exchanges from the RCMP detachment in Sooke proper and from Victoria. He hoped Mrs. Green or Naqvi had not contacted either, and it seemed very likely she hadn't. The party evidently had the impression that he alone was responsible for all of Sooke in addition to East Sooke. It was the sort of underestimation that would come naturally to them. Or perhaps that was unfair—it would not surprise the constable if Walter himself harbored and conveyed that misimpression, dear man.

Constable Cortland's Mini Mounties were nine to twelve years old. There was only that little window in which to get a boy and shape him properly, redirect his substantial energies. The constable could not abide adolescence, try as he might. He could not accept girls, though some had wanted to join, and would have done fine, very likely. Mrs. Cortland, as it happened, still could not have young girls at hand. Understandable. He took the Mini Mounties on horses down trails. He took them out in canoes—on the basin, or sometimes along a gentle river. He and Mrs. Cortland had invested in a large van some years ago which a tourist operation out of Victoria was selling at good value. He'd had the Mini Mounties to every point of historical interest on the southern island. He neglected to take them to points of cultural interest—the fact is, a boy (unlike a girl) does not naturally concern himself with culture, and shouldn't yet. But most often, the constable simply had them over to the house—two afternoons a week in summer, one in winter. He and Mrs. Cortland possessed a large front room, a converted porch, lined with south-facing windows and fitted with a squat and powerful woodstove, which was the troop's designated game room. It was crowded with mismatched tables of the proper height for boys on which board games and

bones and dice in all shapes and cast-metal figures meant to lend substance to imaginary scenarios were left in place between visits. In the plot
of land behind the house he had built a track: cut a winding circuit of
packed dirt twelve hundred meters long with moderate grades and
undulations and one perilous hairpin. The constable had access to a
bulldozer through a friend. The turns were protected by hay bales.
There were lights rigged to a generator in a shed, to combat fog and the
early darkness of winter, but the proper bulbs were terribly expensive so
the number they could afford only managed to bathe the track in a
species of yellow haze. The children were equipped with buggy helmets
and well strapped down, and though some evenings of racing ended in
tears of one variety or another, no Mini Mountie had ever been seriously
injured. It was all quite safe. The children must pay to use the track, of
course. Mrs. Cortland always said it was a shame she and the constable
were not made of money. Mini Mounties who could not pay—with parents who would not—lined the course behind the hay bales and sipped
cocoa which Mrs. Cortland prepared for them, and cheered with envy. It
was an effort to get proper races organized. Pole positions might be
neatly established, and a set number of laps agreed upon in advance, but
the races would nevertheless degenerate. The buggies simply would not
operate at comparable speeds, no matter what the constable did to them,
so that the Mini Mounties who had arrived too late or fought for their
rights too weakly and had been left with the lesser buggies might be
lapped a number of times too large to keep count of. By the conclusion
of most races there would be buggies running in both directions or out
of petrol or puttering about the infield. But there were only two boys—
Jeffrey Colhane and William Billington—who especially concerned
themselves with winning, so one or the other generally did.

Constable Cortland once had neighbors, Americans, who complained about a stench from the track and the fine, obligatory buzz.
They had moved here from Ann Arbor, Michigan, of all places, and
had evidently thought they would find pristine emptiness—just themselves and the eagles and bears, very likely. How disappointed they were
to discover that other families had gotten here before them and were
already going about their humble lives, crowding the Raughleys' dream

of retreat. Canadian lives, no less: how *unfair*, they felt. What a *nuisance*.
These were two of the Raughleys' favorite words. In any case, they did
not last. They were caught exceeding posted limits on a number of
occasions—tearing around in their four-wheel drive American vehicle
with the Michigan tags on it still. They were written up for that. They
were a young couple, about the ages of this missing man and his wife,
with a very young son—a sweet little tot, truth be told. They were
caught once in one of the provincial parks after sunset, and written up
for that as well. They possessed a general sort of disregard. Perhaps, in
their view, Canadian laws were roundly unfair, or a nuisance—were an
imposition upon their retreat into the wilderness. They had rented the
house beside the Cortlands' rather than buying it, fortunately. Suddenly,
one day, they were gone. And then the Billingtons moved into the
house, with their four sons, and bought it for a fair price. Mark and
Colin were too old, but William Billington became a Mini Mountie, and
Brent, too (though he was an ill-fated child—the only Mini Mountie in
a dozen years who had managed to get himself thrown from a horse).
The Billingtons never once complained about the track. On the contrary: they found it quite extraordinary. They had come down from
Comox—islanders, born and bred. Mrs. Cortland made a gooseberry
pie for the Billingtons, just as she had for the Raughleys, but the difference was that Mrs. Billington had returned the favor next day with her
blueberry cobble, which was superior. Things got better all the time,
week to week, in every little corner of the Lord's green world. You had
merely to tend to your own plot—point things in the right direction—
and trust the Lord to manage the rest.

Look, they didn't come here to be parasites. Constable Cortland
would take this line with anyone in any establishment in Sooke—with
old-time locals who outranked him, even. The constabulary position lent
a certain latitude. They meant well, he maintained—these visitors. They
didn't think they were parasites, or foulers of a clean well—they didn't
mean to be. Nine times in ten they just didn't know what they were. This
was the way not only with cottagers but with criminals in general, large
or small. The constable might deal with only the smallest variety out
here, but he would remind his audience that he had had adventures with

his share of "heavies" back in Birmingham, too, when he was a young man new to law enforcement—and it was all the same. People had no sense, quite. (And not all of them, please. You can't name a set of people who are all bad to the core.) But each was as well-meaning as your next man—don't doubt it.

Now, your Mr. Green (he was thinking, while driving): he may have run away, for instance. He may have meant to go missing. Could be escaping from, or to. Statistics would tell you it was most likely, a man that age and of that background, perfectly healthy, able to care for him-self—you didn't need to consult a book to know this would be true. In the photograph of the man that the wife had provided, he had that par-ticularly American look of glamorous irresponsibility. If he *had* run away, would the constable try and find him? That could prove an entertaining challenge, and a real service to his poor family. Or there could be foul play. It was not beyond consideration. Mr. Green's friend, Mr. Faber, would have to be your prime suspect, as the last to see him. Or the miss-ing man could be more foolish or clumsy or unlucky than usual. He could be dead on a pointy rock somewhere along the shore, or simply drowned, and in that case he might never be glimpsed again. The best of swimmers drowned up here by underestimating how cold the water was, or the tug of the current. In fact, the constable's theory was that your stronger swimmer from another climate—accustomed to the balmy beaches and heated Jacuzzis of America—was the most likely of all to drown: he was the one with the leather to go for the swim in the first place. The constable had known of cases, in Port Renfrew—they froze up, sank like a stone—though it hadn't happened in East Sooke yet. This could be something new. The truth was, no one had become lost under the constable's watch since that poor girl and her starfish—it might well have been "Jenny": that name did ring true in his memory, still.

But you couldn't be simply pleased with such an assignment, invigor-ating as it was to the end of a dull week. You couldn't help but think of this poor daughter, named Hilda, and of his foreign wife (if they were in fact married), who had not seemed firm on her feet, quite. Sometimes the foreign women were more dependent than any of your Anglo stock—they learn subservience in their cultures—and that was exactly the attraction to a certain sort of man. A not uncommon sort, very likely. Not the constable's cup of tea, but you had to worry for the pair of them. Mrs. Cortland would be examining the husband's photograph and saying a prayer for them tonight.

But very likely Mr. Green would turn up, posthaste. Even now the constable had been keeping an eye open on this drive back home. He would stop in on Walter to tamp down the story, keep the old bugger from spreading it too far. He could swear his troop to secrecy tomorrow morning and probably trust it to last a day or two—long enough. At any moment the missing man might step out from the woods, after all, and that was for the best nine ways out of ten. You never wished for tragedy to visit your corner, though if you were smart and responsible to the practical expectations the Lord placed upon each of us, then you prepared for such a visit and when it came you faced forward squarely and rose to meet the challenge. They were lucky people to lose their man here, under the constable's watch—it was not a thing he would ever say to anyone, of course, not even to Mrs. Cortland, but he could think it, here by himself in his car—and the cottagers would not recognize this or deign to acknowledge it, very likely, but that wasn't necessary. A policeman does not work for credit or gain to self. He would be good to these people—sweet as peaches. Expect the best from them. He could afford to. If the expectation was not met, Constable Cortland did not actually have any innocence concerning human nature left to lose.

18

T HERE WAS A tremendous tree stump bobbing in the water. As the tide had lowered, the stump had half beached itself on the shallow shelf of the cove. Nicholas rolled his pants up a bit farther and waded out, climbed onto the slick surface. He stood and managed to rock the stump free of the shelf. It bobbed with surprising stability. While he was sitting on one edge and momentarily dangling his feet in the frigid water—for the pleasure of the shocking cold—one of his sandals slipped from his toes. He tried to catch the strap with his foot but ended up pushing the sandal farther away instead. He waited for it to drift back to him. He could still wade and fetch it without getting wet much above the knees, but his feet were already half numb and the air was cooling, too, as the sun set behind clouds. There didn't seem any need.

As it turned out, he was wrong: instead of pushing in with the waves, the sandal quickly drifted out from shore. He supposed it must be pulled by the tide. Now he couldn't retrieve it without actually swimming, but they were decent sandals, bought just for this trip—*chappals* in his mind, the Urdu word for them, which with its clicky "cha" and thwap-back "pulls" seemed more onomatopoetically accurate than "sandals"; as good as "flip flops." He would have to walk back to the car with one bare foot—

not the worst notion, but a little creepy. There were enormous slugs in this part of the world. It seemed the *chappal* might float within stick's reach of the little island, but then it didn't. He was still on the stump, watching it sail out to sea, when he saw a person from the corner of his eye, on the path above the beach. He expected it to be Greg, and when it wasn't he thought it would be a stranger, but after a moment, though this person had his back to Nicholas, walking away, he recognized Cyrus.

"Cyrus," he called without thinking, though as Cyrus turned and found him he suddenly wished he'd just let the boy go. "How are you?" he called—a little stupidly, he thought. He still felt he ought to make up for being a jerk to Cyrus the night before, over dinner. And an image had formed in Nicholas's mind: Cyrus stripping his shirt off, diving in after his *chappal*. It seemed vaguely possible that Cyrus would welcome such a challenge.

The boy smiled in his way, seemed to consider his options, then plunged into the trees there and scrambled awkwardly, half falling, down the steep slope to the beach. Nicholas waded back in from the stump to meet him—the boy crashed through the last bit of brush and fell to his knees on the beach stones. "My goodness, are you okay?"

Cyrus said, "Uh-huh," and brushed his knees, wiped his palms. "What's up?" he asked—in a tone that suggested he had understood that Nicholas had a favor to ask him.

"Oh, nothing. Greg brought me out here," Nicholas said. For some reason. After a moment, he added, "He's off exploring," and gestured, vaguely in the direction of Greg's hidden path.

Nicholas said, "This is a beautiful park you've got, Cyrus." Cyrus smiled—not quite accepting the compliment. "Really amazing," Nicholas added.

Cyrus looked out at the strait. "Getting dark soon," he said.

It seemed just enough of an opening. At least he was already looking in the proper direction. Nicholas told him, "Actually, I lost my sandal." He held up his left foot, with the other sandal still on it—to indicate. "It just sort of drifted away from me. You can still see it out there." He pointed. "Just off the island there?" But Cyrus wasn't looking where he pointed. Cyrus didn't like Nicholas much. "I'm half tempted to dive for it," he said.

"Did they cost a lot?" Cyrus asked.

"Oh, no." They both appraised the one on his foot now. "But they're good sandals. They're comfortable. I don't usually like sandals." Cyrus wore a pair of ancient running shoes—his big toes showed through matching holes. Nicholas said (even though he knew he probably shouldn't), "Actually, when I saw you I suddenly had this idea that you might be itching for a swim. A heroic rescue of the sandal, or something to that effect."

Cyrus met his gaze and smiled wider, then laughed—but congenially, it seemed.

Still, Nicholas backpedaled immediately: "But you'd have to be crazy," he said. "That water's freezing."

Which might have sounded like a further provocation—an attempt to challenge his daring—so Nicholas said, "No, it's my own damn fault. I could have gotten it easily enough at first. I just thought it would drift in to shore instead of out to sea." Cyrus laughed a little more. Nicholas joined him.

"Tide's going out," Cyrus said.

"Yeah. Dumb," Nicholas replied. "*Chappals* is the Urdu word for them," he said. "Or Hindi—I'm not sure. They overlap a lot when spoken, the two languages. Although they have entirely different scripts, oddly."

It sometimes seemed to Cyrus that the cottagers had absolutely no sense of the height from which they looked down upon the locals—no self-awareness about their free-floating, chronic contempt, the childishness of their vacationer's sense of license—and in this, Americans, naturally, were worst of all. What did Americans *really* think of Canadians—the few Canadians who ever flitted across their pissy, city minds? How could anyone *stand* to be an American? Good god, to be in their brains for just an hour, to look out from their eye sockets—to know exactly the spot from which they spoke to a Cyrus: how far above it was. Were they all busy contemplating their extraordinary *freedom* through the course of a day while picking their clean American snot or purchasing whatever was within reach or running around with their wives' best friends? But what was the use in getting angry? They had no idea! And in that they weren't alone, god knows.

But he *was* angry, today. He'd been cranky all day, thinking about his evening with the cottagers the night before and about how in all his hours of watching them through windows he'd never yet heard his name mentioned—not once. He'd been feeling disgusted with himself, today, for the stupidity of his fantasies: for thinking a person like himself might be liked—cared for, to a meaningful degree—or even just missed, when they'd gone back home, by people like these. Unless he broke in on them in the middle of the night and screamed like an idiot, he'd never make any real impression on cottagers. And just now, up on the trail, he'd tried the same test he'd given Samina—let Nicholas see him walking away and find out if he would call to Cyrus or not: see if there was any chance that Cyrus was wrong and in fact Nicholas liked him or was interested in his life. He'd stupidly imagined, for just a minute, that Nicholas had passed the test. But he should have known that if Nicholas called Cyrus down it would only be to ask a favor—an errand for the errand boy. He *hated* how often he still found himself naïve like this—still, at nineteen. "How's your wood supply?" he asked. "I don't need to split you some more yet, do I?"

"Oh, no, we've hardly made a dent." Nicholas nodded. "Thanks."

Now he wishes he hadn't called me down, Cyrus thought. If I wasn't going to *rescue* his fucking shoe . . .

He took a deep breath and looked for something else to occupy his mind. Everyone took liberties with metaphors—a little too casually, if you were asking him. He wandered to the tide line. A "dented" woodpile: see, people didn't think before they spoke. There were driftwood sticks and logs, uprooted seaweed—more debris than usual, after the storm. The water was still that roiled, dark shade, with foam caught in protected places. Sometimes you could find something valuable on a day like today. Once Cyrus had found a waterlogged watch. Another time an expensive bass lure in good shape still.

Nicholas asked, "Do you come to the park all the time?"

"Not so much."

"I think I'd be here every day if I lived in Sooke."

"It's a long walk from my house."

Nicholas nodded. "How far does it extend?" he asked, gesturing in the direction Cyrus had been heading—or pretending to head—when Nicholas had seen him.

"Oh, it's big. It runs the whole length of the peninsula. Quite a few miles that way." "Is that right?" "Yeah, it's pretty. You should come back with your wife and take a hike. There's a cormorant rookery down there. You can see seals. There's an old copper mine up one of the trails."

It was just *easier* to play the role—which *didn't* make it right, perhaps: you could argue just the opposite. Some days Cyrus could not help but know that his whole life thus far had been a waste—a drift along the grain, unremarkable and unintended, and with what promise for the future, after all? This was just one of those days. Could you blame the Americans, though? The cottagers? Was Canada worth fuck-all to anyone? Maybe he had to break it off with these people. That would be Ginny's advice: get away from them, let them go. They aren't doing you any good.

Poor Columbia, he thought—denied its Cyrus.

"Beautiful," Nicholas said. He was skipping stones on the still cove, but poorly. What an idiot.

Cyrus said, "You've got a hell of a good life."

Did he say "wife"? He thought maybe he had! And the possibility turned him bashful again. He said, "No, I mean—*you* know. I think you and Samina are really . . . good, you know? You're in a really good place it seems like. I mean—you guys have done some things right, I bet. Along the way."

Nicholas smiled (from way, way up on high—oh, he could hardly be seen way up there!) but didn't stop throwing his stones.

"Hilda's a really great little person," Cyrus added.

Nicholas said, "Yeah, she is, isn't she? Thanks for saying so." He had poor wrist action was the problem. One of his pants legs was rolled up farther than the other, and he still had his one damn sandal on—totally ridiculous. He said, "She really likes you, too, Cyrus," and flung another stone. *She really likes you, too, Cyrus*—his voice bleeding contempt: it coiled and curdled in Cyrus's mind: *She really likes you, too, Cyrus*. The way they said your name, alone. . . .

Cyrus turned away and went back to hunting up the beach, along the tide line. He picked up a thick stick to poke among the debris. There were swarms of sand fleas who leapt out of the beached seaweed when you messed with it. Nicholas threw a stone into the water and Cyrus picked one up and gave himself a little toss and batted his stone past Nicholas into the cove. Cyrus said—aloud, surprisingly—"You've got no idea how lucky you are." There was a real quiver to his voice—it was a big voice rising like a balloon out of his mouth. It forced his jaws apart to say this.

Nicholas actually stopped and turned to look. He grinned. What was he going to say? Cyrus wondered—and with no notion, really: he knew nothing about this man's weird mind. Instead of speaking, Nicholas came up the beach and sat on the driftwood log at Cyrus's feet. He should just leave, Cyrus thought—in this mood. Just head up the path without saying goodbye. It would be a relief to both of them. Nicholas was below him, bent at the waist, his knees apart, poking among the stones at his feet now—looking for the prettiest ones to take away. Cyrus tossed a stone up over him. It would have fallen on Nicholas's back except that Cyrus had a nice, even, high-contact swing, and he sent the rock spinning out to sea.

Nicholas said, "I'm sure you're right." Then—the pause between these two sentences, like the long pause before it, was not accidental; it was strategic and timed (teacherly, parental)—he said, "I think you're pretty lucky, too. Living here." Of course. To the cottagers, Cyrus was nothing but a dull smudge in a pretty landscape.

What a good weight the thick stick had in his hands—what a good drag on his arms. He chose a little round stone and tossed it in the air. He swung the stick, getting his shoulders into it, even though dumb, oblivious Nicholas was unbending just then, sitting up, in the way. Cyrus missed his stone and swung the stick right through Nicholas's head. *Not* through it, of course—but that was the impression: as if the head had just flown out of the way, like a baseball, a grapefruit, with give—not like a stone, not at all like a person's head. It made a thick, different crack, with a little sponginess to it. It was a perfectly acceptable sound for the tiniest instant of time, but then it was really very awful, once your brain put it together with a human head. Nicholas's whole body pitched forward. It was as if he were leaping up onto his feet. In fact, for another instant, Cyrus's brain had enough time to imagine that was what Nicholas was doing: leaping up for a fight, about to turn around with his fists up. But instead, he sort of dove headfirst into the stone beach, forcefully enough to dig a furrow with his face, and his arms were weirdly useless, hanging from his shoulders, and his legs just followed his torso into the landing, still half folded—a doll, a puppet. The stones flew out in front of his skull. A few pinged into the water. Immediately his whole body began shaking, convulsing—it rattled the stones. There was a certain pulpiness in a crease on his skull where Cyrus had hit him and blood began to well up into his hair there. He made a very weird squeaky sound—Cyrus couldn't tell if it was coming from his mouth or his chest. "Hey," Cyrus said. "Hey!" The squeaky sound turned wet, then turned into a vomit, and a bloom of blood fanned out into the stones around his head, under his face. The little waves were lapping just a foot or two past him—the blood leaked toward the water. Cyrus wasn't breathing, he realized. He had tried to speak again—to say Nicholas's name this time—but no, no air there. His vision was narrowing, getting black at the edges. He half sat/half fell down onto the stones right behind Nicholas. Nicholas's leg, still pitching around, kicked Cyrus, and Cyrus leapt back out of its way.

That got him breathing again. He looked up at the path that he knew was there, though not quite distinguishable, on the slope above the beach on both sides. His eyes felt puffy, though. Nicholas stopped moving—all at once, more or less. One of his arms was folded under himself awkwardly, but the other seemed almost comfortably bent, by his head—a sleeping position. The legs were entirely wrong. The head was most wrong of all—still buried in the stones, face down. His shaking had seemed to dig his face deeper in. But that one arm was just comfortably placed enough to make Cyrus try again. "Nicholas?" he said aloud, but quietly. *What were you thinking*, Cyrus would ask next—*why did you sit up?* He waited. A piece of the stick was still in Cyrus's hand. It had shattered. He realized his arms hurt. The mind takes things in sequentially at times, and it lies. "Nicholas!" he said, more demandingly but still quietly. Equally ineffectual.

He was beginning to see again. The darkness had pulled back from the corners of his vision. He scanned the forest behind him—slowly, carefully. He stood perfectly still to listen. "F-f-f-uck," he said to himself, very quietly. But what he meant was: *Think! Think, Cyrus, think.*

19

A BRIGHT DAY, Constable Cortland could see, though it hadn't arrived just yet: bright and ragged, a Saturday, the sun gleaming soon, the trees scrubbed after all-night rain. The cataracts would be falling through the forest and the insects would be out. There was in fact a raw and saturated morning on the wrong side of his windows, a thick stew with only the first seasoning of dawn stirred in, but the constable's talent at reading the intentions of fog and the promise lurking in dreary prospects was widely envied. Troop days were always a blessing, an occupation to take the mind off one's steady if not precisely rapid demise. Mrs. Cortland had been baking. The kitchen was a haze of scone scent and Linda Ronstadt on Mrs. Cortland's portable. A surprise mission—a mobilization: an exciting morning for everyone. They would rescue a man today, very likely, and how grateful he would be, or if he wasn't, well, that would make for fun, too. The constable had been up and down the basement stairs half a dozen times, gathering supplies. A moment over tea, and then he'd go and put the battery in the van. He reached to stretch his aching back and groaned. "Speaking to you already?" Mrs. Cortland inquired. "Oh, we're in constant communication, madam," he said, "constant communication. All lies, I'm afraid, from the back's side."

AN HOUR EARLIER, Samina had woken Laurel with her bustling, but Greg had been awake already. He lay still, propped on one arm—they shared an uncommunicative look. You glanced out the bedroom window and could not help but see poor Nicholas, his bald head shedding rain down his neck and his glasses fogged.

"We're going to find Daddy," Hilda said the moment Laurel emerged, and it seemed a healthy step. "That's right," Laurel told her, "we sure are, sweetie. What's the plan?" she asked Samina, rubbing her friend's back—a plank of muscle. "What can I do first?"

"Why don't you take over for me?" Samina said. She had been making sandwiches. "Is Greg up?"

"In the bathroom. Got a plan?" But Samina hurried away.

Hilda sat in her booster seat at the table, with her bowl of dry cereal and her no-spill cup and a sheet of bright stickers arranged before her. She had evidently been waiting through the interruption of her conversation with Laurel. "He's lost," she continued now. Laurel said, "Yes, dear, but we're going to find him." Hilda drank from her juice and set the cup back down in its place. "I didn't know *where* he was," she pointed out. "We'll find him, dear," Laurel said, "you wait and see. We'll bring him back home and then won't he be happy to see Mommy and his Hilda?" Hilda seemed to consider. "You're supposed to stay with me," she said.

Which turned out to be true. When they were all together in the kitchen Samina divulged her plan. Laurel would stay to look after Hilda and to be here if the constable called or if Nicholas appeared on his own. Samina would go back to the park with Greg. On their map—of Victoria and vicinity—the park was a featureless yellow rhomboid, reassuringly small, and Samina was determined to cover every inch of it before nightfall, if necessary. First, she wanted Greg to take her to the trail map posted in the parking lot.

Off they went—and what a change. It was good to see Samina emerged from the resentful silence of the night before—good for her— but it wasn't quite a sensible plan, to Laurel's mind: Laurel was the stronger hiker on any ordinary day, much less on a day after Samina hadn't slept, and who would Hilda rather stay home with? "You're being very neat this morning," she told Hilda now, a stone dropped into the silence brimming again between them. Hilda stared in reply, and fed herself a Cheerio.

Samina came back with two sketches she'd made of the trail map and Greg had traced on these where he and Nicholas had been. The beach he'd left Nicholas on was at Iron Mine Bay, and beside it here was the unnamed promontory that Greg had gone to alone—the very corner of the park. The wide, initial trail was called Pike Road. And across the rest of the slick page a web of smaller trails wound and smudged between entry points along East Sooke Road and the coastline. Samina drew the route that she and Greg would follow on both copies of her map, up and down in systematic closed circles: this loop first, this second. Laurel would keep this copy. When she and Greg came out onto the road—here and here and here—they would knock at the nearest house and phone to check in. Laurel would have the car and would be able to coordinate between their search and the constable's, presuming he was searching, too. It was a plan too detailed to be tampered with. Samina seemed flung into a high pitch of practical competence that Laurel hadn't known she was capable of.

At the trailhead Laurel made Greg take just a second to bend down to her window and kiss her goodbye. He pulled away, nervous and distracted, and off they went, strapped into their backpacks. Of course he felt guilty, poor Greg. Of course he hadn't slept, either. This would all be over so soon and so suddenly, though. It was not mysterious, in all likelihood, Laurel felt: you hiked and hurt yourself or got lost, and while everyone else wondered or panicked, you simply kept walking, and found your way, or stayed put and waited until they came upon you. You might feel, momentarily, as if you'd stumbled through a seam, or down a hole—it would always appear that you had from this end, among the searchers—but let's face it, hardly anyone was ever very far from being found. Anyone who wished to be found. (That was the only possible complication, of course, but it couldn't really be true. Could it?) For now, Laurel only wished that she and Greg might prove as helpful as possible:

dependable, inventive when necessary. Samina was lucky that they were here, and that would always be true, always part of the story. Laurel spied on Hilda in the rearview: a little girl strapped down alone in the vast reaches back there. It was a cold safety, she felt—car seats. "What shall we do, honey? When we get home?"

Hilda had already decided. "Visit crabs," she said immediately. And she asked, "Can Cyrus come over?"

THEY WALKED SIDE by side along the Pike Road. A more substantial gray had advanced, a lit cloud, but it was difficult to say if the sun had cleared the horizon yet—such a distant event, it might take a long time for the repercussions to reach them here. Samina startled Greg the first time she called out Nicholas's name. She evidently had nothing to say to him, about the morning or this forest she was seeing for the first time. She was all business.

At the coast, coming down the steps, she startled him again—she sprang backward, into Greg. She had made a quick, terrible sound. "What?" he asked—he instinctively whispered. She'd grabbed hold of his arm. It was a sob rather than a scream, the sound that had leapt out of her. He leaned down and saw something lying on the beach, a vague heap, half in the water. But it wasn't a person. It was too compact first, then it was furry. Samina had evidently reached this realization also, and had let go of him. It was a dog—a dead dog lying in the stones with its head in the ocean. White and thick-furred (Greg didn't know breeds). The waves ruffled its fur forward and then back again. There was a crust of dark blood that ran in a chin strap, down from the exposed ear, and its lips were pulled back grotesquely, its tongue stuck between its teeth. "What in the world . . . ?" Greg said aloud. Meanwhile, a small part of his brain was reflecting on the feel of Samina clutching him—her fingers dug into his arm.

She asked, "Was it here last night?"

He shook his head, looked around—but for what, exactly?

"What happened to it?" she asked—naïvely, he thought. "No idea," he said. "This is your beach, though? Definitely?" "This is it. This is where I left him—right over that way, by the rocks. I went up that path."

He pointed. "At first, when we got here, we both crossed over there to that island."

"There wasn't a dog around?"

"No. There wasn't anyone."

"Nicholas!" she hollered.

They inspected the beach and the brush at the edge of it, trusting that they'd know what they were looking for when they found it. The fog began to lift out of the treetops and off the ocean. Greg rolled his pant legs up and crossed the causeway. The tide pulled at his calves with a muscular cold. He stood for a minute on the hump of the island, trying and failing to think more clearly. Samina was wading out as he crossed back. *Nothing out there*, he began to say, but she would want to see for herself. Eventually, they both ended up beside the dog again.

"I don't understand," she said. "What is it doing here?"

He supposed she must not really expect him to answer. (Or did she actually think he knew something about the dog that he was keeping from her?) "Why would it die here?" she asked. "Did somebody just leave it?"

"It has a collar." He stepped into the freezing stones where the waves broke against the dog and used a stick to work the leather around until he could read the tag. It said "Sasha" in script, and on the other side were two numbers, one of which appeared to be a phone number. Samina had packed a pen and pad—she wrote these bits of information carefully. *Clues.* He asked, "Where was next for us?" and she consulted her map, which she had zip-locked into a plastic bag.

"To the other beach. The one you went to when you left him."

He couldn't decide—he'd been going back and forth in his mind, both last night and this morning—whether she meant every shred of implied accusation that she directed his way (when she chose phrases like "left him"), or if, more likely, he was listening through the filter of his own porous guilt. If the accusation was intentional, what could she be accusing him of? Only of leaving Nicholas—of the same charges he'd been leveling against himself: one count of misplacing him, one of wanting to be alone. Nicholas would be guilty of his share, too, and charged, Greg hoped, when he was finally safe and available for sentencing. By and large, Greg's thoughts ran in that direction.

But on the other hand, it was impossible to quite keep the canned phrases borrowed from television dramas out of his mind—*the last person to see him* or *the only witness*—and he had even carried these backward to what would certainly be additional facts highlighted in the script: who had suggested this trip to the park?—Greg had; did he invite anyone else to come along?—no, he didn't; had he specified *where* they were going? "Want to go for a little drive?" he had asked Nicholas (*in front of witnesses*), intentionally vague, hoping to keep his park just between the two of them, one day longer. Ungenerous: at the very least, he'd be proven guilty of that. Had Nicholas been to the park before? they'd ask. Had any of them, apart from Greg? Why not? And what *were* they to think? Where *was* Nicholas? What was that dog doing there?

20

THERE WAS A gap at this point. Cyrus had been sitting there, breathing—empty-headed. He had just told himself to think. But instead he had evidently slipped into a gap of some kind. For how long? He didn't know. Now he could see again. He could breathe; he had a mind again. Here he was—there was Nicholas. And over there was Greg, at the headland. Or he might be on his way back already, or he might be above Cyrus on the trail at this moment, looking down, trying to put what he saw together. ("What is Nicholas *doing?*") The day did seem incrementally darker than it had before. Before the gap. *Go ahead— carry on. Do what you will. It doesn't matter anymore—you're done, Cyrus. A loser now, a wasted possibility. Carry on.*

He took his shirt off and wrapped it around Nicholas's head. It was a flannel shirt with buttons: he folded the long front flaps under and doubled the shirt at the back of the head where the wound was. Images tiptoed through his mind—stealthy pictures that were not true and were not happening, but felt as if they were: Nicholas waited for Cyrus's hand to reach across his open mouth and then he bit it. Nicholas opened his eyes. Nicholas panicked—what's this shirt doing over my face! These things were happening in Cyrus's fingertips but that didn't make them

so. The cloth slipped on a certain slickness to the skull in the back. A
gooey blood darkness began to infest the fabric there, and a wet, water
darkness bled around from in front.

Cyrus sat back again. He flexed his fingers, tried to shake the pictures
out and the feeling of the face. *Look at this!* he thought—*My goodness, what
do we have here?* There was the replaying picture of Greg, on the trail,
strolling toward them. Attached to this picture was a kind of practical
mind-set—lots to do.

He slid his forearms under Nicholas's chest and flipped him onto his
back. The face was acceptable, covered. There was only a little unfortu-
nate hollow to the cloth where it pulled down from the nose over the
open mouth, and a dab of blood in the wet fabric there. It was too cold
to be bare-chested. A shiver began where Cyrus's forearm had gotten
wet and slid up into his shoulders, through his nipples. He stepped over
the body—*the body*: that would help. He took the left arm and pulled the
body around, away from the lapping edge of water. Cyrus was listening
now to everything that wasn't between himself and Nicholas—to all the
articulate near-emptiness, the bit of blowing in trees and the small water
mutterings. He bent at the knees and got his forearms under the shoulders, right up to his own elbows, and lifted—the head lolled uncoopera-
tively but Cyrus managed to wedge it forward onto its chin with his knee.
He locked his hands together across the chest. It was heavy, but more or
less manageable. (*How clumsy you've become, Cyrus*, an observer remarked,
cut to size. You're a teenager!) He took two steps up the beach, then had a
better thought. He dragged the body down into the water so that he
might not leave a trail. His jeans wrapped clammy against the back of
his calves and there were shivery little tugs to the water—it had a will
and a slippery life, after the storm. Nicholas was wet up to his butt.
There was, of course, the splashing sound this was making. But Cyrus
tried to hurry. He dragged Nicholas across the length of beach, to the
end opposite where Greg would soon return. Nicholas was slipping.
Cyrus pulled him half onto dry beach again and had to put him down.
There is a certain kind of hard looking—it's what birds of prey do, but
all his life, Cyrus had also been capable of it—in which you pick your

target and stare, then reel in, concentrate, and by stages, if you're patient
and dedicated, you can see more there, and then a little more. You would
have to know where that path to the headland was to see it along the top
of the rise opposite, but if you did know, then it was visible as a thread of
hollow space through the mesh of trees and salal and sea grape. There
wasn't anyone in the thread. His breathing had come down. His shoulders ached. He should drag the body backward to the steep slope that
Cyrus had scrambled down earlier, in his prior existence.

Then he did hear a dull, forest-floor thump, steps, just where he had
known they'd be. But he couldn't see Greg—not even now, while hearing
him. It was too dark. He'd been kidding himself. The body (in fact, it
wasn't a friendly term—it made things worse) was laid upon the apron of
beach stones, the legs still in the water up to the calves. "Nicholas," Greg
called, from the top of the rise. Cyrus slipped into the cover of the brush
behind the beach, making small sounds despite his care. "Hey,
Nicholas!" Greg called. ("Over here!" Nicholas would shout, through the
shirt—and he would leap up, and tackle Cyrus—Cyrus wouldn't fight—
Greg would come running: "Good work, Nicholas!")

He heard Greg trot down the steps at that end. He saw him emerge
onto the beach—not so far away, but in the dark he was a vague form.
Nicholas was exposed and gray at the edge of the water, just below
Cyrus. Greg took a few uncertain steps, which made the stony sound of
this beach. "Nicholas?" he tried again. What was he seeing? Cyrus
couldn't even be sure which way Greg faced—he did not have a face,
quite. What would he do without an answer?

But then he turned and disappeared up the same steps. Cyrus listened. He heard Greg on the trail above. He leaned back to look up the
slope—Greg might come all the way around the corner, past the Pike
Road trail, and if he did, he'd be standing directly above Cyrus and
Nicholas, and would look down on them. "Hello," Cyrus would say. But
he didn't appear there. The little noises that Greg could not help but
make (just by being a live thing) slipped away. Cyrus left Nicholas to
scramble up the slope and follow. It was darker here than at the beach.
He never saw Greg, but then he heard him—a funny sound: he was

banging something on a rock. Or banging two rocks together—not far enough ahead to be quite safe. Cyrus stood still, the sound pulled away, and when it was as tiny as could be, he turned and walked back.

There was a kind of jog in the logic going on, as a matter of fact—a sort of wrinkle somewhere, half perceptible. Something had been seriously misaligned in that gap. Why had Nicholas sat up just at the wrong moment? Who was to blame? You do *one* thing, give in to one little craving—you never have before; is a person not owed one, at some point?—but the world wrinkles and gathers around the act, and suddenly you've got a body. And so much more than that, too, of course—it was only beginning to take shape in his mind now: how much he'd just inherited. Do you think Nicholas deserved this, say what you will about him? No. Of course not—no. Cyrus doesn't deserve this. He never intended . . . it was an accident. It isn't right. Nicholas might actually be gone when Cyrus got back: and instantly, there you are, there's the whole picture of it: Cyrus stands at the top of the slope but he doesn't see the body; he scrambles down, and what do you know: no body! There's the spot where it was lying. Guess he was okay.

When he stood on that slope and looked down he could see the body. It was a darker lump in the darkness and not itself from here—a solid shadow in the mixed shadows, a heap, a log. Cyrus didn't want to go back down to it.

He looked out across the strait, at the layers of gray and the just-discernible mountains. It was a tremendously large world. It never ended, you could argue—layers within layers, anywhere you went. He shivered. He checked his pants pockets, though he knew what was in them: his little crumple of money, the coins wrapped in a bill, and a lighter, and in the other pocket his driver's license and gum, and a lucky shell in the fold that was meant to hold his change. It added up to nearly nothing, but all along the way out, between here and Sooke Road, there were depots—places where he could get almost anything he needed. It didn't seem sensible to think about his situation too deeply. That seemed crippling and perhaps the source of age-specific clumsiness and ineffectuality. He felt unnaturally cold.

He went around to the steps and down, across the two smiles of beach. Nicholas was moving—his knees moved, writhing. That was how it looked, until Cyrus, standing still at a distance, realized it was only the motion of the waves lapping at him. "Nicholas?"

Cyrus unbuttoned the shirt Nicholas was wearing and pushed him through the very awkward series of rolls required to get the shirt away from him without smearing it in whatever had developed around his head. It was a gray chamois—a little too big for Cyrus, but warm. He went back around and up onto the coastal trail again. There were four trails branching off this one and out of the park. The closest and best was the way Greg had gone, of course, and that was impossible. The next best would be either of the two exits all the way at the other end, which would both put him out beyond Walter's and that much farther toward Victoria, farther from the cottage where Nicholas would soon be missed. It was probably a six-hour walk, but almost all of it along the coast: certainly not a flat route, but no large hill to climb, and he'd be at the edge of the tree cover, better able to see the trail. On the other hand, he'd also come out past most of East Sooke and all the depots he had in mind, which wouldn't do. It was one thing to break into a house you knew well—while people who knew you were having their dinner in front of a television you'd sat at and watched—but it was something else to break in on strangers. He'd have to take the middle path out—he was already moving down the coast, away from Nicholas, as he sorted the options—which was a pain in the ass, since it cut right through the dark forest and over the hills in the middle of the park. But it would put him at the top of Copper Mine Road. He could be among his neighbors before anyone went to bed, while houses were still busy and loud and turned in on themselves.

Everything, it seemed, was now turned in on itself, turned away from Cyrus. He would slip through it all and off the backs of it, unremarkable. It did not sound unattractive to slip away, though he would miss Ginny. How quickly that came to him: yes, he would miss Ginny, good god! But there must be something to miss and carry into the submerged channels and what must be lonely anonymity, something that had been important to you back when you existed. The smell that Cyrus had been smelling, he now realized, was from Nicholas's shirt—not a bad smell,

not cologne, just sweat and personhood. But that whole region of thinking would not do. For instance, it was totally unprofitable to recall the
pale boniness of Nicholas's bare chest lying a little too intimately in the
stones, which must be very cold. *Be responsible, Cyrus.* It began to rain. Or
it had been raining.

He knew this trail well enough not to need to see it very much—fortunately, since he couldn't. It rose rather steadily from the coast trail, past
the old mine site, before leveling off at the swamp and crossing the
Anderson Cove Trail. He had the feeling that what people did wrong
when they did what he was about to do was mainly to cling to the paths,
still—or, put another way, they still found themselves craving the life up
on the surface and they stepped up from the hidden layers, which were
safely shadowed but so disconnected and futureless. So they poked their
heads up, eventually. When that seemed okay, they came out and met
their neighbors again. You heard of this once in a while: of a person
who had disappeared for years and might never have been found except
he couldn't stay under. He got married, bought a house in a lovely sub-
division, and ran for first selectman. They were all over Canada: draft
dodgers, or only ordinary criminals from the States who looked up on
the map and saw forgiving emptiness—towns no one had heard of,
surely—but without the hassles of Mexico. If they thought that, then
they were already doomed to one day be caught. They were already
craving the surface. Why did so few people take proper advantage of all
that a little imaginative reasoning had to offer?

For instance, it occurred to Cyrus now that what he had half-consciously
assumed he was presently walking toward, on the other side of the visits
to his neighbors and the hitched ride—which was a ferry, one or another
(he'd been contemplating the ferry from Nanaimo, which was heavily
traveled but far enough away, up-island, to be safe, or the one from
Sidney to Anacortes, which would be nearly empty at this time of
year)—it occurred to him that this was travel on the surface still, and all
wrong. There would be customs to pass through, but more than that, it
was the wrong foot to get off on when he could instead go to the fishing
boats docked at Esquimalt and offer himself for the day. His griminess and
mismatched clothes would protect him there instead of marking him

out. He'd be off-island before sunrise. He would slip away at the docks in Seattle. No customs to fret over. It would not be difficult to have made himself trusted by then, enough to be allowed to go piss in the market washroom when the holds had been unloaded. There were people living invisibly everywhere in the world, but you had to train your eyes to see them, or only be one of them. He didn't need a passport. People went from America to Mexico without a passport every day, he believed, and from there it would presumably get easier still, continuing south, into whatever came next. He had a sense of where to find these under-layer people. How different could they be, one place to another? Were there train tracks everywhere? Were there fishing boats, farms, city emptiness? He might be killed—Cyrus was not tough; he had no delusions about that. He tended to annoy people unexpectedly. He felt a shiver of fear, and nearly stepped into one of these holes—he couldn't do this; who was he kidding?—but he hit the side of his head with the heel of his hand in a way that often knocked the sand out of the gears and then he felt he could again, and besides, would have to. Would it be such a loss if he did get himself killed?

But it was an accident. (*You should tell, Cyrus—you didn't mean it.*)

He would miss Ginny. He *loved* her—that was the right word. He always had. You slip behind things and you can see them more clearly, of course. Or did he love Samina? But that wouldn't do.

The trail rose up the hillside in earnest. He had underestimated how much darker it could get still, until the moon rose, and now he found himself losing the trail—he kept thinking he was on it but then finding he wasn't. He stopped and backtracked until he realized there was no reason to follow the trail—he struck off from it, straight up the hill. He would meet it again at the top or he wouldn't—it hardly mattered. There were dozens of proximate and available sounds to indicate that he was alive and what he was in the midst of, but the darkness under the trees, with the rain in the leaves creating an umbrella of steady and unrepeatable sounds, set him apart. He was already invisible. He could see his hand, but not as a hand—it was only a figment or shimmer.

They would find Nicholas with his shirt missing and his head wrapped uncomfortably. They would unwind Cyrus's shirt and underneath there would be the face to make it very forcefully Nicholas again. *An accident—* very funny. Who would "they" be? (He shouldn't go this way, but he couldn't help it.) Would it be Greg and Laurel and Samina who found Nicholas? Just Samina? Would it be tonight, at the terrifying end of a flashlight? Or tomorrow morning when the sight would only be awful? Samina would think, *Cyrus.* Who else could it be? She might even recognize his shirt. He misstepped and slipped and hit the ground hard—his bent wrist and then his chin—and saw stars and slid backward down the slope. "Fuck. Fuck. Fuck!" There was dirt or something stuck to his cheek. He pounded the black ground, but it didn't help one bit.

Chick would be expecting them when they arrived—he would see the police car turn in from his upstairs window and find all his fears confirmed at last. He might feel relief. Everyone, in fact, would be deeply unsurprised, and would go all over town saying, *I knew it—didn't I always say so?* Oh, think of Paula Purebred! How she would go on. She would shiver at night, and break down in Don's arms—*I slept with him,* she would say to Don, horrified. *What was I thinking? Get up,* Cyrus told himself. *Get going, asshole.* He had leaf slime ground into his palm and wrist on one side and his forearm on the other. *Fuck you.* "Fuck you," he said, wiping it off. *Up the hill. Fuck you.* What time was it? What could be happening to time, exactly? Nicholas had been wearing a watch, which he certainly didn't need now. Cyrus was a fucking idiot.

It was nice to think that Ginny would say, *No, I don't believe it, Cyrus could never do such a thing,* and she would require the proof that no one else required and that, who knows, might not be so forthcoming; that she would speak out on his behalf to anyone who would listen. She *would,* too, if it was what she believed—he had never, actually, seen her take what might be called "a stand" on anything, or get in anyone's way, but her capabilities in that direction were inherent. She might take that line for an hour or a day: it would be her first instinct to be loyal. But she would tell the truth, of course, and she would end up better capable of the addition required to put the stray sums together than anyone. It was a fucking awful, awful thought to think of Cyrus disappointing Ginny. At last, he would have managed to disappoint everyone—no exceptions left! He just had to stand still for a minute and he found he had to scream.

His face shook with the force of this scream—it *hurt*. And he *meant* it—he really did—so it was just pure cruelty the way his mind so quickly wrapped around and regarded him there, a boy screaming in the woods, a little murderer, and found him unconvincingly dramatic, only acting. *A bit heavy-handed*. He sat down and cried. This lasted for some time, until he became tired and resigned again. The sound of rain falling into a forest at night could make you feel miserable. No one was interested in his screams or in what Ginny thought of him, or Samina. No one ought to be.

He stood and fought his way up the slope, where he seemed to rejoin the Copper Mine Trail. When he only kept walking (he had been so good at this underappreciated talent in his former existence) he did top the hill, and lost the trail but found it again, several times, until eventually he emerged onto the gravel crown of Copper Mine Road and saw the back-porch lights of the houses that hemmed the park. He'd sensed the first light from a great distance through the forest. It had seemed like evidence of something strange—a civilization he wasn't aware of. No one was on the road. He walked down the center of it—not sensible, but he felt apart and protected. A dog barked far away. He came to the house with the wraparound porch, with the chainsaw back where it belonged in the crawl space, never missed. He sat down in their hedge to have a comfortable look at the situation. All the windows were lit—in this house, that was often true. Some families loved light, and did not want to walk into or even out of a dark room. The kids were still up. *It wasn't late at all*, Cyrus realized. This realization calmed him. It was after dinner, not the middle of the night. Cyrus had known these two boys since they were little people. After a promising beginning, they were not developing well, in his opinion. They suffered from some unexamined aggressions. Their mother was mousy and her head was too narrow— her eyes seemed almost to slip off the sides of her skull and she didn't have the width of cheek available for a proper smile. The father was dull but friendly. They had finished dinner. In the kitchen, the mother scrubbed. The father was upstairs with the younger boy—they could just be heard now and then but not seen from this side of the house. Downstairs, the other boy looked into the television. Oh, it was such a simple, native pleasure to sit here and watch the inside world, just to look into lit windows and be with the people there when they were alone. The boy in front of the television was examining something on the bottom of his foot. It would be a scab, you supposed, or some stain, some tar or pine sap pressed into the skin. He had his foot in his hands and bent toward his little face. He was himself at this moment—purely alone and unobserved. Cyrus could hardly imagine summoning the energy required to do what he had to do here. He didn't want to touch it—to interact with any of it, or disturb it. He'd be caught if he tried to in this mood. The mother called to the boy: you see, she *knew*: between rooms, inside a house, people sensed things, wandering minds, a kid involved in something not worthwhile like his feet. The boy was calling back to her lackadaisically. These boys didn't respect their mother and everyone in town had seen it. How could they give so much up so early? The kid stalled as long as he could, but eventually she came to him, drying her hands in the dish rag, and snapped the television off, and he was driven upstairs, into the flow toward bed.

But there would be more to see. Cyrus didn't want to move, wet as his ass was. If he could beg God for something it would just be to allow him to sit right here tonight and watch—maybe also to keep them up late tonight, at least the parents. He hated the moment, sitting up with people, when they turned the last light out and cut themselves off. He wouldn't ask for more than that. *In the morning* (he would promise God), *I'll still be here. I won't disappear, or try to. I'll tell the truth—I'll tell* these *people first. I won't wait to be found. It's a good deal, God,* he would argue—he'd be right—but of course there wasn't any God. Or probably there was but He wouldn't be inclined to bargain with Cyrus.

He had to stand up and walk back. He wasn't, probably, quite capable of disappearing—when it came down to it, he was a nineteen-year-old from a small town on an island. He didn't know much. He wasn't up to this. It had to not have happened, or at least as much of it as could be taken back, still. What had happened wasn't fair—Cyrus would never kill someone. He had to protect Ginny—her precious delusions. He couldn't sit in hedges any longer. That was over. He would be inside the windows now, unhappily, until they caught him, and it was his own fault—he had done this to himself. It was truly incredible to think (but it was *true*—and this clinched it for him: he *did* have to go back) that this person, this Nicholas Green—the whole life attached to that name—was not in his own lit cottage right now, or with his wife, or even where he belonged, in what must be his tasteful apartment in New York City, reading quietly under a lamp. Samina would sleep or not sleep without him tonight. Hilda was done with him, an early memory. No part of this Nicholas was in any of those places, because he'd made one mistake. He was only there, where only Cyrus could see him, lying on stones, in the rain, with no shirt on. He needed Cyrus.

So Cyrus went back. He walked three hours more to reach the coast again, the moon risen behind clouds.

But Nicholas wasn't there. Cyrus stood in the same gap between trees on the trail in the rain and looked down exactly as he had looked down earlier, but there was no foreign shadow on the beach below. He threw himself down the slope and splashed into the water where he'd left the body. The tide was coming in and had reduced the beach considerably—Cyrus kicked about, hip-deep. He stood still again, and small waves grumbled and picked through the stones as if searching for something, too. But no Nicholas.

21

IT WAS NOT the worst idea in the world, Laurel felt. She knew—or guessed—that Samina wouldn't like it (because Samina, being Samina, would not want Cyrus or anyone else involved—would think, illogically, of even this search as something to be kept private). And initially Laurel resisted the idea. She brought Hilda home and explained to her that they had to stay by the telephone—in case Daddy called, or someone who had found Daddy—so they couldn't go check on her crabs quite yet. They had more breakfast together, then she tried to occupy Hilda with a book—with her favorite, featuring Mr. Brown and Miss Porridge. But Laurel was more engaged by the story than Hilda was, today. Hilda had been running back and forth between her bedroom and the living room, each time bringing a new toy, a new prop for whatever game she was playing. Now, with the story over, she was back in her room, having missed the entire denouement. Laurel had begun to wonder why the constable hadn't called. "Hilda," she said. But when she got up from the couch she saw that the sliding glass door was open. "Hilda?"

She hurried to the bedroom—no Hilda. From the deck she couldn't see her, either. "Hilda!" She ran down the stairs, and down the lawn. From the top of the short steps that connected the lawn to the beach she could see the girl, squatting and staring into the ocean scenery. "Hilda," she said, when she was on the beach with her, "I told you we couldn't come out here, now, didn't I?" Hilda was not listening. "I'm very angry at you." She crouched at the edge of the water and the hem of her dress hung in the sand. "Hilda?" Laurel stood beside her, modulated her voice (this was what she hated about children—the uninventive performances they so often demanded of one). "I'm speaking to you." But Hilda wouldn't acknowledge Laurel. She actually stood up and began to walk away. Laurel grabbed her arm—"Hilda!" Which provoked a terrifying scream from the girl, and made her lean away from Laurel's grip (rendering it that much tighter, of course—perhaps actually painful). She burst into tears. Laurel instinctively let go, though she was mad at herself for being so easily bullied. "Stop that!" she said, but Hilda already had. She'd let herself fall when Laurel had released her—plop down in the wet and filthy seaweed. "This is not like you, sweetie. What would your mother say if she saw you now?" Hilda's little face was rather miserable, maybe even contrite. "Come on, let's stand up. Do you want me to carry you?" But when Laurel tried to touch her she screamed again, and this time began to cry in earnest.

"Fine. We'll sit here," Laurel said, letting go. "Bad girl."

Not everyone should have children, as almost everyone acknowledged. But those same people would make you feel ungenerous and brittle, or at the very least, unfeminine, if you happened to count yourself among those who shouldn't. Hilda sat and cried, then pushed herself onto her feet and began to walk away, down the beach. She took a stone into her palm for close inspection (pretending Laurel was not there at all) and threw it in the water. She turned around to dash past Laurel, then strolled back toward the steps and the black rocks where her crabs lived.

Would they hear the phone ring from here? Laurel tried a couple of different carrots—new suggestions for indoor activities, and the generally reliable promise of food: they could bake cupcakes! She was just getting disgusted enough with the whole game to grab Hilda and carry her in, no matter the protest, when she remembered Cyrus. It wasn't unreasonably early—it must be close to nine by now. It would mean leaving the telephone and the house for a few minutes, but then one or the other of them, Laurel or Cyrus, could follow Hilda's whims (well, it would be Cyrus, of course) while Laurel stayed by the phone. When Samina and Greg called, if Nicholas wasn't with them, Laurel would convince Samina to trade places for the next leg of the search, and this way she could leave Hilda at the cottage with Cyrus while they made the exchange. When Nicholas was found he might need a hospital. Cyrus would know where it was. And the timing was good: it was too early for Greg and Samina to have finished their first loop yet.

"Shall we go see what Cyrus is doing?" she asked. "See if he wants to come play?" Hilda hesitated, clung to resistance, considered her pride, but soon relented.

They drove to Walter's and he obliged with directions. Cyrus's driveway was winding and thickly covered—a driveway down which unexpected visitors would be long anticipated. There were lights on in the house, thank goodness. Laurel parked close to the front door and left the car running, with Hilda in it. She could hear scratchy orchestral music—it must be the radio. An older man answered her knock: Mr. Collingwood. One of those men whose gray hair worked against a broader impression of youthful restlessness and concentration. "Good morning," he said—the kindly-without-smiling type (a favorite type of Laurel's; she could feel, by contrast, the exaggerated width of her own foolish smile). He did seem nervous, or wary. "Mr. Collingwood," she began, "my name is Laurel Faber, and we haven't met yet but your son Cyrus has become a friend of ours." This only left twice as much to explain; the anxiety in his eyes seemed to deepen. "My husband and I are renting a cottage just down the road, along with another couple. That's their daughter in the car—" She indicated. And seeing Hilda, all his resistance melted. He interrupted her to say, "Oh, goodness, yes, of course. Please bring her in. Please."

"Thank you."

"Cyrus is here," he said. "Have you had your breakfast yet?"

THE WHIP OF wind funneling down the strait and the gather and pound of waves at the headland darkened their mood. They called out Nicholas's name but couldn't expect to be heard over the ocean's racket.

It wasn't beautiful today, Greg decided. And they had only to return a short distance into the forest for the unnatural quiet to reopen around them like a tomb. A couple of days earlier, Greg had been imagining he might live here in Sooke. He could stay behind when Laurel went home—become a Canadian, of all things (as if they'd have him). There was a patch of trail back above the first beach where they lingered a moment to look at the dead dog. The tide had lifted, and the little heap of fur sank and reemerged in a swirl. Who was he kidding? He'd only ever be among the prey in a place like this, the quarry, the dupe. Today he couldn't wait for his next deep breath of the stale, safe air of a city street.

Samina's plan called for them to turn away from the coast onto a trail called the Copper Mine. It rose into the forest, gradually at first but steadily, with a stream snaking back and forth. Strange the way you formed a mental image of a trail or a road from a map, based on its name and something about the shape of its course, or on what it looked as if the route might pass close enough to view, but you were always wrong. When you were on the trail you could picture your position on that map and know that the ocean was only a short distance in that direction, or that a named peak should be rising now on your left, but from where you stood you'd have no hint of either. "Nicholas!" they called, getting tired of the sound of it. The trail became steep and Samina slowed. Near the top of the hill there was a trickle running in a culvert with a strange, copper-orange silt in it, and around the next bed they came to the mine. A muddy ditch ran from the trail to the black mouth of a cave carved into the hillside—it was roughly circular and not quite the height of a man. There was standing water perhaps a foot deep at the entrance to the cave, and dripping echoes came from within, along with a dead, clay smell. They both wondered, Greg believed, if they were obliged to go in. "We'll come back later with flashlights, if we need to," he said, the first words either had spoken apart from the chanted name in a long time. Nicholas could only be in there as a result of the worst one could imagine—the hollow of the cave was an invitation to imagine the worst—and Samina must be giving in as well. Tiny drops had pearled along her dark eyebrows. "Should we eat something?" Greg suggested, and when she met his eyes, for just a moment, her face seemed to burst open—such a quick, utter disintegration that he reached for her instinctively and spoke her name, even though she'd recovered already and his hand hung between them.

Turned away from him, she adjusted the pack on her shoulders.

"I can get that."

She stood still and looked around them through the trees. "Where the hell are you?" she asked, quietly.

She kept her back to him. When she said, "Why don't we keep going?" her voice was her own again.

They climbed to the top of Mount McGuire, where a wooden bench, faded by weather, faced a wide south view. They came down off the peak, Greg as relieved to be headed downhill as Samina must be, and took the Anderson Cove Trail toward the Pike Road to finish their loop. The first hikers they'd met all morning startled Samina—human sounds on the trail ahead—and then must have disappointed her: two boys, nine or ten, who stared rudely at Greg as they passed. Were tourists so very unwelcome in this park? Maybe by this time of year.

Soon they came upon another pair of boys, and these wore the same red bandannas the first two had, tied loosely around their necks. It had seemed like something imposed upon the first two, but these boys, a little older, wore it with a Gaelic flair. They, too, passed in staring silence. "Where are their parents?" Greg wondered aloud. A moment later, the boys called out, high and mocking: "Niii-chol-asss!" Samina stood still. Greg looked back. They were out of sight, around the bend, but Samina asked, "What the hell is he doing?" and Greg realized she meant the constable. He ran after the boys. "Hey!" he called out. "Hey, guys." A burst of nervous laughter, and when he rounded the bend they were running away, looking back; one screamed theatrically when he saw Greg.

Samina had gone on without Greg. He jogged to catch up.

Down the hill they heard her husband's name called out from the forest in several directions—his name in the voices of strangers had the same effect as the sight of the cave. The Pike Road Trail was crawling with boys in red bandannas who stopped to wonder if Greg, emerged before them, could be Nicholas. "Where's Constable Cortland?" Samina asked the first group, and after a moment of nervous silence, the smallest boy said, "Down there," pointing toward the beach. She began in that direction.

"Are you looking for the missing man?" the same boy asked her.

She turned to say, "Take us straight to him, will you? It's very important."

"We don't know where he is."

Samina stared, not comprehending. Then said, "I mean the constable. You know where he is?" The boy nodded. "Let's hurry."

They acquired an entourage along the way. "She knows the missing man," the same kid told each of the parties that joined them—whispering initially, but soon not bothering to. One of the older kids had a walkie-talkie. He spoke to someone, saying, "We found some people, sir. They claim to know the missing man." Greg couldn't make out the reply. After a brief period of solemnity, a cloud of banter had developed: walking sticks must be compared, and tested as swords; a trophy seemed to be at stake for the one who found Nicholas, and there was some question as to whether his discovery with the aid of Samina and Greg would constitute a valid win. Farts were being traded over the walkie-talkie. When they reached the constable he was waiting for them at the top of the beach steps. He smiled in his charming and infuriating way; his height was amplified among the boys around him—*more* boys, each tagged with the red bandanna. Greg felt like a prisoner captured by a tribe of miniatures and taken to their chief. "Mrs. Green," the constable called out, when they were still some distance apart. "A lovely day, isn't it? Your husband must be enjoying it as much as we are."

She said, calling back, "We need to talk, Constable Cortland."

"We certainly do," he told her. "There's a great deal my men have discovered already. Mr. Green won't be missing for much longer, I can promise you."

22

M RS. GREEN WANTED to "speak to him," by which she meant apart from his Mini Mounties, and she was upset, a tad fragile, already angry at the constable for not having found her husband yet—he had anticipated this reaction and could not be surprised. He countered her aggressive manner with thrusts of his own, but gently— no more than was called for. "Actually," he said, "I have some pressing questions for both of you as well. You've been out searching, I gather?"

"Constable—" she began again.

"For some time already," he said, "I'd guess by the look of you both. And on your own. Which is no less than understandable—entirely— except it isn't helpful, to be frank. Having multiple parties tripping over one another, buggering up the evidence."

Mr. Faber said, "The more people out looking for him, the better, I would have thought."

But she cut in. "You don't think I should be looking for my husband?" A pretty if conventional tartness she gave it—she'd soured a bit overnight.

"Mrs. Green," he replied, "you'd be surprised how seldom I tell any- one to do or not do anything in the course of a day. It's not my style. I'm merely offering advice for everyone's best interest and what you do with it is entirely up to you."

"Why are you searching for a missing person with ten-year-old boys?" she asked. The boys, unfortunately, capered about her, half listening, half bored, in a way that was native to them and couldn't properly be faulted but was sure to make a poor impression on someone in her state of mind. She wasn't a person, though, who appeared to possess the proper forthrightness of gesture—she leaned away more than into her challenge, and her pretty, foreign face conveyed more sad confusion than disdain. But perhaps she was a little treacherous, less predictable than he might have hoped. "My men," he said, winking at them, "are easily underestimated. They could teach a course in search and rescue, as a matter of fact."

To his frustration, he could hear some sort of thumping being delivered just behind him. The squeals of the victim were familiar: Brent Billington.

"But that's not true," she was saying—pleading, really. "They're only boys."

"Mini Mounties," he told her. "It's similar to your Boy Scouts."

"Constable—" Mr. Faber began.

He said, "I can't cover the ground I used to, with the back what it's not." The walkie-talkie on his hip crackled with indecipherable gibberish.

Mrs. Green said, "*They'll* tamper with the evidence, if anyone will"—whining a bit now. "They won't mean to, of course"—already she backpedaled—"but they're kids, Constable. I don't know what you're thinking."

"Mrs. Green—"

"Her name is Naqvi," Mr. Faber said. "His is Green."

She said, "I'm sorry to contradict you and I don't mean to doubt your ability to do your job, but this just isn't appropriate. Are there *any* other adults out searching with you?"

The constable was losing control of things. And his troops attended closely now. He said, "In fact, if you'll pardon me—if you'll indulge me for just a moment, both of you—we've collected quite a lot of evidence already. In what I presume must be much less time out here than you've already spent—though this isn't a competition. And I'm sorry to say that some of that evidence has already been compromised by less-experienced hands, which—stop me if I'm wrong—I take to be yours. The dog, for instance." Their faces betrayed the knowledge he'd anticipated. "Which my men—correctly, I see—guessed that you'd already discovered. And probably handled."

"We didn't," Mr. Faber said.

"You're telling me you haven't seen the dog?"

"No, we know about the dog—"

"Well, I have to tell you," he broke in, before Mr. Faber could get a head of steam up, "there are tracks leading this way and that on the beach down there and we'll gain fingerprints from off the poor animal if the tide hasn't scrubbed it, but we've had to waste a great deal of time already in determining which of these tracks are significant and which— we'd already guessed it—must be only yours, Mr. Faber. And Mrs. Green's. Pardon me, Mrs. Naqvi's."

Tim Phelan said, "We don't even know who killed Sasha."

"He means the dog," the constable explained, while silencing Tim with a look. "Have you a guess, Mr. Faber?"

"No, I haven't," he said. A touch of cheekiness had bled into his tone. But it was interesting that his anger rose more slowly than hers. He added, "It wasn't there last night, I can tell you. And Nicholas wasn't in the habit of killing dogs, if you're wondering."

"My goodness, I had never imagined he might be. No, Mr. Faber, please: you must try not to get angry at *me*." The constable gestured, his hand against his own chest. "It's a natural reaction—*only* natural. It's self-protective. But it's unproductive, too. We must all work together, you understand."

"Why do you say the dog was killed?" Mrs. Naqvi asked.

"Oh, but that much is plain," he said. "Shall we go have a look together?"

"Who could have killed it?" she asked—defenseless again. "Why?"

"Mrs. Naqvi, those are my questions, too. I'd hoped, to be frank, that Mr. Faber would have answers."

"Well, I don't," Mr. Faber said.

"No, I see that. I can see that clearly. Mr. Green himself may still have answers, no doubt. Look," the constable told them. He took a deep breath. The sun—as bright and lovely as his prediction—fell slanting across his cheek. "Let me lay it out for you now, may I?" he asked. "Let me lay the whole thing out." He gestured—he could sense them relaxing. "You must trust me," he said, and gave that its pause. He said, "The circumstances are these, presently: we have a good Point-Last-Seen from Mr. Faber. That's number one." He held his pointer finger in the grip of his other hand. "That's tremendously valuable. It means we're halfway to the man already. When we find him, Mr. Faber, half the credit must still go to you. Now, number two," he said, "we have a good description of him, and a photograph, which all my men have studied, as you'd expect. We have, number three, several promising trails—clear leads—which branch away from the PLS. It's not ideal, naturally, to have so many leads, and we had hoped to be the first party here this morning so that our job would be easier and quicker. But who can fault your eagerness to help? On the contrary, it's commendable. When I ask you to go home now to your rental cottage, as I will in a moment, I anticipate you'll still resist the idea."

"Constable Cortland—" Mr. Faber began.

"I'm nearly finished, Mr. Faber—please? Only a moment longer? Then you can have your say, of course—then I'd like to hear from you.

"Now," he continued. "We will trace these leads. We've already begun to. When I say 'we,' I do mean the troops and myself—yes, you're right, Mrs. Naqvi, these boys here. Exactly so. But may I just ask you—by way of . . ."—he searched—"of confidence-building, say. Not as a challenge. But may I ask if the two of you, for instance, noticed the evidence of someone having recently scrambled up the slope at this end of the beach here?" He pointed. "Where, of course, there is no trail?" He only waited a moment. They stared—malevolent, vaguely, but giving in. "Well, I didn't, either," he said, "until one of my men pointed it out to me—and I say 'men,' but of course you understand I mean these boys." The troops were his audience as much as Mr. Faber and Mrs. Naqvi. "Did you notice the candy wrapper in the bushes just over there, I wonder? Did you happen to note the splinters of a stick down on the beach, which do fit together, and which make up, very likely, the weapon used to do in poor Sasha? Again, I admit to you that I missed these things myself, at first. I wish I could claim I hadn't."

The boys around them were silent—attentive as could be. Enlarged, you'd have to say: you give a boy credit, you see, for the best he's done and even a bit more, and you wait and watch if he doesn't expand to meet your description of him, and soon surpass the hopes you'd risked. It was true of *his* boys, at least—of the boys he accepted as Mini Mounties, of those who lasted. "We have," he said, "I'm sorry to repeat, wasted some time just walking in your footsteps, following leads that were only yours. And unfortunately, where that lead I've mentioned comes out on the coast trail, just over there, we noticed that your footsteps have superseded, in a manner of speaking. Yours are much fresher, of course, having come after the rain." This had landed—Mr. Faber looked guilty, underneath his more accessible anger and haughty dismissal. "But that couldn't be helped and it's done with now. You'll describe for us the trails you've been down, though I believe we already know, and then we'll let go the leads that head in those directions. We'll just all hope you didn't accidentally destroy the most important evidence. But here, we've this third fact, too—this dead dog, exactly at the PLS—and I'm sure you'll both agree that we'd be foolish to think it was unrelated to our case. What is the relationship? we ask ourselves. Who has killed Sasha? We all know this dog, you see—please remember, it's a small town. We know it was a sweet dog, good-natured and trusting. We'll go and speak to Sasha's owners, just as soon as we can. We may find new leads from their yard."

They just wanted to be free now—away from him. Sent home to sit on their hands. He'd drained them of their fight while lathering up his own men. "So all I'm saying, and then I'm through, is simply this: That we have done this before. That we know from experience we'll find your man twice as quickly if left to our own devices. And that our goal is to find him sooner, not later—before lunch, we still intend. Because he's going to be tired and hungry, wet, perhaps injured—we all know that, I think. Ready to be home. And that's just where we'll bring him. Now."

On closer inspection, perhaps he didn't have them. He had his boys, though. "Would *I* trust me, I ask myself, in your place? This foreigner, an older man, in charge of a bunch of rough-leather boys? Canadians, to boot?" He laughed a little, to keep it pleasant. "You're both too gracious to say it, but we understand. And the fact is, I'd have a hard time rising to that trust, thanks very much. Don't imagine I can't sympathize. But you give us just four hours—"

The walkie-talkie on his hip squelched and spat at this point, and William Billington burst in with, "We got him—we found him, sir! We got him!"

The news was met with a touch of disappointment among the boys at hand, of course—who had not only wanted to be the heroes themselves but had hoped, above all, that anyone except William Billington or Jeffrey Colhane should win. Behind the constable, Brent Billington was helped into some brambles. "Stop it," the constable said. On the walkie-talkie he replied, "Are you sure, Group One? Where are you, precisely?"

But there was no response because William held his button down still, a mistake which everyone had been specifically taught not to do. He wouldn't hear anything the constable said until he let the button go, and in the meantime they could hear what was happening at his end. There was William calling out something to Craig and Rory—"Why not?" was the portion that was clearly audible. Their reply was too distant, but then William said, "Are you shitting me?" The constable glanced at Mrs. Naqvi and Mr. Faber—who hung on every word—and tried breaking in on William again, though he knew it wouldn't work.

"—some other guy!" William was saying into the walkie-talkie, when the constable let his own button go. "He's named Nicholas, too, but he says he's not lost, Commander. He's with some person." (This was already evident—the other person, a woman, could be heard in the background, rather vigorously protesting.) "She won't tell us her name."

"I see," the constable attempted to reply—but to no avail.

"—doesn't look much like the photo."

"William!" the constable tried once more—pointlessly.

"—let him go?" the boy was saying.

Perhaps he'd follow a question with some common sense? "William?"

the constable tried again. "Yes, sir," came the reply, thank God. "William, what did I tell you—"

But Mrs. Naqvi was speaking to him. "Who is your superior, Constable Cortland?" she had asked—with calm, unmistakable vindictiveness. He would kill William Billington. He held one finger up to Mrs. Naqvi and said into the walkie-talkie, "One minute, William, please stand by. Stay off the line entirely, please." Politely, he asked, "You had a question, Mrs. Naqvi?"

"I want to know who your superior is."

He smiled as best he could. "I do wonder why."

But she evidently changed her mind. She turned and began stalking away. Mr. Faber meekly followed her, not meeting the constable's eye. "Oh, Mr. Faber," the constable called, when he was a short distance off. "Would you do me a favor? Would you not go anywhere, please? Not leave town, I mean? Just until we've found your friend?"

Mr. Faber took it in, then turned away again, following the woman like a spanked puppy. Of course he fled. Of course they both did. Now the constable would be pressed for time. It was his own fault. He'd really believed it would be a simple case, only a lost hiker. You had to expect the best of strangers. You had to give suspects at least as much trust as strangers, initially—if you didn't, you were fouling the investigation before it had properly begun. But nothing was right here. Nothing had been right yet. Lost hikers didn't brain dogs, and the families and friends of lost hikers didn't generally do everything they could to impede the search. Where was *Mrs.* Faber? Why were these two such a team, all of a sudden? But he caught himself immediately, getting too far ahead, venturing out where there wasn't a plank of evidence yet. *Stick to now,* the constable told himself—*expect the best, only a little longer. What does it cost you? Have William ask to see some identification from this party of his—but* politely, *for God's sake.* It was time, the constable admitted to himself, to stop thinking along conventional lines.

23

ON THEIR WAY out of the park, when Greg and Samina were nearing the end of the trail, they saw a woman in the distance coming toward them, and something in the swing and openness of her walk let them both know who it was. "Laurel, where's Hilda?" Samina called to her.

"With Cyrus," she called back proudly. "Boy, I really hoped I'd find three of you instead of two," she said.

It didn't sit well with Samina. Greg was near enough to see this but Laurel wasn't. "How far have you been?" Laurel called cheerfully. "Just finishing the first loop?"

Samina did not answer and seemed, in fact, to be fighting off tears again. Greg said, "There's been a wrinkle in the plans." "Not bad news, I hope?" Laurel asked. She wore her still-new hiking boots, bought for this trip. She had her hair pulled back into an all-business ponytail.

Samina asked her, "Why is she with *Cyrus*?"—and lost the fight, did begin to cry.

"Oh, dear, Samina." Laurel came forward the last few steps and touched her. "It's okay—truly. I just left them this minute. Hilda couldn't be safer."

"Laurel!" she replied—exasperated, diminished, a person who wasn't getting any proper help at all. "I *asked* you to stay with her," she said through her tears—but not with anger so much as dismay. "Didn't I? That's all I asked."

"DO IT AGAIN," Hilda demanded. She was slumped down on the leather sofa, watching. Cyrus looked for another prop. There was a napkin on the glass coffee table: he lifted it with two fingers, acting surprised to find it, pleased—ah, just what we need—and shook it out before her, then very carefully unfolded it to gain the larger square. Turned it to reveal both sides—with great drama. She sat transfixed. She was a whole creature, an entity unto herself: yes, sure, the product of these two people, of their flesh and tending. (Say, for instance, they had given birth to her but then she'd been given to Chick to raise: well you could guess how different she'd be and how misshapen by Chick's shy and tentative touch, and his fear of children.) But she was something apart from Nicholas and Samina, too. She was better off not knowing; no, she deserved the truth: a fork in his reasoning. He wasn't quite sure what to do with the napkin but luckily it didn't matter much. He felt inspired to turn in profile and tip his head back and pretend to feed the napkin, painstakingly, into his open mouth. He pretended to swallow, gag a bit, to be unsteady on his feet. He'd be discovered, very likely, so Hilda would know, but it was something quite different to confess. She didn't believe in the illusion—Cyrus wasn't good enough to pull it off, really—but that was okay in her brain, didn't seem to diminish the entertainment value. Who could guess what Hilda needed or would be better off without? Nicholas was dead but Cyrus was not a killer—a fork. He could, quite honestly, not imagine killing anyone. There should be a different word to accommodate the subtlety here. He stood up straight and pretended to swallow the napkin. He bowed with a flourish in a manner that he thought might be Shakespearean, provoking the applause from her that was a part of the act. *Wait*—he held up one finger. Her eyes lit. It was clear that he should confess and set them free. He began to cough, held his fist with the balled napkin to his lips—out it flew. He picked it up and unfolded it again with a great flourish, revealed both sides. She clapped for him.

"Thank you," he said, bowing deeply. "Oh, thank you—*merci, merci.*"

She laughed a little—only as much as he deserved. They stood still, looking at one another. "More," she insisted. He required a new prop.

At first Laurel had sent him down to the water with Hilda. But the crabs weren't out this morning, and when they had come back into the house Laurel had wondered aloud why Constable Cortland hadn't called. She was restless and annoyed about being left out of the action. She told him she would trade places with Samina when they telephoned but he suggested she might just go find them now. No, Laurel had said, Samina wouldn't like that. Cyrus should probably be the one to go looking, she said, except that Hilda (off she went—speaking as if the girl was deaf) liked him and couldn't really stand Aunt Laurel. In a few minutes, she convinced herself he was right after all. Nicholas might need her help.

He'd taken the coins from his pants pocket. Two fat five-centers, five pennies, and a gold loony. "Examine, please," he had whispered, bent down, spreading them out on his palm for Hilda. Foreign currency, to her eye—she was fascinated. She took each coin into her hand for closer inspection and then put each back into his palm, quite properly. He stood up, took deep breaths, adjusted his feet to find a good base. He bent his knees, turned in profile, bent his elbow, and held his forearm up level with his chin. He let the whole pose go to look at her and gesture— *just a moment, please; your patience . . .* —then elaborately stepped into the pose again. The coins were on the coffee table. He bent down carefully and, with his left hand, stacked them, one at a time, onto his outstretched forearm, close to the elbow. Samina would remarry. He stole a glance—Hilda watched him nervously.

A talented actor, who makes his profession that way—well, he's a professional liar, of course. He told the world one thing or the other: either, *It's not me, that role and that one—the one where I play the psychopath with the hatchet or the one where I'm the adorable retard—none of them are me at all, only acting, though I'm glad I managed to fool you. Don't worry, though.* Which was the same, roughly, as saying, *Liar—professional liar.* And shrugging: *It's a living.* That was A. B said: *Well, sure, yeah, that* was *me, some of me—a little, at least.* Although maybe more likely he would have to say, *Most of me, actually,* since so much of one would be necessary to summon all that scenic self-display, wouldn't it? *Sure,* he'd tell his loved ones and his little people, when they grew up seeing Daddy raging in Technicolor, *It's true, you should probably be a bit worried, to be honest. It's lurking,* he would admit, if he was actor B. Now, which was better? Who could love such a person— either A or B? Cyrus would be A. This he knew.

The coins were neatly stacked and he paused, made her as nervous as possible—acted nervous himself—then said, "Would Madame count to three, please?" His accent was meant to be French. They said Mademoiselle, though, not Madame. Hilda said, "One"—paused (so good at her role!)—"two . . . three!" He flung his arm, unbent it at the elbow. Cyrus would like to respectfully point out that, awful as the whole situation was, Hilda would get to keep Samina, which was not nearly the same as it would have been to keep only Nicholas. And Cyrus truly believed that Nicholas would have failed his family, sooner rather than later. It even seemed possible he'd been up to something already, with Laurel. The coins flew from Cyrus's arm straight into his hand—too quickly to be visible. The coiny sound of them hitting his palm provided the main drama of it. He didn't know why it worked. He bowed and she clapped, with indulgence this time. "Again!" she said.

They came home when he was halfway into his repeat performance. He heard the car pulling into the driveway, doors opening. He mussed his hair, assembled his face. "They're home," he whispered to Hilda, who stared up at him with deep comprehension. All his instincts screamed: *Run, Cyrus.*

Samina came in first, in a hurry, and scooped Hilda up. The little girl wrapped her arms around her fiercely. You did get the feeling Samina meant to save her daughter from a threat, but then she cobbled together a sort of smile and tossed it to Cyrus. She grabbed the cordless and hurried toward the bedroom.

"Everything okay?" Laurel asked Cyrus, quietly and morosely, as she came in. She'd had a piece bitten out of her—it couldn't be clearer if she'd sported a black eye. "Fine," he said. "Hi, Greg." Greg said, "Cyrus, how are you?" wearily, and added, "Thanks for coming over." They all spoke quietly. They could hear Samina down the hall, talking to the police in Sooke. "Coffee?" Greg asked. "Thanks, yeah," Cyrus said.

Samina—everyone—I have something very important to tell you, I'm afraid. I have a confession to make. It's awful—unintentional, too, not that it matters.

Samina came out saying, "I don't believe it. I don't be*lieve* it." But Cyrus could actually hardly breathe, much less speak, standing in the same room with her.

The constable, she'd finally discovered, was only one of many constables. He hadn't even contacted the main police detachment in Sooke yet. "They didn't know what I was talking about," she said. "They had no idea anyone was missing."

Cyrus swallowed. "Unbelievable," he chose to corroborate, except the syllables didn't quite line up properly.

"So what do we do now?" Laurel asked sourly.

"We drive over there and fill out a missing persons report, first of all." Samina got her wallet from the backpack. She shook her head and whispered, "I'm so *stupid*." In a full voice, she said, "There's a whole search and rescue team for the Sooke area—people who are trained to do this." Cyrus could tell she'd been crying—at some point not very long ago. Greg turned the nearly boiling water off. "I just don't believe it," Samina repeated, her hands busy tugging a coat onto Hilda, whom she had stood up on the kitchen table. She was all aflutter.

From the first moment Cyrus had seen her, weeks ago, he had sensed there was something brilliant in Samina—some dormant force—and here it was, finally.

"How do you want to do it?" Greg asked.

"You have to come with me." Obviously Hilda was coming, too, this time. "Laurel," she said, "can I *please* ask you to just stay here while we're gone? In case he walks out on his own?"

Laurel was offended. "Now, why do you put it that way? You *know* I'll do whatever you want me to."

"I'm sorry," Samina said briskly. "I'm sorry, I'm sorry, I'm sorry," she added. "To everyone, I'm sorry."

Cyrus simply waited. He was a speck in the corner of these people's eyes. Into the jittery quiet he said, "What can I do?" The very sound of his voice was inappropriate in the same room with her. It hit the air through which she moved and fell flat, noxious. Samina did not glance at him—hadn't time. "Nothing, Cyrus," she said, "but thank you—thank you for coming over. Can we call you again if we need you?"

He was going to cry. He said, "Uh-huh."

"Thank you," she said.

He followed them out the door, leaving Laurel behind. He walked up the steep driveway while they got into the car and got Hilda settled. He was on his way down the road already when they passed by him—no horn or wave. Not even Hilda had looked at him as they passed. So it *was* over—but not in the way he'd expected. Samina didn't suspect him or need him, either, and if he had any role to play at all now it would be only as the head-hanging culprit when they came up the driveway and knocked at Chick's door, except it wouldn't be Laurel knocking, or Samina. It would be only the police, impersonal, unimportant. So he was free.

24

SAMINA SPENT THE evening on the telephone. Her first call was to their answering machine at home, but the messages she found were unrelated and rendered meaningless and she didn't care for the image of them playing aloud in the empty apartment—of Nicholas's voice there, especially, directing the message-leavers with his casual confidence in which hints of dissatisfaction or a shade of boredom could nevertheless be made out. Next she called Nicholas's parents in Cambridge. They were both in their seventies and more fragile each year but still self-sufficient, their busy if constricted lives still intact. Mr. Green still put on his chalk-stripe suit each morning and drove his Peugeot with agonizing caution through Harvard Square to his office on campus. Mrs. Green had half a dozen appointments to fill a day. They had recently installed a chair elevator on the lower flight of stairs in their three-story house but Mr. Green couldn't always be persuaded to take advantage of it. He no longer taught but he wrote and published and his consultation was still sought by the State Department or by foreign governments in the midst of "insurgencies." Fairly regularly, Mrs. Green bundled them both in an old-fashioned Yankee brand of formality—her very high neckline, his bow tie—and herded him to a ceremony of some kind at which he would be honored. Afterward, on the telephone, she would speak about the interesting gentlemen at their table or about the chandelier that hung above it, and Mr. Green would grumble about the meal, but neither would mention his honor. Mrs. Green was nervous and warm and overconcentrated. She had answered the telephone—she always did. Samina had rehearsed her lines. She said that Nicholas had gone for a hike and had not come back yet and they were beginning to worry about him. How long ago? Mrs. Green asked, as Samina had guessed she would. It seemed best to parcel the information this way. By stages, she told Nicholas's mother most of what she knew. She said she had not wanted to worry them unnecessarily or she would have called earlier. "Robert!" Mrs. Green shouted into their house. "Come here!" (He would have shouted back from his study upstairs, not wanting to be interrupted. Their lives were formed around this dynamic: his desire to be protected from interruption and his mistrust of her judgments about when it was necessary to interrupt.) She wasn't panicking—she wouldn't. But she did sound frightened.

Samina didn't mention Constable Cortland. Instead, she told Mrs. Green—and then Mr. Green also; he wanted to hear the whole story himself—about the afternoon search: the police and the impressive SAR team in their practiced formations, with their dogs. Tomorrow there would be a Coast Guard boat and a helicopter. Where would they look tomorrow? Mr. Green asked. They would look again where they had looked today, but more carefully. Volunteers were being organized in the town of Sooke, who would help. But was there some-where *else* to look? Mr. Green asked. Samina understood how insufficient it all sounded.

She had to warn them that the police here might call them. They said that was fine, but they didn't understand what it meant. It was difficult to hang up.

When she did, it was still too early to call India. Samina spoke to her friends Zachary and Sarah in New York. The most difficult part of each call, already, was breaking the news initially, and reciting the same unpromising details. She asked if one of them—or someone—could go

and stay in the apartment until Nicholas turned up. If anyone found
him, or his wallet, there would be nothing to connect him to this rental
cottage—only to the address and the phone number there. Sarah promised they would arrange things. Shifts, if necessary.

Finally it was late enough to call her brother Khalid in Delhi. His wife
Aisha picked up—sleepy, awakened. Samina had met her on the trip to
India with Nicholas. She had seemed sweet and mild-hearted to Samina,
no match for Khalid's gregarious force but perhaps a good complement
to it. "Hello" was what they answered the telephone with there now, but
when it was Samina she switched to "*Assalaamailakum*" and Urdu: "How
are you, how are you? I *wondered* who could be calling at this hour!"

Khalid listened with as much patience as one could hope for from him
and then interrupted to say, "What do you want me to do?" They spoke
mostly in English, as usual—he had always pretended she preferred to,
and she had always assumed her accent embarrassed him. "Tell me what
to do," he said, "I'll do it. Do you want me to come there? Never mind—
I'm coming there."

"Don't come here, *bhaijaan*."

"I'm coming."

"How?"

"How do you think? I'm getting onto an airplane. Later today, if they
will find me a flight."

"You don't have a visa."

But he did—he'd been sent to Vancouver twice recently for business.
If he had known she was finally on the better coast of America, he said,
he would have come to visit her already. "You're lucky I'm not bringing
Aisha and the boys with me."

"But by the time you get here, he'll have turned up and you'll have
wasted a ton of money for no reason."

"Do you think I'm giving one thought to such things?" It wasn't only
that this was his native manner. He thought it would make her feel better. "Forget this business—I'm coming," he said. And he was right: it did
make her feel better—his decisiveness—although she was afraid of putting another person into motion away from home, into taxis and onto

airplanes. Khalid said, "If I get there and you people have managed to find him already, very good. Less for me to do. Perhaps I will finally teach your husband to fish."

She had begun to cry again. It was evident in her voice when she said, "I don't understand where he could have gone." He didn't know quite what to say to this—he wouldn't, of course. Their relationship consisted of one or two private, pleasant phone calls each year plus the slightly harrowing call at Eid when the phone would be passed to a dozen relatives she hardly knew and she would only get to speak to Khalid in his role as overzealous moderator. "I'm at a loss right now," she said, hoping to sound reasoning and reasonable. He didn't reply, but it occurred to her that it might not be a phrase he would know. There were strict limits to what their relationship had ever been pressed to accommodate, but tonight Samina half resented that. Why should everyone be protected from her? Greg and Laurel had to be, too. At what point did she earn the right to spill over? What had to strike her first? "I'm spending most of my time thinking again and again about the possibilities. Where can he be, what could have happened to him? And nothing seems plausible. Or acceptable. In any way acceptable." She wiped her eyes. Hilda slept beside her in this room. Not far away, down the hall, Laurel and Greg lay awake still, surely, perhaps listening. "They keep asking about his mood."

"Who is asking?"

"The police here."

"Nicholas's mood?"

"They also wanted phone numbers of everyone he's close to."

"Nicholas's mood? I'm not following."

She told him, "They're going to call our friends and his parents, asking them all if he was depressed lately or ever mentioned suicide." She felt calm again, drained. "Or if he had enemies. Or if he ever talked about leaving me." What was the acceptable option, the least painful to anticipate, if the first and best—that he had only twisted an ankle, or gotten lost—was no longer available? She half wanted to make the phone calls herself and ask everyone he'd ever known every question she could think of about him. "Which should I hope for, even?"

After a pause, Khalid said, "I'm coming. Okay? I'll be there as soon as it is possible."

She said, "Okay."

"We will find him," he promised, foolishly, and she was disgusted with herself for believing him.

25

I T WAS TOO dark—the sun had set. The constable should go home. Mrs. Cortland waited for him in the van at the parking lot at the other end of Pike Road. His bicycle waited at this end, hidden under ferns. The other searchers had been more than ready, an hour ago, to call it a day and amble off to their television sets and their cozy, dry beds. But there was a nearly full moon up in a sky with only shreds of clouds. The constable could in fact stay out another hour. And one way or else the other (heaven forbid) the missing man was out here with the constable, doing his best with what was available, though his own wife, too, and his best friend, had left him behind for another night. The missing man must wait impatiently, dead or alive. It made the constable ashamed sometimes to see what law enforcement had come to, hollowed out with gadgetry and impatience.

Mr. Faber claimed he had come here alone, to the headland at the corner of the park. The surf beat in and boiled back vaguely white. Contemplate otherwise—say, for instance, he wasn't alone. Say the two men came this far. It was an immeasurably more likely place to lose a man, in fact—if he fell into that surf. The tide had been toward low but still emptying out yesterday evening (which Americans like these, landlubbers, would have failed to recognize). A person could be dragged under here. There was the man at Port Renfrew, for instance, last winter, who only meant to wade a bit—this was in March, after all—but his poor brother had watched him get swept right off the beach and out and out until he disappeared, and hadn't reappeared on any shore yet. Mr. Faber did not have to touch his friend. They come over—*Take a look at this spot, would you?*—and Mr. Green thinks it's lovely, he takes his sandals off, he wants to stand in the way of a wave or two. But the footing is poor. And if the surf doesn't drag you away, well, then it smashes you back against the rocks. Why wouldn't Mr. Faber admit what he'd seen? He'd be culpable to some extent. He could have saved the man?

The girl had been named Jessica, not Jenny, and though the constable had worked alone on her case, without help from the grand Sooke detachment of the Royal Canadian Mounted Police, wasn't she discovered? She was the strictest test he'd been given thus far—a more difficult case than this one, in many ways: she was a child, after all, and worse yet, a girl, who are snatched by the monsters of our world daily, the Lord knew. Jessica, truth be told, had cut right into the constable's heart. He couldn't fail to think of his own daughter. Mrs. Cortland had, too, and they both knew it without needing to speak of it. She was that much younger than Olivia, but even so, the Cortlands had shivered at night while she was missing, and lain awake, picturing every worst thing imaginable and then wondering at their own minds for being capable of such thoughts. (That wasn't something they shared aloud, either. Who could admit to the ripping and the cries, all your own creation? But each morning over toast and jam Mrs. Cortland would turn away from the constable to hide what the fight had taken out of her.) For this reason it was a sort of blessing to find Jessica, even dead: she had only been alone, and gone to see her starfish. It seemed possible to believe she'd died happily. They couldn't believe Olivia had, too. *I ask you to take this,* the Lord said—*I ask you to survive it and learn from it, and to see into it*—and then that was your duty. You could not look with merely accustomed eyes: a dead girl, a missing tourist, one less American—boo-hoo. It was the constable's opinion that Staff Sergeant Dunn was having thoughts to this effect at this very moment, if he had any thoughts for the case at all while he sat over his dinner in front of the evening news. When Jessica was found and Sergeant Johnston, who had preceded Dunn, was told that Constable Cortland had acted on his own, without notifying his detachment, the constable hadn't been scolded in front of his troops, and no one had suggested that someone else could have found her more readily than he had, or put more into the search. How dare they?

The breeze at this time of evening still smelled, to the constable's mind, of summer trips to Eastbourne. Or was it the particular chill that matched, perhaps? The missing man could, of course, have run away. Mr. Faber may have assisted. If that was so, then nothing would be right—not the PLS or any part of the story, perhaps. It was funny, but the constable had thought he'd seen a moment of peculiar panic on Mr. Faber's face when William Billington had said they'd found the missing man. The constable had—in that instant—thought of it as the reaction of a man afraid the dead had come back to life, but more likely (or less unlikely, at the very least), Mr. Faber had thought, *He didn't get away,* and *What the hell has he been doing all night?* Mr. Faber did not actually strike one as a murderer, only as a man keeping secrets. You had to expect the best from people to satisfy the Lord. The real problem was that evidence was always so difficult to come by. It was as true for the SAR people and the Coast Guard as for him—it was never the way they showed you in the movies and on the television. Seldom. Especially in a rural landscape instead of a city, with so few witnesses available per square mile of crime; especially in a damp place where there was always a rainfall to wash the deed away. The constable wasn't surprised that Mrs. Naqvi and Mr. Faber had believed him—that, until William Billington poked his dull head into the conversation, they had actually begun to trust him. People thought your police were all scientists these days, and no one could get away with anything without leaving a trace. People did and *didn't* believe that, of course—in fact, they knew that criminals got away with all sorts of devilry, all the time, and that if you had your car or your handbag stolen the friendly officer would shrug politely and offer little more; but on the other hand, people maintained this wonderful faith in forensics and the general abundance of invisible evidence. Go down to that beach and try to fit any of the dozens of sticks and pieces of sticks together. Just try to follow footprints in a climate like this, a forest like this, spongy when not plain muddy. It did look like someone had been scrambling up and down the slope between the other end of the beach and the coast trail, but was it last night or last week or every day for the last month? This was the problem with the latest innovations in law enforcement: the officers trusted such evidence so entirely that when it wasn't available they felt helpless and defeated. But the constable's contemporaries had never expected much of that, and had treated the lack of such evidence as only the first bend in the trail, not a dead end: when the physical clues ran out you told stories and then alternate stories to yourself, and then you went out and looked again, and spoke to people again, until one of the stories became compelling, the others less so. Poor Sasha: case in point. Nobody in the detachment had any good guess about what she was doing there, but when they couldn't find any fingerprints on her and they had spoken to the Whittleseys and obtained no help—the Whittleseys said they hadn't seen a thing, and no, they hadn't heard a soul, terribly sorry—well, then these men were done. He wondered what they could think. Dead dog at the PLS—*Hm, well you got me. Let's get the helicopter out.*

Part of the problem, of course, in a landscape as beautiful and rugged as this, was that there were innumerable nooks and tucks and hiding spots. Just this little section of coast at Pike Point, for instance, snaked in and out and in again, with mini-coves only exposed at low tide. He ought to get home. His bicycle had a lamp on the handlebars which was lit by the action of his pedaling—see, that was ingenious. That was a proper gadget, to Constable Cortland's mind. Poor Mrs. Cortland, who'd never complain. The constable looked out at the ocean, lit in streaks and shards. What a place—what a place, good Lord. He saw an object caught and troubled in a scoop between rocks, and his eyes knew what it was before his mind did, long before he could climb over—a treacherous spot—and reach it to confirm. A sandal. So how did it work? he wondered. Was a man rewarded for his patience, as in a test one had passed—*Well done, here you are, then*—or was it only that everything worthwhile in this world lay under the surface in any case, not kept or given at all but always long out of sight, only available to the patient or bull-headed? The sandal smelled of salt water but it wasn't slick with algae yet or faded. It hadn't been in the water for long. And would a man who meant to go missing set out with only one sandal? It sounded like a Bible parable.

26

L ORINA AMONG THE flooded trees, in trouble. Sometimes it felt as if Chick heard them calling as if from behind the page not yet turned, as if his sentences headed not into blank yellow corridors between the lines of the pad but through closed doors of the narrative that had preceded his words, around bends that weren't his at all, in pursuit of girls already there. It was typically inconvenient that he heard the call during a break, downstairs, far from his desk, with the tea water about to boil and Cyrus in the room (so that he couldn't simply turn the gas off and hurry up the stairs after her). The TV dinners were half baked. Invariably, he had these flashes of inspiration when Cyrus was at home. Inconveniently.

Charles had dressed Alice in her slicker and rubbers and they were out in the flood, in a boat, in the scene which Chick had left at his desk. But he had thought they were only surveying the damage and perhaps headed for a picnic under tree cover on the high banks at Nuneham. Number four—he'd had them headed toward number four, he supposed. But the book knew better, it seemed.

"Would you . . ." he began, speaking to Cyrus. The kettle came to a whistle at that instant. He panicked a little, poured, burned himself with the steam. When that had been gotten through, he asked, "Are you staying in tonight? Were you about to go?" Sucked his burnt finger.

"Huh-uh," Cyrus said, not looking up from his magazine.

"Then would you mind getting the dinners when they're ready? Ten minutes, I think. Could you bring mine up to me?"

"Yuppers."

He couldn't hurry on the stairs, with the tea. Always always always—when, he wondered, would he know his people well enough not to make such mistakes? He was always giving in to Charles, not acting in the narrative's best interest—always stealing moments for him, alone with Alice or Xie, or Agnes, letting him drift toward number four, number one: bright pauses. Alice smiling. The canopy effect of rainfall. But of course one's characters are at one's mercy. No one tempts, no one calls—it's all the metaphoric business of living inside the thing. If it doesn't *feel* like a call—if you don't feel the same mix of annoyance and guilty relief that Charles feels, his plans interrupted—then how would you ever get it to come alive? An author had to be in the boat with them. Or Chick did. Dodgson had been this kind of writer also, he felt certain.

At his desk he sat down slowly and took a deep breath. He looked at the pad—neat corridors tracking into it. It *felt* like listening. It felt like rendering yourself available. The metaphors of composition were imprecise and could make one sound like a crazy person. He took a sip of tea and picked up the pencil, began to round the corner toward Ina.

When he heard Cyrus coming up the stairs he put the pad into the drawer and opened a book on his desk. He got up and met him at the door of the study. Cyrus had left the dinner in its plastic tray but had put this on a plate, and had remembered a napkin, a fork, and the box of toothpicks. "Oh, look at that," Chick said. "Smells pretty good." He smiled. "So are you in tonight?" he asked, turning to put the dinner down on his desk, turning back to his son impatiently. "Nothing brewing in the neighborhood?"

Cyrus said, "Too sleepy. You feel like playing a little, maybe? I can set things up."

"Oh, I wish I could." But he should, of course. He hesitated. He covered his mouth with his hand, torn now, and he looked back at his desk, from which Ina called for Charles. He said, "Can I see? See how the work goes?"

"Yup."

"I'd like to—I seem to remember I have you in a hole down there."

"No, no," Cyrus said. "I've got you right where I want you."

Chick offered a smile, looked at his shoes. "I'll tell you what," he said, "set the board up. We'll see. But don't wait for me, okay? It's just that I'm in the midst of something here."

"Yup," Cyrus said. He'd begun to go away.

Another line would be nice—a last note of contact. His impatience was immediately replaced with guilt whenever Cyrus was walking away and had been held off another evening. "Don't touch my chips," Chick tried. His son clomped down the stairs. "We'll see," Cyrus replied. Fine. Good enough.

Alone, he set the dinner safely aside and took the pad back out. But it was all at a distance again. He must sit still and wait.

He cut himself a piece of Salisbury steak. Sit still. Wait.

Hilda—a lovely, old-fashioned name. A lovely child. The poor man. He should be home safe by now? Chick would stop in on Walter tomorrow morning to hear the news. Downstairs Cyrus began playing the piano—naturally, just a little poke at his old dad. Pickles began to sing and squawk in reply. But some nights—tonight—all this set Chick free instead of distracting him: the house full but familiar, Cyrus accounted for. Free of responsibilities, except to Charles. So then:

His oar strokes in the rain-pocked surface of the water. A swish of wind through Alice's hair. On the banks the flooded tree trunks look like soldiers fording the river. From the darkness in among the canals between the tall trees somewhere, Ina calls out. What is she saying? Charles turns the boat into the forest.

27

THE MAN WHO was missing in East Sooke Park was discussed over file footage of searchers in a forest on the last news from Victoria. In the papers next morning there was a proper photograph: Staff Sergeant Dunn directing searchers in blue vests. The missing man's name had been withheld at the family's request. He had been missing for thirty-six hours already, a long time in a park that size. The volunteer spirit which lurked never far from the surface in Sooke sprang forth. People organized into their cardinal affiliations, then telephoned the Mounties to be provided a place and a time to meet with Juan de Fuca Marine Rescue Society personnel or politely thanked and turned away. Volunteers from each shift at the older grocery store (but not at the newer) were given the day off and accepted by the police, as were a contingent from the Sooke Power and Sail Squadron, the Royal Canadian Legion, the Contact Loan Cupboard Community Assistance Society, and the Sooke Community Arts Council. As a result of Constable Cortland's antics, it was thought best to forgo the assistance of the Girl Guides of Canada, and the Steppin' Out Sooke Dance Club was turned away—certain members were known to take direction poorly. The Sooke Community Choir offered a half dozen mild-mannered and right-minded adults but could not be accepted if the Dance Club was not. This was the town at its best, people felt. The coffee shop and a woman who did catering sent in fresh thermoses all day and crumbcake. *That ought to keep your motor running.* The searchers achieved a sober cheerfulness that was respectful yet optimistic, and native to the place. Their worst fear was that some harm had come to the missing man from local sources, but it seemed the least likely possibility. One did not need to have converted one's house into a bed-and-breakfast or own one of the shops that sold Indian sweaters and bentwood jewelry boxes to be relieved that this was happening in October instead of July or August. Nearly everyone had this thought, briefly—a measure of the degree to which the community had converted from its timber and commercial fishing past. A woman from the hospice wished to call the missing man's family to make their services available, but was told the family did not want their local number given out. The character of this family (they were known to be three—husband, wife, and small daughter—and American; there was another couple with them who were only friends, evidently) was examined predictably in the court of public opinion. Sympathy was brightened by intrigue and darkened by suspicion. The privacy they had guarded thus far was understood to suggest mistrust by those who had nothing to hide, themselves. *She wouldn't have his name given out, you know, which is Nicholas. Imagine searching for a man without knowing his name.* By and large, the crisis had a salubrious effect on the community. But a few of the people engaged in the gossip (as well as those who listened with frowns) drove home from town in a poor mood, and all day felt the shape and weight of their safe lives and the polish of the clear day to the extent that one seldom did except in the shadow of crisis. Poor woman, they thought. Others were jealous of her.

Cyrus had missed his father's birthday. It had taken him until that night when he lay on the couch, not sleeping, beside the *über*-game set up but never played, to remember this: they had planned (tentatively, of course, since all plans between them were hedged in an effort to limit disappointment) to have a dinner out the night before, while he'd been with Nicholas instead. What a relief: perhaps his father had only been smarting from that, and had suspected Cyrus of nothing more than his usual insensitivity. First thing the next morning Cyrus telephoned Ginny. Could they invite themselves to dinner? he wanted to know. She hollered out the door of the trailer to her father, asking. "Tomorrow night, how 'bout?" she came back on the line to say. "He said tell your father not to expect any presents. But what are you doing today?" How should Cyrus know? "We should go help look for the missing man," Ginny said.

My god, what was she talking about? "Ginny, what are you talking about!"

"On the television—didn't you see?" And she explained.

"Oh, I don't know," he said, calmly now. "They probably have enough people, right? The park is probably crawling with people."

"How do you know?"

"People banging into each other—I'm just saying."

"Let's go see. If they turn us away, fine. It's a nice day."

He didn't want to have anything to do with any of them, anymore, ever. Dismissed. But what could he tell her? "Okay, but let's go get a cake first."

"Cyrus!"

"Okay, okay—let's go, then. Are you coming here?"

Chris and Ahmer stood with some pride at the trailhead in their blue Juan de Fuca MRS vests and their mirror sunglasses, like bouncers at a concert. "Sorry," they said, and shrugged, "not our idea." Don was already there, half hidden in the shadow of a tree at one end of the parking lot, stretched out in the bed of his truck and smoking. And Paula was with him—recently they hadn't been found apart—plus Paula's little sister, Melanie, and some boy who must be Melanie's boyfriend. "Great minds think alike," Don said, offering cigarettes. "Old Dunn has a tight grip on it, I guess. Ginny?" He smiled at her. "Long time no see. Cyrus, my dear, you look like shit." He put his arm around Cyrus's shoulder, reaching across the side of the truck. "As usual. Have I told you about 'sleep' yet? I keep meaning to."

"Why?" Ginny asked—she spoke toward Paula, but not, surely, because she thought Paula would have answers. Only to kindly keep her involved, Cyrus supposed. "Why wouldn't they want as many people as possible searching?"

"Search me," Don said.

Paula said to Ginny, "They told us"—she indicated Chris and Ahmer with her chin—"because we're gonna mess the trail up or something. But you know who they let in? The fucking art-farts. We watched a whole bunch of them go by in like sweatbands and stuff."

"*I* want to find him," Ginny said. She added, "He's got a kid. A little girl."

Which left a small silence between them, except for the exhales of smoke. "How do you know?" Cyrus asked her.

"It's all over town."

Don said, "He'll turn up. They always do."

"Not always," Ginny replied unhappily.

Melanie sat in the cab, facing sideways out the open passenger-side door, and her boyfriend stood and leaned between her legs. She was touching his hair and they were whispering together, like anyone. Cyrus watched them. It seemed to him a great betrayal, hard not to take personally, and further evidence of broad decline or of his own antiquated dreams and unreliable impressions. Where was innocence anymore?

Don, just beside him, said, "Cyrus has a plan, I bet. Does Cyrus have a plan?"

"We could go up Copper Mine Road," he said. But maybe Melanie should have what she could get, actually.

"Where's Copper Mine Road?"

"It turns into a trail. Probably nobody there."

Ginny took his hand and said, "Oh, let's go. Come on come on come on, let's go right now!"

It was a gorgeous day—the second straight. A little chilly, but clear as a bell. The four of them drove over in Ginny's father's station wagon. Melanie and her boyfriend had decided to stay behind with Don's truck. Cyrus indicated the place to turn off, at the top of the hill. He let Ginny lead the way into the park. Don kept up with her. Paula fell behind them, already a little sulky, and Cyrus came last and gave Paula plenty of room. It was no fun, being back here. He realized he had dismissed this park, too—it belonged to Nicholas now, one big cemetery. Paula didn't want to touch anything. She cringed slipping past spider webs and held branches away with two extended fingers. She looked at the moss hung from the trees and the pink and orange growths on the trunks as though she'd never seen such things, though she'd lived here all her life. "It's fungus," Cyrus told her. "It's gross," she said. Ginny and Don, far ahead, were laughing at something. "Come here often?" Cyrus asked. Paula said, "I'm not much for woods and stuff." They *were* speaking—comfortably enough, Cyrus would have to argue. The sweater she wore was ribbed, vertically, and had little fuzzy balls of nubble around the neck and the ends of the sleeves. The nubble fuzz looked extremely soft. A little later they saw Ginny and Don ducking and skittering off the trail, waving Cyrus and Paula off, too. They all hid behind trees—each behind his own. A party of four adults came through. They could be heard first, calling out his name: "Nicholas!" They were faces familiar to Cyrus, but nobody whose names he knew. Two of the women and the man walked shoulder to shoulder, very neatly, and the other woman came behind them, her head up. She seemed to look at Cyrus, but she was only seeing his tree. Don made owl sounds from his hiding spot when they were nearly out of sight.

"I thought they weren't giving out his name," Ginny said, when their own party of four had reconvened on the trail. Don said, "We're the unknown searchers. The secret searchers." "No reason to stay on trails, actually," Cyrus pointed out, and Ginny said, "That's true." Paula said, "I'm not going off the trail." Cyrus suggested that the missing man wouldn't be on it, very likely. If he was, he wouldn't still be missing. "That's true," Ginny repeated. "You're right. Let's follow Cyrus." Don said, "Let's follow Cyrus. Lead us, Cyrus, lead us!"

But when he began—took the first few steps heading straight west, because it was silly to wander aimlessly this way—Paula said, "I'm not going in there." She was right that he was pushing through branches and stepping over ferns already, and that the way in front of him looked blocked by growth. But that was only the constant illusion—you went ahead and when you got closer a way through would always open up. There were paths everywhere, zigzagging and half hidden.

"Can we do it?" Don asked him.

"Uh-huh." He shrugged.

Paula repeated, "I'm not going in there. I'm staying on the trail, thank you very much."

"You can just go back," Don told her. "Wait for us at the car—"

"Fuck *you!*"

"Fine—do what you want." To Cyrus, Don said, "Let's go, Kemo Sabe."

Cyrus tried to smile an apology to Paula. When they were under way she stood her ground for a moment and yelled, "Fuck you, Donald!"—too loudly—but then she scrambled to follow them. "It's stupid," she muttered. "Ouch! *We're* gonna get lost."

"Not with Cyrus leading us," Ginny said brightly.

Of course, it was pointless to be anywhere in these woods. Cyrus had considered carefully and decided, once and for all, that Nicholas had been dead—he hadn't walked away. He would wash ashore, one supposed. If Cyrus didn't at least point them in the right direction now, then what were they doing here? They weren't even calling the poor man's name out—they were idiots. They fought through the sea grape and climbed over dead trees. After a long time, Ginny asked him quietly, "*Are we lost?*" "Not really," he said, and soon they crossed the next trail, then a bit later, up and back down over the loaf of hill, they hit Pike Road.

Cyrus led the way up the edge hill, near the border of the park. He stopped to get his bearings when they were close. It made him a little sick to be here, but in his mind the pictures were more like a dream than a memory, and it wasn't the same landscape in the light of day, under a blue sky, without the rain falling into the leaves. "Where are we going, anyway?" he asked.

Don cracked up.

Ginny said, "We thought *you* knew, honey," and Paula said, "Je-*sus!*"

"I'm starving," Cyrus said. Though he wasn't.

Don sat down and offered cigarettes. "Smoke 'em if you got 'em, gentlemen."

When they had all lit up and relaxed, Cyrus wandered away, casually, but it took longer than he thought it would to figure out where he'd thrown it. Finally he got to call out, "Hey." The voice was just right—just the way he'd heard it in his head: surprised, but not too surprised. "Hey, you guys," he continued, "look at this"—just interested, slightly proud. He bent down and picked up the leash by the handle. Put his other hand onto it also.

"What is it?" Ginny asked. Cyrus showed her. "It's a leash," she said. "You think it's evidence?"

"Did our boy Nicholas have a dog?" Don asked.

Cyrus shrugged, couldn't think of his proper line. He said, "Maybe we should show it to somebody."

They all hesitated—they were enjoying the game too much, secret searchers. But Ginny said, "Maybe you shouldn't touch it."

"Too late."

"Put it down, Cyrus. Let's go find Dunn or somebody and bring them back here."

They walked to the beach at Iron Mine Bay. Sasha was gone—Cyrus had assumed she would be—and there was yellow tape marking things off: where the dog had lain (they'd driven stakes into the beach to hold the tape up above high tide) and across the bottom of the steps down to the beach; also on the slope near where he'd left Nicholas. By the looks of things they were halfway to Cyrus already. It did depress him, but it would have been worse if they weren't getting anywhere. Don and Ginny stopped at the tape and called to the Mountie there, who wasn't Dunn—just another face Cyrus half recognized from parties interrupted. They led a little group back to the leash: a pair of Mounties and a pair of Juan de Fucas, plus Mrs. Schmidt, who drove the bus, and Mrs. Matteis, who was Augie's mother. It was striking to think that any glancing contact these people had ever had with Cyrus, today or any other day, might become worthy of reexamination soon, and would either appear suggestive or strangely opaque in retrospect. The Mounties required everyone to stay on the trail and Cyrus pointed out the exact spot to them. Then they stepped between the trail and the spot with slow, meticulous, and captivating movements, scanning all about themselves, turning every leaf before they took the next step, circling the tree that the leash lay under before slowly closing in on it. Which was pure silliness, since Cyrus had stood here on this muddy trail, where everyone milled and trampled now—more people were gathering—and thrown the leash.

Constable Cortland was among those who had arrived. "Discovered something, have we?" he asked Don, putting his arm around Don's shoulders. Everyone was speaking quietly, but the constable's voice had a way of cutting through. "Who first found it?" he wanted to know, and he said to Don, "Cyrus Collingwood did?" The Mounties came back with the leash in a plastic bag. "Cyrus already touched it," Ginny pointed out. "Well, that was a mistake," one of them said, "but it's good work, finding this."

"A hand for Cyrus," the constable called out, and began clapping. But what was interesting was that the two Mounties didn't spare a glance for him. A search party was directed north across the hill behind the trail, another south. They asked Cyrus and Don and Ginny and Paula if they would circle out of the park and have a walk through the Sooke Sun Drive area, past the edge of the public land. Constable Cortland said, "I'll join the teens." But Cyrus thought he must have earned some bit of influence, and if he was going to waste his whole afternoon searching where there was nothing to find, he wasn't about to do it in Constable Cortland's company. He said, "Actually, we'd rather go alone" to the Mountie. It was interesting again that the man immediately nodded and said, "Fine," and added, "You want to come with us, Mr. Cortland?" already moving on. "Oh, anywhere I'm needed," the constable replied, with sarcasm.

As they were walking out, a few quiet minutes later, Don squeezed Cyrus across the shoulders. "Actually," Don said, "he's quite an asshole, our constable." Cyrus smiled. Don said, "I was afraid you hadn't noticed." And Ginny kissed Cyrus and pinched his cheek. "You ought to be a detective," she said. He couldn't help but smile—a big, blushing smile, dumb as an ox. He shrugged. Paula said from behind them, "Excuse me, but are we ever eating?"

28

OOKE SUN DRIVE was the last kilometer of East Sooke Road, from the final old and naturally arising house to the windy patch of high ground where the road dead-ended. It had been a dirt road here recently but now all except the last bit was neatly and narrowly paved and unlined—like a golf path. There would be a golf course. Near the end of the drive, by his stone and iron gate guarding nothing, the developer had planted a huge wooden sign with a map of the lots that would be carved and the tremendous facilities: the eighteen-hole course high on the hill (where they had already ripped out great threads of trees), and a marina in a pretty cove, and the resort—a shining hotel and spa—hulking on that final plot, atop the rise at the dead end, facing down the strait. On the wooden sign, many of the lots were nailed with little red "sold" chits. The developer had been fighting and winning legal battles for two years and was said to be broke now, but Cyrus didn't believe it. Evil is never broke. Everything, obviously, would end when this sprang up: when the houses were planted and lawned on the close lots and the docks spiked the shore and the resort drew in its first reservations. There would be dinghy service across the mouth of the harbor to the town of Sooke, but mainly these new people would clog East Sooke Road. They would require more services than Walter's Lickety Split could offer. They would overrun the park: they'd have their own entrance, a new trail sliced into its back, straight to Iron Mine Bay. You would hike to that beach from the other trails and find fat and pale families there under umbrellas, with barking dogs chewing the crabs and children pissing in the sea. East Sooke would become the shunned and crowded cousin of Sooke, with the clogged road on weekends and the shabby roadside stands—the roles would reverse. The development had stood almost still for so long—for over two years now—that Cyrus often allowed himself to half forget the peril they lived under and the nearness of their end. In every new patch of coast they walked to today, he expected to see a man's body bobbing, shirtless and crowned. How putrid would he be by now? What would salt water do to him? But another feathery, chilled sun set into the strait upon the dead still missing: Ginny, Paula, Don, and Cyrus watched it from where the broad windows of the resort would soon protect the guests against the steady wind and people would stand among their luggage or sit with tea, pleased with themselves. They faced discouraging walks home along roads. Don and Paula hitched instead—with quick success, because this was Don.

Ginny, however, came home with Cyrus. Stay to dinner, Chick offered, but she said she'd promised dinner with dear old dad, though she'd take a cup of Mr. Collingwood's famous tea. She told Chick how Cyrus had navigated through the forest without the aid of trails and then found the leash, and although the begrudged smile and wrinkled, worried brow were only the way Cyrus's father's face came day to day, when they heard a car in the driveway (Ginny hadn't heard it and kept speaking), Cyrus and his father both sat still to wait for the knock with exactly the same thoughts (Cyrus believed): the same picture of a stern Mountie in their minds' eye, and then Cyrus in handcuffs.

It was only Greg. All alone. Introductions were made—"Ah yes," Chick said, "I believe I met your daughter earlier?" Greg said, "No, not mine, I'm afraid, though that was my wife she was with." "Oh, yes," Chick said, and stupidly, "You're right, yes. Will you join us for a cup of tea?" Greg said he would.

He said that he was here to ask if Ginny and Cyrus and their friends would be available to help with the search again tomorrow. He'd heard that they'd discovered the leash, which was, unfortunately, the only worthwhile thing discovered all day. He told them it had belonged to Sasha—he told them about poor Sasha's fate. Chick and Ginny were fascinated, troubled. "Of course," Ginny said. "We wanted to help. Cyrus knows that park like the back of his hand." Greg looked upon them with bright eyes and this fake smile. Why in the world wouldn't he put two and two together and leap to Cyrus? Perhaps he had seen something, however half perceptible, that night in the park—or heard something, someone not Nicholas, or only had a feeling that did not require the imprecise senses? Perhaps he had half seen the body across the beach. The longer his friend was missing, the more time he'd have to worry the little impressions, put people into the shadows.

Greg lingered and Chick asked him about the missing man; Cyrus made a new pot of tea and listened from the kitchen. Was it only meant to be a short hike? Just a walk, Greg said—just a break from writing their books. Are you writing a book? Chick asked. (Did he sound just as stupid to everyone, in these moments, or was his old man's gift for lending grace to the obvious so powerful that no one but Cyrus quite noticed?) Greg explained, lackadaisically. Ruskin, he mentioned—a biographer, a historian. "Cyrus told us you're writing something yourself," he offered politely, and Chick said, "No, not really." "About Lewis Carroll," Ginny provided. "Hot tea!" Cyrus said, carrying it in on a tray.

They milked and sugared and held the steam up to their faces. There was a cozy charm to life in houses, in the web, which Cyrus would miss when this was through and he was caught, or else, if he was unfairly spared, he would begin to appreciate these charms and no longer dismiss the sedentary pleasures. It was Ginny's presence that made the difference, mainly. She was lovely tonight, her hair wild and knotted. "How *is* your book?" Greg asked Chick, surprisingly. "Cyrus said you had old family papers? Old letters, I guess? Dodgson was quite a letter writer."

"Yes, he was," Chick allowed. He smiled impenetrably. "Yes, he was." Eventually, he said, "The book goes slowly, Mr. Faber. Always the same—slowly. I imagine you understand."

"I certainly do."

Ginny asked, "How many pages do you have, Mr. Collingwood?"

"You know, it's positively silly," Chick said, "yet even that can be a difficult question to answer. Not that it matters. Mine," he said to Greg, "is not really a book so much as a hobby. Not like yours."

"Mine may be less than that," Greg said.

Chick smiled. "You're modest."

"What's your friend's book about?" Ginny asked Greg.

"The Shakers, mainly." "How far along is he?" Chick asked, and Greg replied, "The early stages, I guess. He recently published a chapter." "It's been going well, though?" "His books always do," Greg said. Chick asked, "He hadn't taken it into the park with him, of course?" "Oh, no, no." They sipped their tea. Chick shook his head and said, "Where in the world can the poor man be?"

When Greg spoke again, it would be to the point—he would seize the opening, swing things back around to Cyrus. He would ask if any of them had been out the night Nicholas went missing. Someone (he would say) may have seen something; this is why he asked, he'd say. The opening was just as clear to Cyrus (his father here to confirm he wasn't at home; Ginny to confirm he wasn't with her, either), and it would work: Greg's suspicions would mesh with Chick's, a path would form, and they'd find their way down it, eventually.

Cyrus sipped his very good tea and watched Greg intently. He wasn't obliged to make it easy. But when Greg did speak, he asked, "Have you found his diaries?" and Cyrus (after a moment of utter confusion) adjusted. "Dodgson's?" Greg clarified. "I seem to remember there were volumes missing, weren't there? Or pages, at any rate?"

His gaze had risen from his tea to Chick, not to Cyrus. Chick (as surprised as his son, perhaps) eventually said, "That's right. You're right." There were the usual difficulties, he explained—the missing pieces—no more than with another subject, he imagined. "Sure," Greg said, relenting, "and anyway it won't do to talk too much about a book in progress."

Very shortly, having given up, he left. "See you in the morning, then," he said to Cyrus on his way out—with no accusation at all implied: an emptiness there, a man forgotten.

As it happened, they didn't see him, next morning. Don drove over from Sooke, giving Ginny a ride (Paula was not interested, or invited), so that he could drop her at Cyrus's house later, where she would need a ride home. She would get it from Chick—Cyrus would come along— and she'd find a pretext to invite them into the trailer for a minute, where Mr. Mallet would have Chick's surprise party ready. First, though, they faced the long day of fruitless searches. The park was crawling again, though possibly not as full as it had been the day before. The constables coordinated, but there was no sign of Cortland. Cyrus wanted to search the shoreline, but when the three of them were sent inland instead he hoped for the only worthwhile possibility—to see Samina. He was disappointed in that, too. Everyone was disappointed. The day passed without event. Cyrus had a great deal of time to think because Ginny and Don chatted and fell behind him and he wondered if there was any chance that Nicholas was alive. Had dragged himself away from the beach—any chance at all?

The birthday surprise came off without a hitch. Mr. Mallet had collected a cake, had lit the candles and turned the lights out when he heard them drive down the dump's entry road. He had pizza warm in the oven. Ginny got Chick through the trailer door first: "What's this?" he asked, and they all yelled, "Surprise!" For an hour there was no mention of the missing man. "You can cut the cake," Mr. Mallet said, "but no one's eating it. I made the mistake of telling Connie who it was for and she felt obliged to donate it, so we got the one that's been in her window for a week." Mr. Mallet was thin and yellowish. He shivered now, though the trailer was stuffy with heat. "How generous," Chick said dryly, and added, "A lovely gesture." Ginny said, "See what you inspire, Mr. Collingwood?" Mr. Mallet said, "That knife won't do. Get the hacksaw, Cyrus, would you?"

This is it! Cyrus thought. *My God,* he thought in a flash, *this is it! This is all I need. This is where I'm needed. Oh, let's go,* he thought. *The four of us— everyone—let's get this trailer operational and leave town tomorrow. Please! Let's not be found. Let's have nothing to do with this place.* Mr. Mallet should die somewhere beautiful. Everyone should. Greg would never find them. Ginny and Cyrus could get work. She'd given up the violin—she'd said so—she was free now; she could take it along, of course, and play for pleasure or comfort in the evenings, or possibly for income if she was comfortable with that. He was in love with her—it was simply true. She might fall in love with him, given the proper environment, although she never would here, in this place where nothing changed and people only ran down and ferns grew up around them, or were trampled under Americans and other survivors in shiny vehicles. Let East Sooke be overrun with golfers. Let it go to hell.

It came to Cyrus as a first-class revelation: *he'd had it all, already*—all he needed. Something so much purer than the mess of cottager intrigues and jealousies he'd been wasting his autumn envying. He'd had to accidentally kill a person to realize it, so now he didn't deserve it, but was that necessary?

He felt his father forget what he knew about Cyrus and the night of the murder—his father always wanted to forget. He was changing out his suspicions. When the conversation finally came back there, as of course it would—it was the talk of the town—his father looked upon Cyrus with all the forgiveness and high-ground optimism (Cyrus would *change*, he must be thinking; this phase would pass) of his best days. How well, he asked, did Cyrus know these people? What was his opinion of Nicholas and what did he think could have happened to him? He would not be asking if he didn't expect to like the answers. And Cyrus, who never wished to hurt his father, said, "I wonder sometimes if he could have run away." His dear father nodded—so sadly! "Abandoned his family," Cyrus elaborated. "It's terrible," he said, "but I don't know what else to think. And somehow—you know?—he kind of seemed the type? Nicholas, I mean?"

Ginny *tsk*ed sadly. "He has a little girl," she pointed out again.

"Hardly makes a difference," her father believed.

Chick, in his deep and lovely voice, full of rugged and empty compassion, said, "But I've been having the same exact thought, Cyrus."

After they'd cleaned up (Mr. Mallet did not even bother to help anymore—he sat still, giving directions, wrapped in a blanket), Chick walked into the dump yard with Ginny and Cyrus. "Heading out, then?" he asked Cyrus. "Or maybe coming home with your old man tonight?"

There was heartbreaking hopefulness in his voice.

This was the thing—it *wouldn't* be easy. The challenge of the life that Cyrus had just begun imagining rose up before him anew, because he would actually do *anything*—anything at all—not to go home with his father. Not tonight, with him happy this way. Not to suffer through a long evening of well-meant calculation behind his father's every move: his kindly, saved-up questions (*How are the French Suites coming along, by the way? What are you reading lately? How is Don?*—there were so few questions he could think of, and Cyrus would have to feel his father searching for new ones), and his gentlemanly back-pats, and his happy and attentive quiet when they sat together playing the *über*-game, both of them aware of his father's distracting gratitude. When they parted—when Cyrus went to bed—he would feel his father's burdensome hope that tomorrow night might be like tonight, and that Cyrus *had* changed. Had changed again, rather.

"I think we're going out, actually," he said—a lizard; a worm; not fit; "Dad," he added, by way of compensation. He would try his best again tomorrow night—he promised himself he would. "Aren't we?" he asked Ginny. His father's mild smile had not budged, though his eyes had emptied into ashes.

Ginny said, "I'm just supposed to meet Don, actually. Nothing special." She wouldn't help Cyrus in such cruel work. He said, "Yeah, I'll come along."

They walked in silence to where Chick's car was parked. When they were there, Ginny leaned to kiss Chick. "Happy birthday, Mr. Collingwood."

"Thank you, Ginny," he said. "I enjoyed my party immensely."

Cyrus, just behind them, leaned forward and kissed his father, too. He kissed the man's ear. "Love you, Dad," he said. His father said, "Thank you"—he didn't know quite what to say, getting into his car, though he added "Be careful, Cyrus," but too late: Cyrus had closed the car door on the sentence. Cyrus waved to him through the window to indicate he understood. His father drove home alone.

29

L AUREL SAT IN front of the television, flicking through the very few channels. She had resigned herself to neglect—no one here trusted her: not Greg; least of all, Samina—and now that Samina's brother was in town, she and Greg would soon be superfluous. Khalid had flown in from Delhi via Vancouver. Greg and Laurel had been to Victoria earlier in the evening and dropped Samina at the garage, where the Jetta was ready at last. Samina had picked her brother up at the airport. They should have all been home by now but it didn't surprise Laurel that they weren't. "Don't put your feet on that," she told Greg, not taking her eyes from the television. Samina would be busy telling her brother all about Laurel and Greg—how she longed to be rid of them. "Do you want to make dinner?"

Greg took his feet from the coffee table. "Shouldn't we wait for them?"

"They're not coming back." Since their conversation with the police sergeant earlier this evening, Samina had been listlessly and differently remote. "Do you know what I think? It's obvious, though. I really think she's never liked either of us much. Not me, either."

"You already knew she didn't like me?"

"You never liked her, Greg. That's always been clear as day."

He laughed contemptuously. "To you, maybe."

"No, actually, to all of us. You think they didn't know it?"

"Oh, dear." He sighed.

This evening Laurel was suddenly, swiftly (and belatedly) feeling certain that there was something enormous Samina knew but wouldn't admit to. "Why did they invite us, then?" she asked aloud. "Why stay in touch? Why put up with us all these years? Pity, I think. I think they thought we would be heartbroken if we lost touch with such dear old friends."

Greg rolled his eyes. "What can I make you for dinner?" he asked. She said, "Old friends are overrated. I'm sticking to new friends from now on." "Good plan." "I'm changing them out, like tires." "What a trail of tears you'll leave behind."

It was a game—it was some kind of game, someone's game, which they had used Laurel to play. A stupid pawn. Nicholas had used her, certainly. Had he been planning to abandon his wife and wanted Laurel to reassure him that Samina wasn't aware of this? Laurel was meant to tell him, *No, my goodness, nothing is wrong! Everything is fine. She loves you! She doesn't suspect a thing.* He might have used her more directly, then—to occupy Samina at the proper moment on the proper day; or when Laurel had followed the script, he would have told her how reassuring it was to hear that, how deeply in love with dear Samina he still was!—something Laurel would be sure to communicate to Samina later, when Nicholas was gone and presumed dead. He'd wanted Laurel to cover for him.

On the other hand, couldn't he have been leaving Samina because there *was* something terribly wrong? Leaving her before she left him—so that the lies Laurel had told him had been just what he'd expected and all he needed to carry through? Wasn't it even possible Laurel had accidentally told the truth about Samina?

"I *wanted* to help," she said aloud, sincerely. "I *still* want to, Greg. God, I want to find that bastard! *Why* won't she let us help?"

Greg could say, *What could we do, after all?* She might agree. He could say, *I want to help, too. I feel useless.* It was probably true. But instead he said, "Maybe she doesn't want your help because you're self-centered and needy around her. And competitive. And nosy, and pushy. She brings out the worst in you, somehow."

She picked the remote control back up, flicked at the screen. "I *hate* talking to you lately," she said. "*You* bring out the worst in me." What a vacation. She and Greg should have spent this sabbatical at separate ends of the earth. "Why don't you go away?" When he didn't, she said, "Fine, I will."

But neither of them moved quite yet. The television chattered between them. "I'll make dinner," he said.

SERGEANT DUNN HAD been a tall, pale man with light red hair and invisible eyebrows. His cheeks flushed easily and often. He had asked them—all three of them—to come to the station in town at the end of the day, and there he had sat them down and explained why he would be scaling back the search tomorrow. He spoke slowly, with agonizing pauses, but kindly, quietly, while leaning forward across his desk, with his great, pale hands parting and folded before him. He looked into his hands frequently, as if for certain words. The essence of their job in a case like this, he said, was to narrow the possibilities. The fewer they had to consider, the better they could concentrate their efforts and resources on those that remained. To this end, he said, he wished to speak plainly about the reasoning he and his constables, along with the search and rescue team, had worked through over the last three days. "Now, if," he said, "at any time, while I'm going forward here"—he spoke especially to Samina, of course; his pauses broke his sentences into packets of words—"I get ahead of myself, or start down a road you'd rather not go down yet, you'll just let me know. All right?" "All right," Samina told him. She seemed calm, but unnaturally attentive. She'd left Hilda in the outer room (the sergeant had insisted), in the care of a female constable. He said, "I wish the possibilities we had to discuss . . . were better." She said that he probably couldn't mention anything she hadn't thought of yet, but tears sprang from the corners of her eyes. She wiped them away impatiently. "It's fine," she said, her voice unchanged. "I'm sure you're right," Sergeant Dunn replied.

When seventy-two hours had passed since the missing man was last seen and he had not walked out on his own, the search coordinators found themselves reduced to only three broad theories, which they could arrange from least likely to most. Number three: that Nicholas Green had suffered a debilitating injury, or had been rendered unconscious, or had (Sergeant Dunn looked away from Samina and blushed) killed himself, or died accidentally, on land in a remote corner of the park. That was, by now, least likely. Number two (he held up fingers, paused): that he had drowned and been washed from land. Or number one: that he had never been injured—had merely walked away. They *would* search again tomorrow. They could not keep the Coast Guard or the helicopter any longer, and most of the police force would have to return to the regular duties they'd been neglecting, but there were a number of volunteers from the community who would be back out and well organized, and who would focus on the more remote sections of the coastline. Mr. Green might turn up yet. They weren't going to leave him stranded somewhere, waiting for help. But the first possibility, Sergeant Dunn explained, had gone from most likely to least because someone had already passed within shouting distance of most of the park, two days in a row, and they had searched almost every spot anyone could think of where a man might fall far enough to do real damage to himself. They doubted they had an exposed body in the park because they'd been keeping an eye on the vultures. There had been vultures patrolling the forest the last two days, as there always were, but they hadn't behaved as they would if there was something large dead or dying. "Should we take a break?" he asked Samina. "No." But she did look frightened. "You hadn't thought of vultures?" he said. "No." "How about a cup of coffee?" he asked. "No," she said. "Thank you."

More likely, the sergeant continued, was drowning. The waters off the coast of that park were full of odd currents after a storm. If he had drowned, there might be evidence or there might not be. Two private boats—again, volunteers—would search the coast once more tomorrow, plus the shores of Donaldson and Wolfe Islands. But the hard thing about a drowning was that the body might present itself tomorrow, next week, or next April. A terrible patience was sometimes required. On the other hand, most often a drowning victim did *not* go far, and it was discouraging to this line of speculation that they hadn't found any evidence yet: in the form, for instance, of footprints that led to the water but not back from it, or bloodstains below the cliffs of the coast trail. Mr. Green was a fit man in good health, and a strong swimmer. That never ruled out drowning—none of these points did—but for these reasons, they had to consider it less likely than the last possibility. Which, again, was that Mr. Green had, for some reason, walked away.

Here the sergeant sat back. He faced Samina sheepishly. Not only was he disinclined by temperament to press her on this point but there was no reason for him to: it was her problem, not his, and the answers, if they were available at all (where had he gone? why? with whose help?), were beyond Sergeant Dunn's reach and responsibility. "You've made it clear, Mrs. Naqvi, that this seems highly unlikely to you. All three of you have agreed on that. And, to be honest, so has everyone else—Mr. Green's family and acquaintances, the contacts you gave us. I certainly don't claim to know better. But for what it's worth to you, the longer we go empty-handed, the more likely abandonment becomes. Logically." Nudged in this direction, there might be clues this woman would discover or remember, days or months from now. If it was true, the missing man was a bastard—the search coordinators all agreed. It was clear that the abandonment had taken his wife completely by surprise, and there was the daughter as well. She must have thought they were happy together.

Mr. Faber said, "I'm not sure why you haven't considered some sort of violence, Sergeant. Someone or something attacking him."

"Oh, yes, we have. Certainly. Not 'something'—there aren't any bears or cougars left in that park. But homicide was the fourth possibility, or kidnapping—some sort of assault. I didn't mention that. It turns out to be the least likely of all."

This was the second time that Mr. Faber—who happened to be, of course, the only passable suspect for a homicide—had brought it up himself. Which did not, in the sergeant's mind, enhance Mr. Faber's potential innocence, nor compel the sergeant toward a suspicion of his guilt. Mrs. Naqvi had never expressed any suspicions of Mr. Faber, and nothing about his alibi had appeared false or slippery. Many of the questions the constables had directed toward the family and friends in the

States over the telephone yesterday and today had been meant to flush out problems between Mr. Green and Mr. Faber, but nothing had emerged. Mrs. Naqvi had provided the contacts, but she had left none of the gaps one looked for—no siblings or old friends she'd failed to mention. Aloud now, Sergeant Dunn explained the obvious: there was no one resembling a suspect at hand, and no clear motivation, either. Mr. Green hadn't had his wallet with him, or even a backpack. There were thieves who sometimes worked these parks but they merely broke into parked cars and stole what careless hikers had left behind. The last thing such cowards wanted was contact with a fit, adult man.

"But there's the dog," Mr. Faber said.

"That's right. The one detail that suggests violence is the dead dog on the beach. But it's very hard to interpret by itself." It had been at its owner's house until at least eight o'clock that evening, the sergeant explained (corroborating Mr. Faber's word that it hadn't been at the beach when he'd been there—and the presumption that he almost certainly hadn't killed it), but the Whittleseys lived at the edge of the park and their dog was known to wander as far as that beach on its own. Sasha sometimes followed hikers. "She was a good dog." (The sergeant blushed at this, too, for some reason.) "We all knew her." Someone had certainly killed her, he said—had hit her on the head with a stick or a bat. Who? So far, Mr. Green was the only person known to have been in the park that late, but it was against the law to stay past sunset, so even without the suspicions attached to a missing man and a dead dog, anyone else who may have been there would be unlikely to come forward. If Mr. Green had been attacked, then his assailant may have killed the dog: it may have been barking too much, calling unwanted attention.

Mr. Faber said, "Or it may have been attacked in the same spot Nicholas was, to cover up evidence. Or someone might have killed it there out of cruelty. It could be a boast—if this person took Nicholas from that beach. Or if he followed us into the park in the first place."

"You said earlier you hadn't believed you were followed."

"Well, no, I didn't see anyone. I don't *feel* like we were followed. But that might only mean the person was good at it—it doesn't mean he wasn't there."

"Yes," the sergeant said, "you're right. Everything you've mentioned has occupied the team members for the last two days, and our investigation will continue in that direction." (It did seem likely by now that Mr. Faber was a man who sensed a bear in every bush.) "But what you don't know, Mr. Faber—how could you?—is that young people sometimes come into this park at night. And when they do they often enter at the Pike Road and walk to this beach." In fact, he said, they'd found evidence—a half-buried campfire and a beer can—of a party, not far from Iron Mine Bay. It might have been from that night or another recent night—impossible to say for certain—but someone had taken pains (more than these teenagers usually did) to cover up the evidence. They might be more likely to do that if, for instance, things had gotten a bit out of hand at this party. If someone had perhaps killed a dog. The tide and the rain that evening had probably been responsible for cleaning any evidence from the fur. But the tide and rain would both have washed the beach of human bloodstains or other evidence as well—one would hardly need to kill a dog for that purpose. And in fact, it would be a blunder, since the dog was now the only evidence of a crime that they had. Of some crime, at least. This killer they were imagining would have to be stupid. "The fact is, strange as it sounds, these two things—the dead dog and the missing man—do not necessarily have anything to do with one another. And then one does wish for a motivation, in any case. If you're right, Mr. Faber—if you and Mr. Green were stalked—then 'Why?' is as difficult a question to answer as 'By whom?' " (The answer, again, might have come from America along with Mr. Green, despite the lack of enemies his friends had been willing to mention. But that wasn't what Mr. Faber meant. Mr. Faber, being a cottager, had in mind some sort of local madman.) "Even if there is no good reason at all—if we're talking about some inexplicable act, and the two of you were no more nor less than in the wrong place at the wrong time (which, I must tell you, as rare as it is in your cities, is even less common out here)—even then, if you'll allow me, we wonder why the killer might choose Mr. Green as his victim instead of you yourself, Mr. Faber. He's the larger man, as you've said. Perhaps the more physically fit? And how often, getting right down to it, is this sort of killer we're attempting to construct interested in random men instead of young women? Forgive me. But if the missing person was a woman, or even a child, our mindset would be different, I can tell you. But an adult man"—he spoke to the wife again now, gently—"in good health, with no known enemies, no outstanding threats . . . left alone in a park he'd never been to, and known to have been wading shortly before he was last seen . . . a man, to speak plainly—please stop me if you wish—but a man already far from home, or from anyone who might recognize him hitchhiking, or boarding a ferry, or climbing, as prearranged, into someone's car . . ."

"True," Mrs. Faber admitted. "You're right," she said.

And it was sinking in with Mrs. Naqvi, too: she looked both angry and defeated. Mr. Faber (who was really only a suspect to them in this capacity, still: who may have helped the man go missing) stared out the window of the sergeant's office now, at the sun shining on the parked cars. "Well," the sergeant finished, "this inexplicable and—yes, nagging— dead dog aside, I think you can see how difficult it is to assume murder when an accident, or abandonment, are so undeniably more likely."

30

CONSTABLE CORTLAND DID his best to wash his hands of it. He stepped through a pleasant Monday as if he'd never heard of poor Nicholas Green—why should he be the only one kept up at night?—and took care of lingering errands for Mrs. Cortland and got back to the fouled buggy. He had the Mini Mounties over for their regular troop meeting and found they had entirely moved on (dear and resilient creatures): not one of them mentioned the search or the missing man. After he'd delivered the Mounties to their parents and waved to each from the driveway, back in the house, upstairs, he found Mrs. Cortland in one of her funks. Oh, it's only silliness, she said, wiping eyes on her apron: "It's only that you told me about their little girl, you know—Hilda, I believe you said—and didn't I end up right back with our Olivia? Oh, dear me, Constable," she said when he held her. "Silly old woman," she called herself. He said, "There, there." How about a trip to America? he wondered. Weren't they due, after all? That would be lovely, she said—or she'd become interested in Australia, as a matter of fact. Was he, at all? "Kangaroos?" he asked. That's right. And Nicole Kidman was from there, interestingly enough. And Russell Crowe as well. "Well, then, by all means," he told her. "Let's look into it."

An hour later he'd lost her for the evening to her Internet and her
happy search for deals. So he dropped down to the pub, where the talk
around the fender in the back room was still of the missing man, and no
one but the man himself could have been a more welcome sight than the
constable stepping through the doorway. There was a rumor abroad that
the missing man had been murdered—a dead dog had been invoked in
support of this—and another that he'd merely abandoned his family (for
which the same dead dog was somehow employed). "I shall confirm the
former," said the constable, settling at his table—"Cheers" he told the
young man tending, who'd drawn and delivered his pint already—"and
dispel the latter. Though I speak so freely only for the reason that I speak
without authority, understand. The man you see before you has no offi-
cial role in this search any longer. That's number one."

He was asked why that was, and he explained. He spoke of it as a
judgment call by well-meaning men, but his equanimity in the face of
injustice and ineptitude was nevertheless conveyed. He developed the
narrative of his own search then, from his earliest, most humble supposi-
tions—from incompetence through injury, abandonment, drowning—
on past the sergeant's reach to the night when the missing man's sandal
bobbed into the constable's view in the moonlight. He had not shown
the sandal to anyone yet because, to be perfectly honest, no one was
interested. He'd accept a second pint. Next he carried his audience
through the complicated deductions and left them seeing that when you
took a sandal in the ocean half a kilometer from the Point-Last-Seen
plus the dead dog and three days' search empty-handed, you had
nowhere left to go but murder and cover-up. Neat as a whistle.

Then who killed him? his audience wished to know, and the constable
admitted: That's your question. There you are. Your best suspect was
obvious—the friend, of course—but perhaps too obvious? The constable had seen plenty of that bloke the last three days and the fact was, he
simply didn't *act* like a guilty man. (Which was as vague as the constable's
feelings about Greg remained. Sometimes he wondered why he didn't
suspect him more.) But on the other hand, this dead American might
have imported his enemies with him. In New York City they may have
good guesses to offer you.

He was done with his second pint and knew his limits. Already he had regrets. He hated to tell a secret. Not the telling itself—the telling was delicious, a strong temptation—but when it was told he always felt bereft and exposed. "Well then," the constable said, and slapped his palms down on his knees. "Good evening to you, gentlemen." He stood, and left his money. "And listen, will you? Don't believe a word of it. Right?" He winked broadly. On the drive home his thoughts returned to local business—to Don and his brother Marty, who were not getting along in life as readily as they ought to, and then to Cyrus Collingwood, who was perhaps a bad influence on Don. Who demanded a bit of attention. There were these summer break-ins, the menacing of tourists—you hardly wanted to put the cottagers above your local sons, but it was possible to give a young man too many second chances. There were the shoes the constable had found in the bushes not far from the Flaherty cottage, the morning after the people from Winnipeg were harassed—they were in a plastic bag in the constable's closet. He still suspected old Cyrus would turn out to be Cinderella. Back to basics, he thought. Mrs. Cortland would be asleep. So he drove down to the Collingwoods' and parked his car in the driveway of an empty cottage down the street and approached by the neighbor's woods. If anyone was awake—if he saw Cyrus through a window—he would knock, and probably scare the wits out of the boy, this time of night. A bit of the boy's own medicine. But the house was dark. The car was parked under the cedar tree. Mr. Collingwood was a strange if mild man—he meant well, very likely—but he was not quite to be trusted, either. He was overmatched by that son of his, and always had been. There was a time when Constable Cortland had thought that he himself could repair the damage of an overlenient and motherless childhood—he'd put his oar in, God knows, and Cyrus had been worth it, after all: no one denied he was bright. But Cyrus had quit the Mini Mounties and run away from proffered help. He was a quitter by nature, unfortunately. And Mr. Collingwood could be disagreeably mealy-mouthed and secretive, and had not seemed to work a day in his life. It was family money, people said, but no one knew for sure.

And so who was that, then, tiptoeing up through the woods on the other side of the house? Or no, he wasn't coming up the hill—he was going down it now, toward the ponds. He'd already been by the dark house, or in it. The constable thought it must be his man—it must be Cyrus, off to something nefarious. He circled around stealthily and hurried to get to the road first. His back complained and complained, but he wouldn't have any of it. He saw the man clearly when he came out at the road and set off the trip-light at the Hannah cottage—not who the constable had thought, yet he *should* have known.

GREG HAD LAIN awake for a long time, wondering what he had left to look forward to except the emptiness on the other side of all he'd recently been. (Which he welcomed, in a way—that emptiness.) He wondered, bleakly, if there was any way he could get Melanie back—if it was at all possible he might be more attractive to her divorced. With his wife would go most of his friendships, not only Samina and Nicholas. What more could this trip mark the end of? It certainly had emerged as a turning point. And so he wondered if it was somehow possible to do the ridiculous thing he had longed to do since yesterday evening. It was cruel and selfish to even be occupied with the notion, much less act on it—that was the easiest part of the dilemma to sort out. How could he be thinking of books and long-dead authors when his friend (Laurel was right, he supposed: his oldest friend) was missing? But he just kept asking himself that question without bothering or expecting to answer it, and so it had become as much a balm as a prod to his guilty feelings. He could get out of the cottage easily. He was always getting up without Laurel noticing lately, and Samina had arrived home exhausted. She'd spent the evening with her half-brother, whom she'd presumably left at the bed-and-breakfast. Greg was sure she would sleep tonight, however unhappily— the meeting with the sergeant had taken the wind out of all their sails. This first part—sneaking out of the cottage—was so easy that eventually he just got up and did it. He set off the trip lights in his own driveway and then in another, staying off the road a bit, but too far into dark yards. He avoided the Collingwoods' driveway and took the path through the woods that he'd discovered earlier, past the two tiny ponds still as photos. The night sky was littered with stars and hemmed by the silhouettes of evergreens. My god, where was Nicholas? What had Greg done, just by leaving Nicholas alone—what opportunity had he provided? Would he himself be missing now, too, if they hadn't parted?

The house was dark but they were home—the car was there. Mr. Collingwood, Greg thought, had acted exactly like a man who guarded a worthy secret, yet could you have much confidence in him finishing his book? "Hobbies" didn't lend themselves to completion. When he died, his treasure would fall into the broad trust of a library, where second-rate biographers would tear the whole into scraps and race to get their half-baked volumes out first; or worse, into tighter family fists than Mr. Collingwood's. But it would be a slow, delicate process to win him over— that had been clear, too. First of all, Greg would have to publish his Ruskin book, establish his credentials. But it would be foolish to embark on a courtship that might last years without knowing for certain that there was a worthwhile prize at the end.

Greg had used their bathroom the night before, and on the way down the hall he had pushed open doors, looking for Mr. Collingwood's study. He'd decided it must be upstairs. In his mind's eye, in bed a few minutes ago, he had imagined a climbable tree that might lead to an upper-story window left ajar, but there wasn't a tree close enough and now, looking at the house, the whole idea was quickly fading from daring through unlikely toward idiotic. He crouched among oversized ferns. The house hunched and sagged, the roofline dipping down past the upper windows like drooping eyelids. Everything was wet, though it hadn't rained in days.

He'd lost his mind, he thought—he had lost his way, recently. *Look at me*, Greg suddenly thought: *Look what I'm doing.* He sat here, a predator, staring into the dark rooms where people slept. He'd turned into just what he feared. And that thought made him recall his own fears, and begin to half imagine someone else out in the woods, watching him. He couldn't even do this well, he told himself. He wasn't even adept at his vices. He forced himself to sit still, pointlessly, for a long time, growing cold. *Remember this*, he told himself. *Make this the low point. Don't go down from here, for god's sake.*

How lonely the house seemed. Not only now, dark and silent as it was, but yesterday evening, too, when Greg was inside of it. The room that should have been the dining room was full of floor-to-ceiling bookshelves instead, plus a desk that was piled with more books, and stacks of journals on the floor. In the front room there were two pump organs and a piano crowded together and all the chairs but two were occupied by dusty boxes or more books. One could hardly walk through the clutter—only a narrow path was left clear. The paintings on the walls hung by long lengths of dark string from an old-fashioned molding. They were framed, but without glass, and they were of artfully mangled landscapes, or caves—a man in a boat held a lantern up to see—but lamps or stacks of papers or shadows were in the way of them. There were all these rugs, in all the rooms but the kitchen—beautiful rugs in drab colors and simple patterns, some battered, two layers deep and haphazardly spread across the creaking floors. It was a house that Greg would have found immensely appealing, so recently. His own house might resemble it—atmospherically, at least, if not quite in any of the specific details—twenty years from now, if he parted from Laurel and remained alone. Was that what he wanted? He had better decide soon, he thought, before he ran out of choices.

SAMINA KNEW IT was him at the end of the corridor though his back was turned to her—there was a physicality to the striding shift of his shoulders in his shirt, a bunching of muscle, though he was walking away from her and in no hurry at all. She should call out. She hoped to lay Nicholas down and climb on top of him. The swell and shift under her feet meant a boat, at night. He opened a door and stepped through it, then closed the door behind himself, but quietly, as if to keep from waking the crew. A light had been shining down from a helicopter or an airplane flying low over the boat—she was on deck. Was he in the airplane? Was she meant to row? He'd just been here—what a pleasure it would be when she had his skin under her fingers again, his bulk and precise shape. She could still hear his footsteps receding, or was that a memory? The light went out. She held Hilda at her breast (an infant) and looked up, though it was very hard to see into the night sky. The shape of something, floating and shrinking, could be detected only by the way it blocked out the stars there. She heard insects in wood, fingers clicking. He'd disappeared. I'm dreaming, aren't I?

Part
III

31

SHE HAD TAKEN the telephone into her bedroom. One of her persistent fantasies was of a late-night phone call. Best of all, it would be from him: at a cottage somewhere nearby, or in a hospital (but safe now—well enough, now, to call her; he would have called sooner but he was unconscious and had no identification on him, they hadn't known who he was). Or, even, from the next life, across the divide of a choice he had made, to explain it to her. So that she would know he was alive. Possibly even with contrition already, already wishing to come back. But it didn't have to be him. It could be anyone else, saying he'd been found.

"Mrs. Naqvi? Have I woken you?" She knew the voice immediately, the accent, and after a moment she had attached it to the person. Had he woken her? She sat up. The room took shape around her. "Yes? What is it?"

"It's terribly late," the constable said, "I must apologize. I hoped to speak to you alone—privately, if possible." He spoke quietly, as if to keep from waking someone on his end. There was silence behind him—he didn't seem to be in a police station. He wasn't supposed to be involved at all, any longer. "We haven't found your husband, Mrs. Naqvi—I should make that clear. I do wish I could be calling you with that news."

"What time is it?" She couldn't see the clock, for some reason. But then she found it, covered over by the bedspread. "It must be past two," he replied. It was ten of three. "In the morning," he clarified. "I have woken you—I can hear that. You'll need what sleep you can get now, I suppose."

"Mr. Cortland, why are you calling me? I don't want to keep the line tied up."

"You're expecting another call at this hour?"

"Constable—"

"Of course you are—I understand. I'd like to speak with you, though, madam. There are things I ought to tell you. It needn't be now, but I would prefer if we spoke privately. Is someone else there listening? Is Mr. Faber with you?"

"What should you tell me?" Her mind was clearing, slowly.

"I think it may prove too involved to begin now. And it isn't the best news—perhaps not worth sleeping on."

"Constable, forgive me for being blunt, but I understood from Sergeant Dunn that you weren't involved in the search anymore."

"I call you in an unofficial capacity—entirely. You're quite right."

"But why are you calling me at all?"

"Perhaps this isn't the best time—"

"It's three in the morning. Why do you have bad news to tell me? It must be something Sergeant Dunn could be calling to tell me instead?"

"Not at all, as a matter of fact."

She should keep him hemmed in, keep him from holding forth. "I would really rather not receive a call from you at this hour, Mr. Cortland." In fact, she should just hang up, except that whatever he knew, she wanted to know, too. "Frankly, it's a little cruel," she said. "You probably can't guess how disappointed I was to hear it was you."

"But I can, in fact."

"We're not on speaking terms, really, you and I."

"I remember what it's like exactly," he said, "waiting for the telephone call—"

"I don't think you understand how much you hindered the search."

"—assuming it would come in the middle of the night. Such calls always do."

"Don't do that." She had meant to remain polite and curt, but she'd raised her voice. Hilda slept on. "I'm sorry, Mr. Cortland, but don't try to guess what I'm thinking, or whatever you were just doing. Please don't do that."

"I never would. But you and I have more in common—"

"Does the sergeant know you're calling?"

"As I've said, I'm speaking to you in an unofficial capacity, madam. It has nothing to do with Sergeant Dunn."

"Why won't you just leave me alone? Wouldn't that be easier?"

"You're right," he said. "Perhaps I should." They were both quiet for a moment. He said, "Then consider this merely an invitation, will you? I have things I could tell you, which you might care to know. I'll hang up now, but if you ever wish to speak to me you will please feel free to call me at home. Any hour is fine. I'm sure I've given you the number?"

"Constable." She closed her eyes. She'd had all the sleep she would get tonight. She did want to know everything. Useful or not quite, good news or bad, facts or speculations—what someone had found or seen or remembered; what Nicholas had said to anyone, however vaguely suggestive or unlikely to be relevant—she wanted it all, as a matter of fact. Hilda, it seemed, would sleep through. It was possible Greg or Laurel had been awakened by the ringing telephone and were listening in but she had decided that she couldn't let them get in her way. All week her thinking had felt cold to her, almost cruelly pragmatic, yet at the same time not quite efficient or incisive enough. If for just one moment she could take the entire situation in—hold it all clearly in her mind with balanced comprehensiveness—she imagined she would know where he was. "Mr. Cortland, I just don't want any games," she said. "I'm sorry, but can I ask you to tell me what you want to tell me—as succinctly as possible—and then we can both go back to bed?"

"Another time," he said. "I'm anxious to tell you, madam, or I would never have disturbed you at this hour, but another time would be better—it wouldn't prove succinct enough for you, I'm afraid. I can't sleep myself, and imagined the same might be true for you. I took the liberty of calling. But sleep is precious at a time like this, Mrs. Naqvi. If you can get it, you must."

Maybe it would be best, she thought, to simply wait for him. He wanted to continue, of course, if on his own terms.

She should let them all rant or speculate—let everyone speak his mind. She adjusted the pillows and sat back against the headboard. "Mrs. Naqvi?" She didn't speak. "Are you there still? I think I hear you breathing."

"I'm here, of course," she said. She said, "I'm awake, too."

"Ah." It was a fine voice, deep and humming with easy confidence. "Let's see, then." He seemed to wear his accent with pride. "Well, I haven't hindered the search at all, I should tell you. That's by the way. You're not inclined to believe me, evidently—as you wish—but quite the opposite is true." He waited for acknowledgment, so she said, "Okay." She ran her fingers down Hilda's hair. He said, "I've been through something like what you're going through, Mrs. Naqvi. Not the same. Certainly not. It's never the same suffering, as everyone knows. No one will ever endure exactly what Mrs. Cortland and I were made to endure, nor understand what we felt, and how could they, after all, when we hardly understood it ourselves? No one, that is, but the Lord, if you'll permit me." Samina wondered if she had the strength for her new policy. There was a good reason why one didn't collect everything, or invite people to hold forth. "But allow me to say that our suffering—my wife's and my own some years ago, and yours now—they're not entirely different. They're congruent, if you will—quite congruent. For instance, my wife and I have lived for months of our lives expecting the late-night telephone call, as you do now. It is a purgatory, I think. Will it be good news or bad, we have been kept up wondering—will it be her, or rather some stranger to tell us she's dead?"

"I don't know," Samina admitted, "if I can listen to your story right now." It was probably silly for her to feel cruel, saying so. But she did. "I'm sorry—I don't mean to be insensitive."

"Not at all."

"But I'm afraid it would probably be too much for me right now."

"I understand. It nearly kept me from calling you. Mrs. Naqvi, I can still hardly bear to speak of it myself."

"I imagine," she offered. "Yes." Neither of them spoke for a moment. "Was there something else you called to tell me, or was it mainly to sympathize? You mentioned bad news?"

"I'LL SPEAK GENERALLY." He could feel the odd swelling back of his eyes, and through the bridge of his nose, which accompanied a too-thorough return to Olivia and events in the past. It was once a pressure that must have led to tears, he supposed—a vestigial reaction now. He said, "But I do think it will help, you see, if you understand, first of all, that when you telephoned me—initially, I mean—and when it was about a missing loved one . . . well, let me say I entered into your case with particular sympathy and determination. I always do now, when someone is missing—however briefly. Whomever the missing may be. You will, too, I should guess. From now on." He waited, listened. The woman's breathing was quite articulate. He'd learned to interpret such things in his work, in Birmingham: how to hear the lies when speaking to suspects or witnesses over the telephone. It was unkind to take her where he must— she was right about that. He wasn't convinced she was ready. "I was determined to find your husband, safe and sound, and bring him back to you. I have had the pleasure of doing that for two or three families over the years—a wife and daughter once, once a wayward son. There's no part of my work I take more pride in." Mrs. Cortland sat behind him on the bed, rubbing his back in small circles. She had pressed him to call— not to wait. She'll want to know, Mrs. Cortland had said—one wants to know, good or bad, remember. He'd thought she was right. But perhaps not for this woman. Or perhaps not yet. She must be in the early stages—still too hopeful, perhaps, for the truth. He said, "The last thing I ever wished was to bring bad news. You can imagine. Shall I skip ahead, Mrs. Naqvi? Perhaps I should."

"Please do," she said—a small voice, defenseless. He ought to be protecting her, not delivering the blow. Sometimes he hated his work. He said, "I stayed late two nights ago—in the park, searching still after the others had gone home for the evening. It was already dark. They were probably sensible to have given up for the day. You'd gone, too. But I myself . . . well, I've explained already. In any case, I did discover something. In the sea, around the headland from Iron Mine Bay—not very far from where your husband was lost. It was a shoe. A sandal. It's gray and black, a rather thick sole. It has a nylon strap across the front— adjustable, I suppose—and a thin strap that would be around the heel. I'm holding it in my hand, as a matter of fact." "Velcro," Mrs. Cortland whispered. "I'm sorry," the constable added, "with Velcro—on the front strap. I'm guessing it might be your husband's sandal?"

"Yes," she'd said. "Where was it?"

"As I say—"

"Have you given it to Sergeant Dunn?"

"Sergeant Dunn is not interested in my investigations, Mrs. Naqvi— we've already established that. And in any case, he doesn't figure in. It would make not the slightest bit of difference at all if I gave it to him."

"Mr. Cortland—" There was a touch of whining to her voice now. And she'd gotten out of bed—she was moving about, busy at something else, perhaps dressing.

"I shall hand it over to him first thing in the morning if it would make you feel better, but I wish I could—" "Please do," she interrupted. And said, "It's illegal." He chose to ignore this. "I wish to make you see," he continued, "that it hardly matters. What the sandal has to tell us, it has already said, you see. Because, I think you'll agree, your husband is not likely to have tossed his only footwear into the sea before setting off to abandon you, Mrs. Naqvi."

Silence. Then she was bustling at something again—yes, getting dressed, very likely. Where did she intend to go at this hour? he wondered.

He said, "I'd appreciate it if you would listen carefully to me now, madam—it won't be for much longer. But what I have to suggest to you is something you're bound to resist, at first. And as you yourself say, we're hardly on speaking terms, you and I. We share something, secretly—we do both know what it's like to have a loved one go missing, as you've no doubt guessed. Not to know what has become of him or her—to have to hold all the terrible possibilities in one's mind, all together. I would only ask you to trust me to the extent that, perhaps, you can imagine someone else who has been through that nightmare may be trusted—not to contribute to it for anyone else, poor soul, and to *help*, if one can. To replace the unknown with the known, if possible—though you know as well as I do, already, that what the unknown is replaced with may offer very little comfort. Still, closure—closure, most of all—is what my dear wife and I craved, when our daughter was missing. Most of all. We thought you might share that craving."

SHE'D CARRIED THE cordless outside, onto the deck. The chairs were wet with dew—she intended to stand, anyway. Hilda had turned and mumbled, and then someone—Greg or Laurel—had come out to the bathroom. Samina had put some layers on. When she had heard whichever it was—Laurel or Greg—tiptoe back into their bedroom and close the door, she'd opened one of the French doors in her bedroom, as quietly as possible, and slipped outside. She said—she wanted to clarify the conversation as much as she could—"I don't even know if I believe you, Constable."

"About which? About the sandal? I can bring it to you in the morning, if you'd like. In fact, I will—you may give it over to the sergeant or not, as you wish. It belongs to you now, after all. Or do you mean about our daughter? You don't think I would manufacture that, surely?"

She thought he would, somehow—but also that he hadn't. The harbor was visible under the moon. It was still and unreal—a vision. An image in her mind now was of a dark spot in the water, someone floating, his dark back. It had been in her mind before. She made herself look away, though, into the trees beside the cottage. "How old was she?" Samina asked.

"Our Olivia? Oh, goodness, she was fourteen. Fourteen when she left us—she was seventeen when she was murdered."

"I'm sorry."

"No, you needn't be, of course—we're all sorry. We're both beyond the reach of that small word, too, I'd venture—you and I. Now, if that's true—if this man's kind, sweet daughter ran away to an awful and filthy life and then was murdered, for no adequate reason—well then wouldn't he be too quick to look for violence everywhere, you might be thinking? That's what I would think, in your place, I'm certain. Even if he means well, can he quite be trusted? To see clearly, I mean. Could he be rendered a bit morbid by an experience like that? It's a question, you see, that I struggle with myself. And with my minister, and my wife. All alone, of course, when I should be sleeping and still can't. But the fact is, I do love life, Mrs. Naqvi. I do believe in good coming from bad—not in the ordinary way that is sometimes spoken of, but in the Lord's way, if you will. I'd never wish to impose, though. Never mind my religious convictions, if you like—or make them fit whatever it is you believe. In any case, my point is that I have seen how things do improve on this earth, despite terrible losses—how good prevails. But only in truth. With truth comes the light, as the man says. And it's never easy to face the glare of truth—would that it were, I often feel. I'm stating the obvious here." She longed to hang up.

He said, "Very well. Hear me out, now. You are thinking, he may have drowned. Yet you know he hasn't. You know what he was like—a sensible man. He'd been to the ocean, he'd been on trails. He could swim. He was strong—wasn't he? You've been to that beach. There are currents, that's true, but it is also a protected beach. A man would have to be less than sensible to drown there, I must tell you. Does that sound like Nicholas? On a cold day, dressed in long pants and a jumper, all alone? Going for a swim? And there is the dog, of course. Have I seen a dead dog with its head bashed in lying on a beach in this part of the world in the twenty-three years I've lived here, Mrs. Naqvi? No, I have not. Please stop me, of course, if I'm ascribing thoughts you don't share. Are we on the same page so far at all, would you say?" He paused. "Someone killed a dog," he said. "He bashed its head in—let's say it is a 'he' for now. That's unavoidable, and it's the same person who knows where your husband is. I think we both accept that. It's the last person to have seen your husband, we're talking about.

"Mrs. Naqvi?" he asked—very gently, as if he'd wake her. The damp chill had reached through her layers. She'd decided to sit. She was reminding herself that she was not required to consider anything he said true—he was no one she could trust. Put it all into a file in your mind marked "Constable Cortland" and keep it with the other files, each together and apart. Nothing can hurt: no information can, nor anyone's opinion. But no one can be trusted, either, since no one knows yet. Nicholas might be phoning right now, hearing her busy signal, wondering. He might walk through those trees there and wave to her in a moment—a weak wave, his bemused and sad, apologetic smile. When the image in her mind's eye was as precise as this, the speculation seemed not only possible but likely—as it had for the floating body, too, though.

"Mrs. Naqvi," the constable said, "please tell me to stop when I've gone too far. Won't you?" He waited, then said, "Very well. I'll finish off. Who is the person, Mrs. Naqvi? Who knows where your husband is? Someone out there does. Everyone, of course, was obliged to begin with the same suspect—myself and Sergeant Dunn, and surely you, too, however briefly. However quickly you disposed of the thought—and you'd be a lesser person if you hadn't, frankly. But we have always known the person who is at least the second-to-last to see your husband alive. Who led him to that beach. We have known from the beginning that he had the time and the means. The motive, we may not know. You may have guesses available to you, but perhaps you don't. It is as obvious as can be that one—a detective, that is—must question the source of the story. It has all been Mr. Faber's story, all along. But that does not make a suspect guilty in the slightest. You must be thinking by now that I've called to tell you that Mr. Faber killed your husband. But as a matter of fact, I haven't. That I still don't know. Instead, I've called to ask if you know where he's been this evening?"

This made her turn, for some reason, and look through the sliding glass door into the house—and she leapt up and screamed, or half screamed. For there he was, there at the door. "Mrs. Naqvi!" the constable shouted in the telephone. Greg held his hands up—he looked frightened himself. He stepped forward and slid the door open (this, too, frightened her now—stupidly). "I'm so sorry," he whispered, "are you all right?" "Yes—you scared me." "I didn't mean to." "Mrs. Naqvi," the constable said on the telephone, "who's there? Are you safe? Make a sign if you're not." She said, "I'm fine, Constable—hold on a minute, please." She held the phone against her sweater.

"Is it Constable Cortland?" Greg asked. "Do you want me to speak to him? They haven't found him, have they?"

More and more each day, they had all avoided invoking his name. But they had all known when the particular 'him' or 'he' was meant. "No," she said. "I'm almost done with him. You can go back to bed."

Greg lingered. "He's not bothering you?"

"No." She could not quite hold his gaze. It was too dark to interpret his expression.

"Okay," he said. "I can't sleep," he said, backing away now, "so don't hesitate to get me if you need me. Okay?" He'd stopped in the doorway.

"Uh-huh." She nodded.

"You want a blanket?" he asked. She shook her head. "Sorry I startled you," he said. He slid the door closed behind himself.

"I'm here," she said into the telephone. She remained standing—had turned away from the house, but felt compelled to glance back to it after a moment. She saw the shadow of Greg's back through the window, heading away.

"It was him?" the constable asked.

"Constable Cortland," she whispered, "he and my husband have known one another for many years. I'm starting to feel like an idiot for listening to you, to be honest."

"But we're done. I won't ask you to leap to anything, Mrs. Naqvi—I told you I wouldn't. We're done now. As you know, I'm off the case—I'm no longer searching for your husband. I wasn't searching for him tonight, in fact. I went instead to Cyrus Collingwood's home, hoping to speak to him. Another affair entirely. This was after midnight. We had one or two things to discuss—it had nothing to do with your husband. The house was dark, though—they were asleep inside. What surprised me was to find Mr. Faber there before me. He was just leaving, in fact—having done what, I can't say. He was creeping through the forest behind their house when I saw him. He'd walked there, evidently—I followed him back to your cottage. Then I came home myself. My wife and I couldn't sleep, you see. I did wonder if you'd known where he was going—I had seen that there weren't any lights on in your cottage then, either, you understand. But perhaps you did. I take it you knew he was awake?"

She did know, now—some of it had been dreams, but some hadn't: the sound of him coming through the door, returning. The trip-light had flicked on and lit her window. "And that was all?" she asked. "That was everything you wanted to tell me, I guess?"

He sighed. After a long pause, he said, "That's right. You will know more than I do, of course—you always have. One always does. One knows things one doesn't want to admit, and all the things one intuits or has tucked away. It takes time for one to get free of the original story of what happened—perhaps false from the start, after all—so that the bearer of the story can be properly examined as well. It all takes time. I wish I could have done more, Mrs. Naqvi, or had more to offer you. I am finished, though—we may not speak again. Shall I bring the sandal to you, or give it to the sergeant? Perhaps I'll just slip it in the cottage mailbox this morning?"

"That's fine."

"It may be someone else we're looking for—I suppose it must be. Some stranger. Someone you don't know at all. Is it less terrible to think so? I don't know—I can't say it is, for me."

"Thank you—" She meant to stop him. Enough.

"To think of someone who never knew your husband killing him for no reason at all, I mean," he said, "—not for money? Not for anything, evidently? Someone you or I will never meet? He left no evidence, this person. Someone almost invisible. *I* know that person, Mrs. Naqvi. My wife and I have had to live with him. I don't know that it's any better, I must tell you."

"I'll hang up now, Constable."

"Good night, Mrs. Naqvi," he said, hanging up first.

32

S HE STEPPED INSIDE the cottage and sat down at the little table in the dark. She sat still, thinking, for some minutes, and then Greg came out again—he'd been listening for her. He was careful to make a bit of noise on his way from the bedroom. "I'm sorry I startled you," he whispered, a shadowed figure in the dark.

He asked what the constable had wanted and she wondered what to say. "I don't know," she said. "I suppose he wanted to sympathize."

"In the middle of the night?"

"Will you have a cup of coffee with me, Greg?"

He examined her, possibly to assess her need, then glanced back over his shoulder before nodding and retreating into the bedroom, holding up a finger: one minute.

She put the water on and lit a single lamp. She *did* "know" him, she felt—a simplistic and imprecise term. What was the implied calculation? He could surprise her, but who couldn't? Was it that she thought she understood the framework within which the contents of Greg were given his shape, even though ninety percent of those contents—or ninety-nine percent—were mysterious to her? Everyone recognized these dynamics, of course, but until now they had never bothered Samina. Trust had filled the gaps, she supposed, yet she wasn't an especially trusting or credulous person. Had she imagined that she needed to "know" (by which she must have meant to be able to anticipate, recite the highlights of their personal history, know their secrets; most of all, to have depended upon them, or to trust that she could) so very few people?

She had, of course. She did. They both did, though it was an attitude she'd acquired from her parents before Nicholas. She was the child of a romantic, disgraceful second marriage, and her parents had come to the States in exile rather than pursuit of opportunity. Her father had left inherited privileges and glamorous, indigent, cosmopolitan Delhi for a split-level and a lawn in Providence, and before that he'd left the chinar trees and almond groves on Anchar Lake in Kashmir for the city (the first and maybe the more devastating compromise). It had seemed to Samina that his life could only be described as a slow, dispiriting decline, and if her mother had shown up halfway down the hill to tip the angle and speed his descent, then her own birth had marked his arrival at rock bottom. When she was a freshman at college, away from her parents for the first time, she had flown back for Thanksgiving and been stunned by how palpable the depression was in every room of the house—it darkened windows, dulled conversations, oozed from the walls to encase the three of them, forming a shell. (The windows were always closed in this house—the heat, or else the air-conditioning, was always running, muffling whatever sounds the street might have offered, departing from whatever the day's weather may have conveyed.) "Depression"—a terrible word. It was for someone else, of course—for Americans, for "white people" (though that was another term which had never been spoken in her house). But it was her family. They were who people described on daytime talk shows. Her father with his self-defeating philosophies and his poor diet and his fear of the unexpected; the absence of change or potential for change; the twelve-hour nights—all that thick sleep congesting the house; their lack of friends or neighborly relations or dinner engagements, or of family beyond the three of them (plus occasional phone calls from Khalid, his son by the first marriage, which were brief and inexplicably devastating: although no one ever brought up the past or spoke of anything personal and Khalid was invariably cheerful and curious, the household would be in a state of shock for a day or two after his calls, Samina's father almost unreachable, Samina and her mother stepping delicately between rooms). Depression. Two of Samina's roommates at college had known one another since third grade and their parents had been playing poker together weekly for decades— the casual, unimaginable ties people made! Depression was what had kept Samina from speaking about her family there at college. No use getting into it all with friends who weren't Indian, she'd thought—too much to explain, and they were often interested in the wrong details (the servants or the mangoes or the exotic logistics of arranged marriage)—but the real inhibition was just the fact that it was a tawdry history: her parents' affair, her shameful birth, the hasty exile and the left-behind son. They were regretful immigrants, not chasing opportunity so much as tugged abroad in the wake of disgrace. Her parents would be mortified if she ever exposed them. Depression, she had thought, was why she would never marry. Her mother could hardly dig up one eligible boy a year to press upon her, and even these came through distant connections and back channels, from uninformed families.

At some point after she had fallen in love with Nicholas she'd decided that the whole history—the whole grubby, ill-defined, outmoded drama— was of little consequence to her any longer. Now that she had Nicholas, it all became surprisingly unimportant. She and Nicholas did what they could for her parents, of course—they visited often, Nicholas was kind and patient with them (despite their forthright disappointment in him), they helped discreetly with finances when her father's eyesight deterio- rated. But at the same time she and Nicholas seemed to Samina a unit as resilient and discreet and dent-proof as a metal cube. How clear this became on their trip to India together, early in their marriage, before Hilda. They had plowed through pilfering touts and taxi drivers and hawkers and first-met relatives equipped with ungenerous implications. Unreliable train schedules and uninformed guides and rain and even a freak dump of hail in the mountains, at Mussoorie, had all bounced off of them harmlessly. They were never out of one another's reach, even when they weren't in the same room. They didn't have to touch or speak— they didn't require eye contact, even—to flick the busy world away. Yet they *did* touch—touched in public because Nicholas was American. Pretended ignorance. And it was a fluent touch. They had never had to fumble as strangers as her father had with his first wife and almost all her cousins and uncles and aunts had. When they whispered together it was with jokes (seldom at anyone's expense, but how would they know that?) or intimate forms of slang that no one in her family would have understood—they spoke their own language. It was his language, naturally, but a gurgling dialect of their own, built on unspoken allusions and ever-extending metaphors, free of explanation. Marriage was meant to extend the family—in India it was. It was supposed to bind you tighter to all of them. They picked your spouse with this in mind, the two families conspiring above the couple, then they put you in a room in his house with this chosen stranger and of course you were meant to fail. You were meant to need them still, miss them, long for what they provided and he couldn't. You were not supposed to marry and find yourself happily free from them.

On the airplane coming home from India, Samina had decided she was free of everyone except this person she had chosen, who had chosen her—no blood or shared background and very little approval to ease those choices or poison them with responsibility. His family—his parents—had failed to disapprove, but his relationship with them seemed so casual, unimpassioned, and occasional as to almost be negligible. Samina liked his parents, very much, but exactly as she would have liked them if they were merely much older friends of his, or perhaps friends of his parents (and they seemed to take just that sort of tidy, mild interest in her). No, she had made her own family, small as could be. Let it replace the families that had come before it, she had decided. She'd grown up missing India, longing for crowds and customs and a substantial history, the press of tradition with its limitations. When she was a girl she'd looked forward to an arranged marriage, romanticizing the hardship and taking a self-righteous pleasure in the idea that she'd be doing things correctly and as differently as possible from her parents. And at the same time, all her life, when anyone said the word "Kashmir," although they usually spoke it in an infamous and banal political context, a mental image with the quality of a memory had come to her mind: of the shade her father had described under the chinar trees in a courtyard overlooking a lake and the mountains. The place where she imagined she belonged. She'd been wasting her time—on the flight home from India this had seemed so clear. If she'd never met Nicholas, she had thought, she'd be doing it still. She had felt angry and happy—blissfully belligerent. "Let's have kids," she'd told Nicholas. "Right now!" Strange that it had seemed like a deliciously cruel and selfish idea—a way to cancel out both of their pasts and erase the world beyond themselves.

SO IT HAD been her idea, first and most, to set themselves apart the way they had, and then she was the one who had taken the idea back. If what the sergeant had proposed this afternoon was true—if Nicholas had actually walked away from Samina and Hilda—it must be partly for this reason. But she'd been right, it *was* a mistake they'd made, not to mention unsustainable, and if he had come to see their life together as a burden somehow it was certainly one which could be lightly set aside. Not much here to disentangle himself from. But could he really have wanted to? Could she have known him that little? What portion of what there was to know about Nicholas had she ever bothered to take into hand? She couldn't fathom now why she hadn't been greedy about every scrap of his past—invited every confidence, pursued every anecdote. Nicholas must have felt her lack of curiosity about him.

When Greg returned to the kitchen, she had decided that one approach would be to say (still whispering, of course—a more conversational whisper now, over the small sounds the water made on its way toward a boil), "If you don't mind, let's not talk about Nicholas"—setting loose his name in the room. Maybe a mistake: it clattered about and lingered. "Or the search," she said. "Not for a few minutes, anyway."

"Sure." He nodded. "Of course." Greg was too agreeable with her, too pliant—too eager to please and vaguely contrite for some reason. This had been more or less true for as long as they'd know one another, and she had always if apprehensively interpreted it as a bit of a crush. The water came to a boil and she poured. She asked him, "How's your book? Were you able to work on it here?"

"A little." The book was fine, he said. But then he paused and adjusted: okay, it was awful, actually, only a month ago—dead on the table—but he'd had a few notions since then, and he'd lowered his standards, and now it seemed to have revived. "Nicholas helped," he said. "He gave me a nice pat on the back one day, in the library." He had stolen a glance at her while pronouncing her husband's name. Everyone did now—probably everyone always would. She set his coffee before him and sat down. He must not have been put off by what he saw in her face, since he continued. "To tell you the truth, I also got an idea for the next book. It's a half-formed idea at this point, but it does help, if only because I have to finish the first book to get to the second."

"Good."

"Yeah."

But he frowned and sipped—felt guilty for speaking happily of anything, she imagined, much less the future. "What's the new book about?" she asked. He smiled crookedly and shrugged. "I know, I know," she said, "but it's the middle of the night, and just me—not even a fellow writer. Anyway, I'm so tired I probably won't remember what you tell me by morning."

"We should both try to sleep."

"I can't. I've tried enough, for tonight."

She'd noticed (it had been only three and a half days—but an eternity as well, already full of different phases with their attending impressions and adjustments) that she *could* relieve any conversation of the burden— only she could, of course—but this was the first time that she had. If she did (she was recognizing now), the act itself—her setting the burden aside, no matter how briefly—would come under scrutiny. Was her mind wandering, they'd wonder—was she forgetting about Nicholas already?

Greg gave in. He did want to, after all. He said, "Well it's that kid Cyrus's fault—he got me thinking about Charles Dodgson again. Dodgson has always been a minor character in my book, you know—in the first one. A while ago, I actually thought I might write about him instead of Ruskin. He was closer than Ruskin was to the other two people I'm most interested in. So it might be something that could pick up where this first book ends, extend some of the same ideas. We'll see."

"He's the same person Cyrus's father is writing about?" "That's right." "It would be a sequel to the one you're finishing, then?" "I suppose it might be. An odd sort of sequel." She asked, "Do you think Cyrus's father really has old family papers? Something important?"

Greg shook his head. "No idea." "But you think so, don't you? You suspect he does?" He smiled—he'd warmed to the conversation. "Yeah, I do," he admitted. "He really might." She nodded. Whispering still, she asked, "Is that where you went tonight?"

He'd been looking at her, and he continued to for a moment, registering, then glanced down into his mug. "It certainly was," he said—honesty, he seemed to have decided. But how *could* they imagine you might forget, even for an instant? Is that really what they wondered? If you'd forgotten? Of course you'd have set the burden aside to relieve *them*, not you—because *they* forgot, of course, through most of the day, and had so many other busy things happening in their still-clear minds. "Was anyone awake over there?" she asked.

He said, "No. Dark house."

"Did you think he would be awake? What time was it?"

Greg smiled, and sat back. *Honesty*, he'd told himself. Or else he was only stalling to think of a better route. But then he did say, "No, I didn't think anyone would be awake. I half thought I might sneak in and poke around a little. Just to see what he had. I can't believe I thought I'd do something like that—even as I say it out loud, it seems ridiculous." She nodded, shared his smile. "I didn't, of course," he said. "I came to my senses under a tree. I sat there feeling like an idiot, thinking a thousand thoughts all over again about Nicholas, and then I came home to do the same thing in bed. I guess you heard me?"

"Do you want more coffee?" she asked.

"No, no."

"Do you think he drowned?"

Greg took the turn easily enough. He had a picturesque manner when considering a difficulty, or when consulted for advice: his gaze would narrow, and focus, but on nothing tangible—on the issue, of course—and a hand would often come up to hold his chin. They were mannerisms he'd had for as long as she'd known him, but she thought they did convey an additional anxiety now. Naturally, though? Anxiety didn't necessarily suggest guilt; even guilt probably didn't always suggest guilt, the feeling so often running out in front of actions. Eventually he said, "I still think he's alive."

She had never believed that Nicholas would have enlisted Greg's help, if he'd left her, but that was possible, too. "But where?" she asked.

"Right. I have no idea."

"Where do you picture him?"

"I don't at all. It's just a feeling more than a thought. What are *you* thinking?"

She shook her head. "I don't know," she said. Then she said, "No." She shrugged. "That's the feeling I'm having, tonight. No—he's not alive." She was responsible—somehow she would be. Over the last few days she'd begun to feel that she'd done everything wrong and made poor choices at every single turn in their lives together, but so quietly and timidly that she'd been capable of not even noticing. Just one gaudy mistake might have woken her up, but instead she'd merely drifted, blithely, in the wrong directions. At the same time, she was just capable of seeing around this thought and recognizing its untrustworthy drama.

"The whole thing is incredible," Greg said. He shook his head as if they were done, as if that was as far as they could go.

"Don't you feel that, too, actually, Greg?" she asked. "You don't really think he's alive, do you?"

He rubbed his cheek up to his sideburns—but only deciding what to admit, she supposed, not contemplating the question. "Be honest," she said. "I've already thought of it, anyway—whatever you're thinking."

He said, "I have stupid thoughts. They're not reasoned out—they're just . . . thoughts. Not logical or systematic like that policeman's today." He spoke toward the table. "I worry that someone killed him. I don't know why. I've been a little afraid of this place and how isolated we are ever since I got here. But those aren't even really thoughts—they're just fears, and pessimism."

"Greg, why did you split up? You and Nicholas." He stole a quick look at her—to gauge how much accusation was behind the question. She said, "I know, I didn't want to talk about this. And you've already told me why, I know. But tell me again?"

"I went to the other beach. Or not a beach—the headland, that you and I went to, where the waves come straight in. To be honest, I wanted to be alone. I was thinking about Charles Dodgson, actually—I just wanted to think. We must have been apart less than an hour, Samina. This is why it's all so amazing to me."

She nodded, accepted.

"What else?" he asked, kindly, but she could tell he wanted to flee.

"Why didn't you take all of us to this beach of yours? Why did you decide to take him there that day?"

He was fully on guard again, as he'd been when she'd first seen him through the glass door. "I just don't have any better answers," he said. "I only have the same ones."

She said, "They're just the things I've been asking myself—or keep asking. These questions that lead to him being lost. Why didn't we all stay home that afternoon? Why didn't the two of you go to the nice, safe library instead, as usual? Why didn't I keep him home, or ask to come along? Whatever has happened to him, I feel like it wouldn't have happened if I was there. And then why did you and he go *there* in particular, and split up. . . . It feels like I might discover there isn't really an answer to one of these questions, or not a good enough answer, and then the whole chain would break and it wouldn't have happened."

A long pause. Greg said, "When I was a kid, watching basketball or baseball, and my team would lose tragically—in the last inning—I would watch the replays with hope still, half believing that it wouldn't quite happen this time. It was such a wrong ending that on one of the replays it would have to come out right, wouldn't it?"

"But who would kill him, Greg?" It wasn't fair of her (*she'd* lightened the conversation, after all), yet she did want to punish him, a little, for comparing this to baseball. "Why would anybody want to kill him?"

"I can't imagine."

Samina had spoken too loudly—Laurel emerged. She squinted against the lamplight, but Samina wondered if she'd been awake already, waiting for an opportunity. "Why is everyone up?" she whispered.

"We couldn't sleep," Samina said.

"What time is it? I thought I heard the phone ring." She sat down in the last chair at the little table. Greg told her, "It was Constable Cortland calling."

"What did *he* want?"

"Do you want a cup of coffee?" Samina asked her.

"Goodness, no. I shouldn't."

"I'm having another. You won't join me?"

"Well, okay, then," Laurel said.

"Greg?" Samina asked.

"No. Thank you."

She set about it at the counter. Laurel whispered to Greg, "Do you have your watch?" "It must be around five," he said. Then they were all quiet, as if waiting for something. Perhaps Laurel really had been asleep—she seemed as if she might fall asleep now, sitting up. But from her fog, she asked, "Why did Constable Cortland call?" Greg looked to Samina.

"Well," she said, taking a deep breath, rinsing out a cup for Laurel, "I guess he called to tell me his theory. Everyone has a theory today, don't they? His is that Greg killed Nicholas."

When Samina looked at them, Laurel was staring at her through eyes still droopy, squinting. Greg studied his hands on the table. Laurel said, "But you don't *believe* that."

"I don't believe anything. No, that's not true—I seem to believe everything. Everything everyone tells me sounds convincing, and then I have all my own fantasies, too."

Laurel was dissatisfied. She was waking up quickly. "I don't know what that answer is supposed to mean," she said. But then, in another tone, she said, "I don't believe that man. He's amazing to me. How did he come to this conclusion? What did he say?"

Greg said, "That I was the only one who could have. It's all obvious—he's not crazy. That I was the only one with him, that the whole story of his disappearance came from me and no one else, that I had only invited Nicholas into the park with me, alone. Were you asking me just now because you believed him?" he asked Samina. "What could I say to prove myself guilty or innocent? Did I seem one or the other to you?"

Laurel asked, "What have you two been talking about?"

"He also saw you tonight," Samina said. "He was there, too—hiding in the woods along with you, apparently." The water boiled: hoarse and velvety mumbling.

"When tonight?" Laurel asked. "What are we talking about?"

Greg asked, "That made me guilty of killing Nicholas, for some reason?"

"To his mind, I guess."

"What was *he* doing there?" Greg wanted to know.

"*Where?*" Laurel asked. "One of you stop and tell me what you're talking about, please."

"Please keep your voice down, Laurel," Samina said.

Silence. She poured the water over the grounds—the little cottony *thwap* and the tinkle as it fell through into the empty mug. "Hilda's sleeping," she added, in case Laurel hadn't known that that was all she meant. They remained quiet, and after a few minutes, she offered: "How could I suspect you, Greg?" She brought their coffees and sat down. "I really mean it—I just find myself believing in everything right now. Nothing seems possible, so what would be impossible?"

Laurel leaned forward. "Then have you thought about what the sergeant said, Samina?"

She seldom entered a conversation without having an agenda in hand. When Laurel found herself in a conversation in which she had no stake or strong opinion to express, or without an underhanded plan to pursue, she either grew bored and left it or she changed the topic, or sometimes she developed an agenda on the spot. It often made her a good conversationalist, though. "That Nicholas might not be hurt at all?" she continued now. "That he might be alive and healthy and just somewhere else—as difficult as that is to believe, too, of course?"

Samina nodded. "I have."

"Have you thought more about why he might have left? I mean, it seems almost inexplicable—it's certainly surprising, to all of us. It certainly seems to be surprising to you, too. But if you think that maybe it *is* true—if you begin to entertain the possibility—are there things that come to mind? Things he said lately, or did? Or didn't say? You guys seemed"—she hunted about—"*tense*, I guess, just before he left. At that dinner with Cyrus, for instance—the night of the storm? Wasn't he angry about something? Did he talk to you about why?"

Samina had always been both flattered and put off by Laurel's attention, because she had never done enough to earn it. The balance was uncomfortable—she felt vaguely dishonest, when flattered (and there were

once days when she would seek Laurel out just for the hit of attentiveness),
because the pleasure she took was undercut by skepticism: why had Laurel
picked her? In her least generous moments Samina worried that Laurel
hoped she would become like her other friends—the women Samina had
met on visits to St. Louis—who were pleased to be bossed around by
Laurel, and were always subject to her criticisms presented as wit.

But Laurel couldn't be blamed for Samina's lack of interest in her
right now: it was only that Laurel had no information to offer about
where Nicholas might be. She hadn't been with Nicholas that day, as
Greg had, and she had never been someone whom Nicholas might have
confided in.

"What do *you* think, Greg?" Samina asked. "Did he seem pleased
when you said you were going to leave him alone? Did he seem nervous
that day, or—"

Laurel said, "You have to stop doing that. You have to stop acting as if
Greg knows any more than the rest of us about what happened to
Nicholas, Samina. Or where he went."

"But he does," Samina said, shrugging. "He might."

"No—that's nonsense. If he knew something he would have said so
already. You know that."

Greg said, "Actually, *I* keep wondering if there is something I've
missed or forgotten. I keep thinking about it all again, too. But there's
nothing there. No hints or anything. It's part of why I don't buy the
abandonment theory."

Laurel had been shaking her head. "No, but look—listen, you two: if
Constable Cortland is saying he thinks Greg is responsible, they could be
at that front door any minute now. This isn't just idle speculation we're
involved in. He's a police officer—of *some* kind. You don't know what he
can do."

"I don't think he'll do anything," Samina said.

"How do you know? If he has this idea—if he gets this bee in his bonnet—I mean, if it's making him call you up in the middle of the night?
What do you know about this man? *We* don't know him. Who knows
what he'll decide to do by morning." She paused, and seemed to gauge
how her argument was landing. "And who's going to defend Greg?

There aren't any witnesses," she said, "it's just Greg's word. He's from out of town—no one here will believe him. Why should they? Trust me: I have some experience with how people like this think. Who knows what the police here have found, or imagine they've found? I don't trust them. And none of us should, Samina—it's too dangerous." She said, "Look, I'm not asking you these things in order to pry. *I* don't care what was going on between you and Nicholas. But you have to tell—"

Greg said, "He didn't leave."

"How do you *know*?"

"Oh, for a thousand reasons, Laurel," Greg said. "Come on. Because I know he loved her—loves her—and loves his daughter. Because he can't stand to be apart from them. Because he's not a person who would do something like that, even if he *didn't* love them. And because I was there. Samina's right. Because he *wasn't* acting nervous or strange or anxious. He didn't expect us to separate. He thought it was a little obnoxious of me, actually, to go off on my own. That's the only signal I got from him. And anyway, come on, *think*: Nicholas didn't even know he was going to the park that day, or anywhere else, for that matter. *I* invited him—I didn't even tell him where we were going before we left. He didn't have a plan. If he did, he could have driven away from the cottage with whatever excuse he wanted, any day he wanted to."

Laurel said, "No, but that's just it—he *couldn't* have. Then he'd have the car. Wherever he left it, there might be someone who would have seen him." She was, again, speaking too loudly. "He didn't *need* a plan. Or he may have had the plan all set, and you just gave him the little helping hand he needed, accidentally."

"Come on. . . ."

Samina said, "No—go on, Laurel. I want to hear this. Just . . ." and she held her finger to her lips, smiling—tried to deliver the gesture as mildly as possible.

"If he was doing that . . ." Laurel began, in as close as she could manage to a whisper. "Look," she said, interrupting herself. "I'll be the first to admit that it's hard to imagine any of this—that he *could* have done any of it. Of course. We all know it's only easy for Sergeant Dunn to believe in it because he doesn't know Nicholas, *or* Samina. He just sees some rich

American guy renting a cottage for the season. God knows what he thinks. Which is exactly what the constable sees when he looks at you, too, Greg, and exactly why he'll be just as quick to believe something even crazier about you, given half the chance. You know, I was *on* that side of the fence. I was the local. But what I'm saying is if you *do* suppose Nicholas could have run away, and he really did intend to abandon his whole life and start over again—and as you said, Samina, why not consider it, why not consider everything—well, then he couldn't have asked for a better opportunity. First of all, no, he doesn't want to have the car with him, or his wallet—nothing to identify him. Nothing to attach him to Nicholas Green if he's stopped, or spotted somewhere. If he just drives off one day and leaves the Jetta or the rental car somewhere with his wallet in it, then we'll all *assume* he's run off. Isn't it better to leave from this beach, with nothing to ditch—where he could have drowned, he could have gotten lost in the park?" She looked at Samina—gauging the penetration of her ideas so far. She was desperate to convince her, Samina felt. "Granted, he needs someone helping him for this to work. Sergeant Dunn suggested it. He needed someone waiting somewhere not far away"—what did she see in Samina's face?—"who he could call when he got to a pay phone. Who would come and pick him up, and have cash, maybe even a new passport or something. It's easier than we think, I'm sure. And that's not even necessary—they could stay in Canada. He'd only need someone else to have a wallet full of cash and credit cards and a driver's license. And *why* would you know, Greg? If this is true, if we want to *truly* grant it as possible—then '*think*,' " she said, imitating him, "—I *am* thinking. *You* think for a minute. If this is true, then he's been faking it well enough for the past few days or weeks or months to totally fool his wife, right?" She looked at Samina, but didn't wait for an answer. "And probably plenty of other people. What makes you think he couldn't fool you, too, in the moment when you finally set him free just by wandering away from him for a few minutes?"

"*Ammi?*" Hilda called, from the bedroom—a sleepy, frightened voice.

"Oh, goodness, I'm sorry," Laurel said, dropping all the way back to a whisper again.

Samina—confused, a little disgusted, strangely engaged—said, "Just a minute. I'll be right back."

33

HER FATHER'S STATION wagon had massive dials with massive numbers—as if to accommodate the legally blind drivers aboard—which lit a lovely and sinister green at night. Where are we going? Cyrus wondered—Ginny drove. To the pub, she said. To meet Don? he asked. Yes, after nine—he was working tonight. "Sorry I kind of invited myself," Cyrus said. Ginny reached over and hit him in a friendly way. "Shut up, freak."

The pub was surprisingly busy for a Monday out of season. The search, Cyrus supposed—people gathered to trade rumors. It was an old building divided into several small and dark rooms like a house, one with a fireplace and a beaten-copper fender (farthest from the jukebox) which belonged to the old men of the town after eight, one with a pool table, one by the kitchen. He and Ginny would settle in the room with the jukebox, as the youth of Sooke always had, it seemed (though Cyrus and Ginny were still fairly new to it—there was still a little thrill, stepping into this dark and busy world). The bar was handy from here, and they could see who came in before anyone at the door was likely to have made them out yet. Tonight there were three girls arranged at a tiny round table who could sometimes be friends of Ginny's but who wouldn't approach when Cyrus was with her. Ginny nodded prettily. She took the table with the curved booth in a corner. Cyrus got the two of them beers at the bar. He would drink tonight, he'd decided—he might need whatever assistance was available in order to keep the role up. Don would be here soon, and when he arrived others would as well, in his wake. Cyrus had these few minutes alone with Ginny, but couldn't think of how to most profitably spend them. It wasn't the way one was with Ginny, of course—that is to say, strategic. Or in a role, in costume.

"What do you think of him?" she asked him first, meaning her father, he knew. "He looks worse, doesn't he?" "Yeah." "Boy oh boy," she said. "What am I supposed to do, Cyrus?" "Yeah," Cyrus agreed.

She wouldn't want an answer, actually, but nevertheless he soon decided to say, "I got this crazy idea tonight, by the way. Should I tell you?" Ginny wasn't looking at him. He said, "We ought to get the trailer operational and just take off, you know? The four of us, I mean—you and me and the fathers. Go someplace far away and unimaginable. Like, say, Winnipeg."

"They just had a blizzard there."

He didn't have her proper attention tonight. "Take in the sights," he said, "keep the fathers on their toes. I was kidding about Winnipeg. Don't you ever want to get the fuck out of here lately? We could go back to Massachusetts and you could introduce us to your friends."

"There he is," she said, and brightened—smiling at what must be Don. Cyrus moved across to the booth by Ginny's side, facing the door. Tony had come in as well, and hung behind awkwardly while Don made his cheerful and delayed way through, greeting the bartender and a fisherman who had come from the pool room and the three tidy girls at the other table: a politician, you had to call him, if with his own versions of handshakes and backslaps, which were meant to be lined in irony. "Blue team," he greeted Cyrus and Ginny finally, nodding. "Look what I found by the side of the road."

"Blue team?" Tony asked nervously—afraid, perhaps, to greet Ginny yet. What Cyrus liked about Tony was that he was shy; what he didn't like was how little difference it made in Tony's efforts. But Ginny explained: "In the park. We were searching today and Don seemed to think we needed a 'handle.'"

"Secret search team," Don said briskly, all seriousness. "Mercenaries. Full contact. Saved our lives a number of times, the handle did. Anyway, you folks mind if we join you here?" He was squeezing into the bit of booth on the other side of Ginny.

"We're awfully busy," she was saying, pushing back. "I don't know if we can accommodate you, sir. *Sir*, no vacancy!"

Cyrus, like poor Tony, smiled through their shenanigans. Alisia arrived to serve them now—a quorum, she must have determined. And the party and the evening fell into patterns too familiar to resent. Don was busy and distracted, the loose center of everything—he never lacked for chatter or let a silence drop between them—and people roughly attached themselves to the table from his end (he was center and hinge), and stood for long stretches during which it was difficult for Cyrus not to itchingly anticipate their suggested departures. They bent away to blow smoke and lost track of which drinks were their own on the table, or sometimes they sat, gathering chairs from nearby, creating clogs in the traffic which Alisia loudly complained about, to no avail. Tony could not meet people's eyes but laughed at anything and stuck by Don. He was scrupulous in his avoidance of Ginny—frightened. Ginny often hosted someone in the opposite direction, a conversation that took place across Cyrus. It would be someone who had broken off from the knot around Don, and they would not bother to include Cyrus much, but Ginny would lean close to Cyrus and rest her hand with her cigarette on his slumped shoulder, sometimes only the heel of it touching him but sometimes, when a louder song played and everyone had to lean in and scream in order not to let their vacuous and repetitive conversations come to any harm, then her whole and thinly clothed forearm would rest along Cyrus's back, a proprietary gesture that seemed to him more loving still for being so casual, though not at all romantic. Cyrus watched, but hardly figured in. It was all he wanted, of course, nine nights in ten, but the tenth night he saw it for what it was: a slight and pitiful existence. And eventually Don would catch Cyrus's eye (but *why?* why did he care about Cyrus? Cyrus never knew, except perhaps it had to do with Don's wish to be unpredictable; unless it was only that Don actually was as big-hearted as people wanted you to believe), and would gesture—such privacy in it: one did feel shone upon—and without a word they would stand up and extract themselves from the clog and head to the men's room together.

They peed to kill time until the big handicapped stall was free. When it was, Don put the seat down and took the throne—Cyrus closed the door and leaned back against it—and Don produced his little mirror (it had been a rearview mirror on his brother's car) from an inside shirt pocket and his bag from his pants. When they'd both had a turn, and a lull came—they were alone in the room—Don asked, "So what'd you see, bub?" It was a thing he said, a thing between them.

"Did you see the constable?" Cyrus asked. "Cortland?" Cyrus nodded. "Did he see me?" Don asked. Cyrus shook his head: "Straight to the nostalgia lounge," he said. "I haven't seen him emerge from there. Did you see Brenda's tits?" "Am I blind?" Don asked. "If you cut me, do I not bleed?" Cyrus said, "She digs you." "No, she doesn't." "Who you gonna believe," Cyrus asked, "your eyes or mine?" He didn't like the way his own voice modulated when he was around Don—not to replicate Don's so much as to suit it—but what could you do? Don asked, "You think she does?" "She wants to get sloppy with you," Cyrus affirmed. "You think Ginny likes me much these days?" Don asked. Then he said, "Am I trespassing, bub? Stop me if I'm being uncool." "No," Cyrus said—in a way that shouldn't have been convincing, except Don wished to be convinced. "You're sure?" Don said, and added, "I never know with you two." Cyrus asked, "What's up with Paula, anyway?" He'd begun to feel the indestructible happiness now. Steel-plated, generous as a king. Don laughed and said, "It's not as if you didn't warn me. I blame myself. But she does wear thin, doesn't she?" "She grates," Cyrus agreed, giggling a little. "She grates like hell," Don said, "and you told me. I wouldn't listen. But my god, let's talk tits, please." Then he looked at a point just beside Cyrus and said, "Goodness gracious. If it isn't Lars!"

This was the thing about Don—this had to be granted: he got such matters correct, every time. He had a certain improvisational gift which you had to admire. Because the head that was there, peering at them over the stall door (the body attached to it must be awfully tall), which neither of them had ever seen before, was very clearly a head that should belong to a Lars. He was blond and large-nosed and possibly Scandinavian, with tiny wire-framed glasses, and a neutral mouth that nevertheless implied a smile. Cyrus pretended to duck and cover when he saw him there, and cracked up. Don cracked up, too, but sat still. "Where've you been, Lars?" Don asked (so that for just a second Cyrus wondered if they *did* know each other), and because Lars had been staring at the mirror still in Don's lap, he added, "Shall we dial you a line, dear?"

Lars said, in a ridiculously—tragically, comically—deep voice, in an accent that was exactly right, "I thought you'd never ask." They both died laughing, while Lars waited. Cyrus unlatched the door, when he'd caught his breath. "Please," he said, gesturing like a maître d'.

Lars was Dutch. He took two lines. He said "Lars" was fine, but no, it wasn't his real name. They wouldn't be able to pronounce his real name, he said. He was touring Canada—the length and breadth. He declared his love for Canada. "Hold it, hold it. Say again?" Don told him, holding a hand to his ear. Lars got the joke (which was surprising—his deep voice and lack of expression made you think he might be slow on the uptake), and instead of repeating himself, he said, "No Canadian can understand this when I say it. This is not like Holland." In March he had quit his job and flown to Toronto. The return flight left in April, but without Lars. He was older—that hadn't been clear at first, but now it was. He had great bags under his eyes, which the wire frames seemed to rest upon. He was big in every direction—broad and rounded from chest to belly—but not quite fat. Soft. Yes, he said, he knew he was here at the wrong season. "Not many boats," he said. "It isn't much fishing now, I think. I am always," he continued, "arriving at the wrong time. I go to Montreal and to this city of Quebec in March and April but there is spring blizzards and melting all the time and people tell me it's nicer to the north. So I go in north of Quebec but is what mosquito season. They are so bad I would want more blizzards. So I go to Northwest Territories but there I miss the elk coming." "You went to the Northwest Territories?" Cyrus asked. "Yes," Lars said, only he slurred it, in his deep voice: Yee (down) -ees (up), as if to say, *Of course I did. Naturally.* "How did you get there?" "I hitchhike." "What's it like?" "People are good here. They always pick me up." "No, I mean the place, Lars—what are the Northwest Territories like?" It was odd to speak to a person who must be ten years older than you this way, but it felt right with Lars. "Coo-ll-d," he allowed. "Ugly towns. The bears are very big. I was chased." He shrugged. "Well, Lars," Don said, "I can see why you stuck around. Sounds like a marvelous journey. Sounds like Canada has rolled out the red carpet for you." Lars said (with a deadpan frown and a different shrug—this one coy and immodest), "You should like to see my life in Holland."

Back at the table, Cyrus began to drink with great speed, but to no effect. He continued to ask Lars about his travels. The crowd around their booth was ragged and began to re-form with two overlapping centers, one around Lars and one around Don. Ginny seemed to like Lars, but not as much as Cyrus wanted her to. She was sharing cigarettes with Don, a little drunk, in her commentator mode. Cyrus heard her say, to something in the other conversation, "I once pan-seared a man just to see him fry." She had her feet up on the vinyl seat and her knees tucked against her chest. Lars hunched over his beer and it disappeared in his hand. The chair was sticks beneath him. He ordered a salmon dinner for himself. He had a bulging backpack which he kept beside him and sometimes leaned on. He had been all over Ontario and to Saskatchewan and Alberta, in Jasper and in Banff and Yoho, to the Queen Charlotte Islands, to Cape Scott Park at the north tip of Vancouver Island and through Nanaimo, and then in Victoria for most of September. Just now he'd been partway up the West Coast Trail. Cyrus made a number of failed attempts to share a look with Ginny over Lars—*Do you believe this guy?*—but though they failed and he recognized, distantly, how stupid the effort must appear, he couldn't keep himself from trying again a few minutes later. Lars had plans for Nova Scotia and Newfoundland next. "Take me along," Cyrus told him. "You'll take me with you, Lars, won't you?" "Yee-ees," he said. Ginny said, "I once jeered a man just to see him cry." "She is funny," Lars pointed out to Cyrus—with so much abject sincerity they all laughed. Ginny said, "I once toweled a man just to see him dry," and Don wrapped his arm around her head to put his hand over her mouth while she laughed and laughed at herself. "Forgive her," Don said to Lars. "We're not sure where she came from. We think she may be a stray." They ordered more drinks and Lars insisted on paying. They toasted Lars—and "To Canada!" Don said. Lars added, "Prince of Nations!" Cyrus loved him! "I love this guy," he said. What did he care? Was Ginny his? No! Was her little itch for Don a thing to be jealous of? God, no! She and Don had been together before. It never lasted. It *meant* something that she'd never expressed a wish to sleep with Cyrus—it meant more good than bad. Lars wondered if they knew that there were Dutch settlements all over Canada where you could still get proper pastries. Cyrus had been watching, in vain, for the constable. The peripheral vision was the best thing about cocaine—best of all the wonderful things. Did they know, Lars wondered, that a man had disappeared very near here? Cyrus said yes, they knew that. "This happens in Norway sometimes," Lars said. "Family goes on holiday and the man enters the forest. Doesn't come back. Wood fairies got him. That is what they say. This man here—I would say wood fairies got him." "Would you?" Cyrus asked. Lars said, "This man had family, too. They want to leave, so they go to the wood fairies. Do you know what Oscar Wilde said?" "No, Lars." "You know of Oscar Wilde?" "Yes—we've crossed paths." "He said, 'To lose one parent may be regarded as misfortune, but to lose both looks like carelessness.' " Cyrus smiled—what was he doing here? "Tell us another," he called out from his pit. Ginny, just beside him, had nothing to do with him. Lars said, "Let me see," in his slow, deliberate, almost malfunctioning way: empty gaps, each word dropped like lead in his deep, dumb voice: Let . . . me . . . see. Did Cyrus know that Germany called itself Deutschland, not Germany? Had they noticed that in English God spelled backward—"That we knew, Lars," Don said, his attention swinging back just then. "Are you still informing us?" He had his arm around Ginny. She smoked and drifted. "Professor Lars?" Don asked. "Class still in session?" And Ginny *smiled* at this. Oh, Ginny. What happened to her in these little stretches with Don? Why wasn't it something that Cyrus could provide? "Gentlemen," Don said then, standing. "I piss. Anyone?" he asked. Lars said, "Class dismissed," in an undertone, standing to join him. Don put his arm around Lars's great shoulders. "Cyrus, my boy?" he asked. But Cyrus laughed and smiled and shook his head. "Suit yourself," Don told him. "Now, Lars . . ." he was saying, as they walked away.

Ginny was sleepy and still. Sometimes she fell deeply asleep at the table when they stayed out too late. She was trying to keep herself up tonight, Cyrus thought, waiting for Don. She sulked a little, quietly, pretending to smile and listen to the music. Cyrus listened as well.

On the other side of Ginny, on the other side of where Don had been, Tony still sat, with a couple of other boys. They were half turned away. Their conversation was just audible—it had to do with bands. Cyrus peered at Ginny from his pit, but she failed to notice his love, or else she wished she wouldn't have to.

He was done. Dismissed. To her, he was pure comfort, familiar as mud, a thing around, a part of life, no genius (*for god's sake!*), not a lover, not the one who would take her out of here, and no particular compensation for the limits of her own genius or the loss of her violin. Cyrus hadn't come through, after all. He'd failed her. He leaned toward her, and Ginny saw him coming from the corner of her eye and leaned her ear toward him just a bit, kindly. He whispered, "I know where he is." She raised her eyebrows, waiting. Smiling blandly. "Who?" she asked, when he didn't go on. When he still hadn't spoken, she finally had to turn and look at him properly. His face, which must be bleak, dampened her smile. "Who?" she said again, but differently this time. "The missing man," he confessed. She let go of her knees and let her feet drop to the floor. "What do you mean?" she asked, confused—perhaps already apprehensive. He said, "I killed him, actually."

She just stared at him for several seconds. He had no idea if she had taken it in, or if she believed him. She said, "Stop it," and her brow knit—she was angry. "What are you doing? It's not funny."

He said, "I didn't mean to," and had to look away. "I totally didn't mean to," he said. "I had no intentions, Ginny. It was an accident, a terrible accident."

When he looked up at her again she believed him. She had slapped both hands over her open mouth, and she almost shrieked. She was a dramatic person. Her gestures were often large, and she didn't hold her emotions in well. The beginning of something that may have been a kind of shriek did emerge through her fingers. But then she looked from Cyrus to the roomful of people, or maybe specifically toward the washrooms, and she shut her mouth tight and dropped her hands and sat back and very straight, not looking at him now. "What are you doing, Cyrus?" she asked, whispering. He said, "I'm telling the truth, I'm afraid. No joke, Ginny. I'm just confessing."

"Where is he?" She'd shut down, it seemed—a blank wall, speaking.

"I don't know. I killed him accidentally at the beach, at Iron Mine Bay. But when I came back later he wasn't there."

"So he's alive?"

"No, I don't think so." His own voice was whining, and very, very young. "I think the tide got him."

"You left him in the ocean?"

"Not really."

"Oh, my god, Cyrus, I can't believe this. I can't *believe* this." She sat still, looking at him. "Listen," she said, staring hard into his eyes, "if you're just fucking around with me, *stop . . . right . . . now*. Okay?" She waited, examining him. "You killed him?" she asked. "Yeah." He nodded. "We have to tell, you know," she said. "Yeah, I know." "Oh, my *god*, Cyrus!" And she turned away, her face a terrible scene—crumbling. He said, "I know, I know."

Then Don was beaming upon them, perhaps disappointed to see them leaning so close together. Ginny got up as Don and Lars arrived at the table. She hurried away—out the door, Cyrus thought, and straight to the RCMP detachment. But no, only to the washroom. "Now now," Don said, "have you two been fighting?"

Cyrus said, "No," and giggled nervously.

When she came back (Don and Lars had sat quietly—Don was angry: knew that it wasn't going to happen tonight, and assumed that Cyrus was responsible somehow), Ginny looked awful, and she said she felt sick. She was heading home, she said—sorry.

She had already turned to go, but she looked back and asked Cyrus, "You want a ride, or no?"

Cyrus stood and followed her. He looked back, from the doorway, and thought he made out Don waving, though he couldn't be sure. He waved back, just in case. So long to everything, he thought, melodramatically.

34

"WHERE ARE YOU?" Hilda asked. "I'm right here, *beta*.
I'm right here. Did we wake you?" "Don't go," she
pleaded. "I'm right here, love," Samina said.

"Do you want to come out to the living room? The adults are talking."
"No-o." She was asleep still, almost, and full of that particular warmth.
She needed her sleep, as they all did. Samina sat on the bed with her
for as long as she could, testing her own patience. It didn't take long for
Hilda to fall off again. Then Samina wrapped herself in a scarf from the
bedpost and went to the bathroom. She did her *vazu*: three times washing in circles for each hand, three times for each arm (like a doctor
preparing for surgery, she'd always thought), her mouth and her nose,
the thread of water pulled from the part in her hair down behind her
ears. Her feet. They were neat and tidy gestures, still attached to childhood. It wasn't dawn yet. She went back and lifted Hilda in her blanket.
"Here, put your arms around me, love."

It *did* all seem possible—any of it. And the constable was right, she
hated the range of possibilities. If just some of them could be set aside,
once and for all. What if it was his *chappal*? Would that eliminate abandonment? Could a person (but in her imagination it still almost couldn't

be Nicholas—she had to picture some other, theoretical husband) go so far to cover his escape as to plant evidence, throw his sandals into the ocean? The man who did would never call to say he was alive, much less to beg forgiveness. Could he walk out barefoot? Nicholas probably could, she supposed. It was what Laurel would say, if Samina told them about the sandal. It *was* better to imagine him alive—much better: while Laurel had spoken and Samina had pictured him in someone's warm, dry car, in someone's care, healthy and whole and still available to be met one day, however theoretically, she'd felt a broad if shallow relief. She carried Hilda out to the sofa and settled with her on her lap, motioned for Greg and Laurel to come over. Hilda stared out through her blanket at Laurel. "Hello, dear," Laurel whispered. "I'm sorry I woke you."

They sat quietly while Samina rocked her back to sleep. Laurel and Greg waited, watching the faintest suggestion of dawn out the windows—none of them quite looking at one another. There were layers to a dawn, here as anywhere: a slim line at the horizon and the bluish, bleeding suggestion picking through things, then the gray haze would come before any real light, long before the sun peeked over those hills. There were layers to what Samina could imagine might be true. Uppermost was the conviction that even if he could have left her, and could perhaps have been leaving her for months—if he could have found and fallen for someone else, maybe someone very different from Samina, more like him, or only more pliant and better able to love him as he deserved than Samina had ever been—still, Samina couldn't, for the life of her, imagine Nicholas choosing to never see his daughter again. You could almost argue that she, Samina, might make that choice before he would (though of course she never could, either). That was the top layer.

But beneath that was the layer at which she had to admit that now and then she herself had entertained (or only regarded from a distance, imagined imagining—they never qualified as fantasies) thoughts about what it would be like to step out of her life entirely and start over, empty-handed. Orphaned images: of herself in a headscarf, in another country (it was warm there—perhaps India or a Muslim country, though more likely Italy or Spain), stepping out of a door into a busy street, on her way somewhere mundane—to shop for dinner, probably—but with no one who belonged to her in that building she was stepping from, no one's tastes to shop for but her own. She might change her mind on the way to the market and end up at the ferry terminal or the airport. She didn't seem to be encumbered by suitcases in these images. There was never someone else who came away with her, someone waiting with a car. Quite the opposite: the charm, to the extent that she found them charming at all (but of course she had, or why entertain the thoughts?), had been in the emptiness, and the freedom from loving anyone. A conventional temptation? But hers in particular, too, since at base this was really only the idea of returning to the narrow and deeply defended life that she'd lived for years, before she met Nicholas. And extending that life into a limitless future was an old habit, too: it was the middle of the three fates that she'd grown up imagining for herself, this one the marriageless fate—the balanced option, not without its attractions, and possibly even feasible. Flanking it on one side was the fate by far the likeliest, which had gone from most attractive to least as she'd grown up—the arranged marriage, across that other, no-subtler divide (the one which separated, in this country and among immigrants, the woman who resisted such arrangements from any man willing to take part in them); and on the other side was the last option, the true fantasy, the fate as attractive as impossible, which was Nicholas and Hilda, of course.

If she had entertained such thoughts (even after she'd been granted the fantasy option), then he probably would have, too. He must have entertained his own version—which would include a lover, of course. He would want to be isolated, but not alone. He would want to go to Alaska, or only to some bleak reach of Canada, and leave behind his students and his friends and write books he'd never have to think of publishing (she could imagine his details easily enough, now that she set herself to it)—but he would want to be there with someone else. He'd never been alone. He'd almost never been without a lover. He'd had long relationships at the ages when she was fending off the very few and poor proposals that came her way and waiting to be possessed without any confidence that she'd prove capable of love or of giving herself over properly. He had contemplated marriages before theirs—twice before.

He'd admitted this easily. Which meant (he didn't seem to realize all that he was admitting, or how strange and threatening it would be to her back then) that he had always known that he could be together with someone else, as he and Samina were together. So for him, the escape may not have been a fantasy so much as simply an option.

But how could this be? Samina thought now, interrupting her thoughts—meaning, *Where am I? Will I wake from this? How can this be?* And she found herself saying her prayer again—it was nearly dawn. Only the smallest part of her mind was required for or occupied by the prayer. Why did the three of them ever come here? she wondered simultaneously. What were they thinking? On the trails, in that park, looking for him with Greg earlier today (no—it would be yesterday, now), she'd decided that she and Nicholas should have done anything necessary to stay just where they were, to remain safe and preserve what they already had. It was incredible to her that she had wanted them to go to India. In the forest, something would creak like a door, something else would whine like a child crying, and then something would crack and groan with fluid anguish like a ghost wrapped in leather. They must all be trees, she had told herself—but not quite convincing herself. He could be anywhere in this. He could disappear into it. Once she had heard the thrum of wings beating above her—only for an instant—but when she looked up there was nothing there except the thick mesh of tree limbs and remote bits of sky. Something—it must also be a bird, or some rodent? (it must be *something*)—was very often crackling through the undergrowth to one side of the trail or the other—so often she'd eventually stopped looking to see what it was. It would never be visible, in any case. The wind would be steady, most of the time, but high above them. They hardly felt a wisp of it. She wasn't a hiker before she met Nicholas. She didn't trust the peopleless outdoors. But she had never seen a forest as forbidding as this. Once, a robin dropped from the sky as if shot—straight down into the path in front of her. It landed in a puff of needles. She jumped—it leapt, and flew away—but why would it *do* that? Where had it come from? Where could he be? As they walked and called, exhausted, she'd made every promise she could think of. She *did* believe in Allah. She always had, she insisted, but the new force of her conviction now belied her prior confidence. It was not true (she argued—with herself, with Him—with anyone necessary) that this was a quick faith of convenience, an eleventh-hour conviction. It was only that she had believed *easily* up to now, without effort or great challenge or even need (she had thought she had needed it, of course, and had thought she was being challenged—how naïve she had been). She felt that this prior faith was hardening under pressure, and expanding, filling in the space she'd always reserved for it. She would pray, she had promised. Properly, at appointed hours, and not greedily or with expectations. She would raise Hilda properly—in the faith: Hilda was just getting old enough now. But she would not take him to India, if he would only come back to her. Of course not. Not unless or until he wanted to. She would not wish he was stronger or less accommodating anymore. She would not be jealous and horde him (she could be jealous of a cat he petted, of a stranger he smiled kindly at across a counter, certainly of his students—for having him through too much of the day). They would have another child, as soon as possible, or two more, *inshahallah*. She would live every day from now on in humble gratitude if he would come back, she had promised. *But you won't*, her own voice in her mind had said. *You'll be happy again—it will soften your resolve.* I won't, she promised. It won't. You underestimate how much of me is tied to this, to him—how frightened I am of being alone. *But your fantasies—you've always wanted to be alone, secretly.* No—I've always been afraid of it. Afraid it was all I deserved. "Nicholas!" she would call out, and she only begged for him to answer her. Would that have to be a miracle? If so, surely it was a miracle of the lowest order? Not this time? Very well—then this time, please God? And she would call his name again.

Now, outside the picture window in front of her, the trees were taking back their shapes, separating from one another. She'd pulled the scarf over her hair, but as if she were only chilly. *Neeath kar te hoo mein tho rakat namaaz fajr kee* . . . She'd recited almost without speaking—the Arabic available at the moment when she needed it, as it always was, each phrase slipping forward from wherever it had lodged itself in her memory just as the one before it ended. *Allah hu akbar* . . . She whispered it into Hilda's hair, her lips against Hilda's moist scalp, so that Laurel and Greg might not recognize the prayer for what it was.

Shortly after she'd finished, Laurel said—whispering again—"If there's anything, Samina, anything there at all, you should just admit it to the police." *Oh, yes,* Samina remembered—*we're still here, aren't we?* "You don't need to go into detail," Laurel said. "No one wants you to. I know how you feel about these things. I'd be as reticent as you are, I'm sure. But can't you see that if you wait, and they get this notion about Greg into their minds, and start steering what little they know and every-thing they don't know toward that one speculation—then it'll be too late to stop them? To say, 'No, my husband and I had been fighting, actu-ally'? Or, 'There's someone else . . .' "—Laurel paused—"if that's the case. No one will ask you for details." Greg looked miserable beside his wife, disgusted. "But please try to see that your privacy, which I know you hold so dear, is really hurting someone, this time. Someone else is at stake this time. Tell *us,* if you prefer, and we'll tell the police." She was only a few feet away, yet Samina seemed to see Laurel as if through a screen. As if one or the other of them were hypothetical, Samina wasn't sure which. How desperately Samina needed sleep. Laurel asked, "What was going on? It was something that had started before we all got here, wasn't it?"

Greg said quietly, "Stop. My god, Laurel, stop it. Leave her alone."

Laurel said, "You're so stupid, Greg." Her voice was still a whisper, too, but piercing. "You have some guilty idea that it was your fault because you left him for an hour, don't you? And because you had to come back and break the news to us? But you also think that because you aren't *really* guilty, you didn't *really* do anything, that you're safe. And it's okay or even noble, or something, for you to sit there and just take all her veiled accusations and suggestions."

He said, "My god, shut up. You have no idea how cruel you're being. Her husband is missing."

"I know that—"

He said, "It isn't anything like it would be if you lost me, or anyone else you love in your skimpy way. No, as a matter of fact—you can't imagine at all."

With the day lighting, slowly, Samina felt newly exhausted. She hadn't felt tired at all, when it was still dark. And she agreed with Greg—he was right about that, she felt (from her fog). She said, "Why do you need to find something wrong with us, Laurel? It's like you're desperate to find the cracks and then split them open farther if you possibly can. He could be dead, but you still don't give up. You still need to prove that he didn't love me, for some reason. I don't understand it."

Laurel was the picture of outrage. Her mouth hung open, her eyes were wide. "I don't believe you said that," she said, as quietly as could be. But less quietly, working herself up, she said, "I don't . . . that isn't true at all."

"It *is*," Samina said. Why shouldn't she tell the truth? Why did she still have to accommodate everyone's feelings, even now? "Of course it is—we've talked about it. Do you think we're blind?"

"Well, you were wrong."

"I always stick up for you," Samina said. "Insist that you mean well. . . ." Hilda woke and pushed her head into her mother's chest, began to cry.

"Look," Laurel said, recovering from her outrage and scrambling for position again, leaning forward now, "listen: don't you dare hide behind the cover of what's happening right now and take shots at me from there. Either we're talking about Nicholas or we're talking about you and me and all my terrible failings—don't you tie them together."

She was right. Samina said, "Okay, you're right."

But Laurel hadn't paused. "If you're through with us, Samina—with Greg and me—and never want to see us again, then that's fine. That's fine. Frankly, we probably should have given up on this friendship a long time ago. I think we can all agree on that." "*Ammi!*" Hilda said, beginning to cry in earnest. "I'm sorry we came," Laurel continued, "I'm sorry if, by coincidence, we were here when you lost your husband. I hope to God he turns up, still, safe and sound, and if you don't think that's true or if, even for the briefest minute, you've ever thought that Greg could have murdered Nicholas, well then you're crueler and crazier and more paranoid than I ever imagined. What are you *thinking*?" she asked. "Jesus, what can you be thinking?"

Samina was thinking that if they didn't find him, then she would always be alone this way, as vulnerable as this, fighting alone.

Laurel said, "If somehow you're thinking you'll just lay low and keep to yourself, as always—" "Laurel," Greg said. "—and let the constable and everybody else decide whatever they decide," she continued, "since, after all, you're through with us—since you can't stand the sight of us anymore, as a matter of fact—well, please don't imagine that we're going to sacrifice ourselves for the benefit of the great Samina and her husband. So that the great Samina won't have to have been abandoned. Or even *possibly* abandoned. So that the great Samina won't have to have her precious privacy violated." Hilda sat up, bawling—"Stop," she was saying, and it was Samina's fault, she was a fool—she had always known not to cross Laurel, not to take her on, that she'd be trounced—but she couldn't think of what to do now, or how to get away. And Laurel continued—Greg couldn't stop her, either, or wouldn't. Laurel stood up, she was pointing, and she shouted over Hilda. "I have never done anything to you—" she said, "*anything* to warrant the way you've always treated me, as if I was your fan, the president of your little fan club. As if I was someone who had to be indulged, unfortunately, inviting us to come and spend time with you out of pity—'Oh, we really should,' I can just hear it. 'We really ought to. I haven't called her in weeks. We've avoided them for so long. Oh, I feel bad—Laurel keeps being the one to call me.' Tell me it isn't true. You can't! I can see by your face that I'm right. But I always knew that, Samina—it's how you've always treated me." She was walking away—storming away toward the bedroom and into it, though her speech hadn't paused. She kept shouting, between rooms, over Hilda. "It's how you've always thought of me. And it made no difference if you asked me questions about my life—I *knew* that. That didn't matter. I just kept coming back—stupid, stupid Laurel. Though, to be perfectly honest, you and Nicholas have not exactly been a barrel of laughs lately. You're awfully smug, you know, awfully smug parents, I have to say." "Shh," Samina said to Hilda—she *had* quieted a bit with Laurel removed to the other room. "But you know what I kept thinking?" Laurel shouted. "I thought, if you ever *actually* told me about yourself, just *trusted* me, just to the degree that I was always willing to trust you, then I'd be wrong. I'd have always been wrong, maybe. It *wouldn't* be just pity and indulgence. You wouldn't be so certain of your superiority the way you always seemed to be. But I wasn't wrong. I wasn't wrong." Greg and Samina stared at one another emptily.

"It's fine," Laurel was saying. "It's done, it's fine—we're going. We'll get out of your hair. We obviously haven't helped a bit, and you obviously could have used our help—but maybe you never would have taken it. Maybe I should have known that. I'm sorry, Samina." She was lugging things—suitcases, and loose piles of clothes—out into the hallway, dropping them by the door, returning to the bedroom for another load. "If you don't believe by now how sorry I am about poor Nicholas—if something terrible really happened to him, if he didn't just up and leave you—then I don't see how I'll ever make you believe it. We'll be stopping by the police station in Sooke on our way out. We'll talk to the sergeant, tell him where we're going. If, for any reason—I can't imagine—you still want to speak to either of us, he'll know where to find us. But you know what? You can relax now, too, because your precious privacy"—she'd made her pile, she came back around the corner, faced Samina once more, though Samina couldn't bring herself to look at her (she was truly afraid to, or to provoke her any further)—"will remain intact right to the end. Your prying friend Laurel won't get her dirty hands on any secrets. She won't get to break up your marriage—which, *god* knows, has been her *one* wish and mission all these years. Greg," she said, "if you don't get up from that fucking chair and follow me right now, I don't know what I'll do." And she turned away—Samina dared to look now—and got the door open around her pile of things, and loaded as much of it into her arms as she could. She dropped some clothes—"Fuck!" she said, and stamped her foot—but she bent down awkwardly, her arms full already of bags half zipped and more clothes—and managed to pick up what she'd dropped. She made it out the door. A chilly draft rushed in behind her.

When Samina looked at Greg he had stood up, yet he seemed to hesitate, too. "I'm sorry," he said, his face miserable—he spoke much too quietly for Laurel to hear—and this hit Samina as a terrible blow, for some reason. Immediately she burst out crying, right along with Hilda. She turned away from him and shook her head, hoping he would understand that she just wanted him to leave. It seemed he hadn't—he seemed to hover. She couldn't look to be sure (or see through her tears now, in any case)—but then she did hear him among the suitcases, and then she heard him close the cottage door.

Instantly, her weeping became even worse—and then much worse. It was gross, and physical, and bent her over—like a kind of vomiting. She had to push Hilda off her lap, down onto the floor. She felt wrung, as if by hands. Everything flew from her. She took great gulps of air when she could, between the sobs. She could hear herself, but only distantly, strangely, as if something else—this shrieking—were between herself and what must be her own tears.

She didn't know how long it lasted. Soon—it seemed soon, but it might not have been—she sensed that someone was there with her. Someone required her attention. Then, that it was Hilda—she was below her on the floor. Samina felt able to move, then. The hand had loosened its grip, though she was still sobbing. She got down on the floor with her daughter. She could see that Hilda had fallen silent, too fright-ened to cry. Samina had to speak in order to comfort her and to show some sign of being herself, still. She took deep breaths, and caught up enough to say, "It's me, *beta*. It's okay."

Then they could both cry—lousy tears, but not the kind she'd just survived. Not obliterating. These came with the physical release, as usual. And as usual, in their wake, Samina felt drained and placid. Hilda would not cling to her yet. She was still, Samina thought, a little afraid of her. But she let herself be held and stroked. "They're gone now," Samina said.

In a little while she carried Hilda back to the bedroom and they laid down. Shortly after she was sure they would never be able to sleep, Hilda fell off, and then she did, too. They woke midmorning. Samina did her *zuhr namaaz*. The phone had rung while they slept—she remembered that now. But it might have only been Khalid. She would ask if it had been him when she called him.

When they had bathed and dressed for the day, she told Hilda, "Come here. Stand right here and watch me," she said, placing her in the open doorway. "I'm just going to our mailbox up there—see it? You keep an eye on me." Hilda was still sleepy enough to relent to someone else's plan. Samina waved from halfway up the rise. It was in a plastic bag, a grocery store bag. Samina knew it was his from the shape of it, before she'd taken it out. She shouldn't touch it yet, she supposed. She held the heel through the bag with the rest of the *chappal* exposed. It smelled like seawater and like itself, too—which suggested him, his smell. She put it back in the bag and put the bag in the rental car before returning to Hilda, whose attention had wandered to an ant crossing the step. "What was it?" Hilda asked Samina nevertheless, taking her hand. "*Abba's chappal,*" Samina admitted. She watched this land in Hilda's mind. Questions would follow. She could see them forming in Hilda already— her face had the busy blankness that anticipated a string of questions. How to proceed, then? What does one tell her daughter, in such circumstances? And in which circumstances, of course? How about if it was over now? If he was gone forever?

35

G INNY DROVE BACK down Gillespie for some reason, not toward town or the police, and she wouldn't speak. Also, she kept blinking. "Are you okay to drive?" he asked quietly, and she replied, "*Cyrus . . .*" totally annoyed, as though she'd been set free and a flood would follow. But she didn't say anything more. In his side window Cyrus could just see himself—his face reflected—and he did feel that he was monitoring this encounter—this performance—while involved in it. She drove the length of East Sooke Road to Sooke Sun Drive and parked by the useless gate where the pavement ended. She got out of the car and walked away from him through the salal toward shore. He followed her at a respectful distance. What if he frightened her—what if she thought, for even a moment, that he would hurt her? Unbearable. She had sat down Indian-style on the moss, facing the strait. She said, "I *hate* that you told me. It's not fair." Cyrus thought it best not to reply. "You really did it?"

"Yes."

"You killed this person?"

"You could say I did. It was an accident."

"You don't think I'll turn you in, do you?"

"Yes, I do."

"No, you don't—no you don't. I know you, Cyrus. I'm not the one you have to confess to, I hope you realize. It's the police. And that poor woman."

"I know."

"They have a *kid*, you know."

"I *do* know."

"I don't think you do," she said. "How could you, Cyrus? How could you lie to everyone and not admit what you did and pretend to be *searching* for him when you knew you already *killed* him? How can you *sleep* at night? How can you eat?"

"I can't," he lied. He'd wondered the same thing, of course. It had surprised him, too—that he could. He had been forced to recognize that these were only further misconceptions—the truth was that one could, as a matter of fact, carry on, by and large, and one did, even after what he'd done—but he couldn't very well explain this to Ginny. She'd think he must be the exception, not the rule—that his conscience was faulty. And thus, the misconception was perpetuated, world-over. "I can't," he said instead. "I haven't."

But she said, "*Cy-rus!*" as if he'd said, *Oh, that's no problem—I'm a bit peckish right now, to tell you the truth.*

"I know," he said, "I know. Ginny, I can't believe it myself, still."

She'd gotten up and walked a few determined steps away from him. She kicked at something there. "What happened?" she asked eventually, but with real disgust in her voice. She'd condemned him already, it seemed—which surprised Cyrus. "Tell me the truth," she said, as if he probably wouldn't, and she looked at him with what must be a hard stare, though he couldn't clearly make out her face in the shadows across it.

He said, "It was an accident," which was true, after all, in more ways than it wasn't.

"So you keep saying."

"I was walking by—I happened to be in the park that day. I was walking by, and he saw me and called me over. He was alone on the beach there. So I went on down. We were just talking and stuff. He was a nice guy, Ginny. I liked him. I think he liked me, too. Well, he lost his sandal in the ocean. Then I was like hitting rocks with a stick, like a baseball bat, seeing how far I could hit them, right? And somehow—see, I don't know. He came up behind me. I didn't see him at all. I took this really hard swing, and after it hit the rock it hit his head. The carry-through, I mean," he improvised. "I couldn't believe it, Ginny." She watched him from the dark. "I mean, I couldn't *believe* it. It made a really terrible sound, the poor guy. Just awful. He was bleeding. I said, 'Nicholas! Are you okay?' I asked him, trying to help him. I thought he'd still get up. How could I have just *killed* him? I kept calling him."

"Where did you hit him?"

"On the head," he said. He wondered if she was testing the story, examining the details to see if they fit together properly. He wouldn't have guessed she'd do that. "Right on the back of the head, I guess it was—right here. He must have been facing the other way. That's why he didn't see me, I think. He was picking up rocks, you know? Looking for pretty rocks. He must have been bent over, and just stood up right that second . . ."

"He was dead?"

Cyrus nodded. He'd begun to cry—for poor Nicholas and for himself as well. He let it happen. The tears felt natural and convincing. He'd been so sunk into his guilt the last few days (and he *was* guilty, of course—he ought to feel guilty) that he'd half forgotten how awfully sad and unjust his own portion of this story was, too.

"You're sure he died?" Ginny asked. "How do you know?"

"I saw him, Ginny. I'm pretty sure."

"Did you feel his pulse?"

"No."

"Did you touch him? What did you do?"

"Well, I got scared. I thought someone would come and find us. Anyone could just happen down the trail, just like I did. I've *been* a coward—I *do* know that. I've been really afraid. I just couldn't believe it had happened, and I thought I had to hide him or bury him or something. So I started dragging him away. I mean, I was careful with him—I wrapped my shirt around his wound. Around his head. I was very respectful. I tried to carry him but he was too heavy. So I like dragged him over to the side of the beach, and then I didn't know what to do because the slope up to the trail is so steep there."

"So you threw him in the ocean?"

"No! No, I just—I panicked. I just left him there. I mean, I kind of thought I would run away, actually, and just maybe go to Mexico. I didn't know what to do. I mean, I did know, but I couldn't actually do it—I was a coward. But then eventually I realized what a coward I was and what I had done to this poor person and his family, so I went back to either maybe cover him over with something to keep him dry, or whatever, and then just maybe go get the police. It was raining a lot that night. It was only a few hours later. But when I finally got back . . ." He paused. "He wasn't there."

"You left him below the high-tide line."

"Yeah, I guess I did. Not so far below, actually—I mean, I didn't think about it. But yeah. The tide had come up across where he was. I wasn't *thinking*. You know?"

Ginny sat down—plop—apart from him, still. Perhaps she was afraid of him. "Did he say something to you, Cyrus? To make you angry."

"No! No, Ginny, he didn't," Cyrus said, risking a touch of anger now—*But careful*, he told himself, *you* are *guilty*. "See, that's what I mean—you see? Even *you* think I meant to kill him." He shouldn't be crying—he'd never trusted tears, on the television. He didn't do them well, very likely. "That's why I didn't go to the *police*," he said, "even though I should have—I *know* that. I do know what I should have done, Ginny, okay? Please. But you tell me the truth: do you think they'll believe me? It's me, you know. Come on. People don't believe me. Why *should* they, anyway? No one else was there, no witnesses." After a pause, he said, "It gets harder to tell, not easier. You wouldn't believe how hard it is." Since she was still quiet, listening, he added, "Sometimes I thought, maybe he's alive. Maybe we'll find him." He shrugged. She was right, after all, that he'd never checked the man's pulse. There hadn't even been that much blood, really, he thought now.

"But you said he's dead."

"I *think* he's dead, Ginny. I don't know." Nicholas had lain still and had not responded to Cyrus—that was all—and by that test he may as easily have been no more than unconscious.

"Oh, Cyrus," she said—with some of her native empathy back in it for the first time. Already he felt relief begin to explode from his chest and course through his limbs, though he wasn't there yet. She asked him, "What about Sasha?" and that was an awfully difficult part. What lie could he tell? He thought perhaps (he wasn't certain) he wanted to confess to everything, honestly and completely, but it was a question of how much she could know and still love him. "I hate to admit it," he said, "you'll hate me. You *should*." But no, she wouldn't—that wasn't her nature—instead she would simply lose access to him. He might prove beyond her understanding or her capacity for forgiveness. He'd be alone.

He said, "But when I went back, you know, and Nicholas wasn't there—it was pretty late by then—I didn't know what to do anymore. But I was worried there must be blood. I couldn't see if there was—it was incredibly dark, Ginny. But I walked to the Whittleseys' place and got Sasha, and I got her leash from the hook on the porch since I had to walk her all the way down to the beach, and when we got there I did kill her. I mean, I made her sit in that spot where I had accidentally killed him—" These were true tears now, and they stung, as the others hadn't. He'd been shivering terribly. He'd buried Nicholas's shirt, digging in a soft spot in the forest with his hands. The dog had been pleased to see him and interested in this walk he was taking her on, full of curiosity. She'd stood still while he got her leash on. The Whittleseys had the television turned up. Sasha hadn't barked. She knew him, after all. *Good dog.* She had obeyed him and had sat still in the spot he told her to at the beach and looked upon the water with real dignity. He'd fooled himself—looking at her in those seconds—into thinking she knew her fate, and had accepted it on his behalf. But when he'd hit her with the stick she'd made a high, strangled squeal—desperate, but also aggressive, it had a growl wedged awkwardly into the scream of it—and she hadn't died. Her head had seemed so much heavier and denser than Nicholas's. She had squirmed and attempted to stand up, although her legs were loose and flimsy and her great head lolled strangely. She'd snapped at something—at air. She made an awful noise, as if begging for his help or pity and at the same time cursing him. He'd hit her again, to make her stop, but with her weird struggling and in the state he was in he'd missed her head and hit her neck, or perhaps it was her shoulders. She'd screamed again. So he had to beat her a third time before she stopped trying to stand up, and once more to be sure she was truly dead and not suffering any longer. " . . . and I hit her over the head with a stick," he said, losing his breath to his tears again now. "And killed her. To cover it up, I thought. Oh, Jesus!" he said. "I don't *know*, Ginny." She had come back to him. "Shush," she told him, and sat down behind him to rub his back. She said, "Stop crying," but in sympathy, he believed. It *wasn't* exactly where he'd killed Nicholas—it was a little higher on the beach, since the exact spot was underwater—and he'd been thinking ever since that night that he didn't have to do it at all. He had thought the blood would mingle. There had been an image of it in his head, that night—of two bloods bleeding into one another, hiding their individual natures in the mix. But he hadn't guessed how hard it would be to kill Sasha—how much harder than killing poor Nicholas.

Ginny sat against his back. "This is so awful," she said.

Killing Nicholas had been an accident—a terrible, cruel accident, probably, but wasn't it an act propelled by no more than the foggiest intentions? Sasha, on the other hand, was innocent.

When he'd mostly stopped crying, Ginny asked, "What are we supposed to do?"

"I don't know."

"They'd probably put you in jail."

"Yeah," he said. He wiped at his eyes. "Yup."

Ginny said, "Oh, Cyrus, that poor woman. They have a *daughter*." "I *know* this," he said. He'd changed—Cyrus had. Someone else was here on this side of the gap. He said, "I know this, Ginny, I know this, I know this. You don't understand. Nobody realizes!" he said, and he had to stand up. He looked down at her. "Do you know what she's like—their daughter? Because I do. Her name is Hilda, Ginny—have you ever known a little girl named Hilda? She *loves* me, by the way. I mean, not really love—she doesn't *know* me—but she can't really get enough of me. I'm not bragging—this is just true. From the minute she saw me she ate me up, you know? You know how kids do that, once in a while? Ginny, *I know what I did*," he said, all teary again—she relented and said, "Oh, honey," and reached out to touch his knee—he said, "I didn't *mean* to," letting himself fall back down flat on the ground there. "It isn't *fair*."

As a matter of fact, he felt he didn't know himself yet—he was just meeting this stranger. That night he had misplaced his confidence and what presence of mind he'd once been capable of summoning, and his sense of direction. He felt younger now, and short on will and energy. He felt he didn't know, any longer, everything he used to know for certain—but there had been a great deal, he remembered. But he felt better, too, right now, having told the whole story to Ginny. Spoken aloud, what he'd done didn't seem so bad. Ginny said, "You've got to make it up to them, Cyrus."

He let his arm rest over his eyes. "I know. I've tried."

"What did you try? How?"

"Ginny, I've tried. They don't want me. They're perfectly done with me." He sat up. The moon, late again tonight, was just rising somewhere behind them, behind the hillside and the trees. It lit the strait into a heavy gray shade, and the dark around them had given way, slightly. "I'm a kid to them, right? Just some local kid. They don't even seem to suspect me. I'm like a nuisance to his wife right now."

"But this girl likes you."

"But she shouldn't, should she?"

Ginny shook her head, and couldn't help but cringe from him, still. She said, "I just don't know, Cyrus—what am I supposed to do?" *He* didn't know. "I mean . . . what should we do?" she said.

He loved that "we"—he felt it was the most generous single word anyone had spoken in a long time.

"I wish I was innocent," he said. She said, "Well you're not." "I mean really innocent—like a kid. I wish I didn't know anything." She said, "That's stupid, Cyrus. Don't say that."

They just looked at one another. Her nose stud caught the bit of moonlight and flashed. They would change now—they would have to. This wasn't love, either, but perhaps it was something more than that, more than sex—more pure, Cyrus wanted to think. More than petty romance. Don? Don was fine, probably. Not a bad person at all (Don

had not killed anyone, accidentally or otherwise). But he did not deserve
Ginny, or need her. He would not understand her or value her properly—he'd had chances to, already. Don had a thousand friends. Don
was a confirmed success, with or without Ginny.

She asked, "What if he's alive?"

"I don't know." Then he said (it *was* a familiar feeling: you walked
toward the thicket, off the path, into the branches, and somehow the
way through did open in front of you—a narrow thread you hadn't
known was there presented itself), "Why do you think I've been searching for him the last two days? My fantasy was that we'd find him alive
still. You know? I mean, yeah, then I'd definitely go to jail, I guess, but
who cares? He'd be alive! Hilda would visit him in the hospital.
Everything back to normal, right?"

She nodded.

On that beach, for just a moment, Cyrus had been taken up and
shaken like a rag doll, thrown back down on the pebbles beside a body,
and he'd always known he *would* be one day, that he was a person who
would leap into a new life, so there wasn't a surprise in that. He'd prepared himself. But he had thought his moment would involve rescue
and sacrifice, some sort of self-forging heroism, or artistic consolida-
tion and breakthrough, or a sudden clarity of purpose that wouldn't be
easy to live with, perhaps, but would propel him toward the life of sig-
nificance. He wanted to be good-hearted and generous like Ginny yet
concentrated, too, and more effective, more forceful. He'd imagined
his moment would start him back toward people—he'd be less alone,
as the famous or dedicated must be—although it would set him apart
in a new way, too. Purity. He'd imagined some purity of purpose and
discovered talent.

What he hadn't anticipated was a leap into a mission of compromise
and undoing like this, of taking back one terrible mistake. He was young;
bright enough. He'd prove anything but lazy if he could get himself
pointed in the right direction, he felt. Was it really so naïve and silly to
think he might travel to New York or find a new life in Holland, or India,
where he could entirely shed his history of disappointing people and
prove so indispensably good at something that he'd be respected and

loved? He supposed it was, though he hated knowing this. Up to just a few days ago he'd thought of the world as so many millions of possibilities and himself as a shopper, choosing from among them, but if he'd ever considered more carefully he would have recognized that he didn't know a single person who had really managed to get out of his own narrow aisle of potential. Not even Samina, who had come around the world only to be the housewife to a not-quite-worthy husband and aspire to ordinary vacations in cottages in second-rate destinations where, like all cottagers, she would examine the views from a septic distance and admire the pretty while overlooking the real and take away all sorts of ideas about the locals without understanding the first thing about them. She didn't deserve what Cyrus had delivered to her, and anyone—even Ginny—would call Cyrus heartless or worse if he said this aloud, yet who was to say he hadn't given her a second chance to be something more? To find a purer possibility this time?

But she probably wouldn't take the opportunity. She would probably be only further narrowed by the loss of her husband. And Cyrus didn't look likely to make it out of his aisle, either. In retrospect, one could argue he'd been born a person headed toward cruel and deeply compromising mistakes.

She said, "Oh, I wish you didn't do it."

He gulped and sniffled and said, "Yeah."

Part

IV

36

SAMINA PRAYED WHILE sitting—the plane flew east—and
when she opened her eyes there was land below her, and snow
on the hills of Wales. A white-ice rim was on the sea. The clouds puffed
into streams and hills with gaps to peek through. She'd never been to
England. The landing was late and the connection tight, but Hilda, who
had slept the length of the Atlantic, would not be carried. This winter she
was turning (too quickly for Samina's taste) into a girl who could rise to
occasions, though, and she led the way in front of Samina, pulling her
own suitcase. The route from the gate to the terminal was endless and featureless, abandoned except for the ragged train of passengers from their
flight. No one in uniform to direct or reassure, no gates or groups of chairs
or vending machines. The walls were carpeted. One came toward angles,
rounded them expecting the opening into customs, but would instead face
another endless, muffled avenue to the next turn and promise.

By the time they reached the India flight, it had boarded. They
walked straight on (one last hallway), and Hilda wanted to be reminded
why they weren't sitting in business class, where the seats were artfully
turned forward and back to allow for reclining, and art-deco fans divided
you from the person stretched out comfortably beside you. It was all-but-

empty. Coach was packed. Samina and Hilda squeezed past a *sardarji* with a barrel of a belly and buckled themselves in for seven hours more. That was England. "What time is it?" Hilda wanted to know, but she fell asleep before Samina could calculate an answer.

She'd been feeling lightened, emptied out, launched into air—it must be relief. The farther North America receded behind her—the farther she got from condolences and measured smiles, from exhausting antici- pation, the betrayals of the telephone, and all the accommodations that a "grieving" person (did anyone like that word? only the safe and smug on shore) had to make for the well-meaning and the overmatched—the better Samina felt. *She* would be overmatched in India, she hoped. Lost in the shuffle, swept into the background, stepped past. Even in the fam- ily she hoped and expected to make no more than a small ripple, her troubles too distant and too vague (*Did he die then, or only run off? She's the one who married the American?*) to be lingered over. She hadn't appreciated, until now, the great advantage she gained by being on the periphery of this family. When the telephone rang in Khalid's house, it wouldn't be for her—it wouldn't fail to have something to do with Nicholas. Sergeant Dunn in Sooke didn't even know she'd gone to India. What difference did it make? In three months, he'd never called. A fog of Hindi and Punjabi began to thicken through the airplane cabin. Samina fell asleep.

Khalid had been with her in Sooke in the last, worst days of the search, when it had seemed likely that the only thing they could still hope to find was a body, and he had come back again a month later to stay with her in New York. "Come to India," he'd begun saying then. "Come back with me." "I can't," she'd replied, and when he'd asked, "Why can't you?" she had told him there were too many logistics to manage: the insurance claim, finding a job, making arrangements for Hilda. But she hadn't admitted that she couldn't change anything quite yet or make any large decisions—couldn't take any of the steps that would solidify her new condition—and that a small part of her felt going to India with Hilda, so soon, would be betraying Nicholas. Would she intuit when the statute of limitations on his presumed wishes had passed, she wondered? "But you can't just stay here," Khalid had argued. "Why not? What do you mean?" He'd gestured to the right and left, and opened his palms, as if it couldn't be more obvious. She had held out for two occasionless, meaningless months.

They landed in Delhi exactly at the haphazard hour in the middle of the night when they were meant to—as if the people who scheduled these flights knew that hours on a clock would be irrelevant to you by now. The ramp to this terminal was short and lined in dusty marble. There was immediately a recalled smell—of damp stone, wet concrete.

Past the last stage of inquiry, through the high and windowless double doors, she stepped with Hilda into a corral, rising slightly, with a metal railing on both sides and silent faces, three deep, pressing in. The runway was wide at the bottom and narrowed, ending in a circle—the shape of a keyhole. The people stared with Asian practice and intensity but were strangely silent. New objects of attention broke through the doors and slipped by Samina, up the narrow, empty aisle. She should keep walking, too. There were men alone along the railing, drivers and company errand boys holding signs with names that revealed their penmanship, and families looking for their charges, and taxi drivers quietly soliciting. The trays of light high overhead were weak and yellow. A fog descended from the ceiling. "Taxi, madam?" they asked Samina. Hilda pressed against her leg and Samina struggled with the baggage trolley. Everyone seemed to watch her and to lose heart at the sight. They must keep moving forward, Samina felt, although the runway was coming to an end. She still hadn't seen Khalid. "*Taxi*, madam. *Hello?*" Perhaps they could retreat back down the runway and through the door, onto the next flight out to anywhere—staying aloft seemed like a good strategy. Then they heard their names called and there was Aisha, Khalid's wife, late and hurrying with a boy who must be a servant.

Khalid was in Sri Lanka, she explained—business—but he'd be back tomorrow night. Outside, the air was thick with ash or dust or mist, or was it only pollution? Everything was damp. They drove through an almost empty city of sealed businesses and cook fires surrounded by huddled shadows and busy, heedless trucks. The empty lots on either side of the old house were littered with weeds and crushed water bottles, but inside his high walls Khalid's garden was cool and lovely: mown grass and English beds mounding in the dark, an ivy trained up the walls. Farzana—her father's first wife—stood by the door, where the porch light reflected in her glasses. She appeared at first as severe as she had been on the last visit, but then she took Samina's hand from her salaam, pressed it, and called her *beta* (as she never had), and picked up Hilda with surprising ease. "Who is this big girl?" she asked in Urdu. Aisha offered tea and kabobs, though it was three in the morning, and the offer could have been politely refused if Khalid was here but without him it certainly couldn't be. As they ate, Samina wondered if she would fall asleep at the table. Her Urdu was even rustier than she'd feared. Hilda sat on Farzana's lap while the old woman taught her to say *dadi*— "I am *Dadi*," she could explain, in English—and Hilda nodded, understanding but busy eating. Later, it was clear that the bedroom they'd been assigned belonged to Farzana, and she'd been crowded in with Aisha's sleeping sons (the upper floors of the house were too dusty, and there were too many monkeys, Aisha said). "Oh, no," Samina tried, "no—we can't," but of course it was useless to protest—she was only delaying further the moment when she could politely close the door on them—and when that moment came at last, she found herself wishing once more for a return flight. Nicholas had been evoked—thoughts of him had rattled the cage of her brain—in every indulgence, and Samina had entertained the ungenerous thought that people like Khalid's mother (there would be others, too—much of the family, perhaps) were kind at least in part out of a sense of satisfaction, and vindication. They had predicted an ending like this one. Her father had planted the seed—the divorce, marrying that silly girl (to their minds), the cowardly flight to America—and his daughter had carried through, latching on to a stranger whose values and family no one knew—a disconnected, free, and greedy American, who had finally run off, evidently. Samina should have gone to Africa or China or Finland—anyplace where no one knew what had happened to her, or thought they knew; where no one had a theory.

She was exhausted, but couldn't sleep. When she was restless on the plane she had fondled the two polished images, as she did again now: of Nicholas dead and found and properly buried, first—his family and all their friends were at the funeral, and everyone knew what had happened to him, once and for all, but no one knew more than Samina did; and then, secondly—still better—Nicholas alive right now, living in a cabin, chopping wood, lighting a fire, wearing clothes he had chosen, thinking his thoughts, with his memory intact no matter his conscience, speaking—his voice heard in the world still, his smell still known. He always does feel guilt or longing in this fantasy—for Hilda if not Samina. He's on his way back to them. Soon, a weird light surrounded her—it seemed to come from nowhere. Then she realized it was dawn.

The second day was better. It was very nice to wake beside Hilda in India, and the light in the room was Indian, somehow, sifting down warmly from the high windows that were tucked close to the ceiling. They heard the musical horns of Tata trucks out on the highway—the fast set of acrobatic notes—and Hilda asked, "What's that?" whispering dramatically, her eyes wide, in a parody of surprise. "Adorable girl," Samina said.

All day Aisha and her driver escorted them around Delhi: to a fair in a park at the edge of the city—little tents and straw booths under the trees, and acrobats, and a boy beating a drum strapped to his chest while his younger brother and his father danced—then to the ready-made stores, and the fabric shops. Aisha had a mild-mannered cheerfulness plus the right mix of generosity and self-indulgence. She wanted to take Samina wherever Samina wished to go, of course, but if asked for her preference she'd quickly provide it. And she didn't mind driving in silence. Outside the windows of the air-conditioned car the traffic bunched and gave way without the slightest regard for lanes and men flew by on scooters and motorcycles or were dangerously passed on bicycles and schoolchildren stared from the backs of cycle-rickshaws. There were pigs in garbage heaps and families huddled around a roadside cook fire, or living in a half-built apartment structure with no external façade or windows or doors—just layers of concrete with wooden ladders between them and blankets hung for walls and bouquets of rebar bursting out the rough ends of the floors. Beside these structures might be new marble-and-glass offices, and a Benetton store, then a row of trees covered in dust, then the most common shops: three-sided boxes of concrete with low roofs and a bare bulb and everything on display: handbags beside plumbing equipment, blacksmiths searing and hammering, an Internet café, a man making trunks and briefcases out of what appeared to be the sheet metal from an air-conditioning duct. In every scene there were people working hard, people pointing and correcting and getting in the way, people watching both of the first two parties, and disinterested loungers, staring back at Samina.

That night Khalid returned, and his sons, Saud and Saif, seven and two (who had spent the day at home with their grandmother), were rowdy and full of ideas. The whole household was louder with Khalid home— everyone performed for him, the servants teased him, his wife had things to tell him and spoke over her sons as the thoughts struck her. Hilda seldom strayed from Farzana's side (she had taken up the title: "*Dadi*," she said, "look at my socks."). With Khalid back, the visits to family began. Every day he went to work for a few hours in the morning but arrived home in time to pack them all off to their lunch appointment, and they would return from lunch just in time to change clothes and head out to dinner. The meals were massive, wonderful but overwhelming, the rotis even better than Samina had remembered. The adults Samina's age had little to say to her, but they chatted idly and rapidly between themselves and didn't seem to mind if she listened in. They were just what she'd hoped for. The older people held her hand and shook their heads, and all said "It's good you came," "We've been worried about you," "You must be strong, for the child," and "*Why* didn't you come sooner?" as if her husband had left her because she hadn't taken him back to India. But they, too, moved on, rather quickly, past her and around her, back to themselves. Hilda played carom, or hide-and-seek in the servants' quarters. A few months earlier it would have taken her hours to dare venture out of reach of her mother's knee, but here she was running ahead of Samina from the car, pushing the front door open, presenting herself to the party with a flourish. "Well, look who's here!"

These houses were usually within range of an *azaan*, and when Samina covered her head at the call and disappeared into a back room in the company of the older women present, no one seemed surprised or troubled. She felt closer to God in India, but thankful that in this family He was rarely discussed. She couldn't stand to be told His way or intentions, or what He offered one in her position or what He had done for anyone else, and she had lived too long neglecting and disgusted with her religion (although she'd always felt compelled to defend it when people in America expressed their received ideas about its failings) to share it with fellow believers yet. Still, it felt like getting to the dark heart of things to shuffle silently into these rooms in the company of bowed and unsmiling near-strangers, and when they closed the door the shouts and conversations and clattering of dishes and children beyond it seemed to Samina the false façade, slipped behind at last. She didn't pray in the form of apologies or requests; she didn't petition on Nicholas's behalf any longer. Not a single word she spoke was her own. She recited the litany of Arabic she could have only half translated, but its allure lay in the impenetrability, and sometimes (not always—she hoped to improve), at some point, deep in the midst of the prayer, if she gave herself to it properly, everything she was would seem to slip off her like a loose skin and she would feel an annihilation that she imagined must be what people had meant when they spoke of grace. Emerging again she would seem to have lived her whole life the same way she experienced India—skimming across the surface but with this weird and misleading sense of comfortable belonging and custody—and she would be anxious to find Hilda, and a little ashamed of herself—of her secret death wish—before her daughter.

A WEEK HAD passed. Then a month had passed—impossible, but it was true. Samina never glanced at beggars any longer. Only Hilda still did. They saw traffic accidents—a bus which had hit a tree, with tourists who sat dazed and bleeding on the curb, and, another day, two trucks buckled into one another. Late one night, coming home, they were stopped in the empty road by the spectacle of a hobbling cow being hunted by a pack of dogs. A dog would latch on to its rump and let itself be dragged and kicked a short distance while the cow stumbled and rolled its eyes. Khalid blew his horn, was ignored, watched the cow almost run onto his hood, then finally backed up to the nearest side street. Samina was almost certain she used to be a person who would have been kept up that night thinking about the wild eyes of the cow, or who would have had nightmares featuring the old woman from the crumpled bus trying to wipe the blood from her nose but streaking it across her lips. What about the mothers picking dinner from the garbage, then, their children squatting beside them and munching already? If Nicholas was here she would have suffered it all doubly— once in embarrassment—and she might have been bulging by now, desperate to flee. She never thought, *What does it matter what happened to a man on vacation on a beach in Canada?* In fact, she couldn't seem to truly convince herself yet that anything else was important—that anything this far from that awful beach was of any real consequence to her, or she to it. Living without him was a shield she held in her hand, but grief was an indulgence. It kept everything at arm's reach—suffering, family, even their daughter. No one here, of course, could have a sense of how much she had loved him, and anyway what would they know about love? What experience did they have of this overwhelming circumstance, which had hollowed Samina out and filled her back in, replacing or at least recasting so much of what she might have once shared with the cousins her age? These cousins were Indian Muslims, after all—they didn't have to be told what a kurta was or what length was in fashion; they ate properly, in the proper sequence of courses, saving the rice, making *niwalas* (it was a pleasure not to have to watch someone make a sandwich of his roti, or eat it as a side dish; it had been a pleasure to only hear the word "exotic" applied to things Samina found exotic, too)—yet on some deeper level they kept seeming more foreign to her than her friends in New York. The divide was love: whether one had ever been governed by it, for better or worse, or not.

Before she met Nicholas she couldn't imagine marrying an American. What sort of intimacy could be built out of so much explaining? And he would never properly understand the things she told him, partly because she didn't know them well enough to play teacher, but also in the way that one never does with explained information. She can remember talking to an Indian friend in college about how awful it would be to take your American husband to India, or into a *masjid*—playing tour guide. It would be like marrying a tourist of one's self; *a form of orientalism*, she and her friend had agreed. And what if he *did* take it in, study up, read books behind your back, begin to argue with you about whether the kabobs at a restaurant were good or not or sit there telling his American friends all about what the Koran *really* says or how we should all feel about head-scarves? Terrible. Creepy. He'd better be awfully good-looking, they'd agreed, and keep his mouth shut in the bedroom.

But they'd also had romantic faith in the impractical, transformative force of love, of course, and it had surprised Samina that this was the belief which proved true to experience rather than their cool and doubt-ful presumptions. And it hadn't occurred to them that they might be happy tourists in his life, too.

She probably didn't give her cousins enough credit, and she probably understood as little about the chemical reactions in their form of mar-riage as she assumed they did about hers. But if they had a sense of what Samina had lost, wouldn't it show more clearly in the way they spoke to her, or were afraid to? Another month passed.

One day a letter came. The outer envelope was greasy and wrinkled and had been forwarded by the friend in New York who was collecting Samina's mail. The inner envelope was from St. Louis—from Greg. The pages had softened.

I have hesitated to write this for weeks and weeks, and I hesitate now in part because the apology Laurel and I owe you (and have been making to you for a long time, in our hearts) is so overdue. I'm so sorry about the way we treated you, Samina. I think, in the utter strangeness of losing Nicholas that way, we must have lost our minds a little, too. I hate to think of that trip, and Laurel does also. But we do think of it—all the time, it seems—and we wish we had acted properly and done everything we could have to help you. And of course we worry about you, still. For what it's worth to you, Laurel felt like a complete fool the day after we left you. She would have come to the cottage and apologized immediately (we were still in Sooke), but she was afraid that she'd been so cruel she didn't have the right to. And she was sure you wouldn't have wanted to see her then— understandably.

I don't make these apologies with the hope of inspiring any particular action from your end, though, including forgiveness. Truly. We would like very much to still know you, and to be your friends again, but we recognize that we may have failed you too deeply to deserve that honor, or to earn back your trust. We do miss you, though—Laurel does, especially. And I can't tell you how much we regret that Nicholas hasn't been found yet. We both miss him terribly and can hardly imagine what you must be going through. Please accept our very belated condolences.

But I did hope to ask you one large favor as well. Or at this point, only something to consider, perhaps. I hesitate here, too, but I suppose I should just come right out with it: I would like to write a book about Nicholas, and about our time in Sooke. It would be much more personal with regards to myself than to Nicholas—a sort of memoir—but I hope that, in part, it would be a way to publicly remember him and what a good writer and friend he was. It would also be about biography—about how the lived life turns into the remembered life, I think, and what we have to do to our complex, disordered progress through the world to reshape it into a narrative—and I've been feeling as if the sheer mystery of Nicholas's disappearance is in some way an illustration of all that. Do you know what I mean? As I say, it would be a personal book, and to that end something of an act of contrition, since Laurel and I would appear in it with all our warts. But naturally I wouldn't consider writing such a book without your permission and consent, and I would be happy to give you as much oversight of it as you wanted—you could read it before it went to a publisher, for instance. I'd be grateful for your input, in fact. Of course, if I went ahead, with your permission, I would need to speak to Nicholas's family and friends.

I'm told that you and Hilda have recently gone to India. This has probably reached you upon your return—I hope it was a good trip for both of you. Please give our love to Hilda as well. I hope you're doing okay, Samina. We do miss you, and we think about you—with nothing but sympathy, regret, and warm feelings—all the time.

Your Friend,
Greg Faber

It was strangely incomprehensible to Samina. It wasn't meant to be, was it? She'd never received a letter from Greg, or read his critical articles, but she wouldn't have guessed his prose would be this way—that he'd be the sort to talk about making apologies in his heart or deserving the honor of anything. What about this idea of his? Writing a book about Nicholas? He hardly knew Nicholas—didn't he recognize that? He hardly knew Sooke. Was this a good idea, or at least a relatively reasonable idea (given that he *was*, after all, a writer and a biographer), or was it, as it seemed to her, absolutely ridiculous and offensive? Should she be outraged by this letter, or only conflicted, or pleased and mollified? (*Had* she been angry at Greg and Laurel?) Samina showed the letter to Khalid. "These are the friends you had an argument with?" he asked. "For heaven's sake, what did they do to you, Samina?" "Never mind that," she said, "I'm asking about the book. Is this a good idea or a bad one?" "Well, is your friend a good writer?" Samina said, "I don't know. He doesn't write much of a letter, in my opinion." "Is he someone you want snooping around in your husband's life? Would you *read* such a book, Samina?" "No," she said—she hadn't realized that was ever in doubt. "Would you?" she asked. He shrugged.

"It's up to you, of course," he said. "What do *you* want?"

Eventually, she called Nicholas's parents in Cambridge. Greg had contacted them already, but after Samina got past their respectful hesitations and deferrals to her judgment, it became clear that they were attached to the idea. They thought Greg would have known their son in a way that they hadn't, which was probably true, and they were under the impression that he was going to investigate Nicholas's disappearance. They hoped he might turn something up. They seemed to think he was a different sort of writer. But what was Samina's opinion? they asked. What did she think of this Greg Faber?

Samina could still locate no opinion on the matter. It was almost impossible to believe she'd had the relationship she knew she had had with Greg and Laurel—it seemed like something from a different era and there didn't seem to be the slightest room for it in her life anymore. One day, she supposed, not very long from now, she was going to have to return to New York and sell the apartment, find a new one, find a job, gain substance again, and opinions, and consider a future, like anyone else. She'd have to do this for Hilda's sake, at the very least.

"We want to travel," she told Khalid a few days later. She and Hilda were in the back seat of his car again. Being always in the back seat, this far from the windshield and the carnival coming toward it, was fitting her sensibilities too well. "I think we'll go to Agra."

"Alone?" Khalid turned to ask.

"Just Hilda and me."

"You cannot travel alone."

But he found a way to let them. He called a man he knew, an old friend of their father's, who said, "Put them in my hotel. I will have them looked after." Khalid reported this phrase to Samina with pride, as if she would admire it as much as he had. Before they left, Samina sent a quick letter:

> Dear Greg,
>
> You should write whatever you want to, of course, but I'm afraid I can't be of any assistance. I'm afraid I can't know you anymore. I hope you'll understand. Thank you for your condolences.
>
> *Sincerely,*
> *Samina*

She wondered if this letter would one day appear in his book.

The manager of the hotel met Samina at the train. "Miss Samina Naqvi" it said on his little sign. He had a bellhop along to handle the bags. While the bellhop drove to the hotel, Mr. Malhotra turned in his seat to discuss their touring plans and lend his advice. He had the deep, smooth voice of an actor, and a broad, neat salt-and-pepper mustache. How long would their stay in Agra be? Samina didn't know. Four days at least, he advised. If it suited them, he would hire their guides. "May I suggest the fort this afternoon?" he said. "Tomorrow the Taj—at dawn it is best. The next day, Fatehpur Sikri? I will hire a car, with your permission."

He took care of them all weekend. He paid the guides and the drivers himself so she wasn't involved in any discussion of terms and those terms wouldn't change as soon as they had taken her away from him. When he saw Samina in the lobby the first evening, on her way out toward some destination Mr. Malhotra hadn't scheduled, he asked if there was anything he could help her with. May he lend her advice on a restaurant for dinner? "The directions are complicated," he said, "let me get someone to lead you there." "Oh, no—thank you," Samina told him, "I'm sure we'll find it." But he insisted. A young man in a stiff *sherwani* drove them the four blocks and stood smoking outside the restaurant, waiting to drive them back again.

The monuments were more impressive than Samina had remembered. The fort was a village of complexly connected structures and wide lawns behind a wall of red stone and a moat. There was a view through *jalis* of the river and of the Taj floating on a pillow of haze. Hilda squatted to help some boys with their game of marbles, but they didn't appreciate her help and one said to Samina in Hindi, "She doesn't know the rules!" "Talk English," Hilda instructed.

The Taj, next day, was magnificent at dawn, with morning mist on the river behind it. It took Samina a moment to realize the mist was reminding her of Sooke Harbour. She and Hilda had ridden in a cycle-rickshaw through the last darkness of morning to get to the gates—with the streets empty except for occasional women carrying water, lighting fires, making tea—but when they came out a few hours later, the same streets were clogged with hawkers and tourists—German, Japanese, British. Samina had the idea she and Hilda might walk back to the hotel. It wasn't so far. She remembered the way. But every few steps there was another rickshaw-wallah wishing to give her a ride instead, or someone wanting to sell her a souvenir, or a cow draped across the sidewalk, forcing her to step into the busy street, or a man in a car slowing down to ask with unctuous solicitation if they needed a lift. It evidently wasn't possible, in this city, to "explore"—to stroll down a street and look into the windows, or shop for a restaurant—or for Samina and Hilda it wasn't. Khalid had been right: they couldn't do much of anything without a man beside them.

Safe in the hotel room, Hilda kept falling asleep—sweaty naps plus ten hours at night. She didn't complain often enough, didn't fuss enough. She was too patient for Samina's taste, as if resigned to something. But this was their condition now. India amplified it, certainly, but they'd be alone and exposed in America, too, without Nicholas. How would she do this? How would she keep Hilda from growing up in a house like the one she'd grown up in, shadowed by tragic setbacks that had preceded you and yet would shape your life?

On only their third morning in Agra she called Khalid and told him they were ready to come home (like a child—like a girl still unmarried). He made the train and taxi arrangements from Delhi, and by evening Samina and Hilda were in the back of his ancient Ambassador again.

"You've had a phone call," Khalid said, watching Samina in the rearview. "Just a few hours ago. While you were on the train." He didn't want to say more, or perhaps didn't know what to say in front of Hilda, but Samina knew already. "They found a b-o-d-y," he said, spelling it out. Nicholas's parents had called India with the news. "It was on a beach, very remote I understood. A hiker came upon it. D-r-o-w-n-e-d," he said, and as he spelled the word out (it seemed to take him forever) her mind raced ahead to other possibilities: *Drenched*. He was soaking wet. They gave the poor man a towel. *Drove*—he dried off, then drove to the nearest police station. When the whole word was out, her mind clung to its last quick defense. "How do they know it's him?" she asked. But Khalid said, "So I asked, myself. It was his DNA." She had given the sergeant his hairbrush.

Samina looked out her window, then turned to Hilda, who sat on the other end of the back seat, by herself, with her little arm placed casually on the door's armrest. It would be tough to get her back into car seats. She'd been watching her mother, perhaps waiting for a translation. When none was forthcoming, she asked, "Can we go to the zoo?" They had been once already.

"Next trip, *beta*. We need to go home now."

Hilda turned away to process this. Samina ought to tell her, but couldn't bring herself to open the topic.

Hilda asked, "Can we get a cat?"

Samina nodded. "I think so, love."

"And parakeets?"

"We'll see."

She should have prepared for this, right from the start—from the first time she had kissed Nicholas. It must have been possible: small denials day to day, holding back from the hazardous moments. This was why

you stayed close to the family who preceded the one you'd made, of
course, despite and through the midst of your marriage. But on the
other hand, she felt as if all she'd done was hold back—*not* in preparation or self-defense, but just from short-sightedness and cold-heartedness
and distraction. If she had actually anticipated the worst, she might have
been sensible enough to drench herself in him daily.

There was music playing ahead. Khalid was slowing down. A Hindu
wedding procession was just crossing the street in front of them. These
were as common as could be in Delhi, any day of the week—trains without tracks, slicing streets in half. Khalid stopped, and the cars behind
him immediately filled in all the space on either side, making three lanes
out of one, before grudgingly stopping as well. The band members in
the *baraat* wore their tall hats and white and red uniforms—they played
kettledrums and squealing *shenais*—and men in dhotis carried electric
lights, which they shone onto the wilting groom perched on his horse.
The horse wore a hat with gold tassels. Thick black electrical wires
trailed on the road behind the lights, and a man pushed the loud, smoky
generator, followed at a distance by all the groom's guests and family.
The party was so large, and walking so slowly, that Khalid got out of the
car to chat with the other waiting drivers. "Can we get out, too?" Hilda
asked after a moment. "Okay," Samina said.

They had to be careful not to knock their doors into the cars on either
side. When Hilda tugged on Khalid's pants he stood her up on the roof
of the Ambassador for a better view. The wedding guests were dressed
beautifully and wearing their gaudiest jewelry. They chatted and laughed
in groups. Perhaps they'd already been walking for a long time—some of
the fat men were sweating, and the procession had lost its form. "What
do you see?" Samina called up to Hilda, when the music and the generator had progressed down the road far enough for them to hear one
another. "I see people," she said. She was very happy—bouncing at the
knees a bit, with Khalid's big hand around her ankle. What had Samina
been thinking? Of course he hadn't left them. *Oh, I'm sorry,* she thought,
meaning it for Nicholas. He never would—he would never have left
Hilda. "Be careful, *beta*," Samina called to her, but Hilda didn't hear or
wasn't listening. The drivers farther back on the clogged road had begun

to lean on their horns. "*Beta*," Samina called, but Hilda still didn't hear. "*Beta?*" "I see *Dadi*," Hilda said. She was mistaken, of course—it was only a woman about the same age. Khalid (who would not look at Samina, either, who hadn't since delivering his news), said, "Wave to her, *beta*. Wave." But what was Hilda doing up there? "Come down now," Samina said.

No one was listening to her, though. She waited. It was amazing: not the slightest sign that either of them had heard her.

She opened the door and climbed back into the car. The windows were rolled up and the band and the car horns were muffled. He'd died, drowned—an accident. They were together again—no one had known more about him than she had. No one else possessed him now. Through the windshield, while Samina watched these people streaming by, a group of three women turned to look in her direction. Hilda on top of the car caught their eye first, then they looked into the car, at Samina. They frowned. They were married women, thick with makeup, unsmiling, tired of weddings. Their husbands walked together in front of them. But their frowns had deepened when they saw Samina. To just be left alone—it wasn't so much to ask, really. It occurred to Samina that the women must imagine Khalid was her husband. *What is she doing pouting in the car*, they must be wondering, *while her daughter and husband are out here smiling at us?* An unhappy mother. An unhappy wife. They turned to consult one another about what they'd seen. They said either, *That's just what I'm afraid of* (if they didn't like what little they knew about this bride they were walking toward), or, *Let's hope it won't be one of those.* When they turned back to Khalid their frowns lightened, and their eyes threw him sympathy. What was Samina doing here, where everyone speculated and was mistaken about her? But where would she go instead?

Then she slipped all the way back, to the very first day—it was the day he had died, she suddenly realized—and she found herself thinking, all over again, *Oh, my love, why did you go to that beach? Why did you go without me? Why did you leave me?*

37

THE FIRST SURPRISE was that, shortly after her father died, Ginny did clear out of Sooke—with little notice and few good-byes. But what astonished Cyrus was that she did so in the company of Don. It probably shouldn't have surprised him. In the last days of the search she had been right by Cyrus's side all day long, doing her best to help the sergeant and Samina, yet she wouldn't look at Cyrus properly or speak to him as they did and he'd never felt further from her. It seemed he may have won her—her complicity and full attention, finally—and lost her—her ease and liveliness, her casual trust, everything that set Ginny apart—all at once. He should have kept his mouth shut. He almost felt he'd corrupted her. Then they'd found Mr. Mallet on the floor of the trailer. Cyrus had thought he was dead—he was heaped and awkward in an uncomfortably familiar way—but when Ginny had screamed, her father's eyes opened. At the hospital, Cyrus got in the way, said the wrong things, misunderstood; he dropped whatever was placed into his hands. Don arrived on the second day and Ginny said, "Oh, thank God you're here." She didn't owe Cyrus anything, naturally—his mistakes were not hers to rectify. In fact, she had her own problems to solve, and suddenly Cyrus was one of them.

So he shouldn't have been surprised a few months later. Fair enough.

But wasn't Don a lazy bum the minute he stepped off his boat, unsuited to any sort of land-going or regularly scheduled occupation? And wasn't he as likely as ever to have his head turned by the first pretty girl who shivered against his silky small talk? Shouldn't Ginny know better? Wasn't she the most sensible person you could hope to meet, up to very recently? Where would they go? They were vague about it. They seemed cautious and closemouthed around Cyrus. Had Ginny told Don, then? Would she really do that to him? They weren't taking her father's trailer, of course—Ginny had traded that for a beat-up Honda with many, many miles on it. A conventional mistake, it must be said. But Don had managed to find a buyer for that boat of his, so maybe there was hope for him after all. "We'll miss you," Ginny told Cyrus, and how cruel she was to use that "we" against him now and tamp her own affection down to the level of Don's. Cyrus waved and blew kisses as they drove off. He called her name out, "Ginny! Ginny!" in falsetto. "Don't leave me, Ginny!" Kidding.

Equally astonishing was that Cyrus's father died, without warning, only a few weeks later. Cyrus found him slumped over his desk. "Heart attack," they said, and what a stupid term. People don't seem to think before they model these phrases out of the unfortunately malleable language and spatter the world with them. People said he must have a funeral, but Cyrus didn't know anything about funerals—he had skipped Mr. Mallet's—and he wasn't prepared to learn just yet. Chick, he thought, would not lose any eternal sleep over the lack of a funeral. Cremation seemed right. Cyrus didn't want to take the ashes, but they wouldn't let him leave without them. "Ask yourself," the man advised, "what your father would have wanted. Look into your heart." But Cyrus was more or less afraid to.

He went home and stepped into the empty house with his urn tucked under his arm and walked between the quiet, busy rooms. They were so thoroughly empty now, lacking the slightest expectation and the tang of disappointment and the insult of industry—of his father working hard at something, however worthless, while Cyrus drifted in or out, *killing time* (a metaphor he could get behind)—but on the other hand the rooms had a new, busy, dead life to them. Walking through them now, Cyrus felt his head expand and pulse a bit, and wondered if he should be crying. Parts of his head seemed to be sending the signal, but other parts couldn't understand it: *You want* water? *Flowing from the* eyes? *Where to, for god's sake?* He put the urn down by the front door (he couldn't very well leave it outside). He sat down at the kitchen table—this was the least scandalized room in the house, the one with the least to lose. There was a pack of cards on the table—he played solitaire. He turned the little television by the range on. It received only one less-than-promising channel. He cooked a bit of whatever was there when he got hungry, a bit more in the morning. He'd fallen asleep for a little while at some point, sitting up, while the television chattered. The parrot woke him. He fed it, too. Then began another round of solitaire. He seldom won.

After two days he was just about out of the food he could think of any way to eat. Surprising how much still remained in Chick's cupboard, though. Someone or someones had come to the door—three different times—and Cyrus had silently waited out the knocking. One person—it had turned out to be Walter, from the store—had circled the house, looking into the windows. Cyrus had hid under the table. In the front room by the door, the urn still sat. He found a cheesy mess on the steps outside—it must have been a casserole, but the raccoons had gotten to it before him. It was raining. He tucked the urn under his arm and walked down East Sooke Road. He could drive instead—the car was at his disposal now—but this didn't even occur to him until he was half way to the park. He went in by the Pike Road Trail, down to the beach at Iron Mine Bay. The tide was lowish. He could run across the bit of sand to the island between the feathery surges of water, though his sneakers sank into the stones and still got wet. He climbed over the bald top of the islet and down the bare rocks on the strait side. The hump of rock fell directly down into the water here: it was some feet deep right in front of you. What to say? "We'll miss you, Chick."

But my god, what a lie—who was this "we" now? Who would remember him at all by summer's rush of cottagers? With Mr. Mallet gone and Ginny and Don away and occupied and only meager Cyrus for family . . . he might as well have never existed.

"You did your best," Cyrus said.

But he couldn't get the top of the urn off. He tried holding it between his knees and tugging with both hands. This annoyed the shit out of him—*now* he cried. Lovely. He finally threw the whole thing into the ocean. Luckily, it sank. So maybe that was for the best, too, as a matter of fact. Why would anyone want to be scattered, really, and have to watch his nose ashes float past his rump ashes, while some fish nibbled on his toe ashes, and what would Cyrus have done with the empty urn? *Oh, for fuck's sake, why did Cyrus have thoughts like this*—always nasty and disrespectful and inappropriate? He wiped at his tears. *Just* feel *things for fucking once*, he told himself—*don't deny it or try to examine it or pretend you see through all these feelings that everyone else finds perfectly useful and authentic through the course of a day.*

He retreated to the top of the island. It was a truly unpleasant rainfall—chilly and not especially picturesque. But he watched a sea otter pop up just down the coast and drag an eel to shore, where it held the slithering thing down with one paw and munched on it, head first. He would miss his dad. They'd suited one another, he thought, in a funny way. "Goodbye, beach," he said, for he never intended to come back here. "So long, park," he said, at the end of the trail out. "Good riddance."

He walked home and took his father's car to the grocery store. In a week or so, he ran out of cash, and had to speak to the bank. There were three hundred and twenty-seven thousand of his father's dollars there, which belonged to Cyrus now. It would be a waste of time to wonder how. He opened an account. He went home, feeling newly clear-headed in addition to flush, and put many of his father's things—the saleable knickknacks on his desk and in his bedroom, and all his clothes, and his bedding and towels, his toiletries, his framed photographs (except the two that included Cyrus's mother), and his ugliest paintings and his chess sets—into boxes, which he left at the bottom of the driveway with a sign that said "Free!" But when no one had taken anything some days later, and it had rained into the boxes overnight, Cyrus loaded them in the car and waited until after dark to drive them to the St. Vincent de Paul Society in Saanich. (He'd realized he would actually prefer not to see a neighbor wearing his father's shirts.) He moved things around in the house so that the downstairs could be more nearly his own. He stuffed all his father's books and his clay pots and his blue glass and the rocks his father had gathered from across the globe in his married, pre-Cyrus days, and all the furniture that reminded Cyrus most of his father—all of it upstairs, into his father's bedroom and his study, in addition to most of the rugs, and the paintings Cyrus hadn't given away, and the one mug, plate, and bowl his father had daily used, and the spare pairs of his father's reading glasses, which turned up in every room. His father's bed and dresser were already up there, as were his filing cabinets and box upon box of papers. Cyrus wished there was a door to close at the top of the stairs. He hung a sheet over the opening at the bottom instead. Then he began to feel at ease, and to settle in. He bought some books for himself and took them home and read them. He also bought girlie magazines, and with these as company he mastur-bated often, as the mood struck him, in many of the rooms (though not programmatically or with desecration in mind—only at his leisure). He took a funny pleasure in leaving the magazines out on tabletops and on the raw wood surfaces of the empty bookshelves—these voluptuous women and glossy couples lay exposed in their well-lit worlds, waiting for Cyrus to happen upon them in his.

The parrot he didn't know what to do with. He thought about killing it, only because it was so distraught since Chick had died. It would hardly eat, and it kept plucking its feathers out. It had a big bald patch under one wing already. Surprising that Cyrus had never realized Chick was the bird's favorite. "Goodness me, time for bed," it kept saying, quoting his father—it seemed to be begging Cyrus for a mercy killing. But Cyrus wasn't up to the task. He pressed it upon the pet shop in town, though they weren't pleased with him. Cyrus had to seem distraught himself. He said the bird reminded him of his father—it was driving him crazy. "Pickles, my father called it." They could kill the poor thing if they needed to, he supposed.

So it went. But it went so slowly—one day he heard the date mentioned on the radio and it was exactly the one-month anniversary of his father's death. But he would have guessed a year before he guessed a month.

Often he wasted time thinking about Ginny and Don. He chose to pic-ture them generously: in Vancouver, perhaps, where they had already made friends, and they were sitting over cups of coffee with these friends,

laughing at Don's funny stories about Sooke. One of the funny characters
in his stories was named Cyrus. Or perhaps they'd managed to get across
the Rockies, despite the snow, and now they were in some place hardly
imaginable, like Toronto, or Nova Scotia. Cyrus thought about Nicholas,
and about Samina and Hilda, very regularly—not every day but probably
every other day, often when he lay in bed not sleeping. In the dark he was
better able to picture Nicholas alive and smiling. The cottage they had
rented had stood empty since they left. He thought of the day he'd first
been introduced to Nicholas: Hilda in his arms, flirting with her father,
and if Nicholas had thought about this boy in front of him at all, he'd
thought, *Colorful locals—how charming*. But that didn't sound quite like
Nicholas, really.

Which things would be different if Nicholas had not stepped in the way
of Cyrus's stick? Would the fathers be just as dead already, for instance?
Would Ginny have left with Don? The strangest thing was that Cyrus
could not, for the life of him, conjure up a mental image of Samina. She
was a named entity, and he could place her in the frame of his memories—she's right there making iced tea for him; they're talking about the
Prophet, Muhammad—but he couldn't place her face on her shoulders,
and actually, he didn't have her shoulders or the rest of her body, either.
Hilda was easy, Nicholas was easy—same with Greg and Laurel. Think
the name and there they are: *Hello, Hilda!* Samina had been very pretty.
She'd had black hair with a lot of red in it, if you saw it in the right light,
and big brown eyes, and heavy eyebrows. A good, noble nose. But a face
wouldn't come together with these ingredients. One day when he was in
Sooke for groceries he saw her name on the cover of the little local newspaper in the checkout aisle. They had found Nicholas, on a beach all the
way in the middle of the Pacific Rim National Park. He'd been identified
using DNA testing. Sergeant Dunn said he had drowned—a terrible
accident—and the search for him was recalled in some detail, the community taking a moment out of its decorous grief to pat itself on the
back. No quote from Samina. The very first day—the first moment she'd
arrived at her cottage in Sooke, when Cyrus had watched from behind
the Doug fir—she had spotted him out of the corner of her eye and
turned to stare at him for one moment. Thrown the rope out. And what

Cyrus wanted to know was had she looked at him and intuited tragedy, recognized him as her tormentor, though he had no inklings of this fate yet and had innocently taken the rope, tied himself to her, unable to guess how much better off she'd be without him? He'd like to know.

Another day, as he was pulling out of the driveway, he noticed that the big mailbox was bulging with uncollected mail. Among the fliers and garbage and unpaid bills (that explained the telephone), there were three letters from Greg Faber.

Who is Greg Faber? Cyrus wondered. Then realized. He read them in the order they'd been sent. *Mr. Collingwood,* they said, in essence, *I continue to have a great interest in (a strong wish to steal) your project on Charles Dodgson. Who was Lewis Carroll. I am and continue to prove to be a big shot, in this way and in this way as well, which I expect to render you honored to be stolen from by me, and I hope you will consider my fine offer before something unforeseen happens—like, an attack of your traitorous heart against the rest of your poor, nambly body, for instance, or your own, unimaginable literary success.* The last of the letters was the most interesting. It said that one of the ways in which Greg intended to turn out to be a big shot was by writing a book about his missing friend, Nicholas Green, and the events surrounding his disappearance in Sooke. It called this proposed book a memoir. It said he hoped to speak to Mr. Collingwood's son, Cyrus, if possible. In fact, the letter said, he'd tried to telephone the Collingwoods, but he'd been told their number was disconnected. "I continue to hope I'm not being too forward, Mr. Collingwood," the letter ended, "and in fact, I won't write (or call) again unless I hear from you. I do, of course, wish to respect your privacy. But I hope you will understand my desire to solve the mystery of what happened to my old friend. A mystery which hardly seems diminished, to my mind, by the recent discovery of his body (about which I presume you've heard). I would be extremely grateful for your help. Yours sincerely."

Cyrus paid all except the phone bills. Greg's letters made him realize he would need to get out of here, soon. Out of reach of Greg. Disappear—he'd never gotten around to that. He'd half thought in some distant way that he would stay put until his father's money ran out, but at the rate he was going that would take decades. Sometimes, lately, it seemed to Cyrus that it might be great fun to have a job—of any kind, really. To have hours and paychecks, and to be at the disposal of some boss's ambitions, however mundane. His problem lately was that his days took the exact and perfectly predictable shape of his thoughts.

When he got over being disgusted with Greg as an individual, he realized he quite liked this idea of a book about it all. He would get involved, he supposed, if only his role wasn't that of the secret villain destined to be revealed. One morning in the midst of spring—a bright, beautiful day, with fish bursting upon insects in the basin and early tourists out in kayaks and canoes, wrapped in orange life preservers—he looked at his house through the binoculars while walking up his driveway, into the dormer windows upstairs, where the flimsy curtains were drawn. He remembered the night Greg came to their house not to find the killer of his poor friend but to speak to Chick about Chick's book. Cyrus pushed the sheet aside at the bottom of the steps and went upstairs. There was a hornet's nest between the panes of a window that had been left ajar. The sill was damp and rotting there. He went to his father's desk and opened the drawers. Then he began to poke through the boxes and the filing cabinets. There was so much more paper than he'd expected, than he'd ever imagined. It came in all shapes and varieties: loose pages and note cards and library catalogue cards and bits of scrap in manila folders, and cardboard-cover notebooks and notebooks wrapped in leather, typewritten pages and pages copied out of books and many, many pages covered in his father's handwriting.

Cyrus had seldom been forced to decipher it. Most interesting were the yellow legal pads, which were either notes for his book or the thing itself. There were half a dozen pads full of his sentences in pencil (and of passages poorly erased or shaded out, and of diagrams and what appeared to be poems and even surprisingly adept marginal sketches) in the top drawer of the desk. They were all about *Charles*. There was an *Alice* here and there along with many other names. It seemed to be a huge, confusing cast (it was extremely confusing to Cyrus, at least, skimming through). Most of the characters were women, or girls: here was Ina, Dora, Francine, Isa (unless that was Ina again), and Julia, Nellie and Edith, Elizabeth and Mary, a Henrietta, a Louisa. Margaret, Violet, Beatrice, Evelyn, Agnes, Irene, and Effie. They all seemed extremely busy on the pages. There was a "Xie" who was a girl, and a "Skeffington" who seemed to be a boy. There was a safe-deposit box, which, when Cyrus found the key (it was right there, unhidden, in the desk), turned out to be crammed full of more legal pads. On some pages the handwriting bent around the bottom-right corner and climbed up the margin, planted itself in neat rows across the empty field at the top of page, above the first green line, upside down, and went to seed along the left margin some distance. By the next day he'd found a weird old safe, hidden in a doorless hole in the wall behind one of the filing cabinets. The combination was Cyrus's birthday. This truly touched him. Inside (how could he still be surprised? but he was), there were many, many more legal pads. Dozens and dozens of them. Grossly covered in print. A treasure, except that it struck him as creepy, too. Cyrus would have to finish his father's book.

But it took only a few days to realize he was entirely overmatched. He didn't know anything about Charles Dodgson, and he couldn't follow the story (it *was* a story—that was clear—with scenes and conversations and people's thoughts running on for pages), in part because he had no context for any of it. Also because he couldn't figure out what order the notebooks went in. Where did things begin? In three days he hadn't found a single date yet, and none of the characters seemed to be growing older. Plus, there was something a little unappealing about the story itself. This had to do with there being too many little girls. Cyrus had cultivated a raging headache.

He went downstairs and made a fresh pot of coffee, and then he thought about the situation for the better part of a week, downstairs, in his own half of the house, playing a sort of game in which he pretended to consult his father. (This was easier to do convincingly, for whatever reason, after dark, with only a bit of lamplight in the room.) What was best for his father's book? *It must be published,* his father said, *that's first and foremost. Don't leave my life a waste, son. But profit is not an issue. You'll need help, my boy.* (His father seemed to have acquired a number of new phrases and a more forceful manner since Cyrus had last seen him.) *You're in over your head. You'll need an expert. Someone good—I mean really good. A big shot. Don't let me down, son.*

After these debates, and after he had laid in bed reading for as long as he could possibly stand the sight of print, when Cyrus still generally found he wasn't able to sleep yet, he would some nights turn out the light and lie still and try to banish the marching lines of pencil from behind his eyelids but then begin to suffer from a weird panic. His mind would go into overdrive, working in tight, small spirals of thought and sentences—phrases repeated from his father's book, without any particular meaning or traction but with an urgency that falsely suggested he was getting somewhere—and he would miss Ginny, terribly: her kindness and patience with him and her free-for-the-taking smile and laugh. He missed her stupidest jokes and her glittering nose stud and the three times exactly she had ever kissed him (but never once on the mouth). He missed her hands. He really believed she had loved him, once—she hadn't needed to, she just had. He would begin to miss his father, too—every least attractive thing about him, but mostly just the physical fact of him in these rooms, and in the grocery store with Cyrus, in the bench-style front seat of the car with Cyrus on East Sooke Road, dropping a younger Cyrus off first mornings of the school year (they had both decided, without speaking about it, to let him do this right through Cyrus's senior year). In the house, his father had made the quietest, rainiest, darkest day occupied, still, however slightly. Cyrus even missed his mother, though he didn't remember her, really. He felt so deeply alone in those moments at night, in the too-familiar darkness of what had always been his bedroom, in his little bed, that he had to sort of convince himself he had ever existed at all. He hadn't made his bed since his father had died. He hadn't changed his sheets. He had kicked the comforter to the floor a few weeks ago, the first warm night, and there it lay. He thought he almost might have to kill himself, but what was strange was that he also thought he really, really didn't want to. He felt so sorry.

On the day he finally decided, he waited until after dark again—he felt more comfortable doing anything of real consequence after dark (but that was just human nature, wasn't it? he didn't have to take that one all on his own, too, did he?)—then drove to the pay phone at Walter's with a pocketful of change. Greg had included his telephone number in each of his letters. Laurel answered—"Yes," she said, with sleepy rage (oh, it must be later in St. Louis)—and Cyrus hung up.

He waited a minute, took a deep breath, and dialed again. Greg answered now, with a "Hello" that floated—midway between annoyance and worried curiosity. Cyrus said, "Greg?" No answer. "Hi, it's Cyrus," Cyrus said. "Remember me?"

"Cyrus?" They had known one another at a difficult time.

"It's really me," he said. "How are you, old pal?" he asked. He shivered, waited—it was a cold night. All the lights were out in Walter's except a dim, indistinct glow at the back which Cyrus knew to come from the cold drinks refrigerator. "Sorry to wake you," he said. "How's Laurel? Greg," he said, "I think I need your help."

38

D O YOU WANT a magazine?

"No."

Greg heard them from between aisles, his view blocked by tall book-shelves. They spoke so quietly—they were evidently so close to him.

"For the flight?" Samina asked. "I think you're forgetting how long and boring it is."

"*Cosmopolitan.*" And that must be Hilda.

"*Cosmopolitan?* Think again, my dear."

"What's bad about it?"

Samina mumbled something Greg couldn't hear.

He wasn't sure if he wanted to flee or not. He stepped quietly to the end of the aisle and, very slowly, leaned around to peek. They were three or four steps away from him. He ducked for cover. Hilda was virtually unrecognizable—twice as tall as when he'd last seen her, rail thin, and with her hair cut short and neat (how old would she be now? Eight? Nine?)—but Samina, even in profile, in the briefest glance, was unmistakable. Even in *hijaab*. That's what the scarf was, wasn't it?

Samina said, "Trust me, *beta*, you can't arrive there with a *Cosmo* in your hand. Who's been peddling this stuff to you, anyway?" A woman in Greg's aisle was finding him suspicious. He bobbed his eyebrows at her.

"Can I have *Mad-Libs?*"

"Excellent choice. Look, it comes with the pen now."

"It always comes with the pen."

They were walking away—to the register, presumably. Greg had decided: No. He didn't want to speak to them. The headscarf sealed it. Too afraid—and now that he'd decided, in fact, he wondered if there was a better hiding place in the store.

But then he heard Cyrus (who was supposed to be in the men's room). Cyrus, of course, hadn't hesitated. "Oh, hi," he said, presumably to Samina, as if he'd been expecting her—as if they ran into one another all the time. "Remember me, Hilda?" Greg heard him ask. "Your friend Cyrus? From Canada?"

Someone on a cell phone chatted her way into Greg's aisle, so he missed what came next, but he supposed Cyrus would out him. He plucked a random book from the shelf, tucked it under one arm, and slung his satchel over the other, winked at the suspecting woman, and strolled into the open with a flourish of casualness. "Greg's here some-where," he heard Cyrus say, just as he steered his head around toward them. They had all spotted him at once. He left a second of grinless blankness—that would signify remembering, recognizing—then said, "Samina?"

"Hello, Greg," she replied—and with a much better approximation of happiness to see him than he could have hoped for. She looked amused.

"What a surprise. Don't tell me this is Hilda?" The girl looked more as he remembered her, now, shrinking behind her mother. "You wouldn't remember me, I bet," he offered her.

Samina asked her, "Do you remember Greg and Cyrus? From . . . a long time ago?"

Fair enough. Which unmentionable had she been headed toward: *Canada*—Cyrus's considerate generalization—or *Vancouver Island*, or *Sooke?* Hilda nodded, but not convincingly.

"You were this high the last time I saw you," Greg said. And he was just realizing now that he'd neglected to age Hilda properly in his mind over the years. Samina he'd over-aged, a little. A bubble of silence wedged up between them.

Cyrus told Greg, "They're on their way to India. To a wedding. Has Hilda ever been there?" he asked Samina.

"This will be her second time. I don't think she remembers the first time, though."

"I remember," Hilda said.

Samina looked down at her, smiled up at them. Another silence.

"So what are you both doing here?" she asked. Then added, "It's so strange to see you together."

"Isn't it?" Cyrus said. "We live together."

"Sort of," Greg added. "We were actually here for the book. A panel."

"I live in his garage," Cyrus said. "Part of the year. The U.S. government doesn't want me to get comfortable, so I go back and forth."

"This is in St. Louis, still?"

She hadn't read the book. Maybe she hadn't touched it. Maybe she never got it? But he knew he had the right address—Nicholas's parents had given it to him. Greg felt annoyed, but he ought to feel relieved. She hadn't hated it—she just hadn't read it. "No, we moved to Boston," he explained. "A couple of years ago. Laurel got a job at Tufts."

"Good for her," Samina said. Greg thought that she'd perhaps hoped Laurel's would be another name they could leave out of the conversation. "She's doing well, then?" Samina asked. "Is she here, too?"

"No, no." If Samina was relieved she didn't let it show. "No, she stayed home to take care of the munchkin. We have a son, actually." She hadn't read as far as the acknowledgments page or unfolded the updating letter he'd included with her copy. "James."

"Congratulations," Samina said. "That's really nice. How old is he?"

"Almost two."

"Oh, such a sweet age."

Cyrus asked her, "Did you read our book, Samina? Or maybe you weren't up for it."

"You both wrote it?" she asked.

Cyrus said, "Well, no, Greg wrote it, actually. I just helped out. I'm teasing him. But this panel thing—they asked us both to come, and I kind of stole the show? So, I'm thinking it'll be my book pretty soon, and I'll be able to leave Greg at home." She didn't seem to be sure he was kidding, though, so more soberly, looking at his shoes, he added, "It's getting pretty good attention, actually."

She said, "That's great."

"Yeah, good reviews." Cyrus rallied—smiled at her.

Then she was at the head of the line. She handed her things to the cashier and tucked her smile away. All business with a stranger—she had always been that type. Should this be it? Greg wondered. Are we free now? But for some reason he and Cyrus lingered while she took care of the transaction. Cyrus said, "You remember those crabs, Hilda? The graceful crabs and the big Dungeness?"

She nodded yes.

"But you don't recognize me, do you?" he asked. "No big deal."

She shook her head no.

He said, "Yeah, it was a long time ago. We used to visit the crabs together, you and me," he said, and shrugged. "So, you still big on pancakes, or what?"

Greg was preoccupied with the sight of Samina. The woman he had known seemed hidden away under the cover of fabric—retracted.

"Now I remember you," Hilda said. She clearly resembled Nicholas when she smiled.

Cyrus said, "Oh, great. I can just tell you remember me doing something stupid. Well, what is it, then? Let me have it."

But Samina broke in. "So you're heading to this panel?"

A little pause among them. *Oh, get this over with,* Greg thought—*she doesn't want to be here any more than you do.* "No," he told her, "on our way back from it, actually. In fact, we should probably run." He looked at his watch.

Cyrus asked, "How long will you be in India?"

"Two months."

"Wow," he said. "Big trip."

She nodded.

Greg said, "So you're doing well, obviously? You look great. Hilda, too."

"Thank you," she said. She hadn't changed a bit. He'd never known anyone better than Samina at avoiding a question, gliding past it without an answer. "You look good, too," she added. "You both do."

"Well, I'll tell Laurel we bumped into you. She'll be jealous."

But Samina's nod was so stiff, and her eyes fell from his so haphazardly, he immediately said, "Or—I don't know. Maybe we won't mention it." He looked at Cyrus—to give Samina room to recover. "Maybe we'll keep it to ourselves. A little secret."

After a moment, Samina said, "It was nice to see you both."

Cyrus nodded. Greg waited, gave Cyrus a few seconds, expecting something to arise from him late (he'd become accustomed to the timing), but Cyrus merely waved in his funny way—his hand cocked, down by his hip—and began to back out.

But Greg had to say something. They were slipping from one another too easily, and he could hardly expect to ever see her again. Through the entire process of writing the book he had felt certain she would eventually come around, although he knew it would probably be to fight with him rather than help him. He had fretted for weeks after sending her the manuscript, imagining a thousand objections she might raise to her portrait as he'd rendered it, or to Nicholas's, or to their history as friends, but the only response she'd ever provided was a single-sentence reply to the publisher's lawyers, signing off. He said, "I really hope the book is okay with you, Samina. We never heard, so . . ."

"It's fine, Greg. I told you—you should write whatever you want to write." It had all been easier than Greg had expected—Laurel said he should be grateful—but in some ways he would have preferred a pitched battle with her, a proper reexamination and comparison between memories. He'd debated with her so often in his mind as it was, imagining her best arguments and polishing his rebuttals. Such arguments would have made it a better book.

He said, "I tried to be honest."

She nodded, looking past him. Hilda had wandered out into the airport hallway, where she seemed to be watching Cyrus go.

Greg said, "So you're doing well? You're in New York still, I guess?" Would she give him the smallest scrap of information? Why in the world was she wearing *hijaab*? If there was a new husband, would she be going to India without him? Could be. He could be coming later—they couldn't both take two months off from work perhaps. Did she work? Had she forgiven him? Couldn't she give him some proper sign that she had? "Everything's going well? You're . . . carrying on, and so forth?"

She did the strangest thing: she laughed at him. It began as only a smile, *her* smile—not the polite one she'd been holding against him but her old, real smile. But then that expanded into a laugh. She looked away from him, embarrassed. She'd provoked a stupid grin out of Greg, too—he could feel it. "We're doing just fine, Greg," she said. "Better all the time."

Grinning still—was that a sort of joke?—he said, "Well, good. Good. Everybody's fine."

And she stopped smiling. She didn't look angry or unhappy, she only put the smile and the laugh away. He'd seen her do it a hundred times, so there was no reason for him to still take it as a slight or a gesture that had anything to do with him.

"I better go find Cyrus. Very nice to see you, Samina."

"You, too." The alarm went off as he was stepping free of the store, and he remembered the book still in his hand—his prop. "Oops," he said to Hilda. He held it up for the cashier to see, handed it back to the boy—"decided against it, actually"—and had to—no choice, really—nod once more at Samina. "Good to see you," he confirmed.

THE FLIGHT WAS splendid. No clouds the entire way: Cyrus looked out his window and watched the lights of New York, then Connecticut, then Massachusetts gather and disperse. The loop out over the black ocean—as if the pilot had missed his exit—then the turn and touchdown on what Cyrus liked to think of as the easternmost tip of land in North America, though he knew it wasn't. Greg hadn't cared to talk about her, which was just as well. "Hilda's cute as ever," Cyrus had tried, when they were first buckling in. "I can't believe how tall she is." But Greg had just nodded in his grumpy-Greg way.

Laurel had kept James awake and taken him along to the airport. The minute the kid saw Cyrus he pulled his shirt up and began to giggle in anticipation. Cyrus gave his marshmallow skin a good raspberry—James laughed his head off—and Laurel said, "Oh, please, Cyrus, don't get him started. Not at this hour, dear."

Greg and Cyrus gave her the play-by-play of the conference while she drove. Greg kept his promise and didn't mention Samina or Hilda, at least in front of Cyrus. When they were home Cyrus insisted on carrying the suitcases in. He grabbed a Gatorade from the fridge and a plate of cookies (which Laurel had made just for him), and said good night to the household. His room—in what had once been a garage—had reacquired the funky smell that came back whenever he left it closed up for more than a day or two. He opened the windows and turned the desk lamp on. He'd learned the secret of good lighting: no overheads, just little pools of yellow that you could edge into and out of. Contrast—an underappreciated value.

He unpacked, because he could never think properly or relax until things were in place again. Then he sat down at the desk and gave himself as long as it took him to polish off these cookies to think about Samina and Hilda. A disciplined schedule—he never used to appreciate that, either. It was what had saved Cyrus, though, he often thought, as much as Greg had, or his father's book.

When Cyrus was young—when he was nineteen and Samina had known him (poor woman)—he had, without realizing it, thought he was the very center of the universe. He'd had great faith in notions like fate and genius, but really only with regards to himself, maybe Ginny, too. Why in the world had he looked at this middle-aged American woman, a cottager, and imagined they'd share a future of some kind? It was silly, narcissistic. One of the things he'd learned since then was how difficult it was to ever know who among the strangers you crossed paths with day to day would be lingerers, and who would quickly veer away. Samina had not remembered him, today. Not until he said his name to Hilda. When she still thought of Sooke she thought of all sorts of things and Cyrus was hidden deep in the midst of most of them, but she probably never thought of Cyrus. It surprised him, though it probably shouldn't. And Hilda hadn't loved him, as he'd liked to imagine then—she'd only enjoyed passing the time with him. Just as James did now. "Oh, he loves his Cyrus," Laurel liked to tell people, but if Cyrus left James when he was only four he wouldn't remember this love of his by the time he was five. The fascinating thing to ponder about little people was exactly what hit home and shaped them despite pouring right back out of their leaky memories—what you'd done to them without either of you realizing it. Cyrus had known Samina the instant he saw her in the airport, yet the sight of her had surprised him, too. She was pretty, merely. It was the headgear, in part—not getting to see her hair—but even her face: a nice-looking woman, unremarkable. She was just the slightest bit plump. Cyrus tucked the last cookie away and set the plate aside. She'd seemed content, he thought—that was a mild surprise, too. But why shouldn't she be? Maybe she preferred the single life.

Back to work, back to work. Part of his discipline was to put at least an hour or two in at the desk the first evening he got back to this room from Vancouver, no matter how late it was. Enough to be in the middle of things, his mind settled down, by the next morning. Each time he returned to his father's book his mind slipped and scraped and wandered off, which made these initial hours the most difficult and least pleasurable. But by tomorrow afternoon he'd have gotten his footing and lost his sense of the world, and then the hours would begin to peel away mysteriously. That effect, Cyrus sometimes felt, was what he liked best of all about this work—better than anything it produced.

His father's book was hard to define. Greg had a range of terms for it, depending upon the mood he was in: a "literary fantasia" and a "crazy novel" were what he'd chosen most often at the conference, speaking to colleagues; on his generous days he called it "the most liberal biography I've ever seen," but most often: "a huge act of vandalism." When he said that, he was actually forgetting about the book itself, though, and only thinking of the notebooks—Charles's notebooks, the ones Cyrus's father had inherited and emptied, destroyed. Greg focused too much on the death here, too little on the resurrection. But that was fine since it was of course what made Cyrus indispensable. Greg admitted that he'd never have the patience for Cyrus's work.

He got himself arranged: the legal pad front and center, his own pad just beside it, and on the desk podiums in an arc around his work space he set out two biographies, the second volume of the letters, and the second and third volumes of the Wakeling diaries. In the scene from his father's book that he'd been working on before they left for New York, Beatrice and Evelyn were cooking a stew in Charles's kitchen—or it might be a kind of potion. They had stirred in a lock of his hair and a lens from his telescope, and a black beetle and a tincture (*Lovely word, Chick*) of lunar caustic which they had pilfered from the dark room. "You must taste it first," Beatrice was saying, while stirring, and Evelyn replied, "I do like the smell." Unless that was Beatrice speaking still—it was often hard to tell. It would come clear eventually, in the way that things did. Paths open up—strange ways through. There were ways out of even where Cyrus had been.

What would the potion do to them? he wondered. *A tincture of lunar caustic*—Greg hated shit like that.

But Greg had actually made his peace with Cyrus's father. He'd been furious when he first came back to Sooke and dug up the Dodgson notebooks with nearly all the pages ripped out. He'd actually refused to help Cyrus. But Cyrus had settled down, developed a schedule, put his nose to the grindstone—for the first time in his life, as a matter of fact—and found enough in the scenes on the legal pads to convince Greg that some of it must be days and conversations and meetings that Charles had originally recalled in those notebooks. Greg had realized how much Cyrus needed him, too. Greg loved to be needed. And anyway he wanted Cyrus's help for his book about Nicholas. Sometimes Cyrus forgot that they'd joined forces out of mutual convenience and desperation more than friendship. Greg had become less angry when James was born, and still less this year, with his book published and doing well. But he didn't really believe in Cyrus's project anymore, either. He wouldn't admit it, but at the conference, when people asked Greg what came next, he'd talked about this and that and only mentioned Charles Dodgson as an afterthought when he remembered that Cyrus was standing beside him.

Had she sensed Cyrus's affection for her? She must have had an inkling. He hadn't known how to make a solid impression back then, or how to put people at ease.

He couldn't put his finger on exactly why but Beatrice Hatch, more than any of the other girls, reminded Cyrus of Hilda. He had given her

Hilda's face, even though that wasn't accurate: in Charles's photographs Beatrice had Hilda's long hair from Sooke but a flat nose and a flat, thin smile, and in the colored photograph in which she was naked, she looked too pale and willing. Ella Chlora Faithful Monier-Williams looked more like Hilda, as she'd been in Sooke—this girl had an expression of Hilda's, exactly, in the photo in which she stood by the window and held a cane against her shoulder as if it were a rifle. She turned her toes out in just the way Hilda had. But Ella's role in Chick's book was too small to make her a satisfying stand-in. Why did they love little girls so, you wondered—Chick and Charles? The cloudy mind of the little person, sure, and all that unexplored future before them, all that innocence, but why not little boys, too? Was it all as simple and unseemly as one supposed, for both of them?

Initially it almost felt as though Cyrus had embarked upon a massive campaign to undo his poor father's life's work, but eventually he had come to trust that, in fact, he was only carrying it through—in a different direction, perhaps (the son always takes up the father's endeavors and extends them at an oblique angle; biography teaches you that), but with a kind of dedicated loyalty that made Cyrus feel closer to Chick than he ever was in life. He felt he was making it up to his father, for the disappointment he'd been. He believes Chick would be proud of him. And this is a worthwhile reward to Cyrus now. He doesn't agree with Greg that Chick wanted to bury the real life—that he was a hider, a forger, a destroyer. His father was only a strange exposer, as dedicated as Greg to recapturing, though he thought you could only do it alone. His project was meant for himself—written for one reader—and it'll more or less stay that way, even if Cyrus is successful enough at separating the wheat from the chaff to let Greg write a book. Chick's book could never be published—Greg has made that clear. But Chick had known that he could only really get at a slippery fish like Charles alone. It's a truth that Greg won't face. You get back there into the past, and into someone else's life, only in your private pages with the door closed and the lights out—in your own mind, really, and at its extension, your desk. Who knew Charles more intimately—who had been with him in his rooms and looked out of his eyes—Greg and these legitimate biographers with their published books, or Chick? If that wasn't the biographer's goal, what was? And on the other hand (both true!), Cyrus wanted to know, as badly as Greg did, what was *real*—what had really happened or hadn't to Charles, what he'd ever dared admit to himself and set down in those notebooks. Some days Cyrus felt disgusted with his father's book, too.

Forget it—it's no use. He won't get anything done tonight. He'll wake up early tomorrow and put an hour or two in before he strolls over to the house for breakfast. Breakfast at Laurel's hands was a proper affair: breads or fried batters and salty meats all glazed in syrup.

With the desk light off, the world through the windows reestablished itself. The flow shifted from out to in. He gave the world his rooms when his lights were on, offering a view of himself to anyone interested—he'd realized that when he was only a kid, but he'd never wanted to make the offer. Cyrus's life is the most secret life he knows. Totally undocumented. He's never written a letter or committed a single thought to paper. The notes he takes all day long now have no trace of himself in them (he hopes). Until he came here and found himself plunked in front of Laurel's camera, caught with the photo-magnet baby in his hands, he'd never been captured on film, so far as he knew. He's like his mother in this. There are the two old shots of her, in touching dull colors, a figure leaning timidly into his father, but that's it. Unless she's hidden in his father's book somewhere. Cyrus looks for both of them—his mother and himself—all the time. But there seems to be so little of them among the girls, no more than shadows and hints behind the silly commotion of the scenes, and this makes Cyrus sad for his father's sake.

Sitting with both his father's book and with Charles Dodgson (with the pages upon pages of scribble Charles left behind as well and all his published books and photographs), in which, nevertheless, the nasty, essential secret of both men's inappropriate love is never once admitted or apologized for, Cyrus feels oddly free of his own terrible secret and something like forgiven. Negligence has the feel of forgiveness. If no one remembers him—if Samina never thinks of him, and the mistakes he's made leave no trace out in the world—it's as if it never happened. As if Nicholas merely drowned. Ginny knows, but Ginny has disappeared. Greg probably could have guessed once, if he'd wanted to—all through the writing of his memoir Greg could have. But he has a kid now and wants to be famous. Greg never wanted to know. Cyrus's father could have guessed but he had loved his son in his very small, strong way, Cyrus believes, and did his best to protect him.

In this most of all, Cyrus sympathizes with his father's act—the "vandalism," as Greg calls. Going along, erasing behind yourself. You want to do something important, of course, and to make a difference—you want to leave a mark in the world, and improve things—but unfortunately you're not worthy of the world's attention. You're not willing, in the end, to give yourself away. Cyrus's father was probably just as lonely as Cyrus is. So was Charles—so busy, but lonely—and for some people, that's the way it goes. No one meets Cyrus and thinks he's lonely, any longer. He is a young man who makes a solid impression now. He hopes he came off well in Samina's eyes. *I always liked Cyrus,* he hopes she went away thinking.

Leave Me Alone, that's their motto: Charles and Chick and Cyrus. I'm doing my best, I'm sorry, I'm making it up. What more can anyone ask of them?